"A little comfort for us both." He rolled onto his back then drew her toward him until her head rested on his shoulder and his arm wrapped around her.

She gave a quiet little laugh. "At least I'm not cold now." Unable to resist, she snuggled a little closer and inhaled his scent. Wonderful. And the way her boots were getting warmer, she figured they'd both be safe. Another couple of minutes and they'd have to back away from the fire or completely change position.

But right now she wanted to revel in the rare experience of physical closeness with another human being. With a man. Since coming home she'd avoided it, feeling that she was too messed up to get involved without hurting someone.

Yeah, she was adapting pretty well, but if her paranoia of the past few days didn't make it clear that she wasn't completely recovered, nothing would.

And if she couldn't trust her own mind and feelings, she wasn't fit to be anyone's companion.

D0210026

HER DEADLIEST MISSION

NEW YORK TIMES BESTSELLING AUTHOR

Rachel Lee &

Jenna Kernan

Previously published as *Murdered in Conard County* and *Warning Shot*

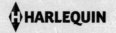

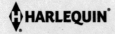

ISBN-13: 978-1-335-42474-7
Her Deadliest Mission
Copyright © 2021 by Harlequin Books S.A.

Recycling programs
for this product may
not exist in your area.

Murdered in Conard County
First published in 2019. This edition published in 2021.
Copyright © 2019 by Susan Civil-Brown

Warning Shot
First published in 2019. This edition published in 2021.
Copyright © 2019 by Jeannette H. Monaco

This edition published by arrangement with Harlequin Books S.A.

For questions and comments about the quality of this book, please contact us at CustomerService@Harlequin.com.

Harlequin Enterprises ULC
22 Adelaide St. West, 40th Floor
Toronto, Ontario M5H 4E3, Canada
www.Harlequin.com

Printed in U.S.A.

CONTENTS

Rachel Lee was hooked on writing by the age of twelve and practiced her craft as she moved from place to place all over the United States. This *New York Times* bestselling author now resides in Florida and has the joy of writing full-time.

Books by Rachel Lee

Harlequin Intrigue

Conard County: The Next Generation

Cornered in Conard County
Missing in Conard County
Murdered in Conard County
Conard County Justice
Conard County: Hard Proof

Harlequin Romantic Suspense

Conard County: The Next Generation

Conard County Witness
A Secret in Conard County
A Conard County Spy
Conard County Marine
Undercover in Conard County
Conard County Revenge
Conard County Watch
Stalked in Conard County

Visit the Author Profile page
at Harlequin.com for more titles.

MURDERED IN
CONARD COUNTY

Rachel Lee

Prologue

Three years earlier

"Have either of you ever heard of Leopold and Loeb? They thought they could commit the perfect murder."

A large fire burned in the huge stone fireplace, casting dancing tongues of orange light and inky shadows around the cabin's sitting room. The wood sizzled and crackled, adding its dry music to the light and occasionally loud pops that sounded almost like gunshots.

The log walls, burnished by the years, added weight to the entire scene. Trophy heads of bighorn sheep, elk and deer hung everywhere, beneath each a plaque memorializing a past hunter.

Clearly this was a hunting lodge, one of generous size, able to house a fairly large party. But its heyday was in the past and now only three men occupied it.

It seemed like the last place on earth three men would plot murders.

Dressed in camouflage, their orange caps and vests tossed onto a nearby chest, they sat in a semicircle of comfortable lounge chairs in front of the fire, sipping brandy from snifters. Two of them enjoyed fat cigars with a surprisingly pleasant aroma.

"It was really cold out there," remarked one of them, a man with dark hair and a luxuriant mustache who appeared to be about thirty, maybe a couple of years older. He'd been the one who had asked the question about Leopold and Loeb, but having received no response, he dropped it. For now.

"Good for the deer, Will," said the man nearest him. His name was Karl, and he looked like his Nordic ancestors, with pale hair and skin and frigid blue eyes. The deer he referred to had been field dressed and was hanging in a shed outside, protected from scavengers.

"Yeah," said Jeff, the third of them. He had the kind of good looks that could have gotten him cast on a TV drama, but he also had a kink in his spine from a military injury and he didn't quite sit or stand straight. He often endured pain but seldom showed it. "It's probably already frozen stiff."

"Like a board," Karl agreed. "Thank goodness we have a sling on our side-by-sides."

"And tomorrow maybe we'll get an elk," Jeff added. They'd won the drawing for a coveted license for an elk, and since they'd been hoping for one for years, this was no small deal.

Silence fell for a while, except for the crackling of the fire. Three men, looking very content, enjoying their hunting lodge after a successful day. Except one of them was not quite content.

Will spoke. "Do you two ever get tired of this hunting trip? Every year since we were boys, coming up here with our dads. Now just the three of us."

"Something wrong with the company?" Karl drawled.

"Of course not," Will answered. "It's just that I was thinking we've been doing this so many years, and we've never gone home empty-handed. Not much of a challenge, is it?"

Jeff nearly gaped. They'd spent the better part of three days tracking the buck that was now hanging in the shed. "We almost missed that mature eight-pointer. He was smart."

"We still got him," Will pointed out.

Karl spoke. "The elk will be even more of a challenge. What do you want, Will? To stop making these trips? I thought we were doing it more for the time away together. Three guys, brandy and cigars, traipsing around in the woods on the cusp of winter… A lot of guys would envy us."

"We aren't a lot of guys. In fact, I believe we're smarter than the average bear. All of us."

"So?"

"So, how about we hunt a different kind of prey? Not to kill but for the challenge."

"What are you talking about?" Jeff asked.

"You ever hear of Leopold and Loeb?" This time Will spoke more emphatically.

Both Karl and Jeff shook their heads. "Who were they?" Karl asked.

"Two guys who thought they were smart enough to

commit the perfect murder. Back in the 1920s. But they got caught in twenty-four hours."

The other two men froze into silence.

"We're smarter," said Will presently. "Think of all the planning we'd have to do, a lot more than hunting deer or elk. And even without the murder it would be a helluva challenging game."

Silence, except for the fire, reigned for a while. Then Jeff said, "You *are* talking about a game, not a real murder, right?"

Will waved the hand holding his cigar. "The game would be the planning and stalking. Just like when we hunt deer. The kill hardly matters at that point. We only follow through because we want the meat and the rack. You can't hang a man's head on the wall."

That elicited a laugh from Karl. "True that." Even Jeff smiled after a moment.

"The most challenging game of all," Will continued. "How do we do it without leaving any evidence? How do we creep up on our prey?"

Karl snorted. "Men aren't as smart as deer, Will."

"But they're almost never alone."

After a bit, Jeff said, "Sorta like playing D&D when we were younger?"

"Like that," Will agreed. "Plotting and planning and stalking. That's all."

Presently all the men were sitting easily in their chairs and began to toss ideas around. If nothing else, it was an entertaining way to spend an icy evening.

Chapter 1

Blaire Afton slept with the window cracked because she liked the cool night breeze, and the sounds of animals in the woods. As park ranger for the state of Wyoming, she supervised a forested area with a dozen scattered campgrounds and quite a few hiking trails, most all the camps and trails farther up the mountain.

Her cabin was also the main office, the entry point to the park, and her bedroom was upstairs in a loft. The breeze, chilly as it got at night, even in July, kept her from feeling closed in. The fresh air seemed to make her sleep deeper and more relaxed, as well.

It also seemed to keep away the nightmares that still occasionally plagued her. Ten months in Afghanistan had left their mark.

But tonight she was edgy as all get-out, and sleep stubbornly evaded her. Maybe just as well, she thought irritably. Nights when she felt like this often produced bad dreams, which in turn elicited worse memories.

Sitting up at last, she flipped on the fluorescent lantern beside her bed and dressed in her park ranger's uniform and laced up her boots. If sleep caught up with her finally, she could crash on the sofa downstairs. Right now, however, early coffee was sounding delicious.

There was absolutely no way she could make her boots silent on the open wooden staircase, but it didn't matter. All her staff were home for the night and she could bother only herself. Right now, bothering herself seemed like a fairly good idea.

The electric lines reached the cabin, having been run up the side of this mountain by the state, along with a phone landline that extended out to all the campgrounds in case of emergencies. Neither was perfectly reliable, but when they worked, they were a boon. Especially the electricity. Phone calls about vacant campsites didn't light up her life, nor did some of the stupid ones she received. Want a weather report? Then turn on the weather.

"Ha," she said aloud. The good news was that she had electric power this night. She walked over to her precious espresso machine and turned it on. A few shots over ice with milk and artificial sweetener...oh, yeah.

And since she was wide awake and had the power, maybe she should check her computer and see if she had internet, as well. Monthly reports were due soon, and if she had to be awake, she might as well deal with them. Reports weren't her favorite part of this job, and sometimes she wondered if some of them had been created by a higher-up who just wanted to be important.

When her coffee was ready and filling her insulated mug, she decided to step outside and enjoy some of the night's unique quiet. It wasn't silent, but it was so different from the busier daylight hours. Tilting her head back, she could see stars overhead, bright and distant this nearly moonless night. The silvery glow was just enough to see by, but not enough to wash out the stars.

Sipping her coffee, she allowed herself to enjoy being out in the dark without fear. It might come back at any moment, but as Afghanistan faded further into her past, it happened much less often. She was grateful for the incremental improvement.

Grateful, too, that the head forester at the national forest abutting her state land was also a veteran, someone she could talk to. Gus Maddox guarded a longer past in combat than she did, and there was still a lot he wouldn't, or couldn't, talk about. But he'd been in special operations, and much of what they did remained secret for years.

In her case, her service had been more ordinary. Guarding supply convoys sounded tame until you learned they were a desirable target. She and her team had more than once found themselves in intense firefights, or the object of roadside bombs.

She shook herself, refusing to let memory intrude on this night. It was lovely and deserved its due. An owl hooted from deep within the woods, a lonely yet beautiful sound. All kinds of small critters would be scurrying around, trying to evade notice by running from hiding place to hiding place while they searched for food. Nature had a balance and it wasn't always pretty, but unlike war it served a necessary purpose.

Dawn would be here soon, and she decided to wait in hope she might see a cloud of bats returning to their cave three miles north. They didn't often fly overhead here, but occasionally she enjoyed the treat.

Currently there was a great deal of worry among biologists about a fungus that was attacking the little brown bat. She hoped they managed to save the species.

A loud report unexpectedly shattered the night. The entire world seemed to freeze. Only the gentle sigh of the night breeze remained as wildlife paused in recognition of a threat.

Blaire froze, too. She knew the sound of a gunshot. She also knew that no one was supposed to be hunting during the night or during this season.

What the hell? She couldn't even tell exactly where it came from. The sound had echoed off the rocks and slopes of the mountain. As quiet as the night was, it might have come from miles away.

Fifteen minutes later, the phone in her cabin started to ring.

Her heart sank.

Ten miles south in his cabin in the national forest, August Maddox, Gus to everyone, was also enduring a restless night. Darkness had two sides to it, one favorable and one threatening, depending. In spec ops, he'd favored it when he was on a stealthy mission and didn't want to be detected. At other times, when he and his men were the prey, he hated it. The protection it sometimes afforded his troops could transform into deadliness in an instant.

As a result, he endured an ongoing battle with night. Time was improving it, but on nights like this when sleep eluded him, he sometimes forced himself to step outside, allowing the inkiness to swallow him, standing fast against urges to take cover. He hated this in himself, felt it as an ugly, inexcusable weakness, but hating it didn't make it go away.

The fingernail moon provided a little light, and he used it to go around the side of the building to visit the three horses in the corral there. His own gelding, Scrappy, immediately stirred from whatever sleep he'd been enjoying and came to the rail to accept a few pats and nuzzle Gus in return.

Sometimes Gus thought the horse was the only living being who understood him. *Probably because Scrappy couldn't talk*, he often added in attempted lightness.

But Scrappy did talk in his own way. He could communicate quite a bit with a toss of his head or a flick of his tail, not to mention the pawing of his feet. Tonight the horse seemed peaceful, though, and leaned into his hand as if trying to share the comfort.

He should have brought a carrot, Gus thought. Stroking the horse's neck, he asked, "Who gave you that silly name, Scrappy?"

Of course the horse couldn't answer, and Gus had never met anyone who could. The name had come attached to the animal, and no one had ever changed it. Which was okay, because Gus kind of liked it. Unusual. He was quite sure the word hadn't been attached to another horse anywhere. It also made him wonder about the horse's coltish days five or six years ago.

Scrappy was a gorgeous, large pinto whose lines suggested Arabian somewhere in the past. He was sure-footed in these mountains, though, which was far more important than speed. And he was evidently an animal who attached himself firmly, because Gus had found that when Scrappy was out of the corral, he'd follow Gus around more like a puppy than anything.

Right then, though, as Scrappy nudged his arm repeatedly, he realized the horse wanted to take a walk. It was dark, but not too dark, and there was a good trail leading north toward the state park lands.

And Blaire Afton.

Gus half smiled at himself as he ran his fingers through Scrappy's mane. Blaire. She'd assumed her ranger position over there about two years ago, and they'd become friends. Well, as much as two wary vets could. Coffee, conversation, even some good laughs. Occasional confidences about so-called reentry problems. After two years, Scrappy probably knew the path by heart.

But it was odd for the horse to want to walk in the middle of the night. Horses *did* sleep. But maybe Gus's restlessness had reached him and made him restless, as well. Or maybe he sensed something in the night. Prickles of apprehension, never far away in the dark, ran up Gus's spine.

"Okay, a short ride," he told Scrappy. "Just enough to work out a kink or two."

An internal kink. Or a thousand. Gus had given up wondering just how many kinks he'd brought home with him after nearly twenty years in the Army, most of it in covert missions. The grenade that had messed him up with shrapnel hadn't left as many scars as memory. Or so he thought.

He was tempted to ride bareback, given that he didn't intend to go far, but he knew better. As steady as Scrappy was, if he startled or stumbled Gus could wind up on the ground. Better to have the security of a saddle than risk an injury.

Entering the corral, he saw happiness in Scrappy's sudden prance. The other two horses roused enough to glance over, then went back to snoozing. They never let the night rambles disturb them. The other two horses apparently considered them to be a matter between Scrappy and Gus.

Shortly he led the freshly saddled Scrappy out of the corral. Not that he needed leading. He followed him over to the door of his cabin where a whiteboard for messages was tacked and he scrawled that he'd gone for a ride on the Forked Rivers Trail. A safety precaution in case he wasn't back by the time his staff started wandering in from their various posts. Hard-and-fast rule: never go into the forest without letting the rangers know where you were headed and when you expected to return. It applied to him as well as their guests.

Then he swung up into the saddle, listening to Scrappy's happy nicker, enjoying his brief sideways prance of pleasure. And just like the song, the horse knew the way.

Funny thing to drift through his mind at that moment. A memory from childhood that seemed so far away now he wasn't sure it had really happened. Sitting in the car with his parents on the way to Grandmother's house. Seriously. Two kids in the back seat singing "Over the River" until his mother begged for mercy. His folks were gone now, taken by the flu of all things, and his sister who had followed him into the Army had been brought home in a box from Iraq.

Given his feelings about the darkness, it struck him as weird that the song and the attendant memories had popped up. But he ought to know by now how oddly the brain could work.

Scrappy's hooves were nearly silent on the pine needles that coated the trail. The duff under the trees was deep in these parts, and he'd suggested to HQ that they might need to clean up some of it. Fire hazard, and it hadn't rained in a while, although they were due for some soon to judge by the forecast. Good. They needed it.

The slow ride through the night woods was nearly magical. The creak of leather and the jingle of the rings on the bridle were quiet, but part of the feeling of the night. When he'd been in Germany he'd learned the story of the Christmas tree. The idea had begun with early and long winter nights, as travelers between villages had needed illumination to see their way. At some point people had started putting candles on tree branches.

Damn, he'd moved from Thanksgiving to Christmas in a matter of minutes and it was July. What the hell was going on inside his mind?

He shook his head a bit, then noticed that Scrappy was starting to get edgy himself. He was tossing his head an awful lot. What had he sensed on the night breeze? Some odor that bothered him. That could be almost anything out of the ordinary.

But the horse's reaction put him on high alert, too. Something was wrong with the woods tonight. Scrappy felt it and he wasn't one to question an animal's instincts and senses.

Worry began to niggle at him. They were getting ever closer to Blaire Afton's cabin. Could she be sick or in trouble?

Maybe it was an annoying guy thing, but he often didn't like the idea that she was alone there at night. In the national forest there were people around whom he could radio if he needed to, who'd be there soon if he wanted them. Blaire had no such thing going for her. Her employees were all on daylight hours, gone in the evening, not returning until morning. Budget, he supposed. Money was tight for damn near everything now.

Blaire would probably laugh in his face if she ever guessed he sometimes worried about her being alone out here. She had some of the best training in the world. If asked he'd say that he felt sorry for anyone who tangled with her.

But she was still alone there in that cabin, and worse, she was alone with her nightmares. Like him. He knew all about that.

Scrappy tossed his head more emphatically and Gus loosened the reins. "Okay, man, do your thing."

Scrappy needed no other encouragement. His pace quickened dramatically.

Well, maybe Blaire would be restless tonight, too, and they could share morning coffee and conversation. It was gradually becoming his favorite way to start a day.

Then he heard the unmistakable sound of a gunshot, ringing through the forest. At a distance, but he still shouldn't be hearing it. Not at this time of year. Not in the dark.

"Scrappy, let's go." He touched the horse lightly with his heels, not wanting him to break into a gallop that could bring him to harm, but just to hurry a bit.

Scrappy needed no further urging.

"We think someone's been shot."

The words that had come across the telephone seemed to shriek in Blaire's ears as she hurried to grab a light jacket and her pistol belt as well as a shotgun out of the locked cabinet. On the way out the door she grabbed the first-aid kit. The sheriff would be sending a car or two, but she had the edge in time and distance. She would definitely arrive first.

The call had come from the most remote campground, and she'd be able to get only partway there in the truck. The last mile or so would have to be covered on the all-terrain side-by-side lashed to the bed of the truck.

If someone was injured, why had it had to happen at the most out-of-the-way campground? A campground limited to people who seriously wanted to rough it, who didn't mind carrying in supplies and tents. After the road ended up there, at the place she'd leave her truck, no vehicles of any kind were allowed. She was the only one permitted to head in there on any motorized vehicle. She had one equipped for emergency transport.

She was just loading the last items into her vehicle when Gus appeared, astride Scrappy, a welcome sight.

"I heard the shot. What happened?"

"Up at the Twin Rocks Campground. I just got a call. They think someone's been shot."

"Think?"

"That's the word. You want to follow me on horseback, or ride with me?" It never once entered her head that he wouldn't want to come along to help.

It never entered his head, either. "I'm not armed," he warned her as he slipped off the saddle.

"We can share."

He loosely draped Scrappy's reins around the porch railing in front of the cabin, knowing they wouldn't hold him. He didn't want them to. It was a signal to Scrappy to hang around, not remain frozen in place. A few seconds later, he climbed into the pickup with Blaire and they started up the less-than-ideal road. He was glad his teeth weren't loose because Blaire wasted no time avoiding the ruts.

He spoke, raising his voice a bit to be heard over the roaring engine. "Have you thought yet about what you're doing for Christmas and Thanksgiving?"

She didn't answer for a moment as she shifted into a lower gear for the steepening road. "It's July. What brought that on?"

"Danged if I know," he admitted. "I was riding Scrappy in your direction because I'm restless tonight and it all started with a line from 'Over the River' popping into my head. Then as I was coming down the path I remembered how in the Middle Ages people put candles on tree branches on long winter nights so the pathways would be lit for travelers. Which led to…"

"Christmas," she said. "Got it. Still weird."

He laughed. "That's what I thought, too. My head apparently plays by its own rules."

It was her turn to laugh, a short mirthless sound. "No kidding. I don't have to tell you about mine."

No, she didn't, and he was damned sorry that she carried those burdens, too. "So, holidays," he repeated. No point in thinking about what lay ahead of them. If someone had been shot, they both knew it wasn't going to be pretty. And both of them had seen it before.

"I'll probably stay right here," she answered. "I love it when the forest is buried in snow, and someone has to be around if the snowshoe hikers and the cross-country skiers get into trouble."

"Always," he agreed. "And doesn't someone always get into trouble?"

"From what I understand, it hasn't failed yet."

He drummed his fingers on his thigh, then asked, "You called the sheriff?"

"Yeah, but discharge of a weapon is in my bailiwick. They have a couple of cars heading this way. If I find out someone *has* been shot, I'll warn them. Otherwise I'll tell them to stand down."

Made sense. This wasn't a war zone after all. Most likely someone had brought a gun along for protection and had fired it into the night for no good reason. Scared? A big shadow hovering in the trees?

And in the dead of night, wakened from a sound sleep by a gunshot, a camper could be forgiven for calling to say that someone *had* been shot even without seeing it. The more isolated a person felt, the more he or she was apt to expect the worst. Those guys up there at Twin Rocks were about as isolated as anyone could get without hiking off alone.

He hoped that was all it was. An accident that had been misinterpreted. His stomach, though, gave one huge twist, preparing him for the worst.

"You hanging around for the holidays?" she asked. Her voice bobbled as the road became rougher.

"Last year my assistant did," he reminded her. "This year it's me. What did you do last year?"

"Went to visit my mother in the nursing home. I told you she has Alzheimer's."

"Yeah. That's sad."

"Pointless to visit. She doesn't even recognize my voice on the phone anymore. Regardless, I don't think she feels lonely."

"Why's that?"

"She spends a lot of time talking to friends and relatives who died back when. Her own little party."

"I hope it comforts her."

"Me, too." Swinging a hard left, she turned onto a narrower leg of road that led directly to a dirt and gravel parking lot of sorts. It was where the campers left their vehicles before hiking in.

"You ever been to this campground?" she asked as she set the brake and switched off the ignition.

"Not on purpose," he admitted. "I may have. Scrappy and I sometimes wander a bit when we're out for a day-off ride."

"Everything has to be lugged in," she replied, as if that would explain all he needed to know.

It actually did. *Rustic* was the popular word for it. "They have a phone, though?"

"Yeah, a direct line to me. The state splurged. I would guess lawyers had something to do with that."

He gave a short laugh. "Wouldn't surprise me."

Even though Blaire was clearly experienced at getting the side-by-side off the back of her truck, he helped. It was heavy, it needed to roll down a ramp, and it might decide to just keep going.

Once it was safely parked, he helped reload the ramp and close the tailgate. Then there was loading the first-aid supplies and guns. She knew where everything went, so he took directions.

With a pause as he saw the roll of crime scene tape and box of latex gloves. And shoe covers. God. A couple of flashlights that would turn night into day. He hoped they didn't need any of it. Not any of it.

At least the state hadn't stinted on the side-by-side. It had a roof for rainy weather, and a roll bar he could easily grab for stability. There were four-point harnesses as well, no guarantee against every danger but far better than being flung from the vehicle.

These side-by-side UTVs weren't as stable as three-wheelers, either. It might be necessary for her job, but if he were out for joyriding, he'd vastly prefer a standard ATV.

She drove but tempered urgency with decent caution. The headlights were good enough, but this classified more as a migratory path than a road. Even knowing a ranger might have to get out here in an emergency, no one had wanted to make this campground easily accessible by vehicle. There were lots of places like that in his part of the forest. Places where he needed to drag teams on foot when someone got injured.

Soon, however, he saw the occasional glint of light through the trees. A lot of very-awake campers, he imagined. Frightened by the gunshot. He hoped they weren't frightened by more.

The forest thinned out almost abruptly as they reached the campground. He could make out scattered tents, well separated in the trees. Impossible in the dark to tell how many there might be.

But a group of people, all of whom looked as if they'd dragged on jeans, shirts and boots in a hurry, huddled together, a couple of the women hugging themselves.

Blaire brought the ATV to a halt, parked it and jumped off. He followed more slowly, not wanting to reduce her authority in any way. She was the boss here. He was just a visitor. And he wasn't so stupid that he hadn't noticed how people tended to turn to the man who was present first.

He waited by the vehicle as Blaire covered the twenty or so feet to the huddle. Soon excited voices reached him, all of them talking at the same time about the single gunshot that had torn the silence of the night. From the gestures, he guessed they were pointing to where they thought the shot came from, and, of course, there were at least as many directions as people.

They'd been in tents, though, and that would muffle the sound. Plus there were enough rocks around her to cause confusing echoes.

But then one man silenced them all.

"Mark Jasper didn't come out of his tent. His kid was crying just a few minutes ago, but then he quieted."

He saw Blaire grow absolutely still. "His kid?"

"He brought his four-year-old with him. I guess the shot may have scared him. But… Why didn't Mark come out?"

Good question, thought Gus. Excellent question.

"Maybe he didn't want to take a chance and expose his boy. They might have gone back to sleep," said one of the women. Her voice trembled. She didn't believe that, Gus realized.

Blaire turned slowly toward the tent that the man had pointed out. She didn't want to look. He didn't, either. But as she took her first step toward the shelter, he stepped over and joined her. To hell with jurisdiction. His gorge was rising. A kid had been in that tent? No dad joining the others? By now this Jasper guy could have heard enough of the voices to know it was safe.

He glanced at Blaire and saw that her face had set into lines of stone. She knew, too. When they reached the door of the tent, she stopped and pointed. Leaning over, he saw it, too. The tent was unzipped by about six or seven inches.

"Gloves," he said immediately.

"Yes."

Protect the evidence. The opening might have been left by this Jasper guy, or it might have been created by someone else. Either way…

He brought her a pair of latex gloves, then snapped his own set on. Their eyes met, and hers reflected the trepidation he was feeling.

Then he heard a sound from behind him and swung around. The guy who had announced that Jasper hadn't come out had followed them. "Back up, sir." His tone was one of command, honed by years of military practice.

"Now," Blaire added, the same steely note in her voice. "You might be trampling evidence."

The guy's eyes widened and he started to back up.

Now Blaire turned her head. "Carefully," she said sharply. "Don't scuff. You might bury something."

The view of the guy raising his legs carefully with each step might have been amusing under other circumstances. There was no amusement now.

"Ready?" Blaire asked.

"Yup."

She leaned toward the tent and called, "Mr. Jasper? I'm the ranger. We're coming in. We need to check on you." No sound answered her.

"Like anyone can be ready for this," she muttered under her breath as she reached up for the zipper tab. The metal teeth seemed loud as the world held its breath.

When she had the zipper halfway down, she parted the canvas and shone her flashlight inside.

"Oh, my God," she breathed.

Chapter 2

Blaire had seen a lot of truly horrible things during her time in Afghanistan. There had even been times when she'd been nearly frozen by a desire not to do what she needed to do. She'd survived, she'd acted and on a couple of occasions, she'd even saved lives.

This was different. In the glare of the flashlight she saw a man in a sleeping bag, his head near the front opening. Or rather what was left of his head. Worse, she saw a small child clinging desperately to the man's waist, eyes wide with shock and terror. That kid couldn't possibly understand this horror but had still entered the icy pit of not being able to move, of hanging on to his daddy for comfort and finding no response.

She squeezed her eyes shut for just a moment, then said quietly to Gus, "The father's been shot in the head. Dead. The kid is clinging to him and terrified out of his mind. I need the boy's name."

Gus slipped away, and soon she heard him murmuring to the gathered campers.

Not knowing if she would ever get the boy's name, she said quietly, "Wanna come outside? I'm sort of like police, you know. You probably saw me working when you were on your way up here."

No response.

Then Gus's voice in her ear. "Jimmy. He's Jimmy."

"Okay." She lowered the zipper more. When Gus squatted, she let him continue pulling it down so she didn't have to take eyes off the frightened and confused little boy. "Jimmy? Would you like to go home to Mommy? We can get Mommy to come for you."

His eyes flickered a bit. He'd heard her.

"My friend Gus here has a horse, too. You want to ride a horse? His name is Scrappy and he's neat. All different colors."

She had his attention now and stepped carefully through the flap, totally avoiding the father. She wondered how much evidence she was destroying but didn't much care. The priority was getting that child out of there.

The floor of the tent was small and not easy to cross. A small sleeping bag lay bunched up, a trap for the unwary foot. Toys were scattered about, too, plastic horses, some metal and plastic cars and a huge metal tractor. She bet Jimmy had had fun making roads in the pine needles and duff outside.

As soon as she got near, she squatted. His gaze was focusing on her more and more, coming out of the shock and into the moment. "I think we need to go find your mommy, don't you?"

"Daddy?"

"We'll take care of Daddy for you, okay? Mommy is going to need you, Jimmy. She probably misses you so bad right now. Let's go and I'll put you on my ATV. You like ATVs?"

"Zoom." The smallest of smiles cracked his frozen face.

"Well, this is a big one, and it definitely zooms. It's also a little like riding a roller coaster. Come on, let's go check it out."

At last Jimmy uncoiled and stood. But there was no way Blaire was going to let him see any more of his father. She scooped him up in her arms and turned so that he'd have to look through her.

"Gus?"

"Yo."

"Could you hold the flap open, please?"

Who knew a skinny four-year-old could feel at once so heavy and light? The flashlight she carried wasn't helping, either. She wished she had a third arm.

"Are you cold, Jimmy?" she asked as she moved toward the opening and bent a little to ease them through.

"A little bit," he admitted.

"Well, I've got a nice warm blanket on my ATV. You can curl up with it while I call your mommy, okay?" Lying. How was she going to call this kid's mother? Not immediately, for sure. She couldn't touch the corpse or look for ID until after the crime techs were done.

"Gus? The sheriff?"

"I radioed. There's a lot more than two cars on the way. Crime scene people, too."

"We've got to get this cordoned off."

"I'll ask Mr. Curious to help me. He'll love it. The kid?"

"Jimmy is going to get my favorite blanket and a place to curl up in the back of the ATV, right, Jimmy?"

Jimmy gave a small nod. His fingers dug into her, crumpling cloth and maybe even bruising a bit. She didn't care.

Walking carefully and slowly with the boy, almost unconsciously she began to hum a tune from her early childhood, "All Through the Night."

To her surprise, Jimmy knew the words and began to sing them with her. His voice was thin, frail from the shock, but he was clinging desperately to something familiar. After a moment, she began to sing softly with him. Before she reached the ATV, Jimmy's head was resting against her shoulder.

When the song ended, he said, "Mommy sings that." Then he started to sing it again.

And Blaire blinked hard, fighting back the first tears she'd felt in years.

Gus watched Blaire carry the small child to the ATV. He'd already recovered the crime scene tape and there were plenty of trees to wind it around, but he hesitated for a moment, watching woman and child. He could imagine how hard this was for her, dealing with a freshly fatherless child. War did that too often. Now here, in a peaceful forest. Or one that should have been peaceful.

His radio crackled, and he answered it. "Maddox."

"We're about a mile out from the parking area," came the familiar voice of the sheriff, Gage Dalton. "Anything else we need to know?"

"I'm about to rope the scene right now. The vic has a small child. We're going to need some help with that and with finding a way to get in touch with family as soon as possible."

"We'll do what we can as fast as we can. The witnesses?"

"Some are trying to pack up. I'm going to stop that."

He was as good as his word, too. When he clicked off the radio, he turned toward the people who had dispersed from the remaining knot and started to fold up tents.

"You all can stop right there. The sheriff will be here soon and you might be material witnesses. None of you can leave the scene until he tells you."

Some grumbles answered him, but poles and other items clattered to the ground. One woman, with her arms wrapped around herself, said, "I feel like a sitting duck."

"If you were," Gus said, "you'd already know it." That at least took some of the tension out of the small crowd. Then he signaled to the guy who'd tried to follow them to the tent and said, "You get to help me rope off the area."

The guy nodded. "I can do that. Sorry I got too close. Instinct."

"Instinct?"

"Yeah. Iraq. Know all the parameters of the situation."

Gus was familiar with that. He decided the guy wasn't a ghoul after all. He also proved to be very useful. In less than ten minutes, they had a large area around the victim's tent cordoned off. Part of him was disturbed that a gunshot had been heard but no one had approached the tent of the one person who hadn't joined them, not even the veteran. The tent in which a child had apparently been crying.

But it was the middle of the night, people had probably been wakened from a sound sleep and were experiencing some difficulty in putting the pieces together in any useful way. Camping was supposed to be a peaceful experience unless you ran into a bear. And, of course, the sound of the child crying might have persuaded them everything was okay in that tent. After all, it looked untouched from the outside.

Scared as some of these people were that there might be additional gunfire, they all might reasonably have assumed that Jasper and his son were staying cautiously out of sight.

Once he and Wes, the veteran, had roped off the area, there wasn't another thing they could do before the cops arrived. Preserve the scene, then stand back. And keep witnesses from leaving before they were dismissed by proper authority. He could understand, though, why some of them just wanted to get the hell out of here.

The fact remained, any one of that group of twelve to fourteen people could be the shooter. He wondered if any one of them had even considered that possibility.

Blaire settled Jimmy in the back of the ATV after moving a few items to the side. She had a thick wool blanket she carried in case she got stranded outside overnight without warning, and she did her best to turn it into a nest.

Then she pulled out a shiny survival blanket and Jimmy's world seemed to settle once again. "Space blanket!" The excitement was clear in his voice.

"You bet," she said, summoning a smile. "Now just stay here while we try to get your mommy. If you do that for me, you can keep the space blanket."

That seemed to make him utterly happy. He snuggled into the gray wool blanket and hugged the silvery Mylar to his chin. "I'll sleep," he announced.

"Great idea," she said. She couldn't resist brushing his hair gently back from his forehead. "Pleasant dreams, Jimmy."

He was already falling asleep, though. Exhausted from his fear and his crying, the tyke was nodding off. "Mommy says that, too," he murmured. And then his thumb found its way into his mouth and his eyes stayed closed.

Blaire waited for a minute, hoping the child could sleep for a while but imagining the sheriff's arrival with all the people and the work they needed to do would probably wake him. She could hope not.

He hadn't known the kid was there. God in heaven, he hadn't known. Jeff scrambled as quietly as he could over rough ground, putting as much distance between him and the vic as he could.

He'd been shocked by the sight of the kid. He almost couldn't bring himself to do it. If he hadn't, though, he'd be the next one The Hunt Club would take out. They'd warned him.

His damn fault for getting too curious. Now he was on the hook with them for a murder he didn't want to commit, and he was never going to forget that little boy. Those eyes, those cries, would haunt him forever.

Cussing viciously under his breath, he grabbed rocks

and slipped on scree. He couldn't even turn on his flashlight yet, he was still too close. But the moon had nosedived behind the mountain and he didn't even have its thin, watery light to help him in his escape.

His heart was hammering and not just because of his efforts at climbing. He'd just killed a man and probably traumatized a kid for life. That kid wasn't supposed to be there. He'd been watching the guy for the last two weeks and he'd been camping solo. What had he done? Brought his son up for the weekend? Must have.

Giving Jeff the shock of his life. He should have backed off, should have told the others he couldn't do it because the target wasn't alone. Off-season. No tag. Whatever. Surely he could have come up with an excuse so they'd have given him another chance.

Maybe. Now that he knew what the others had been up to, he couldn't even rely on their friendship anymore. Look what they'd put him up to, even when he'd sworn he'd never rat them out.

And he wouldn't have. Man alive, he was in it up to his neck even if he hadn't known they were acting out some of the plans they'd made. An accomplice. He'd aided them. The noose would have tightened around his throat, too.

God, why hadn't he been able to make them see that? He wasn't an innocent who could just walk into a police station and say, "You know what my friends have been doing the last few years?"

Yeah. Right.

He swore again as a sharp rock bit right through his jeans and made him want to cry out from the unexpected pain. He shouldn't be struggling up the side of a mountain in the dark. He shouldn't be doing this at all.

He had believed it was all a game. A fun thing to talk about when they gathered at the lodge in the fall for their usual hunting trip. Planning early summer get-togethers to eyeball various campgrounds, looking for the places a shooter could escape without being seen.

The victim didn't much matter. Whoever was convenient and easy. The important thing was not to leave anything behind. To know the habits of the prey the same way they would know the habits of a deer.

Did the vic go hiking? If so, along what trails and how often and for how long? Was he or she alone very often or at all? Then Will had gotten the idea that they should get them in their tents. When there were other people in the campground, making it so much more challenging. Yeah.

He had believed it was just talk. He'd accompanied the others on the scouting expeditions, enjoying being in the woods while there were still patches of snow under the trees. He liked scoping out the campgrounds as the first hardy outdoorsy types began to arrive. And that, he had believed, was where it ended.

Planning. Scouting. A game.

But he'd been so wrong he could hardly believe his own delusion. He'd known these guys all his life. How was it possible he'd never noticed the psychopathy in either of them? Because that's what he now believed it was. They didn't give a damn about anyone or anything except their own pleasure.

He paused to catch his breath and looked back over his shoulder. Far away, glimpsed through the thick forest, he caught sight of flashing red, blue and white lights. The police were there.

He'd known it wouldn't be long. That was part of

the plan. Once he fired his gun, he had to clear out before the other campers emerged, and not long after them the cops.

Well, he'd accomplished that part of his task. He was well away by the time the campers dared to start coming out. But the little kid's wails had followed him into the night.

Damn it!

So he'd managed to back out of the place without scuffing up the ground in a way that would mark his trail. No one would be able to follow him. But now he was mostly on rocky terrain and that gave him added invisibility.

The damn duff down there had been hard to clear without leaving a visible trail. It had helped that so many campers had been messing it around this summer, but still, if he'd dragged his foot or… Well, it didn't matter. He hadn't.

But then there had been the farther distances. Like where he had kept watch. His movements. Too far out for anyone to notice, of course. He'd made sure of that.

So he'd done everything right. They'd never catch him and the guys would leave him alone. That's all he wanted.

But he hated himself, too, and wished he'd been made of sterner stuff, the kind that would have gone to the cops rather than knuckle under to threats and the fear that he would be counted an accomplice to acts he hadn't committed.

Now there was no hope of escape for him or his soul. He'd done it. He'd killed a man. He was one of them, owned by them completely. Sold to the devil because of a threat to his life.

He feared, too, that if they were identified they would succeed in convincing the police that he was the killer in the other cases, that they were just his friends and he was pointing the finger at them to save his own hide.

Yeah, he had no trouble imagining them doing that, and doing it successfully. They'd plotted and planned so well that there was nothing to link *them* to the murders except him.

At last he made it over the ridge that would hide him from anyone below, not that the campground wasn't now concealed from view by thick woods.

But even if they decided to look around, they'd never find him now. All he had to do was crawl into the small cave below and await daylight. Then he would have a clear run to his car to get out of the forest.

All carefully planned. He'd be gone before any searcher could get up here.

Damn, he wanted a cigarette. But that had been part of their planning, too. No smoking. The tobacco smell would be distinctive, so they avoided it unless campfires were burning.

Who had come up with that idea?

He couldn't remember. He was past caring. He slid into the dark embrace of the cave at last, with only a short time before dawn.

Past caring. That was a good place to be. He envied the others. Instead he kept company with the remembered cries of a young boy.

Blaire wished she could do more. She was the kind of person who always wanted to take action, to be useful, but right now the police were in charge, using skills she didn't have to look for evidence, so she kept an eye on the little boy in the bed of her ATV and on the scene where some officers were busy questioning other campers and the rest were busy photographing the scene and hunting for evidence. Pacing back and forth between the two locations, she imagined she was creating a rut.

At least Jimmy slept. She hoped he slept right through when they removed his father in a body bag. She hated the thought that such a scene might be stamped in his mind forever.

She knew all about indelible images. She wished sometimes for a version of brain bleach. Just rinse your head in it and the dark, ugly stuff would be washed away.

Nice wish. She was old enough, however, to realize how unrealistic such a wish was. Life was the accumulation of experiences, and you could only hope that you'd learn from all of them, good or bad.

Gus stayed close to the line, attentive as the officers questioned the witnesses. Dropping by from time to time, she heard the same story repeated by everyone. They'd been asleep. Awakened suddenly by the loud, sharp clap. At first they hadn't even been sure they'd heard it.

Some had sat up, waiting to see if it came again. Others considered rolling over and going back to sleep.

Then came the sound of Jimmy's crying. Yes, he sounded scared but that might be a reaction to the sudden, loud noise. He was with his father, so he'd be okay.

Only slowly had some come to the realization that perhaps they'd better look outside to see what had happened. By then there was nothing to see, and the night had been silent except for the little boy's sobbing.

Which again they ignored because he was with his father. Except for Wes.

"I was in Iraq. I'll never mistake a gunshot for anything else. When the boy kept crying, I knew. I just knew someone had been shot. Maybe suicide, I thought. I was the first one out of my tent. The others took another couple of minutes. Regardless, I'm the one who ran to the emergency phone and called the ranger. No, I didn't touch a thing."

Wes paused, looking down, saying quietly, "It was hell listening to that kid and not acting. But his dad might have been okay. My appearance might have just scared the boy more." His mouth twisted. "They don't make rules of engagement for this."

"I hear you," Gus said. Several deputies who were also vets murmured agreement.

The sheriff spoke. "You did the best thing."

Except, thought Blaire, she'd moved in, opened the tent, stepped inside and took the boy out. She'd interfered with the scene. Next would be her turn to be grilled.

By the time they came to her, however, they were allowing the others to pack up as long as they were willing to leave contact information with the deputies. The early morning sun cast enough light on the world that details had emerged from the night, giving everything more depth. Making the trees look aged and old and maybe even weary. But that might be her own state of mind. Usually the forest gave her a sense of peace, and the trees offered her a stately temple.

The sheriff, Gage Dalton, and one of his deputies, Cadell Marcus, she thought, joined her just outside the roped area.

"Yes," she said before they even asked, "I touched the front of the tent. I was wearing gloves. I pulled the zipper down partway, poked my flashlight in and saw the scene. I had to get the little boy out of there."

Dalton nodded. "Of course you did. So what did you first see as you approached?"

"The zipper was pulled down from the top. I don't know how familiar you are with camping gear, but these days you can get tents with zippers that open both ways. A top opening allows in air while keeping protection down low from small critters. Anyway, it was open six or seven inches. Then I opened it more."

She paused, closing her eyes, remembering. "I didn't think about it at the time, but the inner screen wasn't closed. Doesn't necessarily mean anything because we don't have much of a flying insect problem up here."

Gage nodded. "Okay."

Cadell was making notes.

"Anyway, almost as soon as I poked the flashlight in, I saw the victim and I saw his son clinging to him. My only thought at that point was to get the child out of there as fast as I could. I asked Gus to pull the zipper down the rest of the way. I entered, trying not to disturb anything, and picked the boy up. I carried him to my ATV, where he's sleeping now."

"Did you notice anything else?"

She shook her head and opened her eyes. "Frankly, once I saw that man's head, I was aware of nothing else but the little boy. I seem to recall some toys being scattered around, the boy was out of his sleeping bag which, if I remember correctly, was pretty balled up, and that's it. I was completely focused on removing the child while trying not to step on anything." She paused. "Oh. I turned so Jimmy wouldn't be able to see his father."

Gage surprised her by reaching out to pat her upper arm. "You did the right things. We just needed to know where any contamination might have come from."

"What about Jimmy?" she asked. Concern for the child, kept on simmer for the last couple of hours, now bubbled up like a pot boiling over.

"Sarah Ironheart has called child services. They're contacting the mother." He paused. "Do you think Jimmy trusts you?"

"Insofar as he can. He let me put him in my ATV to sleep." She smiled without humor. "I think the space blanket did it."

"Probably. I'm wondering, if I put you and him in the back of my car, we can take him to town to the social worker. His mom should be on the way."

She hesitated, hating to walk away from what was clearly her job. This campground was her responsibility, and once the cops left…

"Go ahead," said Gus. "I'll meet your staff when they arrive in the next hour and explain. I'm sure they can fill in for you."

The sheriff spoke. "And after the techs are done I'm leaving a couple of deputies up here so the scene won't be disturbed. You're covered."

He gave her a half smile as he said it.

"Yeah, CYA," she responded. "Okay." She couldn't bear the thought of waking Jimmy only to turn him over to a stranger without explanation. The car ride to town would give her plenty of opportunity to reassure him, and maybe by the time they reached Conard City his mom will have arrived.

She looked at Gus. "I promised him a horse ride."

"We might be able to work in a couple of minutes when we get to your HQ. If that's okay with Gage."

"Fine by me. That little boy needs everything good he can get right now."

Chapter 3

Jimmy woke quickly. At first he looked frightened but he recognized Blaire and when she told him they were going to take a ride in a police car, he seemed delighted. Not once, not yet, did he ask the dreaded question, "Where's my daddy?"

They sat in the back of Gage's official SUV and Gage obliged him by turning on the rack of lights but explained people in the woods were still sleeping so he couldn't turn on the siren.

Jimmy appeared satisfied with that. Then Blaire began the onerous task of explaining to him that they were taking him to his mom and finally he asked, "Where's my daddy?"

Her heart sank like a stone. How the hell did you explain this to a four-year-old? It wasn't her place. He'd need his mom and a social worker for this.

She cleared her throat. "He can't come with us right now."

After a moment, Jimmy nodded. "He's helping the police, right?"

She couldn't bring herself to answer and was grateful when he didn't press the issue, apparently satisfied with his own answer.

Which gave her plenty of time to contemplate the kind of monster who would shoot a man while his young son was nearby. Only in battle when her comrades were in danger had she ever felt a need to kill, but she felt it right then and memories surged in her, the past burst into the present and she wanted to vomit.

But Jimmy fell asleep and they sailed right past her headquarters building without offering him the promised horse ride. Gus, who had been following them down, pulled over and gave a hands-up signal as they drove past. Letting her know he'd figured it out.

It was good of him to offer to stay and inform her staff what was going on. She could hardly stop to call and radio, and she couldn't wait for them herself, not with this trusting, precious little boy cuddled up against her.

Just as well. She wasn't sure what world she was inhabiting. Afghanistan? Conard County? The state park? Images, like mixed-up slides, kept flashing in her mind and she had to make a huge effort to focus on the back of Gage's head, on the fact she was in his vehicle. On the boy curled against her so trustingly.

That trust was killing her. Nobody should trust her like that. Not him most especially. He was just a kid and when he found out and finally understood what had happened, he might never trust another soul in his life.

Almost without realizing it, as the town grew closer and the day grew brighter, she was making a silent promise to herself. Somehow she was going to find the SOB who'd done this. If the cops didn't get him first, she wasn't going to give up the hunt.

Because someone deserved to pay for this. Someone deserved to die.

Miles away, the killer was hotfooting it down a mountainside to his vehicle. The cries of the child rang loud in his head and he thought bitterly that he should have just kidnapped the kid and carried him along.

He'd been angry at his friends. He'd been scared of them, maybe even terrified. But now he loathed them. He wished he could find a way to get even that wouldn't involve putting himself in prison for life.

Thoughts of revenge fueled him as he raced toward safety.

Gus had loaded the ATV onto Blaire's truck and brought everything down to her HQ, where he waited patiently. As staff members reported for their day's work, he explained what had happened and told them to avoid the upper campground, so they wouldn't get in the way of the police.

While he was telling them, an ambulance brought the body down. Silence fell among the six men and women who were about to fan out to their various jobs. They stood, watching it pass, and for several long minutes, no one spoke.

Then Gus's radio crackled. It was one of his own staff.

"You coming back today, Gus, or you want me to stand in?"

"I'm not sure." He was thinking of Blaire. She might need more than a cup of coffee after this. "You take over, Josh. I'll let you know what's up."

"Terrible thing," Josh said. "You can bet we're going to be on high alert today."

"Good. We don't know which direction the perp took off when he left. Or whether he'll shoot again."

That made the local crew shift nervously and eye him. *Oh, hell,* he thought. He'd just messed up everything. What could he say? He couldn't very well send them out to patrol the other campgrounds. Not after this. They were seasonal workers, not trained for this kind of thing. And he was still more used to talking to other soldiers than civilians. He needed to guard his tongue.

"You got stuff you can do nearby?" he asked, scanning them.

One spoke. "Blaire's been talking about replacing the fire rings at the Cottonwood Campground."

"Nearby?"

"Yeah."

"Then do that."

"We'll need the truck to cart the concrete and the rings."

Gus nodded. "Okay. Good idea. Stick together. I'm almost positive the threat is gone, though."

"I'll feel better tomorrow," one said sarcastically.

He helped them unload the ATV, then fill the truck bed with bags of concrete and steel fire rings. Finally, he turned over the keys and watched them drive away. East. Away from the campground where the shooting had occurred. Not that he could blame them.

Then he went inside and made a fresh pot of coffee. He eyed the espresso machine because he loved Blaire's espresso, but he didn't know how to use it. Maybe he'd remedy that when she got back, ask for instructions.

While he waited for the coffee he went outside and whistled for Scrappy. Five minutes later, the gelding emerged from the woods to the north, looking quite perky. He must have picked up some sleep during all the uproar.

When the horse reached him, he patted his neck, then was astonished—he was always astonished when it happened—when Scrappy wrapped his neck around him, giving him a hug.

The horse was a mind reader? No, a mood reader. He patted and stroked Scrappy until the horse needed to move and pranced away.

"You getting hungry?"

Scrappy bobbed his head emphatically. If that horse could talk...

He had some feed in one of the saddlebags and put it on the edge of the porch, making sure Scrappy's reins wouldn't get in his way. Water. He needed water, too.

He went back inside and looked around until he found a big bucket in a supply closet. That would do.

A little while later, cup of coffee in his hand, he perched on the step of the small porch and shared breakfast with Scrappy. Maybe his best friend, he thought.

But his mind was wandering elsewhere, to Blaire, to the murder, to the little guy who'd lost his father.

It had been a while, thank God, since he'd felt murderous, but today was shaking him back into that old unwanted feeling.

A sleeping man. His child nearby. What kind of person would take that shot without a threat driving him?

And how offensive could a sleeping man be? Kid aside, the killer had to be the worst kind of coward.

Afraid of where his thoughts might take him, because he'd spent a lot of time getting himself past the war, he forced himself to notice other things. The play of the light on the trees as the sun rose ever higher. The bird calls. Even more entertaining were the squirrels darting around, jumping from branch to branch and walking out on slender twigs, looking like high-wire daredevils. Even at times hanging upside down while they gnawed a branch. Weird, they usually did that only in the spring and fall.

Blaire returned in the late morning, looking absolutely wrung out. A police vehicle dropped her off, then turned around and headed back down the mountain. Gus rose as she approached, but she lowered herself to the porch step, eyeing Scrappy, who'd found a clump of grass to investigate.

"You must want to get back," she said.

"I most likely want to get you a cup of coffee. Regular because I don't know how your espresso machine works." He lowered himself beside her and asked, "Awful?"

"Awful," she agreed. "That poor little boy. At least his mother was already there when we arrived. But then he asked the question he didn't ask before."

"What's that?"

"Where's Daddy?"

"Oh. My. God." Gus didn't even want to imagine it, but his mind threw it up in full view, inescapable.

"Yeah." She sighed, leaned against the porch stanchion and closed her eyes.

"Your crew is out working on fire rings at Cottonwood. They didn't seem too eager to split up."

Her eyes opened to half-mast. "I don't imagine they would. I'm not too eager myself. God, what a monster, and it's too soon to hope he's made his way to the far ends of the Earth. He could be hanging around out there."

He couldn't deny it. "Look, we've both been up most of the night. If you want to sleep, I'll stand guard here until your people are done for the day. If not, let me get you some coffee."

"Coffee sounds good," she admitted. "I may be overtired, but I'm too wound up to sleep. What I really want is to wrap my hands around someone's throat. A specific someone."

He could identify with that. He'd just finished brewing a second pot of coffee so he was able to bring her a piping mug that smelled rich and fresh. He brought one for himself and sat beside her once again.

"I'm still trying to wrap my mind around the kind of person who would do something like that," she said. "It had to be in cold blood. Nothing had happened as far as anyone knows."

"His wife?"

"She's already been gently questioned. Nobody who'd want to kill him, nobody who'd had a fight with him recently, Gage told me."

"Well, great. The trail is awfully lean."

"If it's there at all." She sighed and sipped her coffee. "You must need to get back."

"My assistant is filling in. Unless you want to get rid of me, I'm here for now."

She turned her head, looking straight at him for the

first time, and he noted how hollow her eyes looked. "Thanks. I'm not keen on being alone right now."

"Then there's no need." He paused. "We've shared a whole lot over cups of joe."

"That we have." She tilted her head back and drew several deep breaths as if drinking in the fresh woodland scents. "I'll share something with you right now. If the police don't have much success quickly, I'm going to start a search of my own. I know these woods like the back of my hand. He can't have come in and out without leaving some trace."

He turned his mug in his hands, thinking about it. "You're right. If it comes to that, I'll help you. But we can't wait too long. One rain and everything will be lost."

"Yeah." Again she raised her coffee to her lips, and this time she nearly drained the mug. Rising, she put her foot on the step. "I need more caffeine. If you want, I'll make espresso."

"Only if I can watch and learn. Then you'll never get rid of me."

That at least drew a weak laugh from her. Once inside, he leaned against the narrow counter with his arms folded and watched her make the beverage. From time to time she told him things that wouldn't be immediately obvious, like turning the handled filter to one side to create the pressure.

"Espresso has to be brewed under pressure."

But her mind was obviously elsewhere, and to be frank, so was his.

"People get murdered," she remarked as she finished and handed him a tall cup holding three shots. "Doctor as you like. Ice in the freezer, thank God, milk in the fridge, sweetener in these little packets."

"Ice will water it down," he remarked.

"Yeah, but I like mine cold unless it's winter. Your choice."

He went for the ice, saying, "People get murdered… But what? You didn't finish that thought."

"No, I didn't." Her own cup in hand, she scooped ice into it and topped it with milk. "People get murdered, but not often by strangers while sleeping in a tent with their little son."

"Agreed."

"Outside?" she asked.

"I hate being stuck indoors." Another leftover from years in the military. He never felt all that safe when four walls held him and cut off his view.

They returned to the front steps. Scrappy looked almost as if he were sleeping standing up. Usually, he curled up on the ground, but not today. The tension the two of them were feeling must be reaching him, as well.

"I like your horse," she remarked. "Wish I could have one."

"Then get one."

"It's not in my nonexistent budget. And I don't get paid enough to afford one. Besides, I'm so shackled by things I need to do he might not get enough exercise."

"You're even more understaffed than I am."

"No kidding."

It was easier to talk about budgets and staffing than what had happened during the wee hours this morning. He sipped his espresso, loving the caffeine kick because he was tired, too, from lack of sleep, and waited. There'd be more. They were both vets. Memories had been stirred up, especially for her because she'd had to see it all.

Yeah, there'd be more. Because she'd had to help the kid.

But as noon began to approach, she said nothing more, and he had nothing to say. He was cramming the memories back into the dark pit where they belonged and he decided she must be doing the same.

Unfortunately, burying them wasn't a permanent solution. Like zombies, they kept rising anew and they were never welcome. And sometimes, like zombies, they'd devour you whole and all you could do was hang on. Or give in because there was no fighting it.

He glanced down into his cup and realized he'd finished his espresso. He'd have liked some more but decided not to ask.

At long last she turned to look at him, for the first time that day her blue eyes looking almost as brilliant as the sunny western sky. "That kid is going to have problems. He may not have seen the mess, he may not understand what happened, but he would remember that he left his dad behind in a tent on a mountainside. His mom will tell him about it later, but he's going to remember leaving his dad."

Gus nodded. "Yeah, he will." Of that he was certain. "The question will be whether he believes he abandoned his father."

She nodded and looked down at the mug she held. "More espresso?"

"I'd like that."

Those blue eyes lifted again. "You sure you don't have to get back?"

"Not today. I have a good staff. But even so, I'm in

no rush to face the inevitable questions about what happened over here."

"Me neither." Her eyes shuttered briefly. "So my crew are out replacing fire rings?"

He'd told her that but under the circumstances didn't feel she'd slipped a memory cog. Overload. She must be experiencing it. "Yeah, it was the first thing they thought to do when I explained what had happened. Besides, I exceeded my authority."

Her head snapped around to look at him again. "Meaning?"

"I suggested today would be a good day to stick together."

After a few beats, she nodded. "You're right. I didn't even think of that. The creep could still be out there."

"I don't think there's any question that he's still out there. The only question is, did he leave the forest or is he hanging out somewhere?"

Her charming, crooked smile peeked out. "Correcting my precision now?"

He flashed a smile back at her. "You know why."

Of course she knew why. With a sigh, she rose. "Let's go make some more coffee. If I tried to sleep I wouldn't rest anyway, so I might as well be wired."

Inside the cabin was dim. Because of the harsh, cold winters, the builders hadn't been generous with windows except at the very front where visitors would enter. Consequently, the rear room that housed the small kitchen and dining area was dim and needed the lights turned on. Blaire flipped the switch, then turned on the espresso maker.

"How many shots?" she asked Gus.

"It's funny, but I'm not used to thinking of coffee in terms of shots."

That drew a faint laugh from her. She picked up and wagged a double shot glass at him. "How many of these?"

He laughed outright. "Okay, two."

She nodded and turned back to the machine.

"You gonna be okay?" he asked as the pump began pushing water through the coffee grounds. Noisy thing.

"Sure," she said, leaning against the counter and watching the espresso pour into the double shot glass. "I'm always okay. It's not necessarily pleasant, but I'm okay."

Yeah, *okay* was a long way from being happy, content or otherwise good. He shook his head a little and pulled out one of the two chairs at the small table, sitting while he watched her. "This day is endless."

"What brought you this way this morning?"

"I was restless and couldn't sleep. Scrappy was agitating for a ride so I decided to saddle up. I think he was feeling my mood."

"That wouldn't surprise me. Animals are very sensitive to energy, at least in my experience." She placed his mug in front of him again. "You know where the fixins are."

Making himself at home in her kitchen felt right. At least at the moment. He dressed up his espresso and waited for her to make her own. "Plans for today, since you can't sleep?"

"I'm probably going to run this morning like a broken record in my head." She finished pouring milk into her mug, added a few ice cubes, then turned. "Outside, if you don't mind. The walls are closing in."

He knew the feeling well. He held open the front door for her and resumed his perch on the step. She paced for a bit on the bare ground that probably served as a parking lot when people checked in and were directed to their campgrounds.

"I keep thinking," she said, "that the crime scene guys aren't going to find much that's useful. The ground was a mess, did you notice? People had obviously scuffed it up pretty good last night even if they didn't this morning."

"I saw," he said in agreement. "What are you thinking?"

"That this guy knew what he was doing. That he didn't just walk into a random campsite and shoot someone through an opening in their tent."

He sat up a little straighter. He must have been more tired than he realized not to have thought of this himself. "You're saying stalking."

"I'm suggesting it, yes. No bumbling around in the dark as far as anyone knows. Certainly some of the people in the other tents must be light enough sleepers that they'd have heard activity."

"Maybe so." He was chewing the idea in his head.

"So, if he planned in advance he had to watch in advance. He'd have done that from a distance, right?"

He nodded. He'd done enough recon to know the drill. "Say he did."

"Then the cops might not find anything useful at the scene."

He nodded, sucking some air between his front teeth as his mouth tightened. "What are your plans for tomorrow? Got any time for reconnaissance?"

"I can make it."

"Can you ride?"

"Sure."

"So shall I borrow an extra mount or do you want to walk a perimeter first?"

She thought about it. "Walk," she decided. "We don't want to miss something."

"This assumes the cops don't find something today."

"Of course."

Their eyes met and the agreement was sealed. They'd do a little searching of their own.

That made him feel a bit better. He hoped it did for her, too.

That evening, Jeff pulled his car into the lodge's small parking area and went to face the music. He'd made a mistake and wished he could figure out a way of not telling Will and Karl. Desperately wished. Because things were going to get worse now.

But Jeff was acutely aware that he was a lousy liar. He could see them when they arrived tomorrow and pretend that everything had gone off without a hitch, but it wouldn't take them long to realize he was being untruthful.

The bane of his existence.

He let himself in and began to build a fire on the big stone hearth. That task was expected of the first to arrive, and given that the nights were chilly at this altitude, even in the summer when it had been known to snow occasionally, a small fire burning all the time was welcome.

The heavy log construction of the lodge acted like an insulator, too. Once it had caught the chill, it hung on to it until it was driven out.

The others weren't expected until late tomorrow, though. Fine by him. There was plenty to eat and drink and maybe he could find a way to omit mentioning his oversight. His major oversight.

Besides, it might amount to nothing. One shell casing? How much could that tell anyone? That he'd used a hollow-point bullet in a .45? Lots of folks bought hollow points and even more owned .45s. Hollow points were less likely to pass through the target and cause collateral damage, while still inflicting far more damage on the target than a full metal jacket.

He couldn't have been sure what he'd be facing when he opened that tent a few inches, but he knew he wanted to kill his target without killing anything else.

They'd find the remains of the bullet at autopsy anyway. A popular brand that could be purchased in an awful lot of places. No, that wouldn't lead to him.

But the shell casing automatically ejected by his pistol? He should have scooped that up, but in his panic to get away, he'd clean forgotten it was lying on the ground. What if it had retained his fingerprints?

Not likely, he assured himself. The way he'd handled those bullets, any fingerprints should be just smears. The heat of the powder burning before it ejected the round from the shell should have wiped out any DNA evidence.

So yeah, he'd made a mistake. It wasn't a god-awful mistake, though. Hell, they couldn't necessarily even link it to the shooting, regardless of bullet fragments they might find at autopsy. No, because *anyone* could have been shooting out there at any time. That brass casing might be months old.

So no, it wasn't a catastrophe.

He spent a great deal of time that evening sipping beer and bucking himself up, dreading the moment tomorrow when his friends would come through the door.

Friends? He wasn't very sure of that any longer. Friends would have taken his word for it that he wouldn't squeal on them. Friends should have trusted him rather than threatening him.

Thinking about those threats put him in the blackest of moods. He wasn't a killer. He *wasn't*. He'd killed, though. In self-defense, he reminded himself. Because failing to take that guy out would have been signing his own death sentence. Yeah, self-defense, not murder.

That proved to be a small sop to his conscience, but he needed one. While the cries of the child had begun to fade to the background, the memory of them still made him supremely uncomfortable.

He'd caused that. Did self-defense justify that? He hoped the kid was too young to understand what had happened.

Because he hated to think of the nightmares he'd caused if the kid wasn't.

Chapter 4

The morning was still dewy when Blaire awoke from troubled, uneasy dreams. At least she'd finally been able to crash after a day that had seemed like a nightmare that would never end, a day during which she'd become so exhausted she had often felt as if she were only slightly attached to her own body.

She'd had the feeling before, in combat and the aftermath, but not since then. Not until yesterday.

It hadn't just been lack of sleep that had gotten to her. Jimmy had gotten to her. He had caused her an emotional turmoil unlike any she had felt since one of her comrades had been hit in a firefight. Or blasted by a roadside bomb.

All she could remember was how he'd been crying and clinging to his dead father. Yeah, he'd perked up well enough after she'd carried him away, singing to him, and he loved the silvery blanket, but how much trauma had he endured? How much had he understood and how much of that would stay with him forever?

She had no idea how good a four-year-old's long-term memory might be, but she suspected those memories were stronger if they carried a huge emotional impact. Heck, that was true for most people. Some events just got etched into your brain as if by acid.

Her staff showed up, trickling in around 8:00 a.m. The first thing they wanted to know was news about the shooting. She had none. Then they asked if they could keep working on the fire rings as they had yesterday.

Of course they could. It wasn't like the job hadn't been done, and from what she'd seen yesterday afternoon, she figured there was hardly a camper left in the park. When she climbed into her truck to check out all the sites, she found she was right: only one hardy camper remained, a guy who always spent nearly the entire summer here. He was friendly enough, but clearly didn't want to strike up any lengthy conversations. Most days he sat beside a small fire drinking coffee. Beans seemed to be his preferred meal. Sometimes he went fishing in the tumbling stream a couple of hundred yards behind his campsite, and she'd occasionally seen a couple of freshly cleaned fish on a frying pan over his small fire.

"Nothing better than fresh fish," she inevitably said.

"Nothing," he always agreed before they went their separate ways.

Finally, because she couldn't ignore it any longer, she drove up to the site of yesterday's horror. She left her truck in the small parking lot next to a sheriff's vehicle but eschewed her ATV. She needed the walk back to the site, needed to stretch her legs and try to clear the air. When she got there, she felt a whole lot better.

The deputies Gage had promised stood guard. Seeing them, she wished she'd thought to bring a thermos of soup or something with her. Their only seat was a fallen log outside the taped-off area, and neither of them looked as if they were having a good time.

"Boring duty, huh?" she asked as she approached. Her uniform identified her as theirs identified them. She couldn't remember having met either of them before. They looked almost brand spanking new. Together they formed a sea of khaki, hers interrupted with dark pants and a dark green quilted vest over her shirt. Both of the deputies looked as if they wished they'd brought a vest or jacket with them.

"I suppose you can't light a fire?" she said. "The firepit is outside the crime scene area and you guys look cold."

"We ran out of coffee," one admitted frankly. His chest plate said his name was Carson. "We'll be relieved soon, though, Ranger. Only four hours at a stretch. If they need us up here tomorrow, we'll both be better prepared."

"You're not from around here, huh?" That seemed apparent. Anyone who lived in these parts knew how chilly it could get up here even at the height of summer.

"That's obvious, I guess," said the other guy. His last name was Bolling and his face was so fresh looking he could have passed for eighteen. Which she guessed was possible, however unlikely. "I'm from a small town in Nevada and I got sick of being hot."

Blaire had to laugh, and the two men joined her. She looked at Carson. "You, too?"

"Different town, more Midwestern. I wanted mountains. Visions of hiking and skiing. That kind of thing."

"I'll bet you never thought you'd be standing guard like this in the middle of nowhere."

"Not high on my list," Bolling said. "So is the skiing good?"

"We still don't have a downhill slope right around here. Something goes wrong with every attempt. But if you want to off-trail cross-country, that's great. So is snowshoeing. Just check in with me or with the national forest before you go. I need to know you're out here and you need to know if we have avalanche conditions. Mind if I walk around a bit?"

Carson chuckled. "I think you're in charge of this place except for the roped-off area."

"Yeah, that's yours."

She circled the campground, eyeing the signs of the hurried departures yesterday. And they had been hurried. Sure, it was unlikely the shooter was around or they'd have known it for certain, but she couldn't blame them for wanting to get the hell away from here.

Death had visited a few tents over. And it was not a natural death. Uneasiness would cause almost anyone to want to get as far away as possible.

She knew she and Gus had planned to check out the area together, but he also had responsibilities at the national forest. Her load was a lot lighter, for the most part. She could afford to set her staff to replacing fire rings, especially now that they were empty of campers.

She had no idea what she expected to find that the scene techs hadn't. They'd probably applied their version of a fine-tooth comb to most of the area, even beyond the circle of yellow tape.

But she kept walking slowly anyway. A campground was an unlikely place to pick up a trail, though. People were in constant motion at their sites and places in between. All of them had to traipse to one of the two outdoor chemical toilets, which meant they either walked around tents or passed between them. Kids, especially, scuffed the ground and kicked up needles and duff.

She paused at one spot where she had to smile. It seemed some kids had been laying out roads, probably to use to play with miniature cars. There were even a couple of twigs broken off trees and firmly planted to make the road look tree-lined. Clever.

How many kids had she seen last night? Not many, but that didn't mean they weren't there. Their parents might have insisted they stay inside tents.

Then she spied something red that was half-buried in earth and squatted. A small metal car, she realized as she brushed the debris away. She hoped it wasn't someone's favorite.

Just in case she got a letter in a week or so from some youngster, she slipped it into her vest pocket. It wouldn't be the first time she'd heard from a kid who'd left something behind and who couldn't come back to retrieve it. Usually it was an inexpensive, small item that the parents didn't consider worth the time and effort to return for. She could understand both sides of that issue, but she didn't mind sending a toy back if it made a boy or girl happy. In fact, just doing it always made her smile.

Since Afghanistan, her smiles had become rarer and far more precious to her when she could summon a genuine one. Gone were the days when laughter came easily. She hoped both would return eventually. She had to believe they would. A battlefield was a helluva place to lose all your illusions, and while humor had carried most of them through, it had become an increasingly dark humor. Something that no one on the outside would ever understand.

Swallowing her memories yet again, she forced herself to move slowly and sweep the ground with her eyes. The guy had to have come from somewhere. He wasn't a ghost.

There was a basic rule to investigation: whoever took something from a scene also left something behind. She'd first learned that in Afghanistan when they'd been tracking the people who had attacked them or one of their other convoys. Nobody could move over even the rockiest ground without leaving traces, however minor.

But this damn forest floor was a challenge unto itself. So much loose debris, easily scuffed and stirred. Even the wind could move it around. Moreover, under the trees it was soft, softer than a carpet, and footprints would disappear quickly unless boots scraped. Weight alone didn't make a lasting impression, not unless it rained, and rain here at this time of year was rare enough. They certainly hadn't had any in the several days leading up to the murder.

Eventually she called it a day. A wider perimeter would need the help that Gus promised and it might be a wild-goose chase anyway.

The killer was obviously skilled, had clearly taken great care not to leave a trail behind him.

Which left the question: Why Jasper? And why when his kid was there? Was Jimmy an unexpected complication for him? Too late to back out?

She seemed to remember one of the campers saying

Jasper had brought his son up here just for the weekend. Yeah, if someone had been stalking him, Jimmy was probably a complete surprise.

She found herself once again hoping Jimmy could forget that night. If he retained any memory of it at all, she hoped it was of a space blanket and a ride in a police car. Not what had happened inside that tent.

Heading back, she passed the two cold deputies again. They no longer sat, but were moving from foot to foot. Too bad she hadn't picked up another survival blanket to offer them. "Much longer?" she asked.

Bolling looked at his watch. "A little less than an hour."

She nodded. "Keep warm." As if they could do much about it without lighting a small fire, which they didn't seem inclined to do. Maybe they didn't know how.

Shaking her head, knowing their relief was already on the way, she headed back to her truck, walking among the tall trees and the occasional brush that looked parched.

The peace she usually found in these woods had been shattered, she realized. The niggling uneasiness she'd been trying to ignore hit her full force during her walk back to her truck. A killer had stalked these woods. He might still be out there. He might be watching even now. And he could always return to repeat his crime.

She told herself not to be fanciful, but she'd spent time in a place where such threats were as real as the air she breathed and the ground she walked on.

The guy could be out there right now, savoring his kill, enjoying his apparent success, wanting to see everything that happened. Hadn't she read somewhere that criminals often came back to the scene, especially to watch the cops?

Or it could be another kind of killer. The kind who got a kick out of reliving his actions. Who enjoyed the sense of power the killing gave him. Or the secret power of being so close to the very cops who were supposed to find him. Cat and mouse, maybe.

His motivation scarcely mattered at this point, though it might become useful eventually. No, all that mattered right now was that these woods were haunted by the ghost of a dead man and the evil of a murderer. That a little boy's cries might have soaked into the very trees and earth, leaving a psychic stain.

God, was she losing it?

But her step quickened anyway. Back to HQ. Back to check on her team. To call the sheriff and ask if they'd learned anything at all.

Despite every effort to ignore the feeling, she paused and looked back twice. The sense of being watched persisted, even though she could detect nothing.

An icy trickle ran down her spine.

A thousand yards away in a small hide left by some hunter in a past season, Will and Karl peered through high-powered binoculars. They'd happened on this point during reconnaissance during their spring planning and were delighted with it.

Here, below the tree line, there were few spots where one could see any great distance through the grid work of tree trunks and the laciness of tree branches. Not much brush under these trees, but not much open space for any appreciable distance.

This was a natural forest, not one neatly replanted by a lumber company, which would have given them

corridors to peer along. No, here nature did her best
to scatter the trees everywhere, giving each a better
chance at a long life.

Some saplings added to the screening effect, huddled around the base of mother trees that, science had
learned, actually provided nutrients to their offspring.
On occasion, an older tree would sacrifice its life to en-
sure the growth of the new ones. Roots underground
were carriers of messages and food.

Will had read about it. It tickled him to think of
how much a forest was invisibly intertwined. When
he was in a fanciful mood, he'd sometimes close his
eyes and imagine a brightly lit neural-type network
running beneath his feet, messages passing among the
sheltering trees.

Then there was that massive fungus scientists had
discovered under the ground that turned out to be a
single organism covering square miles. As he started
thinking about that, however, Karl spoke, shattering
the moment.

"Jeff did it."

Yes, he'd done it. The solitary tent surrounded by
crime scene tape and the two deputies wandering
around as if they wished they were anywhere else… It
was all the diagram he needed. But he remained anyway, peering through the binoculars, both enjoying the
success and wanting to annoy Karl, who felt no appreciation of the miracle under them, buried in the ground.

Once he'd tried to tell Karl about it. Once was
enough. It didn't even matter to him that it was actual
science. Not Karl. He prided himself on being hard-
headed. Will could tell him about it, and Karl would

absorb the information factually and move on, finding nothing entrancing about it.

That was the only thing he didn't like about Karl. Had never liked, even though they were good friends in every other way. Karl had a distinct lack of imagination. A trait that proved helpful in this endeavor, were Will to be honest about it.

While he himself might see a network of patterns and possibilities and race down various avenues of attack, Karl remained firmly grounded in their scouting expeditions and what they knew and didn't know. He wasn't one to make even a small assumption.

Although sending Jeff on this expedition had left them both wondering if he'd just walk into the nearest police station.

They had that covered. Two against one, if Jeff tried to nail them, the two of them would nail him. They were each the other's alibi.

Not that they'd need one. This was their fifth kill in the last two summers, and neither he nor Karl had ever left a shred of evidence. Hell, the murders hadn't even been linked to one another.

They'd vastly overshadowed careless Leopold and Loeb. Funny, though, Will thought while watching the campground, seeing the ranger stray around out farther looking for something. He and Karl hadn't been content to prove the point and stop at one.

No. He and Karl had discovered a real taste for this kind of hunting. Deer could be slipperier, of course, but hunting a human? They weren't nearly as evasive, but they were so much more dangerous to take down.

It was always possible to leave traces, and cops would be looking, unlike when you took a deer during season with a license. They'd be paying attention to anything out of line. And if you weren't cautious enough, your victim might get wind that he was being stalked.

It wasn't the top thing on most people's minds, which had aided them, but one of their vics had had an almost preternatural sense that he was being followed. When they realized he seemed to be taking evasive action, they'd nearly salivated over the prospect of taking him out. A *real* challenge.

He studied the campground below once again, satisfying himself that no one seemed to be acting as if there was something significant to find.

Karl spoke, lowering his own binoculars. "Jeff's a wimp. I still can't believe he managed this."

"We kind of put him on the spot," Will reminded him.

Karl turned his head a bit to look at him. He shifted as if he were getting tired of lying on his stomach on the hard rock. "Would you have killed him?"

"I said I would."

"But he's one of us."

Will put down his own binoculars, lifting a brow. "He's one of us until he screws us. How far do you trust him?"

"More than I did a few days ago."

"Exactly. He's in it all the way now. But if he'd backed off, neither of us would have had a choice."

Karl nodded. "I know. I wish to hell he hadn't found out. Been jumpy since I learned he knew what we're doing. He's always been a bit of a coward. I like the guy, always have. We grew up together, went to college together. Joined the same fraternity, screwed the same girls…"

"Hey, that's almost as much of a crime these days as shooting someone."

Karl afforded one of his cold smiles. "Guess so, but I seem to remember those sorority gals fighting to get an invitation to our parties. And it wasn't a secret we were looking to get laid."

"Usually that was true. I remember a few who didn't seem to be clued in, though."

Karl nodded and lifted his binoculars again.

There *were* a few, Will recalled. Girls who were taken by surprise and had to be silenced before they got someone in trouble. Silencing them had been pathetically easy, though. All they'd had to do was tell them the stories they'd make up about the girls. How they'd come off looking like two-bit hookers. The strength of the fraternity, its numbers.

In a smaller way, he and Karl had that strength now, more so with Jeff actively involved.

God, how had that man pieced it all together from a few snips of conversation he'd overheard between Will and Karl? Why had he even believed it? What had been the clue that had made Jeff realize it was no longer a game?

Someday he was going to make Jeff spill the beans. But not yet. Jeff was entirely too nervous. He didn't want to do anything that might make Jeff take flight.

"I don't like that ranger," Karl remarked.

Will picked up his binoculars, focused them again and found the woman. "Why not?"

"She just picked up something from the ground and

put it in her pocket. She's actively searching outside the crime scene area."

"She won't find anything useful," Will said, although sudden uncertainty made his stomach sink.

"She shouldn't if Jeff did what we said. But she just found something and picked it up. I couldn't tell what it was."

"Hell."

He zeroed in on the woman more closely, but she scanned the ground for a little while longer before waving to the deputies and heading for the parking lot. She didn't seem to be in a hurry, which could well be the best news for them.

At least until she started down the rutty walking path to the parking lot. Her step quickened, then quickened again and he saw her looking over her shoulder.

"What the hell?" he muttered.

She paused again and looked back.

"She senses we're watching," Karl said abruptly. "Look at something else."

"But…" Will started.

"No *buts*. If she'd found something she'd have showed it to the deputies. Instead she just stuck it in her pocket. Let it go."

Will, who'd been letting a lot go without much trouble for the last few years, suddenly found himself unable to do that. What had she picked up? It had been important enough to tuck in her pocket. Why hadn't she given it to the deputies?

Karl was probably right, he assured himself. But the way she'd looked back, twice… His stomach flipped again.

"Let it go," Karl said again. "People can often tell

when they're being watched. It's some kind of instinct. But since she couldn't see anyone, she's probably convinced she imagined it."

"It would be easy enough," Will remarked. His literal-minded Karl might not get it, but Will himself had no desire to be any closer to that campsite. Something might be lurking down there, although he didn't want to put a name to it. He often told himself he didn't believe in ghosts or all that crap.

But the truth was, he feared they might exist.

That was one thing he hadn't considered when he'd embarked on this venture with his friends: that he might be collecting ghosts that could haunt him. Where was it written that they had to stay where they were killed?

He swore under his breath and rolled onto his back, looking up at the graying sky. "It's going to rain. Maybe we should go."

"It rarely rains up here."

"Don't you smell it?" He had to get out of here. Now. Because he honestly felt as if *something* were watching him.

"Well, we're supposed to meet Jeff at the lodge this evening," Karl said grudgingly. He pulled out a cigar from an inner pocket on his jacket. "Just a few puffs, first."

They were far enough away that the tobacco smell should waft away to the west, away from the campground and the deputies if it could even reach that far.

Giving in, Will pulled out a cigar of his own and clipped the end with his pocket tool before lighting it from a butane lighter. Then he held the flame to Karl, who did the same. The cellophane wrappers got shoved deep into their pockets.

It *was* relaxing, Will admitted to himself. Staring up at the graying sky that didn't look all that threatening yet. Lying still, refusing to think about all the worrisome problems that had been stalking *him* since they embarked on this venture.

Would he undo it? No way. He'd gotten thrills for a lifetime the last couple of years.

"What's eating you?" Karl asked after a few minutes. "You're edgy."

Well, there was no way Will would tell him that he didn't like being within range of the scenes where any of the victims had died. He stayed away once the deed was done. It was always Karl, whether it had been his kill or not, who wanted to go back and look the site over. Some quirk or odd fascination.

"Coming back could be dangerous," he said finally, although he didn't say how. No need for that.

"They would never look up here. You know that. We can look down on them, but when we checked it out two months ago, we realized this position was well shielded from below. Different sight lines. You know that. Besides, those deputies look bored out of their minds."

"Yeah." He puffed on his cigar, liking the way it tasted and gave him a mild buzz. "That ranger was acting weird."

"She probably just wants the campground back. Funny, though," Karl added.

"Yeah?"

"Every campground in the park emptied out. Talk about having an impact."

"Kind of a broad-brush response," Will agreed. That hadn't happened before. He pondered that reaction for the next ten minutes while drawing occasionally on his cigar. Maybe it was because this park was so small. While they'd chosen the most rustic of the campsites, farthest from the ranger's cabin and the entrance, the distance wasn't huge. If people thought a killer was hanging out in these woods, yeah, they'd get the hell out.

Abruptly, he returned to the moment as a huge drop of rain hit the tip of his nose. While he wandered in his thoughts, the sky had darkened considerably, and for the first time, he heard the rumble of thunder.

He spared a thought for those deputies standing guard below, not that he cared about them. The rain would mess up the scene even more, covering any inadvertent tracks Jeff might have left. Not that he thought any had been left. They'd picked a time when the campground would be full and well scuffed up by the campers. Probably covered with bits of their trash, as well.

He looked at his cigar, hating to put it out. He bought only expensive ones and felt guiltier about wasting them than he felt about wasting food.

He sat up and Karl did, too, after some raindrops splattered his face.

"We've seen enough for now," he told Karl.

"Yeah. Jeff did the job. If he followed all his instructions, we're clear."

Will looked at him. "Of course we're clear. Why wouldn't we be? He's been doing the stalking part with us since the beginning. He practiced the approaches. He's as good as either of us."

"Maybe."

Will sometimes thoroughly disliked Karl. Not for long, but there were moments. This was one of them. "No *maybe* about it," he said firmly.

The sky opened up, settling the question of what

to do with the cigar as sheets of rain fell. He cussed, ground out his cigar and tossed the stogie to the ground, kicking leaves and pine needles over it. The rain would take care of it. Karl followed suit.

Together they rose, gave one last look back down the mountain, then started heading over the crest and back to their vehicle. Another successful hunt.

Irritated as he'd begun to feel, Will smiled as the rain hid them in its gray veils. Jeff had graduated. Maybe they ought to throw him a small party.

Chapter 5

Gus spent a lot of time thinking about Blaire the next two days. He'd hated leaving her at night, knowing she was going to be all alone in the park. But he didn't want to hover and make her feel that he was doubtful of her ability to care for herself.

Dang, those campers from the other campgrounds had bailed even before the cops had released the folks at the crime scene. Word had traveled on the wind, apparently, and nobody wanted to be camping out here when there'd been a murder.

An unusual murder. It wasn't as if Jasper had been killed by his wife after an argument, or as if he'd gotten into a fight with someone else at the campground.

No, to all appearances this shooter had been a stranger. That might change once the cops dug into Jasper's background more deeply, but the people at the surrounding campgrounds weren't going to take a chance that it wasn't a grudge killing.

Even a few of the national forest campgrounds had cleared out. The farther they were from the state park, the less likely people had been to leave, but there was still a marked quiet.

Weird, especially since people booked sites months in advance to make sure they'd have a place to pitch a tent or park an RV. Weirder still when you considered how hard it was to find a place to camp anymore. Gone were the days he remembered from childhood where you could drop in almost any place and find a site.

Anyway, once he got things sorted out with his staff, leaving Holly Booker in charge of the front office and the rest of his people out doing their regular jobs with guns on their hips and in their saddle holsters, he headed for Blaire's place again. The need to check on her had been growing more powerful all day.

Once upon a time being a ranger had been a relatively safe job. Well, except for problems with wildlife, of course. But that had changed over the last decade or so. Rangers were getting shot. Not many, but enough that anyone who worked in the forest needed to be alert to strange activity.

Now they'd had this killing, and he wasn't convinced the shooter had left the woods. What better place to hide out than in the huge forests on the side of the mountain? And what if he hadn't settled whatever problem had caused him to do this in the first place?

Lack of knowledge about the victim frustrated him, but since he wasn't a member of the sheriff's department he thought it very unlikely they'd give him any useful information. Investigations were always kept close to the vest, and for good reasons.

Reasons that didn't keep him from feeling frustrated nor ease his concern about what might be going on over in the state park. Most of his staff were certified as law officers for the US Forest Service and carried weapons. Things were different on the other side of the line. Blaire was the only park ranger over there who was an authorized law officer. The rest were civilian seasonal hires. Given this was Wyoming, he figured any of them could come armed to work, but he had no idea what training they might have.

He was confident of Blaire's training, especially with her Army background, but come sunset she'd be all alone in that deserted park. The last two nights hadn't worried him so much with cops crawling all over the crime scene, but tonight?

He was worried.

He'd gone on a few solo missions when he'd been in spec ops, but he always had backup at the other end of his radio: a helicopter that could swoop in quickly if he got in trouble. Only once had that failed him, and he'd had to travel for three days as surreptitiously as he possibly could before he got a radio connection and found a reasonably safe place for the chopper to come in. But there was only that once.

Blaire was over there with no one nearby. He was the closest thing to a backup she had, and training combined with the recent murder made him feel he could back her up a whole lot better over there.

Holly was happy to take over for him. She seemed to like the office work almost as much as she enjoyed taking small groups on tours of the wildflowers and wildlife. She said she just liked meeting the people, and she had a natural way of making everyone feel like a friend.

He kind of lacked that ability. Too much had closed up inside him over the years. Trust didn't come easily, and chitchat was largely beyond him. Holly had a gift, and he didn't mind taking advantage of it when she enjoyed it.

For himself, he preferred to be out in the woods riding Scrappy, occasionally stopping by campgrounds for a few words with people, and if he chatted much it was with hikers. Loners like himself.

Scrappy seemed in no particular hurry this evening. He ambled along and Gus swayed in his saddle, enjoying the soothing sound of creaking leather. During a number of missions in Afghanistan, he'd ridden horseback on saddles provided by the Army, but this was somehow different. Hell, he'd never be able to put his finger on the triggers that could send him into rage or cause him to get so lost in memory he didn't know where he was.

Edginess was a constant companion. He lived with it as he lived with bouts of anxiety. Mostly he controlled it. Sometimes he thought that Scrappy was his personal comfort animal.

They reached the end of the trail and Scrappy turned toward the ranger's cabin and Blaire without any direction from him. He guessed he was getting predictable.

Blaire was sitting on her porch step as the twilight began to deepen. She waved when she saw him and stood.

"Coffee?" she called.

"When have I ever said no?"

He swung down from the saddle as Blaire went inside, presumably to bring him some coffee. He'd just reached her step when she reemerged carrying two insulated mugs. Even in midsummer, when the sun disappeared behind the mountains, the thin air began to take on a noticeable chill. She was wearing a blue sweater and jeans, and he pulled a flannel shirt out of his saddlebag to wear.

Scrappy eyed him from the side with one warm brown eye, then began to explore his surroundings. He'd tossed the reins loosely over his neck so they didn't get caught on something. Probably wouldn't be long before he shook them off anyway.

Blaire sat, and he sat beside her, resting his elbows on his knees, taking care to keep space between them. He didn't ever want her to feel as if he were encroaching.

"You hear anything?" she asked.

"Not a peep. You?"

"Nada. I did wander around up there at the outer edge of the campground. I found where some kids had been making roads in the duff and picked up a miniature red car in case someone calls me or writes about it."

"Really? For a miniature car?"

She looked at him, a crooked smile tipping her mouth. "You had a deprived childhood, Gus. Small things can be the most important stuff in the world to a kid. This is a little tow truck. Even has a hook on the boom."

He felt a smile grow on his own face. "Really cool, then."

"Clearly." She laughed quietly. "You know, this place is this deserted only at the height of winter. An awful lot of people have canceled reservations and most haven't even asked for their deposits back."

"Really? I know we're quiet, too, at least on your side of the forest, but I didn't check cancellations."

"Ah," she said. "Holly is taking over."

Something in the way she said that made him uncomfortable. He decided to take the possible bull by the potential horns. "*Not* because she's a woman. She happens to like it."

"Did I say anything?"

"Your voice was hinting."

She laughed, a delightful sound. Like him, she seemed to have trouble laughing at times, but when she relaxed enough he enjoyed hearing the sound emerge from her. He was glad the laughter hadn't been totally wiped out of her. Sometimes he wondered if *he* had much left.

He glanced up the road that led to the higher campgrounds, especially the one where the murder had happened. "It seems so out of the blue," he remarked.

"I know. Especially with the kid there. I keep wondering who would do a thing like that. Had the boy's presence been unexpected? Did the shooter even see Jimmy before he pulled the trigger?"

"Questions without answers right now," he remarked unhelpfully, then hated the way that sounded. "Sorry, I didn't mean anything by that." He took a long swallow of hot coffee.

"I didn't think you did. It's true, though. I have all these questions rolling around in my head, and the answers are beyond my knowing. I wonder if the sheriff will even share anything with us. Probably not."

"Not unless he thinks it would be useful, is my guess." Gus shifted, watching Scrappy knock the end of a branch with his nose, as if he found it entertaining to watch it bounce. It was probably easier to understand that horse's mind than the killer's mind.

After a few minutes, she spoke again. "One of my seasonals gave me chills earlier. Dave Carr. You've met him, I think?"

"Yeah, doesn't he lead backcountry ski expeditions in the winter?"

"That's him."

"So how'd he give you chills?" Turning until he leaned back against the porch stanchion, Gus sipped more coffee and waited to hear.

"Apparently there was a buzz going around town yesterday and early this morning. Some people are claiming there's a serial killer running around the mountains all the way up to Yellowstone and over to Idaho."

Gus stiffened. "Why in the hell?"

"Five murders in two years. Of course, that doesn't mean much. They were all in different places, and you can't even say all of them were killed in tents. They were all asleep when they got shot, but one guy was in the bed of his pickup, pulled over at a turnout on an access road up near Yellowstone. Sleeping, yeah, but out in plain sight." She shook her head a little. "From what Dave said, there's really nothing to link the killings."

"Other than that they all happened in the mountains and the victims were all sleeping."

"*Presumed* to be sleeping. That's talk. I'd have to ask Gage if he can check on the murders, and right now he's probably too busy to be worrying about what happened hundreds of miles away."

"True." He settled again but turned the idea around in his head. Linking murders was a chancy thing at best, especially if widely spread apart. The killer would have to leave some kind of "calling card." And if he had, wouldn't someone have picked up on it by now?

Blaire put her mug down on the porch, linked her hands as she leaned forward to rest her arms on her thighs and stared into the deepening night. "I was up at the scene. Oh, I already told you that. Sheesh, I'm losing my wits."

"I doubt it. Little car, roads in the duff."

She flashed a smile his way. "Yeah, and they were making little trees out of the ends of branches. I bet those kids were having a blast."

"I would have," he admitted. "I was really into making roads and hills to drive my cars and trucks over. My dad told me once I ought to get into model railroading, build my own scenery."

"Why didn't you?"

"I didn't have a place to do it, or the money, even though I was working at a sandwich shop, and then the Army."

Her crooked smile returned. "The Army would do it."

"Didn't leave me a whole lot of time for anything else. So, you were up at the scene? Why do I feel you have more to say about that?"

"Probably because you're perceptive and I do. Yeah, I was up there yesterday, about midday. Two miserable deputies standing watch, neither of them prepared for how chilly it can get in the thin air up there. I felt sorry for them. Anyway, I felt as if I was being watched."

That definitely snagged his attention. He'd learned the hard way never to dismiss that feeling. "But you didn't see anyone?"

"Not a soul, other than the deputies. It felt as if the

woods were still trying to get back to normal after all that happened. Not quite the same, if you know what I mean."

"Disturbed. Yeah. I've felt it."

"So anyway, maybe it was my own reaction to events and the feeling that some animals have moved away for a while. I couldn't blame them."

"Me neither." He drained his mug and was about to set it down when Blaire asked, "You want some more? I have to admit I'm feeling reluctant to go to sleep tonight."

He eyed her closely. "Did you sleep last night?"

"Mostly. I guess it hadn't sunk in yet. Tonight it's sinking in." Rising, she took his mug and her own. "If you want to come inside?"

"I'm kind of enjoying the night. Unless you'd rather be indoors."

"Not especially."

He stared out into the woods, noting that Scrappy had wandered closer to the cabin again. The horse seemed calm and content, which was a good sign. Nothing going on out there to put him on edge.

Now he, himself, was a different story. Almost always on edge. He wished he could contain it some way so that he could help Blaire relax because despite her outward demeanor, he sensed she was wound up tight inside.

She returned with more coffee and the surprising addition of a small package of cinnamon rolls. "Sugar's good for whatever ails you."

He summoned a smile. "Until you're diabetic."

"I'm not. My kingdom for a chocolate bar. I'm a chocoholic."

"A common affliction." He opened the package of rolls, which sat on a silvery tray, and helped himself to one, waiting for the next development. Because there would be one. They'd spent enough time chatting over the last two years for him to have learned the rhythms of their revelations. She had more to say. She was troubled.

"There's something wrong with this situation," she said eventually.

"No kidding."

She shook her head a little. "I don't just mean the murder. But think about it. The shooter knew to walk up to a tent. I'm betting a specific tent. You?"

He thought about it. "There were plenty to choose from. Okay, let's assume he had a specific target in mind."

"But if it wasn't some guy he knew..." She paused. "Jimmy's presence is bothering me. A lot. If the shooter knew Jasper, he'd know about Jasper's kid. If he knew Jasper well, he'd probably know the guy liked to bring his kid camping with him. So... This is an awful place to take out a man you're mad at if you know he might have a child with him. It'd make more sense to get him near work or home."

"Maybe so." He was listening to her spin a theory and wouldn't interject anything unless he saw a glaring flaw. So far, he didn't. People who were mad at someone didn't usually follow them to an out-of-the-way campground to off them. Unnecessary effort, no special benefit. Bigger chance of getting caught, actually.

As if she were reading his thoughts, she said virtually the same thing. "You want to get rid of someone you hate, do it in a heavily populated area without witnesses. Not out here where you might stand out like a sore thumb. Someone's got to know the shooter was in this area, and I seriously doubt he's a local."

He made a sound of agreement.

"I'm not used to thinking this way," she said slowly. "If I go off the rails, let me know."

"Like I'm used to thinking this way?"

That drew a fleeting smile from her, but it didn't reach her eyes. Damn, he wanted to see her blue eyes smile again.

"Anyway," Gus continued, "what I'm getting at is that the victim may have been selected at random. And that our killer must have done some scouting beforehand. How else would he know how to get in and get out so quickly and easily? He couldn't have just been wandering in the woods in the middle of the night."

He was slipping into tactical ways of thinking, and wasn't at all certain that was the right direction to take with this. It wasn't a military operation. No reason to think the killer had been thinking of…

The thought halted midstream. His mind swerved onto a slightly different track without much of a hitch. "Planned operation," he said. He felt her gaze settle on him, almost as warm as a touch. Damn, he needed to ignore the attraction he felt for her. It wouldn't be good for either of them. Besides, right now it seemed to be important to her to puzzle out this murder. Like they had any real information.

"Planned operation?" she repeated.

"Yeah. It crossed my mind for some reason." The only reason possibly being that occasionally he was distractible. He never used to be that way, but since coming home for good, he had his moments of wandering. To escape unpleasant thoughts mostly, he imagined. "I'm starting to think tactically."

She turned toward him, attentive. "Yeah," she said quietly. Same wavelength.

"So, say this was planned. How long was Jasper at the campground?"

"Two and a half weeks. I checked."

"Long enough to figure out his habits, to get a sense of the area and people around him. Long enough to plan an approach and egress."

She nodded and turned more, pulling up one leg until it was folded sideways on the porch in front of her, half a cross-legged posture. Nodding again, she sipped her coffee, evidently thinking about what he'd said.

Which, frankly, sounded like a load of crap to him now that he'd said it out loud. Was he proposing some kind of mastermind killer? To what end? Even a soldier like him wouldn't be thinking of such things if he wanted to get rid of somebody. Hell no. Get 'em in a dark alley late at night, shiv 'em in the middle of a crowd... Escape routes were easier to come by than on a nearly unpopulated mountain. Any one of those campers might have responded immediately to the gunshot. No killer had any way to know no one would.

"Doesn't make sense," he said before she could raise a list of objections that would probably mirror his own. "No reason for anyone to treat the murder tactically. Habitual thinking on my part."

"But not necessarily wrong." She looked down into her mug, remaining quiet again.

He turned his head to find Scrappy meandering around the gravel parking lot at the edge of the woods.

He loved that gelding. Probably the only living thing he allowed himself to love anymore.

"Love," he said, for no particular reason, "is a helluva scary proposition. Friendship, too, for that matter."

"Where'd that come from?"

He turned his head, meeting her eyes. "The horse, believe it or not. He's got a long life expectancy. Iraq and Afghanistan taught me to be stingy with my feelings."

"Yeah, it sure did." She closed her eyes briefly. "Maybe too stingy. I don't know. That little boy really upset me, his terror and knowing he is going to grow up without his father. But I've seen it before. Half the world seems to live in that condition."

He nodded. Nothing to say to that. It wasn't only lost comrades who haunted his nightmares, though. Plenty of civilians did, too.

"Well," she said, "if you think there's any possibility that this guy was stalking the victim, then we owe it to ourselves and everyone else to take a look-see."

"For a distant sight line."

She nodded. "A place someone could watch from and not be noticed."

He looked up the mountain. "We'll have to cover a lot of territory." No denying it. Hundreds if not thousands of acres.

"Let's start with some parameters. How far out would the guy have to hide? Would he choose upslope or down? Whatever we decide, we can expand the area later if we need to."

"We could be wasting our time."

"It's better than doing nothing at all."

With that he felt complete agreement.

* * *

They'd thrown a party for him. Even a bottle of champagne, decent champagne. Jeff felt pretty good and kept his lone slipup from Karl and Will. He figured that one shell casing couldn't give him away. Like he'd already thought, the heat of the exploding powder it had contained probably would have burned away any oils his fingers might have left behind. No reason to mention it.

At best they might find a partial, and fat lot of good it would do the cops even though he'd been fingerprinted when he joined the Army. A partial wouldn't create a match strong enough to stand up on its own. He knew because he'd looked it up.

But once they parted ways, he began to gnaw worriedly on the idea of that shell casing anyway. Useless, he kept telling himself, but part of him couldn't believe it.

So, without telling the others, he decided to go back and scout around a bit. If they hadn't found the casing, he'd remove it. Simple. Make sure there was nothing there. And he'd drive up just like any other tourist so there'd be no risk.

But that shell casing was haunting him, causing him so much anxiety that he was having trouble sleeping.

Worse, it was probably too soon to go back. He had to be sure the local authorities felt the site had nothing left to offer them, that they were totally ready to release it and forget about it.

And he'd need a cover story in case anyone wondered about him being up there. Time. He had to make himself wait a little longer.

He had a couple of weeks before he started teaching again. If he wanted to. He'd considered applying for a sabbatical for the fall term, and his department chair was agreeable, asking only that he give the department a couple of weeks warning so they could arrange for a stand-in.

But the idea of the sabbatical no longer enticed him. Sitting in his comfy little house on the edge of Laramie was proving to tax him psychologically.

Because of what they'd made him do. Because of what he'd done. Because the cries of a young child still echoed in the corridors of his mind.

Hell, if he were to be honest, the shell casing was the least of his worries. The biggest worry was how he would live with himself now. And an equally big worry was that they would insist he do this again. That they wouldn't buy that he now was so deeply involved he couldn't talk.

Damn, this was supposed to have been a *game*. Not real killings, merely the planning of them. How had Will and Karl moved past that? He'd never guessed they were so warped.

How could he have known them for so long and failed to realize they were probably both psychopaths? No real feeling for anyone else.

And how could they have known him for so long and not believe him when he said he'd never tell. Loyalty would have stopped him. But they didn't believe him, they didn't trust him, and that told him even more about them.

Friends? He'd have been better off with enemies.

Finally, anxiety pushed him to look up the state park's website. He needed to make a plan for going back there, maybe with a metal detector. After all, people still sometimes panned for gold in the streams in these mountains. It wouldn't be weird for someone to want to wander around with a metal detector hoping to find a nugget.

So he could get a metal detector and look around until he found the shell casing and then get the hell out. Easy plan. No reason to tell the others because he still didn't want them to know he'd left that casing behind.

Slow down, he told himself. *Take it easy.* Don't make a mistake that could get him into serious trouble.

He hadn't really looked at the park's website before. They'd taken a brief drive up the road to do recon and that didn't require a website. All he had needed to find was that rustic campground that vehicles couldn't. It had been easier than anticipated, too. GPS was a wonderful thing, as was a satellite receiver to track where he was. No need for a nearby cell repeater.

Thus he really didn't know anything about Twin Rocks Campground. The web page had the usual scenery pictures, one of an RV campsite, another of a rustic site and some general information for day hikes. Clearly nobody had spent a whole lot of time or money on this page.

He was about to move on to something else when he saw a name at the bottom of the page:

Blaire Afton, Chief Ranger.

Everything inside him felt as if it congealed. He had seen her from a distance on their one recon, but had thought he was mistaken.

Blaire Afton. That couldn't be the Blaire Afton he'd met in the Army and asked to go out with him. She'd declined, then he'd been injured in that training accident and mustered out. Turning to her brief bio page, he looked at her photo. It was the same Blaire Afton.

He hadn't really known her.

But what if she remembered him? What if his name came up somehow and she recalled him, either from the Army or from him passing her on his way up the road?

Suddenly a partial fingerprint on a shell casing seemed like a bigger deal. If the cops mentioned that it seemed to belong to a Jeffery Walston, would she remember the name after all this time? What if she saw him at the park and remembered his face?

He closed his laptop swiftly as if it could hide him from danger. Bad. Bad indeed. He knew the ranger, however slightly. She might be able to identify him if they somehow came up with his name. But Jeffery Walston wasn't an unusual name. It could be lots of guys.

Unless she saw him at the campground running around with a metal detector. Unless she connected him to the location of the murder.

God, he'd better stay away from her. Far away. But that shell casing was practically burning a hole in his mind.

If he'd had the guts, he might have killed himself right then. Instead he sat in a cold sweat and faced the fact that he'd probably have to fess up about the shell casing…and God knew what else.

He'd smoked, hadn't he? Thank heaven it had rained. He couldn't have left any DNA behind, could he? Surely that casing wouldn't still hold enough skin oil to identify him, either by partial print or DNA.

Surely.

But he stared blankly as his heart skipped beats, and he didn't believe it one bit. He'd broken the rule. He'd left enough behind to identify him.

God help him when the others found out.

Whatever the risk, he had to go back and make sure he found that casing and picked up any cigarette butts, rain or no rain.

And try to avoid Blaire Afton.

But he knew what the guys would tell him. He knew it with leaden certainty. Jeffery Walston might be a common name, but if Blaire Afton could link it to a face, well…

They'd tell him to kill her. To get rid of her so she couldn't identify him. Or they'd get rid of him. Squeezing his eyes closed, he faced what would happen if he ran into the ranger. He had to avoid her at all costs while cleaning up the evidence. If she saw him…

He quivered, thinking about having to kill another person, this time one he knew, however slightly.

God, he still couldn't believe the mess he'd gotten into, so innocently. Just playing a game with friends.

Until he learned the game was no game.

Terror grew in him like a tangled vine, reaching every cell in his body and mind. He had to go back and remove any evidence. No, he hadn't been able to go back for the casing while the cops were poring over the site, but they had to be gone by now. So he had to hunt for the casing and remove it if it was still there. Then he needed to go to the observation point and remove anything that remained of his presence there. Then he'd be safe. Even if Karl and Will got mad at him, he'd be safe, and so would they.

It didn't help that the kid had screamed and cried until he couldn't erase the sound from his own head. It chased him, the way fear was chasing him. He was well and truly stuck and he could see only one way out that didn't involve his dying.

He needed to calm down, think clearly, make sure he knew exactly what to do so he didn't make things worse. Reaching for a pill bottle in his pocket, he pulled out a small white pill. For anxiety. To find calm.

He had a lot of thinking to do.

Chapter 6

"I'm off the next two days," Gus said to Blaire two nights later. "I've got time to do some poking around if you can manage it."

She nodded. As the night thickened around them, the hoot of an owl filled the air. A lonely sound, although that wasn't why the owl hooted.

She murmured, "The owl calls my name."

"Don't say that," Gus said sharply. "I don't take those things lightly and you shouldn't, either. We've both seen how easily and senselessly death can come."

Little light reached them. The moon had shrunk until it was barely a sliver, and clouds kept scudding over it. Still, he thought he saw a hint of wryness in her expression.

"Superstitious much?" she asked with a lightness that surprised him, mainly because it meant her mood was improving. "I was thinking of the book."

"Oh." He'd reacted too quickly. "Some indigenous peoples consider the owl's hoot to be a bad omen. I was thinking of that."

"That's okay. And really, any of us who've gone where we've been probably pick up some superstitions. Heck, my mother even handed me a few when I was a kid. The *knock-on-wood* kind. And she hated it if anyone spilled salt."

He gave a brief laugh. "Yeah, I learned a few of those, too. You got any Irish in the family? My mom was Irish and I think she picked up a tote bag full of stuff like, *never leave an umbrella open upside down in the house.* More than once I saw her leap up, telling me not to do that."

"I never heard that one."

"It's a belief if the umbrella is open upside down it'll catch troubles for the house and family. There were others, but I left most of them behind." He paused. "Except this." Reaching inside his shirt, he pulled out a chain necklace. "My Saint Christopher medal. Apparently, he's not really a saint after all, but plenty of us still carry him around."

"Belief is what matters." She stood, stretching. "Are you heading back or do you want to use the couch? I think it's comfortable enough."

He rose, too. "That'd be great. Let me see to Scrappy and give Holly a call. And what about you? Can you get some time off tomorrow?"

"I can take two days whenever I want. Given that we're deserted right now, nobody really needs to be here. But Dave's my assistant. He'll stand in for me. I was thinking of going to town, too. I need some staples and a few fresh bits for my fridge."

Inside, Blaire scanned her small refrigerator in the back kitchen to see what else she might need to add to the list she'd been building since she last went grocery shopping. She didn't consume much herself, but she kept extra on hand for Dave, in case he worked late and for when he filled in for her on her days off.

Come winter she'd have to keep the fridge full to the brim because getting out of the park could sometimes be uncertain. Right now, however, when she was able to take a day or two every week, it wasn't as big a concern.

She called Dave on the radio, and he said he'd be glad to fill in for her tomorrow. *Good guy, Dave.*

Much as she tried to distract herself, however, her thoughts kept coming back to the murder. And to Gus. She'd learned to trust him over the two years since they'd met. They had a lot in common, of course, but it was more than that. At some point they'd crossed a bridge and for her part she knew she had shared memories with him that she would have found nearly impossible to share with anyone else.

Now, like her, he wanted to do some investigating up at the campground. Being in the Army had given them a very different mind-set in some ways, and when you looked at the murder as if it were a campaign, a mission, things popped to mind that might not if you thought of it as merely a random crime.

She was having trouble with the whole idea of random. Especially since Dave had told her that people were starting to talk about other murders, as well, and that they might be linked somehow.

Tomorrow she was going to make time to talk to the sheriff. She didn't know how much he'd tell her, but it was sure worth a try. She needed something, some kind of information to settle her about this ugly incident. She'd never be comfortable with the idea that that man had been murdered, never feel quite easy when she recalled little Jimmy's fear and sobbing, but she had a need to...

Well, pigeonhole, she guessed. Although that wasn't right, either. But even in war you had ways of dealing with matters so you could shove them in a mental rucksack out of the way.

This murder wasn't amenable to that because there were too damn many questions. War was itself an answer to a lot of things she'd had to deal with. Yeah, it was random, it was hideous, it was unthinkable. Life in a land of nightmares. But it had a name and a way to look at it.

Jasper's murder had nothing to define it except "murder."

So she needed a reason of almost any kind. An old enemy. Someone who bore a grudge. His wife's lover. Damn near anything would do because just *murder* wasn't enough for her.

She was pondering this newly discovered quirk in herself when the door opened and Gus entered, carrying his saddle with tack thrown over his shoulder. "Where can I set this?"

"Anywhere you want to."

For the first time she thought about his horse. "Is Scrappy going to be all right? I mean, I don't have a covered area for the corral here."

"I used some buckets from your lean-to. He's got food and water. And he's used to this." Gus lowered the saddle to the floor near the sidewall where there was some space. "I often go camping when I can get away, and he's happy to hang around and amuse himself, or just sleep."

"Oh." She felt oddly foolish. "I didn't know."

"Why should you? And, of course, being the nice person you are, you want to know he's okay."

She shook her head a little. "I think I care more about animals than people these days. Sorry, I was lost in thought. I just realized I have a driving need to make pigeonholes."

"Pigeonholes?"

"Yeah." She turned to go to the back and the kitchen. "Beer?"

"Thanks."

She retrieved two longnecks from the fridge and brought them out front. He accepted one bottle, then sat on the edge of the couch that filled one side of the public office space. Her living room, such as it was.

"I always liked this sofa," he remarked. "You lucked out. All I have are some institutional-type chairs."

"The last ranger left it. It doesn't suffer from overuse." She smiled. "In fact, you're the only person who uses it regularly."

"Yeah, I come visit a lot. Do you mind?"

"Of course not. If I did, I'd have told you a long time ago."

He twisted the top off his beer, flipped it into the wastebasket that sat in front of the long business desk that separated the public area from her office and raised it in salute. "Back to pigeonholes."

She didn't answer immediately, but went instead to get the office chair from behind the long bar and bring it around. She sat on it facing him, as she had so many past evenings. "Maybe not pigeonholes," she said finally, then took a sip of her beer. Icy cold, her throat welcomed it. The air was so dry up here.

"Then what?"

"Maybe what I'm trying to say is that I need some context. This murder is so random."

"That it is." He leaned back, crossing his legs loosely at the ankles. "So what do you need to know?"

At that she had to laugh. "Motive. Identity. All that stuff nobody probably knows yet. Nice as that would be, I realize I won't be told until the case is closed. But I still need something. Who was the victim? What did he do? Why was he here with his son and not the rest of his family?"

"Did he have any enemies?" he added.

She nodded, feeling rueful. "Context. I guess I don't want to believe he was chosen randomly by someone with an itch to kill. That makes me crazy."

"It'd make anyone crazy. Anyone who cares, that is." He sighed and tipped his head back as he swallowed some more beer. "I guess we have to wait for our answers."

She leaned forward on her chair, cradling her frigid beer in both hands. "I need to deal with this. It's unreasonable to be uneasy simply because I don't have all the answers. I had few enough of them in Afghanistan."

"It wasn't answers we had over there. It was one big reason. If any of us had stopped to ask *why*, we might have had a bigger problem. But the reason was baked in from the moment we arrived. It was a war. This isn't a war. I don't blame you for being uneasy. Hell, the whole reason I rode over here tonight was because I couldn't stop feeling uneasy about you being alone over here.

I'd have been over here last night but I know how damn independent you are."

"Gus…"

He held up a hand and she fell silent. "Let me finish. This is no criticism of you, or an expression of doubt in your abilities to look after yourself. No, I was uneasy because we've got a big question mark with a gun running around out there and that's a lot more difficult to protect yourself against than some known."

"Known? How so?"

"How many sandbag walls did you sit behind in Kandahar? How much armor did you wear every time you poked your nose out? Can we turn this cabin into a fortress? Not likely. It's a whole different situation, and being alone out here isn't the safest place to be, not until we can be sure the killer has moved on."

She nodded slowly, accepting his arguments. And though she could be fiercely independent and resented any implication that she was somehow less capable than a man, fact was, she was touched by his concern for her.

She stared down at her hands, cradling the beer she had hardly tasted, and remembered her early days here. She'd been on maybe her third or fourth night, feeling a mixture of pride at her recent promotion and a bit of discomfort about whether she was ready for the responsibility. Being alone out here, though, had always felt soothing. Comfortable. A long way away from ugly thoughts, pain and anguish.

Then Gus had come riding out of the spring mist that clung close to the ground that day. Wisps of it parted before him and Scrappy. Except for his green jacket, the brass badge and the Forest Service hat, she'd have wondered who the hell was riding in when the park hadn't officially opened for the season.

Iconic, she'd thought then. Even for a girl raised in the West, he looked iconic.

He'd raised a hand to wave, calling, "I'm Gus Maddox, the head ranger at the national forest next door." He and his horse had come closer. "You must be Blaire Afton?"

Thus had begun a relationship that had started as two strangers with similar jobs, then had been welded by sharing that they were both vets and sometimes had some difficulties dealing with the past. The revelations had come slowly, carefully. Trust was hard won in some areas. But now she trusted him completely.

In all that time, they had remained friends who treated each other as colleagues and occasionally as comrades. When they met up, either at one of their cabins or in town for coffee, they had the kinds of conversations she'd had with the guys in her unit in the Army.

As if there was a line that couldn't be crossed. Had they still been in the service, that line would definitely be there. But that was in the past, and now was now, and she felt ever increasing urges to know him in other ways.

A striking man, he'd have made almost any woman drool. She was a little astonished to realize she was getting to the drooling stage with him.

For some reason, the thought cheered her up, drawing her out of the uneasy darkness that had been haunting her since the murder. It was like a permission slip to get out of the serious stuff for a little while.

She looked at the bottle in her hand and noticed she'd

hardly made a dent in that beer. Good. This was no al-cohol-fueled mood.

Rising from her chair, she went to sit on the couch, not too close, but not exactly tucked into the far end, either. Even from more than a foot away, she could detect his aromas, wonderful aromas, the faint scent of man mixed with the outdoors, a bit of horse and a bit of beer. Very masculine.

Very sexy.

Oh, God, was she about to do something stupid? His gray eyes, eyes the color of a late afternoon storm rolling in over the mountains, had fixed on her and settled. It was a frank stare.

She was crossing the invisible line. He sensed it. All of a sudden she was nervous and afraid to move. She didn't want to make him uncomfortable. She didn't want to risk the precious friendship they'd built, and in her experience taking a relationship beyond that eventually led to a parting of ways.

And what if they *did* have sex? Would they become uncomfortable with one another afterward? It might prove to be a major sacrifice.

But his eyes held hers, drew her as if they were magnetic. "Blaire?"

Frank words emerged. There was little she hadn't told him about the bad things in the past, and dissembling with Gus seemed impossible now. "I'm telling myself not to go where I'm thinking about going."

That made him smile. Man, she loved the way the corners of his eyes crinkled when the smile reached them. "You are, huh? Afraid of repercussions?"

"Aren't there always repercussions?"

"Depends." Leaning to one side, he put his beer bottle on the battered end table. Then he took hers from her hands and put it beside his.

"You," he said, "are the most attractive woman I've known in a long time. Like you, I've been trying not to risk our friendship. But a lot of good things can begin between friends."

She nodded as her mouth went dry. A tremor passed through her.

"I get your reluctance. I share it. But I want you."

Oh, boy. Magic words. They lit her up like a thousand sparklers, tingling in every cell. She felt almost as if she couldn't catch her breath.

He reached out and took her hands. His touch was warm, his fingers and palms a bit calloused from hard work. He looked down at her smaller hands, then squeezed her fingers and drew her over until she sat beside him.

"I don't want to mess things up, either," he said. "But a hug ought to be safe, shouldn't it?"

He was quite a perceptive man, she thought as she nodded and let him gently pull her closer. He'd sensed what she was thinking and had turned out to be thinking along the same lines. As his arm wrapped around her, cuddling her to his side, she felt as if a spring-tight tension in her released. She relaxed, more completely than she had in a long time. She softened.

In the hollow of his shoulder, she found a firm pillow, and she could hear the beating of his heart, strong and steady. The arm he had wrapped around her gave her a gentle squeeze, then his hand began to stroke her arm.

Apparently trying to make sure matters didn't progress further until and unless they were both ready, he began to talk about tomorrow. "Do you have good top-ographic maps for the area we're going to explore?"

"Yeah. Down to a meter or so. Some geology students did it as a class project a while back. There may be some differences, though. The mountain moves."

"That it does. Rocks fall, landslides happen... But whatever you have, let's mark out a plan of action tomorrow."

"Sounds good."

"But first you want to go to town, right?"

"I need a few things, but that could wait. What I really want is to talk to the sheriff."

"I've had cause to talk to Dalton quite a few times when we've had problems. He's a good man."

She nodded, loving the way the soft flannel of his shirt felt beneath her cheek. "He used to head up the crime scene unit before he was elected sheriff."

"And before that, undercover DEA." He gave a muted laugh. "That guy has a lot of experience under his belt. Even if he can't share details with us, maybe he can offer a few opinions or speculations."

"A sense of what might have been going on," she agreed. "He doesn't strike me as a man who likes the idea of a random killing, either."

"Stranger killings are the hardest to solve." A slight sigh escaped him. "More beer?"

"I misjudged my mood."

She felt, rather than saw, his nod, then his movements as he reached for his own bottle and took a few swallows. Tentatively she let her hand come to rest on one of his denim-clad thighs. She felt the muscles jump a bit at the touch, then relax. God, he was as hard as steel. Must be all that riding.

But he didn't reject her touch, nor did he do anything to encourage it. Her hand began to absorb his warmth, and she felt an even deeper relaxation filling her. Like a cat finding sunlight, she thought with some amusement at herself.

"I'm making too much of this," she remarked. "Too much. These things happen."

"Sure, they happen all the time in the desolate woods at a campground. If I thought you were making too much of this, I wouldn't have ridden over tonight. I'm concerned, too. You're right about needing a reason. Without it, we have no idea what this killer might be planning. Not a good time to be hanging out alone."

"But Jasper wasn't alone. He was in a campground with at least eight other camping groups. A really strange place to pull this."

"Which may be the biggest clue we have. Only problem is what to do with it."

Absently her fingers had begun to stroke the taut denim on his thigh. She'd always loved the feel of worn denim, but it never occurred to her that she was self-comforting. Well, possibly in the depths of her mind, but she wasn't ready to face that.

Her self-image was one of toughness. She'd survived Afghanistan and all that went with that. She'd helped lead convoys through hell, and for all she was supposed to be a noncombatant, being female, she'd seen plenty of combat. She could handle a lot, and getting in a tizzy over a random murder struck her as an extreme overreaction.

Until she remembered Jimmy.

"It's the kid," she said presently, her voice evincing the slightest tremor. She hated the sound of weakness.

"I should be able to just let this go, Gus. Let the sheriff handle it. But I can't and it's because of that little boy. Sure, maybe the guy had a ton of enemies. Maybe he was a drug dealer or a mob type, or whatever. But what kind of sick twist would have him shot when he was in a tent with his little boy?"

"That's troubling, isn't it?" Surprising her, he put his beer down then laid his hand over hers, clasping it lightly. "It bothers me, too. When it happened, I could see it might tear you apart."

"It was awful, Gus! That poor little kid! He didn't understand what had happened, thank God. And I'm fairly sure he didn't see how badly his father was wounded. I tried to keep my back to all that. But my God! What kind of sicko would do that?"

Gus didn't answer immediately. "Maybe he didn't know the child was there. But a sicko any way you look at it, kid or no kid. The man was sound asleep in a tent. No chance to defend himself."

"And no chance to protect Jimmy. That shooter could have hit the boy, too. Accidentally or not. Everything about it makes me furious."

"I feel pretty angry myself," he agreed.

But as her thoughts roamed even further backward in time, Blaire remembered her days in the Army. "Too many kids get traumatized," she said after a minute. "Too many. I just hope Jimmy has no clear memories of that night."

"Me, too." He squeezed her hand. "You did what you could to protect him, Blaire. You took good care of him, from what I could see."

"Little enough." She lowered her head, closing her eyes. "It's killing me," she admitted. "I want to get that guy. And I'm sure the impulse has mostly to do with Jimmy."

"Hardly surprising." He turned a little, drawing her into a closer embrace. "We can only do what we can," he reminded her. "Tomorrow we'll check with the sheriff to make sure we won't get in the way. Then we'll build our strategy."

"I don't recall any ops planning that happened like this." Meaning the way he held her. She felt the laugh begin in his belly and roll upward until it emerged, a warm, amused sound.

"Nope," he agreed. "I remember always standing, or if we could sit, it was on miserable folding chairs around a table that was always gritty with dust. Hell, *we* were almost always gritty. We rigged a shower at our forward operating base and you'd barely switch into a clean set of camos before you'd be dusty again."

"It seemed like it. This is way more comfortable."

"By far."

She realized she was smiling into his shoulder. She wanted to wrap an arm around his waist but stopped herself. Lines that shouldn't be crossed. She never wanted to lose Gus's friendship.

She spoke. "I appreciate you not coming over last night to watch over me."

"I don't think I'm watching over you now. I've got a higher respect for your abilities, and it's not my place, anyway. I just kept getting this sense that it might be easier for you not to be alone at night."

"Given what happened, you're right." In Afghanistan she'd almost never been alone. That was the whole idea of a unit. But she didn't have a unit here to watch her back and there might still be a deranged killer out there running around in the woods. With everyone fleeing the campground, that didn't leave many targets for him.

"This brings me back to the random thing," she remarked. "If he's still hanging around out there, looking for someone else to shoot, the target population just shrank to next to nothing."

"I thought about that," he agreed. "My end of the forest isn't quite as deserted as yours, but I'm not sure that should make me feel complacent."

"Then there's what Dave said this morning. People have started talking about scattered killings in the woods over the last few years. Some are calling for all of them to be investigated as one case."

"I'm sure Gage would do it if he had some proof."

"Exactly. When my computer is being reliable, I've spent hours today looking up news articles." She fell silent, wishing she could let go of all of it and just enjoy this rare opportunity to be so close to Gus.

"And?" he prompted her.

"I think I found the murders that concern some people." She sensed him grow more alert, a bit stiff.

"And?" he asked again.

"And people might be right. There are similarities but also differences."

"The gang-working-together idea?"

"Makes you wonder." Her heart grew heavy at the thought. "Gang. It sounds so much worse in a way."

"Also maybe easier to solve. More people, more chances for a slipup."

She tilted her head and he obligingly tilted his so they could look at one another from a distance of about three inches.

"You're a glass-half-full kinda guy."

"I try. Wish I could say I always succeed."

She smiled, lifted her hand a bit and lightly touched his cheek. "You're a good influence."

"When I'm not in a dark pit." But he didn't seem to want to discuss that. "So, would it feel more like operational planning if I brought over a folding camp table and sprinkled a little dirt on it?"

The laugh escaped her. She hadn't even realized she was trembling on the cusp of one, but there it came. He had such a good effect on her, Gus did. He could steer a course through the difficult things and eventually bring back a happier mood. At least in her.

She was well aware he carried his own troubled memories, and he'd shared them with her. At least some of them. But like a cork, he always managed to bob back up. She could use a touch of that.

"Sure. I could even cut up the map."

He laughed again, his gray eyes dancing. "Absolutely. After all, every battle occurs at the juncture between four map sections…"

"In the dark and in the rain," she completed for him. An old saying, truer than she would have believed until she faced it.

"We do so much on computers now," she remarked, remembering scrolling through maps that were downloaded from a satellite.

"When the connection worked. I didn't like the limited view on the computer, though. Call me old-fashioned, but I always wanted a big paper map."

"Well, that's what I've got. Better yet, they're rolled, not folded, so no tears, and no corners at a point where we want to be."

He chuckled again. "There we go. I couldn't ask for

better. Do you have any idea how the terrain may have changed since the mapping?"

"Some, but I've never done a complete survey. Basically, I'm here to make sure campers are safe and that no one commits vandalism or annoys anyone else. I know the ground I routinely cover pretty well. Then comes winter and it all changes anyway."

"Yeah. And we're out there with an eye on possible avalanche risks after a heavy snow." She knew he had pretty much the same winter tasks.

"I'm not exactly looking for boulders that might have moved a few feet." Closing a park didn't mean no one would use it. A surprising number of people showed up to cross-country ski on fresh unpacked snow, or to hike around on snowshoes. Hardy types, but they weren't always aware of winter dangers.

Yes, there was a sign out front, and in several other locations, warning people they entered at their own risk. But that didn't mean Blaire didn't keep an eye out. She lived here year-round, including the deep winter months, so if someone needed something and could get to her, they'd find help.

The hard part was keeping out the snowmobilers. The amount of damage they could do, even in the dead of winter, was appalling. It was a constant battle, even though there weren't that many places where the woods opened up to give them a path.

She closed her eyes, though, and thought about what it was like up here in the winter. Beautiful. Quiet. Serene. Almost magical. She found peace here. It filled her and mostly drove away the ghosts that followed her so restlessly.

"I wish it were winter," she heard herself murmur.

"Yeah. Me, too."

She realized he'd helped ease her tension to the point that she was getting sleepy. Much as she hated to do it, she eased away from him. "Let me get you some blankets."

"Tired?"

"I guess I've been more wound up since the murder than I realized."

He smiled and stood, offering his hand to help her up. "Sleep is always good. I think we both learned that the hard way. Where are the blankets? I can get them."

She pointed up to the loft. "My bedroom."

"Then just toss them down to me."

"Okay. You know where the half bath is?" Of course he did. This wasn't his first visit to this cabin. She must be even more worn out than she had thought.

After she tossed pillows and blankets down to him and said good-night, she pulled her boots off and flopped back on the bed. God, how had she grown so tired?

Then she faced it. She hadn't been sleeping well since the murder. She'd been on edge, wound up, and tossing and turning.

But right now, calm seemed to have descended. Gus was downstairs. She could let go of everything and let relaxation seep through her every cell.

Problems could wait for morning.

And almost before she finished the thought, she fell soundly asleep, still dressed, her legs hanging over the edge of the bed.

Downstairs, Gus made his bed on the sofa, glad he'd decided to stay tonight. He got the feeling that Blaire seriously needed company. He could understand that.

Being locked inside your own head with your own worries and thoughts could be crazy-making. He'd been there and now tried to avoid it as much as possible.

Sometimes it was okay. Like her mentioning the winter woods. Like her, he loved that peaceful beauty. Or when he was out taking a lazy ride with Scrappy. But maybe being with Scrappy wasn't really being alone, he thought wryly.

He stepped outside to make sure his horse was okay and found that Scrappy had settled onto the ground, having evidently found himself a soft enough spot to curl up in. Scrappy plainly thought the world was safe tonight.

Back inside he reacquainted himself with the fact that a six-foot couch wasn't quite long enough for his six-foot-two length, but it wasn't impossible. Prop his head up a bit on the pillow and he just about made it.

Judging by the quiet from above, he guessed Blaire had fallen out quickly. Good. He suspected she might not have been sleeping well. Well, why should she? This murder had been bound to reawaken old wounds, even if only to a small degree. He felt some mental twinges himself. But like her, he wondered who could have committed an act like that.

A very sick man.

Which didn't comfort him even a little. It only made the perp more unpredictable.

Then, with nothing else he could do, he scooched onto his side and sought sleep. As with most soldiers, it wasn't hard to find.

Chapter 7

Morning brought the dread visit to Jeff. The champagne they'd toasted him with the first night had worn off. Now they wanted to discuss their next move.

He wanted no part of it, and as they began to talk in the most general terms over coffee and sweet rolls, his mind ran around frantically trying to find a way to step out of this. To get away. To have no further part in their sick game.

Because he finally had to admit it wasn't just shocking, it was sick. He hardly recognized his friends anymore. They weren't the men he'd believed them to be.

Sociopaths. Psychopaths. Whatever. It didn't matter. They were strangers to him now, as if they'd been possessed by demons.

How could he get away from this? He couldn't commit another murder. He didn't want to know anything about what they intended to do next. No way.

But fear held him silent. Maybe too silent because Karl finally said to him, "What the hell is wrong with you, Jeff? You're as silent as a tomb."

That made Will laugh. Maybe in the past a phrase like that would have amused Jeff. Now it only made him feel ill.

Karl dropped his joking manner. "What's going on, Jeff?" This time it sounded like an inquisition, barely veiling a threat.

Jeff's mind, already skittering around like a cornered rat trying to find an escape, was now joined by a wildly hammering heart. He had to say something, preferably something that would get him out of this mess. He'd done his killing. They knew he couldn't squeal. He'd implicate himself as a murderer, not as an accomplice.

But what could he say that wouldn't make things worse?

He had to clear his throat to make sound emerge. "You didn't tell me there was a kid there."

"Kid?"

"Little one. In the tent with his father."

"Did he see you?" Will's immediate concern, Jeff thought bitterly. For his own safety.

"No. Too dark. Hell, I could barely see him. But I had to listen to his screams all the way up the mountain."

The two of them exchanged looks. Jeff was rapidly reaching the point where he didn't care. If they killed him, at least he'd be out of this.

"We didn't know there was a kid," Karl said.

"Great planning," Jeff answered bitterly. "What if I'd hit him, too? You wanna talk about a manhunt?"

The other two were silent for a minute or so. Then

Karl remarked, "They wouldn't be able to find us anyway. You didn't leave a trail."

Didn't leave a trail. Well, that was the big problem,
wasn't it? A missing shell casing. And he was rapidly
getting to the point where he didn't care if they knew.

"I left one thing," he blurted out.

Two heads swiveled to look at him, and neither
looked very friendly. "What?" Karl demanded.

"A shell casing."

Will swore. "We warned you."

"Warn all you want. I forgot it. Do you know how
many people were in that campground?" He was winding up now and didn't care where it took him. "Lots,
and as soon as I fired my pistol, the kid started shrieking and the whole place woke up. I didn't have time to
pull out my penlight and look for a casing. I had to get
the hell out."

Although the truth of it was, he hadn't even remembered the casing. He might well have been able to find
it and remove it. The chance the police hadn't found it
was slim, but he was going to have to go back and look
for it anyway, because he couldn't take the chance that
he'd left evidence that could identify him and that it was
still lying out there waiting to be found.

Bad enough he'd had to commit the murder. He sure
as hell didn't want to *pay* for it.

"It's probably no big deal," Karl said a few minutes
later. "The heat of the exploding powder probably would
have burned it clean."

"And if it didn't?" Will demanded.

Karl shrugged. "Say it's got a fingerprint or two.
Partials at best. And Jeff's never been fingerprinted,
have you?"

Jeff couldn't force the lie past his throat. It was as if a vise clamped it and wouldn't let him speak.

"Jeff?" Will's voice had tightened and lowered until it almost sounded like a growled threat. "Fingerprints?"

Jeff wished he were already dead. He'd like to be out of body, watching this all from the ceiling. He wasn't going to get out of this, though. His silence was already an answer.

"When I enlisted in the Army. They took everyone's prints."

Karl swore and jumped up from his chair.

Will looked at him. "You said there'd be nothing left," Jeff said.

"There shouldn't be. That doesn't mean there won't be."

Jeff cringed instinctively as Will raised his hand. He expected to be struck, and having experienced that once before years ago, he knew it would be painful. The man was religious about staying in shape, and part of that was bodybuilding.

But Will didn't strike him. He lowered his hand and said, "We ought to bury you out back right now."

Jeff felt a flare of anger, a welcome relief from the terror he'd been living with. These men were supposed to be his friends? What alternate universe had he been living in?

He leaped up and glared at both of them. "I never wanted to do this, and you know it. I only killed that guy because you threatened to kill me if I didn't. I'm not happy about it. And if I made a freaking mistake, I'm the only one who'll go down for it, and you know it!"

"How are we supposed to know that?" Will asked.

"Simple, you jackass. No matter what I might tell the cops, you could tell them I'm nuts. There's nothing to implicate *you*. Why would I even bother? I told you months ago I'm not a rat."

"And we warned you about leaving behind any evidence," Karl growled. "Damn it, Jeff, are you missing some screws?"

"No." Jeff was getting fed up beyond containment. "You're clear. What do you care if I get picked up?"

"You need to go back and find it," Karl said. "Because the crime scene people might not have. You need to look for the shell casing, Jeff."

"How could they have missed it?"

"They're not big-city cops. A bunch of rubes. They'd miss their own noses if they didn't have mirrors."

"I can't go back there," Jeff said finally, and sagged into his chair.

"Why not?"

"Because the time we went on recon, I saw the ranger."

Will waved a hand. "Wait a minute. Why were you walking up the road? We told you to avoid that!"

"Remember, you took me on the recon. And the night of the killing. I came in from the back just like you said."

"Then why..." Karl trailed off as if he couldn't find words.

"It's simple," Jeff admitted. "I knew the ranger when we were in the Army. Just briefly. If she saw me when we drove up there, she never recognized me. As far as she was concerned, I was a total stranger."

Karl and Will exchanged long looks, then Karl said, "You're a jerk, Jeff. A total jerk. What if she remembered you afterward? What if she wonders what the hell you were doing there? You should have told us. We'd have found another place."

"I'm telling you…"

"You don't get to tell me anything. There's only one solution for this. You go back and kill her."

Gus and Blaire decided to make a small social occasion out of the morning. Gus took Scrappy back to his corral just as the first morning light was dusting the eastern sky with pink. A half hour later, as the rim of the sun just started to lift above the mountains, he picked up Blaire in his green Forest Service truck. Some of the large tools rattled in the back but that was par.

She climbed in beside him, a smile on her face. For now they were out to banish the ugly things and reach for the good ones. One of the best was breakfast at Maude's diner. For a little while she could allow her concern about what had happened to that man, Jasper, and by extension his little boy, move into the background.

She used to be better at putting things aside. She'd quickly learned when she was overseas that you just couldn't let things weigh on you constantly or you'd wear yourself out, or worse, become useless. Compartmentalizing, she thought it was called. Well, for the duration of breakfast she was going to compartmentalize the murder.

Maybe in a way what made it so hard for her was the protectiveness she felt for all the people camping in the park. As if she were their caretaker or something, which was ridiculous. Still, she handed out bandages, topical antiseptics, advice on a whole bunch of things, like starting a fire in a firepit, and even, at times, how to assemble a tent.

Mothering adults. Did she have an overinflated sense

of her own importance? Or did inexperienced people just decide to go camping?

Only some of Maude's morning regulars had arrived at the café, so they had no trouble finding a seat. Blaire had loved Maude's—or the City Diner as it was properly named—since the first time she had visited it. It was vintage in every respect, right down to the matching tape covering cracks in the upholstery of chairs and booths. The tabletops, some kind of plastic laminate, had been wiped so many times that they showed white spots. And the aromas…ah, the aromas. At this hour, they were mostly of coffee and frying bacon or ham, and enough to create an appetite even on a full stomach.

Her stomach was far from full.

They both ordered omelets filled with cheese and ham. Blaire chose rye toast on the side, but Gus asked for a double helping of home fries with his meal. And, of course, coffee, but this time Blaire ordered one of the lattes Maude had started making a few years ago, from what she understood. One concession to modernity.

It would have been nice to get through the meal without a reminder, but an older man rose from a nearby table and came over to speak to them with little preamble.

"So what's with that murder? You got any leads yet?"

Blaire weighed a response. This would be a bad time to shoot from the hip. Gus was looking at her, probably deciding that since the murder had happened in *her* park, she should answer. "The police are looking into it. Right now, you probably know as much as I do."

The man nodded, rubbing his chin. Calloused skin rasped on beard stubble. "Folks are talking about some other murders, too. Been five of them in the mountains."

"I wouldn't know about them."

He shook his head. "I think people are inclined to make up stories because it's more interesting, if you know what I mean. Well, I thought maybe you could give me some ammo to stop some of that talk."

"Sorry, I know as much as you do."

He glanced at her name tag. "Thanks, Ranger Afton." Then he returned to his table.

"So much for forgetting for half an hour," she mumbled as she lifted the latte to her lips.

"I guess once you poked your nose out, someone was going to ask about it."

"He could have been a bigger nuisance," she admitted and pulled a smile from somewhere. "So much for our little social hour."

"We can try it again around a campfire tonight."

Her smile broadened. "I like the sound of that." And she did. It had been a while since she'd done that, and never with Gus. Sometimes she held campfires with storytelling for guests at the camp, especially when there were quite a few children of appropriate age.

She enjoyed those times, times when all the bad stuff at the back of her mind went into dark corners and stayed there.

After breakfast, they walked over to the sheriff's office. Blaire didn't spend a whole lot of time with the police, but she knew a few of the officers and greeted them. Gus seemed to know everyone there who was getting ready to go out on patrol or settling into a desk. He was, after all, law enforcement himself.

She still found it hard to get to know people. Brief conversations with campers, or informative campfires, were different somehow. Odd, but she hadn't always been that way. Something had happened to her in her time in the Army. It was almost as if she were afraid to commit any real emotion, as if she feared the person would just leave. As so many of her friends had during that year in the 'Stan.

She gave herself an internal shake, telling herself not to go there. It was over except inside her own head. Ghosts. Just ghosts.

Velma, the eternal dispatcher, waved them back to Gage's office with a cigarette in her hand. Over her head on the wall a huge no-smoking sign hung.

Blaire stifled a giggle.

"Skip the coffee," Gus whispered as they entered the back hallway. "Some of the deputies say it tastes like embalming fluid."

Another reason to laugh. Was she ready for that? She guessed she was. But everything changed the instant they stepped into Gage Dalton's office.

The sheriff, one side of his face scarred by an old burn, motioned them to sit in the chairs facing his desk. If she sat just right, Blaire could see around the tippy stacks of paper and the old-fashioned cathode-ray tube monitor on the computer. That thing needed to be put out to pasture, she thought.

"Need a bigger desk?" she heard herself ask.

Gage chuckled. "I need not to have to keep every report on paper as well as on the computer. Don't ask me why. I keep thinking I should make an executive decision to put a halt to the duplication, but then a clerk over at the courthouse reminds me we'll always need a paper trail. What if the computers go down or get hacked? I still need an answer for that one. So, what's up?"

Gus looked at Blaire, so she spoke first. "We want to do a perimeter check, but we don't want to get in your way. And if there's anything you've discovered about the murder that you can share, it'd be really helpful."

Gage looked at both of them. "Don't you have your own park to watch?" he asked Gus.

"Right now I want to help catch this guy so Blaire isn't out there all alone at night wondering if he's still in the woods."

Gage nodded. "I hadn't thought of that. We've been presuming he's long gone. No reason to hang around. And as near as we can tell so far, he picked Jasper at random. He worked as an accountant for an oil company. No reason to have any enemies. God-fearing, churchgoing and nobody so far has a harsh word to say. Although that could change."

She couldn't help herself. "How is Jimmy? The little boy?"

"His mom says he doesn't seem to be aware of what happened, but she's taking him to therapy anyway. He's going to need help, at the very least, with dealing with his dad being gone for good."

"I should say so." She shook her head, remembering that sobbing little boy in her arms on a cold, cold night.

"His mom says she can't separate him from the rescue blanket, so you made a hit with that one."

"Space blanket," she said. "That's what I told him. Maybe he'll dream of being an astronaut." She sighed. "But back to the big questions. I'm hearing from one of my team members that people are talking about this murder being related to others."

"I'm hearing that, too. I have some investigators looking into it and consulting with other police departments. We'll see if we can find any links. God knows we need something more than a spent shell casing."

Gus leaned forward. "He left a shell casing behind? That's amateurish."

"Yeah, it is," Gage agreed. "Very. So the likelihood that he's responsible for other murders that left no evidence behind is pretty slim."

"Blaire had an idea," Gus said. He looked at her.

"It's probably silly," she said, ready to dismiss it.

"Nothing's silly," Gus replied, "and certainly not from you with where you've been. Spit it out."

She shrugged one shoulder. "It seems random. But when you add in the other murders people have mentioned, maybe… Maybe it's not one guy acting alone. Especially since I'm hearing that they're all different, but you say they left no evidence behind."

Gage nodded thoughtfully. "I'm not ready to agree, but it's an interesting notion. Let me see what I get back from other agencies. Then there's the question of what you mean by a perimeter search."

Gus spoke. "We were talking about how this guy had to have somewhere to watch the campground. To make sure when it was safe to go in, to choose his target, whatever. A staging location. We thought we might find something."

"Point is," Blaire admitted almost ruefully, "I'm not good at sitting on my hands. This might turn up evidence."

"You're thinking in bigger terms," Gage remarked. "Tactical terms."

Blaire nodded. "It's our training."

"It's good training. It's also a great idea. The likelihood that he just hung around until everyone went to sleep bugs me. But with kids running around the place, he'd probably be seen."

"Probably," they agreed as one.

"Go for it. At this point the likelihood we'll get anything useful off that shell casing is slim. I'll be able to match it to a weapon if we ever find it, but right now…" Gage shook his head. "Find me a pistol while you're at it."

A few minutes later, they were heading out with Gage's promise to share any information he received on the other murders. Not this investigation, of course. He couldn't breach that confidentiality. But the others? Most were probably cold cases by now. Few secrets he couldn't share.

Before they got out the door, however, Connie Parish and Beau Beauregard, both deputies, suggested coffee at Maude's. Blaire exchanged looks with Gus and got the impression that he felt that might be significant. He nodded to her and she smiled.

"Sure," she said.

Maude's had quieted some after the breakfast hour, and they had no trouble finding a relatively private booth. Coffee arrived automatically, and it seemed Maude had decided Blaire was a latte drinker, because that's what she received in a tall cup. Not that she was about to complain.

"Primarily," Connie said, speaking first, "I'm worried about you being out at the campground all alone, Blaire, especially at night. So is Beau. This was such a random killing, and the guy could still be out there. Wouldn't be the first weirdo we've had playing hermit in those mountains."

"Nor the last," Beau remarked. "The *he always kept to himself* kind don't always limit that to the apartment next door."

Despite herself, Blaire was amused. "What do you think we're dealing with here?"

"Damned if I know. The vic was an accountant. For an oil company," Connie said. "Now, how likely is that to get you shot on a camping trip? Oh, I suppose there could be reasons, but I can't imagine any. If he'd angered someone at the company, why follow him out here? This feels so random."

"At least it appears to be," Gus agreed. "But if you really think about it, a lot of life is random. Even so, maybe he had some debts he couldn't meet. Gambling, drugs."

"That's so cliché," Blaire murmured, unexpectedly drawing a laugh from the other three. "Well, it is," she protested. "Easy fallback position. Blame it on the vic."

He shrugged. "You're right. But we have so little to go on, at least as far as I know."

Turning her latte in her hands, Blaire studied it as if it might have answers. Afghanistan had been nothing like this, she thought. Nothing. It struck her as odd that one murder was bothering her so much after all that she'd lived through. Yet somehow this one murder seemed scarier. Maybe because it was so far inexplicable.

Beau spoke. "We were thinking we'd feel better if you had a dog, Blaire."

Her head snapped up. "A dog?"

"A trained police dog," Beau clarified. "I spoke to Cadell Marcus yesterday. I don't know if you've met him, but he trains our K-9s. He's got a Malinois almost ready to go, and he said he'd be willing to pass her to you, or just let you keep her for a while, whichever you prefer."

This was so unexpected, Blaire had to think about it. She liked dogs. Hell, they'd had a few bomb sniffers with them in Afghanistan. She felt great respect for a dog's abilities. But she'd never thought of wanting or needing her own K-9.

"That isn't extreme?" she said finally.

"Hardly," Gus said drily. "I slept on your sofa last night because I didn't like the idea of you being alone out there. I know you can take care of yourself, but that didn't keep me from worrying one bit. Some things seem to be engraved on my DNA."

She might have laughed except right now she felt far from laughter. A man was dead, they didn't know why and some creep might be haunting the woods.

Before she could make up her mind, Gus spoke. "I was also thinking about getting her a horse. At least for now. We want to ride around up there looking for evidence of a staging area or an isolated camp. Gideon Ironheart's the man for that, right?"

Connie nodded. "My uncle-in-law," she explained to Blaire. "In case you don't know."

"I thought everyone in the county knew how all the Parishes are related," Gus said. "It's one of the first things I heard about."

Connie flashed a grin. "For a while we just kept expanding. Anyway, if you want, I'll call Gideon. I'm sure he'll be glad to bring a mount to the park for Blaire. How well do you ride?"

"I'm pretty much a novice," Blaire warned her, but she had to admit she liked the idea of being able to ride around the mountain instead of hiking for a few days while they hunted for any kind of evidence. "I did some riding while I was in Afghanistan but I haven't done much since."

"Gideon will have a gentle, patient horse. He'll take care of everything."

"And the dog?" Beau prompted.

Blaire had to hesitate. Much as she liked dogs, she wasn't sure she wanted one living with her. She'd become attached, for one thing. For another, animals weren't allowed in the park. "You know we don't allow pets in the park. Mainly because people don't keep them leashed. They chase deer and other animals. Then, most people don't scoop up after them. So how can I have a dog and tell campers they can't?"

"Get him a K-9 vest," Beau said. "That should do all your explaining for you."

He had a point, but she still hesitated. "Let me think about it," she said finally. "Right now the place is completely empty, but give it a few days. Fears will subside and there'll be plenty of people around. Then none of you will have to worry about me being alone."

She was touched by their concern. Inwardly she was aware of her own uneasiness because of the incomprehensibility of this murder, but she didn't want to display it. She'd been to war. If she could survive that, even with some emotional damage, she could certainly survive this. And she had a reasonable, tested belief in her ability to look out for herself. Not that she was a superhero or anything, but she could handle quite a bit.

Everything except someone creeping up on her in her sleep. But she had locks and a sturdy building. She wasn't sleeping in a tent like Jasper.

But something else was going on with the idea of getting a dog. "We had bomb-sniffing dogs in Afghanistan."

"Yup," Gus agreed, then waited.

"We lost a few." She closed her eyes. "Getting attached... I'm not ready to do that again, okay?"

"Okay," said Connie. "Let me call Gideon. We'll get you a horse on loan so you can roam around with Gus and check out the area faster. I bet he can get one up there by late this afternoon. Will you be around?"

Gus spoke. "It's my understanding that Blaire wants to lay in some supplies. Then?"

The question was directed at her. "Just some supplies. Gage said he'll let us know what he learns. Beyond that, I have no business." She turned her head toward Gus. "You?"

"The same." He looked at Connie and Beau. "Figure we'll be back in place at the park by two or a little after."

Connie nodded. "I'll call Gideon now."

The trip to the grocery felt almost like emerging from night into day. It was so damn normal, she thought as she and Gus wended their way through the aisles, sharing a cart. She even decided to splurge a little on a box of frozen clam strips and a bag of frozen North Atlantic cod. Her freezer wasn't large, so she had to resist a whole lot more than that and stick to staples like boneless, skinless chicken breasts that provided a good protein base for almost anything, some frozen veggies and canned goods that would keep for a while.

When she was done, she realized she'd bought more than she usually did, and looked at the sacks she piled into the back of Gus's truck.

"I overdid it," she remarked.

He laughed. "You, too?"

She shook her head a little. "I share with my staff

once in a while, but you can't eat everything out of a box or a can. It gets boring."

"Jars," he said. "I depend on jars. Tomato sauce, Alfredo sauce, things like that."

She nodded. "I'm stocked with enough soup cans to feed an army, I believe."

"I love soup."

They were both pretty cheerful as they pulled out of town and began rolling toward the mountains and the park.

Gus brought up the problem of storage. It seemed a safe enough topic, she supposed, because with each passing mile the shadow of the murder seemed to be looming larger.

"Can't you get the state to give you a bigger refrigerator and freezer? It seems awfully small if you can't get out of the park for some reason."

"Mostly I only have to worry about myself," she answered. "I always have some backup in the cupboards during the summer, and come winter I've got the world's biggest freezer."

He laughed. "True that."

The road into the park began to rise before them, and way up above the mountain peak storm clouds seemed to be brewing. But something else was brewing inside Blaire, and finally she decided to address it directly.

"I must be crazy."

"Why?" He turned the wheel a bit trying to avoid a pothole. The truck bumped only a little.

"Because it's ridiculous to think the murderer might still be up there hiding out in the woods. And that even if he is, that he might kill someone else."

"I don't think that's crazy." Surprising her, he freed

one hand from the wheel to reach over and squeeze hers. Just a quick squeeze because as the road grew rougher, he needed both hands to control the truck. "It would be easier to dismiss the idea if we knew why Jasper was killed. A reason for it. But as it stands, the whole damn thing is an ugly mystery, and now the possibility that five other murders might be linked makes it even worse."

"Serial killer," she said. The truck engine strained a little as the climb became steeper. A short distance with a steep grade that the park system kept talking about leveling out.

"Well, we don't know that, either. But as long as it's a possibility, there's no reason to feel crazy for worrying."

"I guess not. I didn't used to be so easy to creep out."

He snorted. "You're not used to this situation. Overseas we knew we were always at risk and the threat could come from anywhere. Here, we don't expect those things. It's so out of place in the park that it's downright jarring."

"So is this road," she remarked, trying to change the subject. She didn't want to give in to the morbid maundering of her imagination, especially since her experience in Afghanistan had given her enough vivid images and memories to fill in the imaginings. The important thing was to keep control of her mind.

Yeah. She'd been working on that for years. It ought to be a perfected skill by now, but occasionally the wrong stuff still popped up and disturbed her.

"We've been talking about resurfacing this road," she remarked as the truck jolted yet again. "I don't think we're high on the state's priority list, though. We're a small campground, comparatively speaking."

"With the national forest right next door, what do you expect?" he asked lightly. "We get the roads. If people want to drive a huge RV in, they come to us. On the other hand, your campgrounds offer a lot more privacy."

"Yeah. We get a lot of tent campers. Pop-up trailer types. Not so many big RVs, but quite a few smaller ones at lower altitudes where we have hookups."

Covering familiar ground, talking about stuff he already knew, probably because she was trying to cover up her crawling sense of unease. Like when she'd been on missions. Knowing the enemy was out there, never knowing when he might strike.

"You looking forward to having a horse for a few days?" he asked, bringing them around a hairpin bend where the road went from pavement to gravel.

"Yeah, except it occurred to me, too late, I know next to nothing about caring for one. Heck, those saddles we used in Afghanistan were nothing like the one you have."

"Well, I'll share a secret with you."

"What's that?"

He flashed a smile her way. "I'll help you take care of the horse. In fact, I'll bring Scrappy over and the two can share your corral for a few days. Make a party of it."

Her discomfort subsided a bit. "A party? Seriously? When we're looking for evidence to lead us to a killer?"

He laughed. "Thought you'd like that one."

At last they pulled through the official entrance to the campground and into the small parking lot in front of her cabin. Dave was sitting on the front porch on a battered lawn chair with his feet on the railing. He waved as they pulled up. A man of about forty, mostly bald, with a friendly face and a personal uniform of plaid shirts and jeans, he made people feel welcome. Blaire sometimes wondered if *she* did.

"Didn't expect you back so soon," Dave remarked. "I thought when you said you wanted a couple of days you planned to be scarce around here."

Blaire smiled. "I do. Someone's lending me a horse and Gus and I are going to take some rides in the mountains." Why did she feel as if she couldn't share the truth with Dave? He wasn't one for gossip, and what did it matter anyway? It wasn't as if she were embarking on a top secret mission where a little talk could cost lives.

She was slipping back into the military mind-set. Whether that was good or bad, it was too soon to say. She guessed she'd find out.

"So you want me to hang around?" Dave asked. "Or come back tomorrow? I don't see two horses and it's getting kind of late in the day to take much of a ride anyway."

Blaire chewed her lip momentarily. "Would filling in for me tomorrow be a problem?"

"I'd planned to anyway. And an extra day if you want. My wife and kids went to Buffalo to visit her family, so it's not like anyone's going to miss me."

Gus spoke. "I need to go over to my place to get my horse and some supplies. If you could hang out here, I'll take Blaire with me and she can drive my truck back over while I bring Scrappy." He eyed Blaire. "If that's okay with you?"

"That's fine," she agreed. She liked the idea that Gus was evidently planning to stay another night, and that he'd help her learn how to take care of the horse that Gideon should be bringing.

"Just one thing," Gus said. "Gideon Ironheart is

bringing a horse for Blaire to ride for a few days, so if it arrives while we're gone?"

Dave nodded. "That I can handle. The corral out back is still good, mainly because I fixed it up last spring. You never know when the state might decide it would help to get us mounts. On the other hand, the way the road paving argument is going, I figure I'll be walking or using the ATVs for years to come."

"They work," Blaire pointed out with humor.

"Sure, but they don't go everywhere a horse could."

She half smiled. "And they tear up the terrain."

"Exactly." Dave pretended to be struck by the thought. "I never thought of that. Sheesh, Blaire, you ought to pass that along to the powers that be. Hey, guys, the ATVs damage the environment."

"Probably no more than the campers," she retorted. "Okay, that's how we'll do it, then." She looked at Gus. "How long should we be?"

"An hour at most. By truck my cabin isn't that far away if you take the wood trail."

She knew what he meant. There was a road between the two cabins, basically two ruts that ran between the trees, but it shaved off a lot of travel time. Gus's truck had high suspension for dealing with the rugged terrain around the forest. It could probably handle it better than most ATVs.

Thanking Dave yet again, she climbed back into the truck with Gus, and they headed along the wood trail toward his headquarters.

Chapter 8

Gus loaded the back of his truck with all kinds of horse needs, like bags of feed, currycombs and so on. He believed in taking care of any animal in his care, and some that simply needed help. When it came to Scrappy, however, it felt as if he were taking care of family.

Instead of taking the trail back to Blaire's place, he took the wood road. He led the way on Scrappy with her following behind in his truck. The day was beginning to wane. The sun had disappeared behind the mountain he was traveling over, and the light had become flat. It was still daytime, the sky above a brilliant blue, but the shadows beneath the trees seemed to have deepened anyway.

The forest didn't feel right, he thought. He supposed that was something left over from the war, but it was a feeling he couldn't dismiss anyway. As if a threat could lurk behind any tree.

Maybe it could. Some lunatic had killed a man in-offensively sleeping in his tent. Killed him with his young son beside him. What kind of person did that? The question had been bugging him since the outset.

The kind of person who would do that was exactly the reason he couldn't bring himself to leave Blaire alone again. He'd fought his instincts the first nights after the murder, but finally he couldn't continue an internal war that clearly wasn't going to sign a cease-fire.

He was worried for Blaire. She was out there alone at night, and if the campground had been full to the rafters, he'd have felt he was extraneous. But everyone had fled after the murder, and there was still no sign of a return.

People had become spooked. Unless they caught the bad guy, Blaire's campground might remain mostly empty for the rest of the season. That meant she'd be all alone out there in the woods at night after her seasonal staff went home for the day. Ordinarily that wasn't something she, or he, would worry about.

Now he was worrying. The woods didn't feel right, and instinct was crawling up and down his spine telling him this wasn't over. How he could be sure of that, he didn't know, but he remained on high alert for anything that didn't seem normal. Anything that might indicate an important change of some kind.

For certain, he was in agreement with Blaire that something about the murder seemed more like a planned operation. An assassination. Which made him truly eager to learn anything he could about the victim, but no one was going to feed that information to him. Police stuff. Civilians not wanted.

Yeah, he was a law enforcement officer, but only in

the national forest. If the murder had happened over there, he'd be part of the investigation. This was different. He didn't have a clear idea of Blaire's role vis-à-vis this kind of thing. But wasn't she, too, law enforcement in the park? But maybe not for major crimes. Maybe she was expected to rely on local authorities. It wasn't as if she had the manpower to do much else.

But still… Maybe she could press Gage a little more. Maybe, given her position, he might be willing to share more with her than information about the other murders that were now worrying people.

And man, hadn't that seemed to come out of nowhere? All of a sudden people worrying about other murders that had happened in the woods over the last couple of years. Linked? How likely was that? He had no idea.

He just knew that his gut was screaming this wasn't over, and he couldn't stop worrying about Blaire.

Tomorrow they'd pack up some supplies and do a survey of the surrounding area. The killing had been planned. Of that he was certain. And that meant someone had spent at least a little time surveying the campground and the victim. Which also meant a greater likelihood the guy had left some kind of evidence behind.

He just hoped his need to protect Blaire wasn't offending her. She had experience in combat, in military operations, and while she hadn't been in special ops the way he had, it remained she was no greenhorn. He'd often felt kinship with the way her mind worked.

So maybe he should ask her if she resented his hovering. He couldn't blame her if she did. Yeah, he should ask. He should do her that courtesy.

He also needed to be wary of his attraction to her. He'd felt it when they first met, and it hadn't lessened any with time, but he honestly still didn't feel emotionally fit to engage in a meaningful relationship deeper than friendship. And from things she'd said occasionally, he believed she felt much the same way: wary.

A misstep could kill their friendship, and he treasured that too much to risk it. Still, sometimes his body ached with yearning when he thought of her or was around her.

Careful, dude. Just be careful.

The radio on his hip crackled and he lifted it to his ear. A satellite transceiver, it usually worked, but occasionally dense woods could interfere a bit. No real interference right now, though.

"Maddox," he said into the receiver.

"Hey, boss," came the voice of Tony Eschevarria.

"What's up?" Gus asked.

"You said you'd be out of pocket the next two days?"

"At least. Over at the state campground."

"Weird, that killing," Tony remarked, his voice crackling a bit. "Listen, a deputy is here. He's looking for you and I can send him over that way if you want."

"Sure thing. I should be there in about twenty minutes."

"I hope he's got good news, Gus."

"Me, too," Gus answered. "Me, too."

He clipped the brick back in its belt holder, then leaned forward to pat Scrappy's neck. The saddle creaked a bit, a sound he'd always loved, and nearly vanished in the shivering of deciduous tree leaves in the gentle breeze. The storm that had appeared to be building over the mountains hadn't materialized, but he swore he could smell it. Tonight, maybe.

The wood road, as they called it, little more than a cart track, had once been used by lumberers gathering wood to build the old mining town on Thunder Mountain, abandoned more than a century ago. Still, the cart tracks had been convenient enough that they'd been kept clear by usage over those years.

At last the track emerged onto a portion of paved roadway just above Blaire's cabin. A truck and horse trailer now filled part of the gravel lot, and Dave was standing out front talking to Gideon Ironheart. Gus smiled. He'd always liked Gideon.

The man had once been an ironworker who'd walked the high beams, but when he came here to visit his estranged brother, Micah Parish, he'd fallen in love with one of Micah's colleagues in the sheriff's office. At least that was the story. Anyway, these days Gideon raised horses, trained them for their owners and rescued mustangs. His two teenage children often led trail rides for tourists, sometimes at the national forest.

While Blaire parked the truck, he dismounted Scrappy and called a greeting to Gideon, who walked over with an extended hand. "I hear you're planning to do a little exploring with Blaire Afton."

"That's the plan. Thanks for the help."

Gideon grinned. "It's good for the horses to have a little adventure every now and then. I might have some big paddocks but they offer little new to explore. Lita will enjoy herself a whole bunch."

"Lita's the horse?" He heard Blaire's footfalls behind him as she approached.

"Most well-behaved mare a body could ask for."

Gideon turned, smiling and offering his hand. "You must be Blaire Afton."

"I am," she answered, shaking his hand. "And you're Gideon Ironheart, right?"

"So I've heard."

Gus was glad to hear her laugh. "Your reputation precedes you," she said. "I heard someone call you a horse whisperer. So, you whisper to them?"

Gideon shook his head. "Most of so-called whispering is knowing horses. They communicate quite well if you pay attention and, if you listen, they decide to please you. Sort of like cats."

Another laugh emerged from Blaire. Gus felt like a grinning fool, just to hear her so happy.

"Let me introduce you," Gideon said. "Then I'm going to ride her up the road a ways to work out the kinks from being in the trailer. After that, she's yours as long as you need her."

"Somebody say that to me." Dave pretended to groan. "We need horses up here so badly I even took a wild hair and repaired the corral for them. Sell that to the state."

"I would if I could," Gideon answered. "I've got some fine mounts that would love working up here."

Gus and Dave helped him open the trailer and lower the ramp, then Gideon stepped inside and led an absolutely gorgeous chestnut out of the trailer.

"Oh, wow," Blaire breathed.

Gideon walked her slowly in a circle, leading her by a rein, then brought her toward Blaire. "Get to know her. Pat her neck first, don't approach her from the front until she gets to know you. Remember, she's got a big blind spot in front of her nose. And talk to her so she'll recognize your voice."

Blaire apparently didn't feel any reluctance to make friends with the horse. She wasn't quite as big as Scrappy, but still large. But then, Blaire had ridden in Afghanistan so this wasn't exactly utterly new to her.

It wasn't long before it became evident that Lita liked Blaire. Five minutes later, the horse wound her neck around and over Blaire's neck and shoulder, a horse hug.

"There you go," said Gideon. "She's yours now. Need anything in the way of supplies?"

Gus recited the list of items he'd brought with him, from bags of feed to grooming supplies.

"You'll do," Gideon agreed. "Call me if you need anything at all."

"You could send another horse," Dave laughed. "As long as you're lending them."

Not ten minutes after Gideon drove off, Dave helped carry the groceries inside, then left to spend the evening at home. He once again promised to take over for Blaire the next day if needed.

Blaire swiftly put away the groceries with an obliging Gus's help. Then the Conard County deputy arrived.

A big man, appearing to be in his sixties, he unfolded from the SUV. He had long inky hair streaked with gray, and his Native American ancestry was obvious in his face. He looked at them from dark eyes and smiled.

"Micah Parish," he said, shaking their hands. "I saw my brother headed on out." He pointed with his chin toward Lita. "New acquisition?"

"A loaner," Blaire answered. "You're storied in these

parts, and I don't even spend that much time in town so I don't get all the gossip."

Micah chuckled, a deep rumbling sound. "I'm storied because I broke some barriers around here."

Gus doubted that was the only reason.

"You talked to my daughter-in-law, Connie," he said. "And, of course, she talked to me. Then Gage talked to me. Seems like folks are worried this murder might be linked to others in the mountains. So, I'm here to share information. Thing is, Gus, I was sent first to you. Somebody's nervous about the national forest."

"The killer, you mean?" Gus frowned. "Has there been a threat?"

"No." Micah looked at Blaire. "You got maps of the whole area?"

"How much do you want?"

"Most of the mountain range on up to Yellowstone."

"On my wall. Come in. Do you want some coffee?"

"My wife, Faith, tells me the day I turn down coffee I'll be at the Pearly Gates."

She pointed him to the large map hanging on the wall and went to start a pot of coffee. For a minute or so, there was silence from the front room, then Micah and Gus began to talk.

"The thing here is this," Micah said. "Can't imagine why no one noticed it before. Hey, Blaire?"

"Yes?" She punched the button to start the pot, then came round into the front room.

"Okay to use the pushpins to mark the map?"

"Go ahead." She didn't usually do that, but the map wasn't inviolate. There was a corkboard beside it, and other than an announcement of a campfire group every

Friday evening, it was simply covered with colored pushpins.

Micah pulled a pad out of his jacket pocket and flipped it open. Then he read from it and began sticking red pushpins into the map along the mountain range. "Nobody's perfect," he remarked as he stuck the last pin in place. "I can only approximate the GPS readings on this map."

He stepped back a bit. "These are in order, marking those five murders that everyone is worried about." He pointed to the highest pin. "Number one."

Then as his finger trailed down along the pins to the one in the state campground, he called the order. There was no mistaking it. The murders had moved southward through the mountains.

"As you can see, it's not anywhere near a perfect line, but it's too close to ignore. All of the victims were isolated, but *not* alone. Like the one in your campground, Blaire. It's as if the killer wanted the body to be found immediately."

She nodded, feeling her skin crawl.

"Anyway," Micah continued, "Gage sent me to warn you, Gus, because the forest might be next in line. Although what you can do about it, I don't know. That's a whole lot of territory. But judging by the previous timing, the threat won't be too soon. You'll have time to figure out what you can do."

"What I can do?" Gus repeated. "Right now I must have thirty hikers out in the woods, plus about sixty families camping mostly at the southern side. I can't just empty the park indefinitely. Not even for this. Damn, I can hear HQ hit the roof."

Micah smiled faintly. "So can I. All you can do is

have your people remain alert. These instances might not even be linked. There sure hasn't been anything like the Jasper murder with a kid in the tent."

Blaire had been studying the map closely and eventually spoke. "It looks as if someone is trying to make these events appear random."

The men looked again, and both nodded.

"Not doing very well," Gus remarked.

"Actually, take a closer look. Every one of these killings occurred in a different jurisdiction, including two that happened across the state line. That would make linking them very difficult because the different jurisdictions operate independently. That's clever."

"If it's one killer," agreed Micah.

"It looks," said Gus, "like a carefully planned operation."

Silence fell among the three of them. Blaire's skin tightened the way it often had before going on a transport mission, knowing that danger lay ahead, but having no idea what kind, or from where.

Micah muttered, "Well, hell," as he stared at the map. "That would explain a lot." He faced them. "Gage was going to send you some of the reports, the ones he can get. I'm not sure who'll bring them up or when. Most of these cases are cold and getting colder. And from what he said, none of them have any evidence except bodies. Very useful."

"But there are two murders every summer, right?" Blaire asked. "That's what I heard."

"So it appears, not that you can be sure of much with a sample set of five. All right, I'll head back on down and pass this information to Gage. Good thinking, Blaire. You may have hit on something important."

"Important but probably useless," she responded. "Somebody with brains is behind this but finding that brain isn't going to get any easier."

"Maybe that'll change," Gus offered. "We might find something useful in our survey over the next few days. Or just thinking about all the murders from the perspective you provided might generate some ideas."

"Criminal masterminds," Micah rumbled, and half snorted. "Word is they don't exist."

Blaire couldn't suppress a smile. "That's what they say. They also say that every perp brings something to the scene and leaves something behind. Nobody's apparently found anything left behind except bodies and the bullets in them. Oh, and one shell casing."

"Yeah. The reports will verify it when Gage gets them, but from what he mentioned this morning to me, all the weapons were different, too. God help us."

Micah stayed just long enough to finish a mug of coffee, then headed back down the mountain toward town. Gus helped Blaire with grooming Lita and feeding her, along with taking care of Scrappy, and she had to admit a certain excitement at the prospect of riding around the mountains with him in the morning.

It had been a long time since she'd been in the saddle, and she'd realized during those days in Afghanistan that she really loved to ride, that she enjoyed the companionship of a horse, and that a horse could be as much of an early warning system as a trained dog. They reacted to strangers by getting nervous, for one thing.

When the horses were taken care of, they headed back inside. "I need a shower," Blaire remarked. "I smell like horse. And since you were here last night, you probably are starting to feel truly grungy."

"I'm used to grungy," he reminded her. "But I'll never turn down a hot shower. You go first."

"It's a luxury, isn't it?"

She'd never realized just how much of one it was until those long missions in the 'Stan. Sometimes she'd felt as if dust and dirt had filled her pores and could never be scrubbed out. She ran upstairs to get clean clothes.

She would have liked to luxuriate in the shower, but she needed to save hot water for Gus. Making it quick, she toweled off swiftly and climbed into fresh jeans and a long-sleeved polo with the state park logo on the shoulder. From the tiny linen cupboard, she pulled out fresh towels for him and placed them on a low stool she kept in the corner for holding her clothes.

In the front room, she found Gus unpacking fresh clothes from a saddlebag.

"Always ready?" she asked lightly.

"That's the Coast Guard, but yeah. A change of clothes is always a handy thing to have around. I'll hurry."

"I'm done. If you want to use up all the hot water, be my guest."

He laughed, disappearing down the short, narrow hallway from the kitchen into her bathroom. A short while later she heard the shower running.

Now to think of dinner. Fortunately that had been at the back of her mind while she'd been shopping, and it was easy enough to choose a frozen lasagna and preheat the oven. She'd gotten lazy. She could have cooked for two, but in the summers she avoided cooking even for herself, except when her freezer gave her fits. She had plastic containers full of things like pea soup and stew on her refrigerator shelf, but none of them held enough for two. The lasagna did.

Gus apparently believed in conserving water, because he emerged from the bathroom, his hair still wet and scented like her bar soap, before the oven beeped that it was preheated.

He looked over her shoulder, giving her the full force of his delightful aromas. "Oh, yum," he said. "I assume you're making dinner?"

"I wouldn't make this much just for me."

He laughed. "So you were thinking about me when we were at the store."

She was thinking about him a lot, she admitted to herself. Maybe too much. But she could deal with that later once things settled down around here.

She put the lasagna in the oven, still covered by its plastic sheeting per directions, then filled their mugs with more coffee. "Front room?" she asked.

"Let me go hang up this towel." He pulled it from around his neck. "Be right there."

She carried the coffee out to the front room, placing his cup on the rustic end table and hers on the counter that separated the room from the workspace. Everything here was rustic, which she liked, but it also felt empty without the usual comings and goings of campers.

She settled behind the counter on her swiveling stool, feeling it might be a safer move than sitting beside him on the sofa. She didn't know why she needed to feel safe as he posed no threat to anything except possibly her peace of mind.

Afraid of damaging their friendship, she didn't want him to even guess how sexually attractive she found him. The pull hadn't worn off with familiarity, either.

It seemed to be growing, and in the last couple of days it had grown by leaps and bounds.

He joined her just a few minutes later and dropped onto the couch. "Okay," he said. "There's one thing I want to know, and I want complete truth."

Her heart skipped a beat and discomfort made her stomach flutter. "That sounds ominous."

"It's not." He waved a hand before picking up his coffee mug and toasting her with it in a silent *thank-you*. "I just want to know if I'm driving you nuts by hovering. You're a very capable woman. You don't need a man for much."

She nearly gaped at him, then laughed. "Sexist much?"

"I don't want you to think I'm *being* sexist," he answered. "That's all."

"Ah." She bit her lower lip, but she felt like smiling. "I don't. I just thought you were being a concerned friend."

"Okay, then. It's just that you've taken care of yourself in some pretty sketchy places and situations. I *know* that, and I don't underrate it."

She nodded, liking him even more, if that was possible. "Thank you, but I'm glad you've decided to help. How much ground can I cover alone? And to be quite honest, I feel uneasy. *Really* uneasy. This whole situation stinks, and I don't care how many pins have marked that map, how do we know the killer has moved on? He might hang out in the woods. And if I were to go start poking around by myself, I might make him nervous enough to act, but he might hesitate if I'm not alone. Heck, despite what Micah Parish pointed out with those pins, how can I know I don't make an attractive target out here if I'm by myself?"

"That's my fear," he admitted. "My main fear. This guy obviously likes killing. You might look like a pear ready to pluck."

"I hear most serial killers escalate, too. Speed up." She leaned forward, her elbows on the polished pine counter, and wrapped her hands around her mug. "I've always hated being blind and I was on too many missions where we were just that—blind and waiting for something to happen. That's what this feels like."

"I hear you." Leaning back on the sofa, he crossed his legs, one ankle on the other knee. "I don't like this whole thing. One bit. I could be completely off track, though. Comparing this to anything we went through overseas on missions might really be stretching it. Those instincts could be completely wrong."

"But what are they telling you?"

"Probably the same thing yours are. There's something more than a single murder going on, and I don't mean five of them." He drummed his fingers on his thigh. "That was a really interesting point you made about the murders all being in different jurisdictions. It's not like there's a free flow of crime information between them. Not unless someone has reason to believe the crimes are linked, or they know the perp has crossed jurisdictional lines."

She nodded. "That was my understanding."

"Cops are like anyone else, they're protective of their turf."

"They don't even like the FBI, from what I hear."

"And if this really does cross state lines, the Bureau could get involved. Another reason not to open their eyes."

"Gage has."

"Gage was a Fed once himself," Gus replied. "I suspect he's less turf conscious than many."

Shaking her head, she tried to ease the tension that was growing in her neck. "There are moments when I feel as if I'm overreacting. I have no more evidence that this killer might act around here again than we have evidence period. And it's driving me nuts not to know a damn thing about why or how this happened."

He put his coffee aside and rose. "Neck tight?"

"Like a spring."

He came around behind her and began to massage her shoulders and neck. "Tell me if I press too hard or it hurts."

At that all she could do was groan with the pleasure of it. "Don't stop."

"I won't. You're tight as a drum."

She could well believe it. Part of her couldn't let this go, couldn't just brush it off. The police were dealing with it. The other part of her wouldn't just leave it alone. They needed more than a spent shell casing. A whole lot more, and if some guy had watched the campsite long enough to know how to approach and when, then he must have left something behind. *Something.* She knew optics, knew how far it was possible to see with a good scope or binoculars. He could have been more than a hundred yards away. All he needed was a sight line.

Her neck was finally letting go. Her head dropped forward and she felt the release. "Thank you."

"Okay now?"

"Yup. For now."

Dinner was ready. The oven timer beeped, letting her know. "Hungry?" she asked.

"Famished. And I suggest an early night. We should start at first light."

From the woods farther up the road, in the trees, Jeff watched in frustration. Wasn't that ranger ever going to go back to his own park? He was all over Blaire like white on rice.

He'd been told he needed to take Blaire out, but he wasn't at all sure she'd even remember their brief encounter or connect him to any of this. Why should she?

But he knew why he was here. This was his punishment for having lost that shell casing. This was his punishment because he'd known Blaire long ago. He shouldn't have told the guys that he'd passed her on his first recon out here. Hell, she hadn't recognized him then. He was probably just another face among hundreds she saw every summer, and he hadn't really noticed her. Why would she remember him any better than he'd remembered her?

But he had his marching orders. Kill or be killed. Damn, damn, damn, how had he walked into this mess? How had he honestly believed his friends were just playing a game? He should have known Will better. Should have recognized the cold streak in him.

Should have? Psychopaths were notorious for being able to hide their missing empathy, for seeming like people you really wanted to know. So many were successful con men because they appeared so warm and likable. Hard for a mere friend to begin to suspect such a thing.

But that was Jeff's conclusion now, too late. And

Karl was probably no better, or else how could they have turned this "game" so deadly? He'd been wrestling with that since he had first realized what was going on, but almost immediately they'd snared him right into this mess. His life or someone else's.

He wished he had more guts. Evidently, for him anyway, it took less guts to shoot someone else.

So now here he was, under orders to kill Blaire Afton, which he *really* didn't want to do, and she might as well have a bodyguard. What was he supposed to do? Take them both out?

He ground his teeth together and leaned his head back against a tree trunk, wishing himself anywhere else on the planet. He couldn't shoot both of them. There was enough of an uproar over the first murder.

And he still had the cries of that child hammering inside his head. He didn't lack feeling the way the other two guys did. He wished he could have shot anyone except a guy with a little kid. Why those two had picked that man…

He'd assumed it was because he was camping alone. And at first he had been, or so it had seemed. Somewhere between the time the details had become fixed and when he'd crept into that campground to shoot the man, a child had arrived. How could he have missed that?

But he knew. In his reluctance to carry out the killing, he hadn't been as attentive as he should have been. No, he'd sat up there higher in the forest, just like this, with his eyes closed, wishing he was in Tahiti, or even the depths of Antarctica.

Reluctantly, he looked again and saw the national forest truck was still parked alongside the state truck.

He wondered about the chestnut horse that had been delivered that day and was now out in the corral with the forest ranger's horse.

Maybe the two were lovebirds. Maybe they planned a nice ride in the forest and up the mountainside. Why else would there be another horse in the corral? And if that was the case, how would he ever get Blaire alone so he could shoot her? He sure as hell didn't want another body to add to his conscience.

He ached somewhere deep inside over all this and was beginning to feel that he'd be hurting over this murder until the day he died. Crap, the Jasper guy had been bad. His kid had made it worse. And now he was supposed to kill someone he had actually known however long ago and however briefly?

This time he carried a rifle so he could shoot from a distance, but he also had his pistol. He pulled it out of his holster and stared at it. All he had to do was take himself out and all of this would be over.

He turned it slowly in his hand and thought about how easy it would be. The victim had died instantly. He never moved a muscle, and while Jeff wasn't terribly educated in such things, he had expected at least some twitching or even moaning, shot to the head notwithstanding.

But the kill had apparently been instantaneous. No muscle twitching, no moan, then the kid had started screaming and Jeff had hurried away as fast as he could without pounding the ground with his feet.

As his more experienced "friends" had told him, no one would dare come out to check what had happened for a minute or two, giving him time to slip away. They'd been right. Except for the kid's squalling, the campground had remained silent and still. Confusion and self-protection had reared long enough for Jeff to vanish into the shadows of the night. All without so much as scuffing his feet on the pine needles, dirt and leaves.

No trail. No sound, certainly not with the boy screaming. No evidence other than losing a shell casing.

And now all because of that casing, and the possibility that Blaire might remember his face or name after all these years, he was back here facing another nightmare.

The night was deepening. Lights came on in her cabin. Smoke began to rise from a chimney. It was getting cold out here, so maybe it was cooling down inside.

Maybe, he thought, he ought to try popping her through the window. Sure, and that ranger would come barreling after him instantly.

Nope.

A sound of disgust escaped him, and he brought his weary body to its feet. He had to find a protected spot for the night. He hadn't bothered to locate one while there was still daylight, and through his distress he felt some annoyance with himself.

He grabbed his backpack with one hand and turned to head deeper into the woods, away from any chance encounter with someone coming up that road. He'd spend another day watching. What choice did he have?

Well, said a little voice in his head, he *could* go back to Will and Karl and confess that he was a complete failure and leave it to them to shoot him.

Except he had a very bad feeling about that. Their little game of not getting caught meant that however they chose to remove him they'd have to make it look like an accident. Which meant he could die in all sorts of ways, from a fire, to a car accident, to a rockfall. Ways that might make him suffer for quite a while.

He wouldn't go out as easily as his own victim had. No way. They'd come up with something diabolical that would keep them in the clear.

It finally was dawning on him that he had plenty of good reason to hate the two men he had always thought were his closest friends. Plenty of reason.

Clouds raced over the moon, occasionally dimming the already darkened woods even more. Each time he had to pause and wait for the light to return. All so he could find a sheltered place where the wind wouldn't beat on him all night and he could bundle up in a sleeping bag.

Maybe his mind would work better in the morning. Maybe he'd find a solution one way or another. A good solution. Hell, maybe he'd find a way out of this altogether.

Vain hope, he supposed. It was hard to hide completely anymore. Very hard. And he had no idea how to stay off the grid.

Damn it all to hell! There had to be a way. And if that way was killing Blaire Afton, what was she to him? Nothing. Not as important as his own life.

Because that's what it really came down to. Who mattered more.

He was almost positive that despite what he'd done, he mattered more. Blaire had gone to war. She probably had a body count that far exceeded anything he could do.

Hell, maybe she even *deserved* to die.

He turned that one around in his head as he finally

spread out his sleeping bag against the windbreak of a couple of large boulders.

Yeah. She deserved it.

Now he just had to figure out the best way to do it.

Feeling far better than he had in a couple of days, he curled up in his sleeping bag with some moss for a pillow, and finally, for the first time since he'd killed that guy, he slept well.

Chapter 9

Dawn was just barely breaking, the first rosy light appearing to the east, as Blaire and Gus made a breakfast of eggs, bacon and toast. They ate quickly, cleaned up quickly, then with a couple of insulated bottles full of coffee, they went out back to the corral and found two horses that looked ready for some action.

Gus helped Blaire saddle Lita, carefully instructing her on the important points of the western saddle. They weren't so very different from the saddle she had used a few times in Afghanistan.

He saddled Scrappy with practiced ease, and soon they were trotting up the road toward the rustic campsite where a man had been killed. They hadn't talked much, but Gus wasn't naturally chatty in the morning, and Blaire didn't seem to be, either.

The horses seemed to be enjoying the climb, prancing a bit, tossing their heads and whinnying once in a while as if talking to one another.

"I hope you slept well," Blaire said, breaking the prolonged silence. "That couch is barely long enough for you. Oh, heck, it's not long enough at all."

"It was fine. And yeah, I slept well. You?"

"Nightmares." She shook her head as if she could shake loose of them.

"About anything in particular?"

"I wish I knew. No, just woke up with the sensation of having spent a frightening night. I probably ought to be glad I can't remember. For too long, I could."

He knew exactly what she meant. Long after coming home, long after returning to civilian life, he'd relived some of his worst experiences in his dreams. "This situation hasn't been good for the mental health."

"No," she admitted. "I'm beginning to feel as if I'm teetering on a seesaw between the past and present." She paused. "Hey, that's exactly the thing I've been describing as being uneasy. I just realized it. Yeah, there was a murder, it was heinous, but that alone can't explain why tension is gripping me nearly every single minute."

"Maybe it could." But he didn't believe it.

Another silence fell, and he would have bet that she was considering her post-traumatic stress and how this event might have heightened it.

Everyone had it to some degree. Some were luckier, having it in smaller bits they could more easily ignore. Some couldn't get past it at all. He figured he was somewhere in the middle, and after all this time he had a better handle on it. Hell, he and Blaire had spent hours over coffee discussing it, as if talking about it would make those memories and feelings less powerful.

Maybe it had. The last few months he'd thought the two of them were moving to a better place. Now this. Not a better place at all.

When they reached the turn to the rustic campground, they paused. "Want to look over the scene again?" he asked her.

"I'm thinking. How much could the crime scene techs have missed? They certainly found the shell casing."

"True. So let's start circling farther out."

But she chose to circle the evident edge of the camping area, with all the sites in clear view. She drew rein at one point and looked down.

Gus followed her gaze and saw the small metal cars in the dirt, roadways still evident. Kids playing. Kids whose parents had been stricken enough by events that they'd left without getting these toys. Maybe the youngsters had been upset enough not to care about them, or had even forgotten them in the ugliness of what had occurred.

"Sad," Blaire remarked.

"Yeah."

They continued on their way, and through the trees he could see the tent where the man had been killed, and the crime scene tape that still surrounded the area. He wondered if anyone would clean that up or if it would be left to Blaire and her staff.

He asked, "Are they done with the scene?"

"I don't know. I need to ask. Then I guess we get to do the cleanup."

That answered his question. "I'll help."

She tossed him a quizzical look. "I thought you had your own responsibilities."

"I do, but Holly's in her element. She always enjoys standing in for me. One of these days, I bet she replaces me."

That drew a smile from Blaire and he was relieved to see it. She'd been awfully somber this morning.

After the first circuit, during which they'd noted nothing of interest, they moved out another fifty yards. The woods grew thicker but when he looked uphill, he saw more than one potential sight line. Not far enough, maybe, before they were blocked by the growth, but they were still there. He felt, however, that a watcher would have stationed himself a much longer way out if he could. Away from chance discovery.

"Kids like to run in the woods," Blaire remarked. "Several times a year we have to go looking for them. You?"

"No different for us."

"They're usually farther out than this. Far enough that they completely lose sight of the camp. Too much of a chance that someone would stumble over our killer here."

"The same thought crossed my mind."

Another smile from her. "Well, we're on the same wavelength quite a bit."

"So it seems." Mental echoes of one another at times. When he wasn't appreciating it, he could become amused by it. Right now he knew exactly what she was doing when she moved her reins to the left and headed them uphill.

"Hundred yards next?" he asked.

"Yes, if you agree."

"Why wouldn't I?" He was enjoying her taking charge and doing this her way. He'd never minded women being in charge, even though he hadn't come across it often in spec ops, and he had no trouble seeing Blaire as a complete equal. They'd walked the same roads, to some extent, and shared a lot of experience. Now they even had similar civilian jobs.

The only thing that troubled him was the attraction that kept goading him. Boy, that could blow things up fast. Then there was the protectiveness he was feeling. Even though she had said she didn't mind him hanging around, he had to hope she wasn't beginning to feel like he didn't trust her to take care of herself.

That would be demeaning. Not at all what he wanted her to feel.

They reached a point on the second circle where she drew rein sharply. He paused, just behind her, and strained his senses when she said nothing. Waiting, wondering if she had heard or seen something.

Then he noticed it, too. At first the jingle and creak of harness and saddle had made him inattentive to sound, but now that it was gone, he could hear it. Or not hear it as the case was.

She turned Lita carefully until she could look at him sideways. "The birds."

He nodded. They had fallen silent.

"Could be a hiker," she said quietly. "I don't have any registered at the moment, but simple things like letting someone know where you're going up here don't always seem important to people."

"I know," he answered just as quietly. "Not until we have to send out huge search parties to hunt for someone with a sprained ankle who can barely tell us which quadrant he's in. Don't you just love it?" Then he fell silent, too, listening.

A breeze ruffled the treetops, but that was nothing new. The air was seldom still at that height, although here at ground level it could often become nearly motionless because of the tree trunks and brush.

None of that explained the silence of the birds, however. No, that indicated major disturbance, and he doubted he and Blaire were causing it, or they'd have noticed it earlier.

Problem was, he couldn't imagine what could be causing the unusual silence. The birds were used to ordinary animals and threats in the woods, and if the two of them on horseback hadn't silenced them, what had?

Another glance at Blaire told him the silence was concerning her. The birds had to feel threatened.

Then, almost in answer to the thought, a boom of thunder rolled down the mountainside.

"Great time for Thunder Mountain to live up to its reputation," Blaire said.

They both looked up and realized the sky just to the west had grown threateningly inky. It was going to be bad.

"Better head back," he said.

She nodded reluctantly.

He understood. This search of theirs had only just begun, and now they were having to cut it short. Who could guess how much evidence might be wiped away by a downpour. Probably anything that there might be.

She started to turn Lita, then paused.

He eased Scrappy up beside her, trying to ignore the electric tingle as their legs brushed briefly. "What?" he asked.

"I just felt…something. The back of my neck prickled. Probably the coming storm." She shrugged and started her mount back toward the road.

Gus followed. Her neck had prickled? He knew that feeling and he seriously doubted it was the storm.

Growing even more alert, he scanned the woods around them. He didn't see a damn thing.

Hell's bells, Jeff thought. He saw the growing storm, although he doubted it would hit that quickly. What annoyed the dickens out of him was that the two were headed away, probably back to the cabin. He couldn't keep up with those horses unless he tried to run, and he figured he'd either make too much noise and be heard, or he'd break an ankle and die out here.

Regardless, any chance he might have found to take out Blaire was lost for now. Instead he had to figure out how to weather this storm without freezing to death. Nobody needed to draw him a map about how dangerous it was to get wet up here. He'd done enough hunting to know.

Having to hunker under a survival blanket while trying to keep his gear dry and hoping he hadn't chosen a place where he'd quickly be sitting in runoff didn't please him one bit.

Thunder boomed again, hollow but louder. Time to take cover, and quickly. He found himself a huge boulder that looked as if it sank into the ground enough to prevent a river from running under it and began to set up his basic camp. Only as he was spreading his survival blanket, however, did he realize it had a metallic coating.

Damn! Would it be enough to attract lightning? Or would he be safe because of the high trees and the boulder? Except he knew you shouldn't shelter under trees during a storm. So where the hell was he supposed to go?

The first big raindrop that hit his head told him he was out of time. He'd just have to set up here, and if he was worried about the survival blanket maybe he shouldn't use it. Just sit here and get drenched and hope the rain didn't penetrate his backpack. Out of it, he pulled a waterproof jacket that was too warm for the day, but it might be all he had to prevent hypothermia in a downpour.

Or use the damn blanket, he argued with himself. Getting struck by lightning would at least get him out of this mess. It would probably be a much better end than going back to his so-called friends without having completed this task.

Task. Murder. *Might as well face it head-on, Jeff,* he said to himself, then spoke aloud. "You're a killer now. You killed a man you didn't even know for no good reason at all except to save your own damn neck."

The woods had lost their ability to echo anything back at him. Maybe it was the growing thickness of the air, or the rain that had begun to fall more steadily. The only good thing he could say about it was that any evidence he'd left behind would be washed away.

He pulled the survival blanket out of his backpack and unfolded it, tucking it around himself and his gun and gear. A bolt of lightning would be a good thing right now.

And he didn't give a damn that this blanket must stick out like a sore thumb. Somebody finding him and taking him in for any reason at all would be almost as good as a lightning strike.

Miserable, hating himself, hating the weather, he hunkered inside the blanket.

Blaire helped Gus as much as she could with the horses. The saddles went under the lean-to to be covered with a tarp that was folded in there. The horses… Well, horses had withstood far worse for millennia, but Gus left the wool saddle blanket on their backs and gently guided them under the lean-to.

Blaire patted Lita on the neck and murmured to her. Her flanks quivered a bit as the thunder boomed, but she remained still.

"If they were free, they'd run," Gus said. "Unfortunately, I can't let them do that. They could get hurt on this ground."

She nodded, stroking Lita's side. "They'll be okay?"

"Sure. I'm positive Lita has been through storms at Gideon's ranch, and I know for a fact Scrappy's been through a bunch of them. I just want them to feel comfortable under the lean-to."

She nodded. "And if they get wet…"

"The wool saddle blankets will help keep them warm. They'll be fine, Blaire. Scrappy's never been pampered and I'm sure Gideon doesn't have enough barn space to bring his animals inside. Nope, they'll withstand it. Unlike us. Can we make some coffee?"

She laughed and led the way inside, but she honestly wasn't feeling very good. This storm threatened to kill any possibility of finding some evidence to help locate the killer. Maybe they'd been asking for too much. "Gus? Espresso or regular?"

"I could use espresso for the caffeine, but on the other

hand regular might give me an excuse to drink more hot liquid, and I feel like I'm getting a little chilled."

"You, too? I think the temperature must have dropped twenty degrees while we were riding back. Maybe we'll need a fire." Then she put her hands on her hips and tipped her head quizzically. "So, coffee? Espresso or regular?"

He grinned. "That was an evasion. I can't make up my mind. Whichever you want."

"Some help."

He followed her around to the kitchen. "Want me to bring in some wood? And do you want the fire in the fireplace or in the woodstove?"

The cabin had both. Blaire didn't know the history, but there was a nice stone fireplace next to a Franklin stove that could really put out the heat. She preferred the stove in the winter, but right now it wasn't that cold.

"Let's start with the fireplace, if that's okay."

"More romantic."

She froze as that comment dropped, but he was already on his way out to get wood. What had he meant by that? Anything? Nothing?

Dang. Her heart started beating a little faster as she wondered if he'd been joking. Since first meeting him, she'd been quashing the attraction she felt toward him, but it was very much alive and well. Those simple words had nearly set off a firestorm in her.

More romantic?

Oh, she wished.

With effort, she focused her attention on making a pot of fresh regular coffee. If he still wanted more caffeine later, it wasn't hard to make espresso.

* * *

Gus gave himself quite a few mental kicks in the butt as he gathered logs and kindling into a large tote clearly made for the task. Hadn't he seen a wood box inside? In a corner on the front side of the room? Serving as an extra seat beneath a tattered cushion? Maybe he should have checked that out first.

But after what had slipped out of his mouth, he was glad to be out here under the small lean-to alongside the cabin. The corral was out back with another lean-to, but this was the woodshed, capable of holding enough fuel for an entire winter. Right now he looked at nearly six cords of dry wood. Good enough.

He took more time than necessary because if he'd walked out on a mess of his own making with his casual comment, he needed a way to deal with it. Problem was, that would all depend on how she had reacted to it. Maybe she'd taken it as a joke. He half hoped so, even though truth had escaped his lips.

A fire in the fireplace *would* be more romantic. The question was whether this was the time or place. Or even the right relationship. She might be no more eager than he to risk their friendship.

And romance could tear it asunder if it didn't work out. Funny thing about that, how a relationship that could be so close could also be a god-awful mess if it went awry.

He ought to know. He hadn't spent his entire life living like a monk. He'd had girlfriends. He'd considered asking one of them to marry him, too. He thought he'd found true love at last. Just like a soap opera.

And just like a soap opera it had turned out that when

he was away on assignment, she liked to fool around. Being alone wasn't her cup of tea at all.

That one had hurt like hell. Mostly the betrayal, he'd decided later. He couldn't even be sure afterward that he'd really loved her. Maybe he'd been more in love with the idea of having a wife, and maybe a kid or two, and coming home after a mission to a family.

It was possible. He might well have deluded himself.

Or possibly he'd been every bit as scorched as he'd felt.

Inside he found Blaire heating up canned clam chowder as if nothing had happened.

"If you're allergic to shellfish, tell me now," she said. "I can make you something else."

"Not allergic, thank God. Life without shellfish would suck."

She laughed lightly as he went out to the fireplace and built a nice fire on the hearth. When he finished, he had a nice blaze going and she'd placed bowls of soup, a plate of crackers and some beer on the kitchenette table, where he was able to join her.

"If the bowls weren't so hot, I'd suggest eating in front of the fire," she said. "You did a nice job."

"You do a nice job of heating up canned soup," he retorted, drawing another laugh out of her. Man, he loved that sound.

"Yeah. I'm not much of a cook. Mom tried to teach me, but I felt no urge to put on an apron."

Which might be what led her to the military. No standard role for this woman. He liked it.

After dinner he insisted on taking care of washing up. When he'd dried his hands and came out to the front room, he found her staring at the map Micah Parish had stuck with pins.

"It's a definite plan," she murmured.

"I agree," he said, coming up beside her.

"But the killings are so far apart in time as well as location, there's no reason to expect him to act again anytime soon."

"You wouldn't think."

"So he's atypical for a serial murderer. Not escalating."

"Not yet anyway."

She turned her head to look at him. "This is so stupid, feeling uneasy that he might be hanging around. He's probably gone home to think about his next move."

"Maybe."

She arched a brow. "Maybe?"

He shook his head a little. "This guy appears to be smart, unless this is all chance," he said, pointing at the map.

"But if he *is* smart?"

"Then what better way to throw us off than by breaking the pattern?"

She caught her breath. "So I'm not crazy."

"Did I say you were?"

She shook her head and faced him. "You feel it, too."

"Call it combat sense. I don't know. I've got this itch at the base of my skull that won't leave me alone. I tried to act like the murder was over, the guy had gone away. That's why it took me two days to start hovering around you. Because I can't escape the feeling that this isn't over. Don't ask me why. It's just there, an itch. A sting like a pinprick in my brain. Anyway, there's no one else here for him to go after, so I started worrying about you."

She dropped her head, looking down at the wooden floor. "Yeah. From the outset I haven't been able to shake it. Something about that murder… My God, Gus, I can't get over it. What kind of monster shoots a sleeping man when his small son is right beside him? He's got no limit, evidently. So what next? My seasonal staff?"

"Or you," he said quietly.

She whipped around and faced the fire, placing her hands on her hips. It was a defiant pose, he thought.

"Let him try," she said. "Besides, this is all speculation."

But neither of them believed it. Not completely. Finely honed senses were pinging and couldn't be ignored.

Will was fed up with Jeff. He didn't bother to discuss it with Karl. He didn't want any kind of debate, even though he and Karl were very much on the same wavelength.

Jeff must be dealt with. Not necessarily killed but hamstrung enough that he'd never murmur a word about any of this. And while Karl might think that being responsible for one murder would be enough to shut him up, Will didn't.

Damn, he hated overdeveloped consciences.

He, Jeff and Karl had been friends since early childhood. Their fathers had been hunting buddies and when the boys were old enough, they'd joined the hunts with them. Always spending a few weeks here at this lodge, sharing plenty of laughter, talk and beer. It had never occurred to him that friendship with Jeff could become an Achilles' heel.

Of course, when he'd started this damn game, he'd never intended to start killing, so it had never struck him it might be best not to mention it to Jeff.

So he'd sat here in this very chair shooting off his

mouth about a game. All because he'd recently come across the story of Leopold and Loeb and had wondered if the three of them could prove they were smarter. Actually, it wasn't really a question, because Leopold and Loeb had been nowhere near as smart as they had believed.

Still, it had been intended to be a game, just as he had said that night. For a while, the stalking and planning had been enough, but then one night Karl had said, "The thrill is going away."

Fateful words. The first few times, they'd simply shot to miss, to cause a bad scare. And they'd been careful not to let Jeff know what was up, because they'd learned long ago that Jeff's conscience was probably bigger than Jeff himself. Besides, they knew him for a weakling. He hated confrontation, and when they were kids he'd been inclined to run away rather than stand up for himself.

Wimp.

So now here they were. They'd managed to pressure Jeff into killing one man just to make it impossible for him to run to the cops. But had they *really* made it impossible?

He had sensed Jeff's fear. Not that Jeff's being afraid was anything new, but the guy was afraid that he and Karl would kill *him*. They would if it became necessary. Regardless, he and Karl were certain they'd left no traces behind so even if Jeff went running to the cops, they could claim they knew nothing at all and Jeff must have gone nuts.

After all, they were, every one of them, respectable people without police records. He and Karl were pillars of their community. Jeff was...well, an underachiever. Not a man to like taking risks even to get ahead.

Now this. Jeff had been in the Army with that ranger woman. She'd glimpsed him on their first survey trip when they'd gone to pick the campground for the hit. He said he was sure she hadn't recognized him.

But Jeff had recognized *her* and that stuck in Will's craw like a fish bone. Not good.

Karl didn't like it, either. There was a link now, and Jeff was that link. They either had to get rid of Jeff or get rid of the ranger. Neither of them especially wanted to kill Jeff. He'd been part of their entire lives, and his father had been like a beloved uncle to them.

But one or the other had to go. If that woman ranger remembered Jeff being there, and found just one thing, anything, that made her draw a connection, there was going to be hell to pay.

Jeff had called just an hour ago on the sat phone, telling Will that a thunderstorm had him pinned down and he couldn't act tonight, especially with another ranger there. Will figured he just needed some goading.

For Pete's sake, pinned down by a freaking thunderstorm? Jeff needed to grow some cojones. If there were two rangers there, so what? Take them both out, then get the hell out of there. At the least, it would make this case stand out from the others in case the growing talk made the authorities think about the murders being linked.

Frustration with Jeff was nothing new these days. Will growled to himself, then pulled his tablet out of its case and looked at the map on which he'd been following Jeff's every move. Jeff had no idea that Will and Karl could track him, not that it probably mattered to him.

But it mattered to Will and Karl. If the man took a hike anywhere near a cop, they wanted to be able to step in. So far Jeff hadn't entertained any such thoughts, at least none that he'd evinced.

But that didn't ease Will's frustration any. He and Karl had agreed that after this murder they needed to take some time off. Maybe a couple of years. Find another way to amuse themselves. If they did that, any links someone might perceive would go up in smoke.

He settled back in his chair, puffing on his cigar, staring at the red blinking dot on his map. It came and went, but he was fairly certain that was because the wimp was huddling under a survival blanket, hiding from the rain. Each time the dot returned, it assured him that Jeff hadn't moved.

But damn it, Jeff, he thought. The rain would make a perfect cover to just get the job done. No one would hear a thing. It was likely any evidence would just wash away if the downpour was as heavy as Jeff had said.

He was also fairly certain that Jeff wouldn't leave another shell casing behind. So, use the high power rifle and take out the rangers and get out of the rain.

Sometimes Jeff didn't think too well.

Hell, maybe most of the time.

Will set the tablet aside and sat smoking his cigar with one hand and drumming his fingers with the other. He needed a way to motivate Jeff. Soon. This couldn't continue as long as there was a whisper of a chance that that ranger might remember him somehow, especially if his name came up. If the cops had found some kind of evidence.

Will sat forward suddenly, unpleasant feelings running down his spine. If Jeff had left behind a shell casing, maybe he'd left even more behind. He clearly hadn't been cautious enough.

Well, of course not. The wimp had been afraid. He'd scurried away leaving that casing behind and who knew what else. One of his cigarette butts? God knew how the police might be able to use something like that.

He picked up the sat phone and called Jeff. "Still raining?" he asked. He hoped so.

God, maybe he should just go out there, kill Jeff himself, then take out the ranger to be extra careful. Yeah, somehow make Jeff nearly impossible to identify because he *could* be linked to Karl and Will.

Hell! He was beginning to think more like a movie or television show. What was he going to do? Murder Jeff, cut off his fingers and face, then murder a ranger so she wouldn't suddenly remember Jeff's name?

No, Jeff was supposed to kill the ranger, tie up the last important loose end, and it was the least he could do considering he'd left that damn shell casing behind. First rule in this game: leave nothing behind. Nothing.

Jeff answered, his voice shaking.

"Why are you shaking?" Will demanded.

"Cold," came the abbreviated answer.

"Man up," Will said shortly. "Take advantage of the rain and just take the woman out. Then you can get inside again and warm your delicate toesies."

"Shut up," Jeff said. It sounded as if he'd gritted the words out between his teeth.

"I will not shut up. I might, however, come out there and kill you myself to close this out."

Complete silence answered him. Then, suddenly, he clearly heard the sound of rain beating on the survival blanket for just a few seconds before the line went empty. He glanced at the tablet and saw that Jeff had disappeared again. The son of a gun had cut him off. Probably deliberately.

But no, a few seconds later he heard Jeff's voice again and saw the dot reappear on the map.

"I'll get her tomorrow," he said. "And you know what, Will?"

God it was almost impossible to understand Jeff with his voice shaking like that. "What?"

"She saw me, all right. I don't think she recognized my face but she might have. Anyway, she knows we went up there five days before I killed that guy, and at some point she's going to put that together."

Will felt stunned. Ice water trickled down his spine. "You lie."

"No, I lied the first time. I don't trust you, and I didn't want to kill *her*, and now that's exactly where I am because you and Karl are goddamn psychopaths who don't give a flying fig about anyone else on this planet. I have half a mind to come to the lodge and kill the two of you for getting me into this."

"You don't have the stones."

"Are you sure of that? But to cover my own butt I have to make sure that woman can't put me together with this mess. That's all on you, jerk. All of it. When this is done, I want nothing to do with the two of you ever again. Buy out my share of the lodge, then stay out of my life."

Yeah, like they'd pay him a dime. But now was not the time to get into that, or even think about it.

"Has it occurred to you," Jeff asked, his voice quavering, "that she may have recognized me, but she also saw the two of you?"

"All the more reason to erase her," Will said sharply.

"No, you're not getting it, you ass. If I turn up dead, she may remember you two and give your descriptions."

That silenced Will. For once he hadn't thought of something.

"And if you think killing me will save you, think again. I turn up dead, everyone knows we're friends… Nah, you'll be under the microscope."

Dang, thought Will, maybe the guy had some stones after all.

Several seconds passed before he spoke again. "Then you'd better take her out and tie off the loose end. We told you that you could be our next target, and we're not stupid. We can make it look like an accident." Will felt his own bravado covering his sudden uncertainty.

"Yeah. Sure."

"Just do it, Jeff."

"I will, damn it. But just leave me alone. I'm not sitting out here in this miserable rain and cold because I enjoy it."

Then he disconnected, leaving Will to listen to the static of a disturbed signal.

After a minute or two, Will put down the phone and picked up his tablet. Jeff was still there. Will looked across the room to the gun rack, which held seven rifles, some good for hunting, but a couple for much longer-range shooting. Damn near sniper rifles. His dad and Karl's had often liked to practice target shooting over a thousand yards.

Jeff had one of those rifles with him right now. He didn't even have to get close to the woman.

But Will thought about going out there and using one of them on Jeff. He studied the map on his tablet, bringing up the terrain. No roads nearby. He'd have to hike through the night, a dangerous thing to do even without a storm.

Hell! He almost hurled the tablet in frustration. If Jeff didn't take that damn woman out by tomorrow night, he and Karl were going to have to do something about Jeff.

No escaping it. Especially since Jeff had pointed out that she'd seen all three of them. They'd have to get rid of him in a way that wouldn't jog her memory so they could stay clear of her.

Or they'd have to kill them both along with that nosy federal ranger.

Either way, if Jeff failed, they'd have to mop up. They should have gotten rid of him as soon as they learned he'd figured out what they were doing. Honoring an old friendship this way had proved to be the biggest headache they'd had so far.

He was coming to hate Jeff.

The wind had picked up considerably and was blowing rain so hard against the window glass that it sounded like small pebbles.

"Will the horses be okay?" Blaire asked.

"Yeah," Gus said. "They know how to hunker together and they've got pretty thick hides. If they didn't there wouldn't be any horses."

"I guess you're right. I know I wouldn't want to be out there in this."

"Not if I can avoid it," he agreed.

She rubbed her arms as they sat on the couch separated by a couple of feet. "This place doesn't usually feel drafty." She paused. "Let me take that back. It can in the winter because of the temperature differential between the glass and the log walls. That's when I put up the shutters. No shutters tonight."

She had already pulled on a cardigan, but now she rose and went to sit on the rug in front of the fire. Closer to the heat and warmth.

"Is that a wood box over there?" Gus asked.

She twisted and followed his pointing finger. "Yes, it is. I think it's full. I should have mentioned it rather than you going outside to get wood."

"I think by the time I got to the door you were in the kitchen starting soup. It's okay." Rising, he went to the box, lifted the long seat pillow off it and looked inside. "I certainly won't have to go out for more wood tonight."

She pulled her knees up under her chin and wrapped her arms around them. "This fire feels so good. But there went all hope of finding any evidence out there. This rain is heavy enough to wash it all away. And the wind will probably knock down the tent and the crime scene tape. Of course, that'll make the area fresh and clean again."

"There are advantages." He joined her on the floor, sitting cross-legged. "There had to be some place he was hanging out to observe from. I doubt the rain will wash that away. And if we find it, we might find something useful."

She glanced at him. "So you still want to go on the hunt tomorrow?"

"If this weather improves. But absolutely. If you're like me, you want to feel like you're actually accomplishing something, not sitting on your hands. I mean, I'd settle back if the police had the guy."

"So would I. But until then…" She turned her attention back to the fire. "I can't stop hearing that little boy cry. It makes me so mad. Furious. Someone needs to pay."

"Yeah. I'm with you."

Watching the flames leap, she thought about what she'd just revealed to him and herself. It *was* about the boy, she admitted. As much as anything, she wanted that boy to grow up with the satisfaction of knowing his father's killer had been caught and sent to prison. Yeah, she was worried he might still be hanging around, and she couldn't blame Gus for being concerned about her safety. Every night, with the campers all gone, she was out here all alone. It wasn't as if she never needed to emerge from this cabin during the hours when her staff weren't here.

Nope. And if this guy was in it just for the thrill, she'd make a great target. Maybe he even thought she might have found some evidence. After all, she'd been the first person to approach the tent.

"Oh, heck," she said in a burst of frustration. She reclined on the rug, staring up at the dancing shadows on the ceiling. "I hate feeling like everything is messed up and I can't do anything to sort it out. Things were a lot clearer in the Army."

"*Some* things were," he agreed. "But that kind of thinking is what makes it so hard to adjust to the return to civilian life."

"I'm sure. I've been guilty of it more than once." She rolled on her side and propped her chin in her hand. "I don't remember my life before the Army being so messy, but maybe that's not true. No way to tell now. And I'm probably misremembering a lot of things from my military days. Nothing is all that clear-cut."

"Except lines of authority, and even those can get muddy."

He unfolded his legs and stretched out beside her, also propping his chin in his hand. "What I'm trying to think about now is how I'm in a warm cabin with a full belly and a good friend instead of stuck in a frigid cave hoping the paraffin flame will actually make the instant coffee hot."

"Good thoughts," she said after a moment. Then a heavy sigh escaped her. "This is a form of PTSD, isn't it?"

"What is?"

She closed her eyes a moment. "I need to face it. A gun report. A man shot in the head, in vivid Technicolor for me, a crying kid and now I've been paranoid since it happened. The paranoia isn't based in any evidence, merely in my past experience."

She opened her eyes and found him staring at her, appearing concerned, his eyes as gray as the storm outside. He spoke. "Then we're both having PTSD. I feel the paranoia. You might be right. It might be a leftover reaction. But what if it isn't? I'm not prepared to stake everything on dismissing this. It's not like I was walking down a street and heard a backfire. This is a whole different level."

He had a point, but she hated not being able to trust her own judgment. "It's awful," she said frankly. "Not being able to trust myself. It's a new thing."

"You didn't feel this way in Afghanistan?"

"Not often. That's what I meant about everything being so clear. There were bad guys, there were good guys, and if there was any doubt, it didn't last long. But this is different. I'm worrying about the stupidest possible thing. That a killer, who has most likely already moved on so he won't be found, might be stalking *me*.

I have absolutely no evidence for that. It's just a feeling. A phantasm."

He reached out to grip her shoulder firmly but gently. "Given how many times a *feeling* has saved my life, I'm not going to dismiss this one, and neither should you. When the guy is locked up, then we can kick our own butts for our reactions. But on the off chance…" He didn't complete the sentence. He just gave her shoulder a squeeze, then let go.

"We're hot messes, Gus," she remarked after a few minutes.

"Sometimes. Not always. We're luckier than a lot of people. Holding steady jobs. Having friends."

"One *real* friend," she said honestly.

He shook his head a little but let it pass. She figured he didn't see any point arguing with the plain truth. She knew a lot of people, but as for counting friends of the kind she could truly share her mind and heart with, Gus was it. He'd been there. He understood. Considering she wasn't a hop away from a support group, Gus was priceless in that regard.

But it was more than his understanding. Gus had been there any time she needed someone. Like now. Running around with this paranoid fear clawing at her, he'd been right beside her, his mere presence making her feel safer.

"Thanks for being you," she said quietly. "Your friendship means the world."

His expression softened from concern. "I could say the same to you. Two slightly bent vets who've spent the last two years sharing things we couldn't share with most people. Then we're pretty much on our own in separate parks, tied up too much to go seeking the company of other vets. There's a support group in town, but how often could we get there? Honestly."

"Not frequently," she admitted. Her days off were generally jam-packed with things she needed to do, and come winter there was often no getting out of here at all. But Gus always managed to find his way over here on Scrappy.

She shifted her position so she could look at the fire again. Staring at him was awakening feelings in her that had absolutely nothing to do with paranoia. She was afraid she might simply leap into his arms.

No time for this, she warned herself. Not now. No way did she want to do something that would make him feel it was necessary to get out of here. He'd never evinced any sexual interest in her that she could be sure of, and she'd been careful to avoid the same.

Sometimes it seemed as if their shared experience was a wall between them. Maybe it was. Who knew what might happen if they knocked down that wall and moved past friendship.

"You ever dated much?" he suddenly asked, surprising her.

She turned to see him. "Yeah. A bit."

"Never found the right one?"

Forgetting her concerns for a moment, she smiled. "Apparently not. You?"

"I got really serious once. It turned out to be a big mistake. When I left town, she found someone else to fill in until I returned."

"Ouch!" She winced. "I don't know that I ever had that going on. Of course, I never got serious. Nobody inspired that in me."

"A tough nut, huh?" But his eyes danced a little.

"Maybe. Or maybe I'm just too damn picky."

"Picky is a good thing to be."

Taking her by surprise, he rolled onto his back, then drew her toward him until her head rested on his shoulder and his arm wrapped her back.

"Gus?" Her heart leaped with delight.

"A little comfort for us both," he answered. "Not that it's going to last long because the soles of my boots are starting to get too warm. You?"

"Yeah." She gave a quiet little laugh. "At least I'm not cold now."

"Always a good thing. Except those summers when we wished we were on an iceberg."

"Yeah. Huge extremes." Unable to resist, she snuggled a little closer and inhaled his scent. Wonderful. And the way her boots were getting warmer, she figured they'd both be safe. Another couple of minutes and they'd have to back away from the fire or completely change position.

But right now she wanted to revel in the rare experience of physical closeness with another human being. With a man. Since coming home she'd avoided it, feeling that she was too messed up to get involved without hurting someone.

Yeah, she was adapting pretty well, but if her paranoia of the past few days didn't make it clear that she wasn't completely recovered, nothing would.

And if she couldn't trust her own mind and feelings, she wasn't fit to be anyone's companion.

Then she felt her feet. "Aw, damn," she said, pulling away from his delicious embrace and sitting up. If the heat from the fire had penetrated the thick soles of her work boots, it would steadily get hotter for a while, and those soles wouldn't cool down quickly. *Been there, done that,* she thought as she tugged at laces. *Bad timing, though.*

Gus half laughed and sat up, reaching for his own boots. "You're right. I just wasn't ready to let you go."

The words warmed her heart the way the fire had warmed her boots. She tossed him a sideways smile, as she pulled her boots off and set them to one side. Stockinged feet were always comfortable in here unless the floor got really cold. That seldom happened so her feet were generally warm enough.

She realized she was growing thirsty. Beer with dinner had been great, but the soup had been salty as had the crackers. "Something to drink?" she asked.

"Sure." He rose with her and they walked around to the kitchen. "This is sort of like a shotgun house," he remarked.

"I think it was built piecemeal by adding at the back, but I'm not sure. At least I have the loft for a bedroom."

"I bet it's toasty on winter nights."

"Oh, yeah." She opened the refrigerator, revealing a couple of bottles of juice, a few more beers and soft drinks. "Or do you want coffee or tea?"

"I told you I never refuse coffee, but if it's too late for you…"

It wasn't. In fact, it wasn't that late at all, she thought as she glanced at the digital clock on the wall. She turned on the espresso machine, then said, "Latte?"

"Perfect."

Outside, the wind howled and rain beat on the windows, but inside all was warm and dry. Blaire was really glad not to be out there tonight.

Chapter 10

Jeff had just about had it. After his reaming out over the satellite phone from Will, the person he most wanted to shoot was Will. Followed, probably, by himself.

But neither of those things was going to happen. Nope. Instead he sat there shivering under a survival blanket that, while it was keeping him dry, was too open to keep him warm. The storm had dropped the temperature fast, and at this higher altitude it never got exactly hot to begin with. His fingers, even inside gloves, felt so cold he wondered if he'd get frostbite. Being reduced to eating energy bars didn't help much, either.

But he had to keep the blanket spread to protect his backpack full of essential items, like food and survival equipment, and even though it *shouldn't* make any difference, he didn't want to expose either his rifle or his pistol to the rain. They should still fire, but… What about the scope he might need? It wouldn't help to have it full of water or steamed up when he found his opportunity.

If he ever found his opportunity.

Don't leave a trail or evidence behind. The first rule, one they had repeated until his brain felt like it was being cudgeled. So maybe Blaire had recognized him. It didn't mean she'd connect him to the murder.

But since he'd admitted to knowing her, other thoughts had danced unprompted through his head. Maybe she had recognized him. Maybe she would wonder why he never registered for a campsite or signed in as a hiker. What if, by chance, she put him together mentally with the murder, or simply mentioned it to the law because it started to nag at her.

The way he'd begun to be nagged by the moment of recognition.

Or what if they found a fingerprint on that damn shell casing. She'd recognize his name if they mentioned it to her. Oh, she'd probably be able to tell them more than the Army could after all these years. It hadn't been for long, but they'd trained side by side for a few weeks. How much had he shared with her?

He couldn't recall now. Too long ago, and he hadn't placed any undue emphasis on avoiding chitchat about personal things like families and high schools and other friends. Hell, for all he knew he'd mentioned Will and Karl to her. What if she remembered *that*?

Oh man, maybe he should just risk his neck and slide down this sodden mountain through slippery dirt and duff, banging into rocks. And once he got there, he could burst into that damn cabin and take out two people before they could react. They wouldn't be expecting him at all.

And he had been a pretty good marksman even before the Army and he'd kept it up with all the hunting trips and target practice.

He *liked* shooting. A target range was one of his favorite places to spend time.

Or it had been before he'd killed a man.

His alternatives had become so narrow since Will and Karl had told him to kill a man or be killed himself. He could go to the police, turn himself in.

Yeah. And if he pointed a finger at those two, which he increasingly wanted to do, they'd have each other for alibis. Friends? Friends? Really? He couldn't think of them that way anymore. He'd told them he'd keep his mouth shut, but they'd threatened him anyway.

Psychopaths.

After the way Will had talked to him tonight, he was beginning to wonder if they wouldn't kill him anyway even if he got rid of Blaire Afton.

He swore loudly. There was no one to hear, so why not? He needed to vent the horrible stew of overwhelming anger, hatred, fear and self-loathing he was now living in. Thanks to Will and Karl.

His friends. Lifelong friends. Why had he never before noticed they were missing something essential? That thing that made most people humane: compassion.

How could he have missed that they were basically ice inside and only pretended to be like everyone else?

Well, he'd missed it until just recently, and now he was paying for his blindness. Kinda astonishing that he could know someone for so long and not see the rot at their core.

Now there was rot at his, as well. When this was over, he swore to himself, he would never again speak to either of them. Never. He would banish them from his life and try to find some way to make up for the ugliness that had planted inside him.

But first he had to get through this, and if he was going to get through this, he needed to act soon or there'd never be any atonement.

He shook his head sharply, trying to get rid of the thought. Atonement? Later. Because right now he wasn't sure there could ever be any, even if he spent the rest of his life trying.

He was a wimp. Will had called him that and he was right. If he weren't such a wimp, he'd have put the gun to his own head.

But then, unbidden, came thoughts of his wife and soon-to-be-born child. He'd managed not to think of them once through this whole mess, managed to keep them separate and clean, and prevent their memories from making him feel any uglier than he already did.

Now they surged to the forefront, and one question froze even his shivering from the cold. How in the hell could he ever touch Dinah again with these soiled hands?

In the cabin, the lattes were almost drained from their tall cups. Gus had drawn Blaire close to his side and kept an arm around her while they sipped and watched the fire dance.

"We'll go out again tomorrow," he told her. "If there's anything left to be found, we'll find it."

She wanted to believe him, but she knew she had to

look, unlikely though it was. She wouldn't rest unless she tried. That was how she was built.

"Promise you won't hate me?" he said a few minutes later.

"I don't think I could do that," she said honestly. He'd been there every time she'd needed him for an emotional crisis in the last couple of years. Every time she'd needed him for anything.

"Oh," he answered, "it's always possible."

She shook her head a little. "Why are you afraid I'd hate you?"

"Because I want to cross a line."

She caught her breath as her heart slammed into a faster rhythm. "Gus?" she nearly whispered.

"I want to kiss you," he said quietly but bluntly. "I'm going out of my mind wanting you. I realize you probably don't feel the same but…"

"Hush," she said, hardly able to keep her breath.

He hushed instantly and started to draw his arm away. That was not at all what she wanted. She twisted around until she was pressed into him and able to look straight at his face.

"Kiss me. Just do it. And don't stop there."

She watched his expression change radically. It went from a little intense to soft warmth. "Blaire, I wasn't…"

"No, but I am. I know I've been trying to hide my attraction to you because I didn't want to damage our friendship, but—" She stopped, all of a sudden afraid that she'd gone way too far, that he might want to get out of here without even that kiss he'd asked for.

Then he spoke, hardly more than a murmur. "I was worried about the same thing. What we have is already irreplaceable."

She nodded, her mouth going dry, her throat threatening to close off and her heart hammering hard enough to leap out of her breast. She'd blown it, and she hadn't been this frightened since her first exposure to hostile fire. "We can keep it," she said hoarsely and hopefully. "We're grown-ups."

"I want a lot more than a kiss from you," he said. "A lot. But if you change your mind…"

"I know how to say no. I'm not saying it."

He started to smile, but before the expression completed, he clamped his mouth over hers in the most commanding, demanding kiss she'd ever felt. Her heart soared as his tongue slipped past her lips and began to plunder her mouth in a timeless rhythm.

Electric sparkles joined the mayhem he'd already set loose in her, filling her with heat and desire and a longing so strong it almost made her ache.

She'd waited forever, and now the wait was over. He was claiming her in the only way she'd ever wanted to be claimed.

She raised a hand, clutching at his shirt, hanging on to him for dear life. This felt so right, so good. So perfect. *Never let it end.* Then she felt his hand begin to caress her, first down her side, then slipping around front until he cradled her breast.

His touch was gentle, almost respectful, as he began to knead sensitive flesh through layers of sweater, shirt and bra. Those layers might as well have not been there. The thrill from his touch raced through her body all the way to her center until she had to clamp her thighs together. She felt her nipple harden, and when he drew back slightly from the kiss she had to gasp for air.

"You're so beautiful," he whispered, releasing her

breast just long enough to brush her hair back from her cheek. "Beautiful. I've had to fight to keep my hands off you."

Music to her soul. When he released her she almost cried out, but he stood and drew her up with him. Then she looked down as he pushed the cardigan off her shoulders and reached for the buttons of her work shirt. She wished she were wearing lace and satin, fancy lingerie, instead of simple cotton, but the wish vanished swiftly as he pushed the shirt off her shoulders and let it fall to the floor.

His gaze drank her in, noting her in a way that made her feel as if he truly never wanted to forget a single line of her. Then with a twist, he released the back clasp of her bra and it, too, drifted to the floor as she spilled free of her confinement.

"Perfect," he muttered, bending his head to suck one of her nipples.

She gasped again as the electric charge ran through her and set off an ache at her center that could be answered only one way. Helplessly she grabbed his head, holding him close, never wanting the sensation to end.

She felt his fingers working the button of her jeans, then his hands pushing them down along with her undies. Then, taking his mouth from her breast, causing her to groan a protest, he urged her back onto the couch.

Her eyes, which had closed at some point she couldn't remember, opened a bit to see him tug her pants off and toss them away. Then without a moment's hesitation he began to strip himself, baring to her hungry gaze the hard lines of a male body at its peak of perfection.

"You're gorgeous," she croaked as he unwrapped himself.

"Not as gorgeous as you," he said huskily.

Man, he was ready for her, and her insides quivered and clenched in recognition. All of him was big, and right now all of him was hard, too.

He reached for her hands and pulled her up until she was pressed against him, front to front, and his powerful arms wrapped around her. As he bent his head to drop kisses on her neck, she shivered with delight and with being naked against his heated nakedness.

There was no feeling in the world, she thought, like skin on skin, like having his hard, satiny member pressed against the flat of her belly, an incitement and a promise.

"Want to go up to the loft or make a pallet down here?" he asked her between kisses.

She sighed, hanging on to her mind with difficulty while he busily tried to strip her to basic instincts. "Climbing that ladder isn't sexy."

"Unless you're the one climbing behind."

Her sleepy eyes popped all the way open as she felt as if she were drowning in the gray pools of his. They wrapped around her like his arms, the color of the stormy sky outside, but bringing a storm of a very different kind. And with them came a sleepy smile.

Teasing her. At a time like this. She loved it as warmth continued to spread into her and turn into heat like lava. Her legs began to quiver, and all she wanted was to feel his weight atop her and his member hard inside her.

He must have felt her starting to slip, because suddenly his hands cupped her rump, such an exquisite and intimate experience, and lifted her. Then he put her carefully on the couch.

"Before one of us falls down," he said thickly, "I'll make that pallet."

Damn, she hated that he'd let her go, but there was nothing she could do except press her legs together in anticipation, waiting for the moment he would satisfy the burgeoning ache inside her.

He grabbed the folded blankets she had given him the night before and spread them on the rug before the hearth, folding them in half for extra padding. The pillow soon joined it. Then before she could stir much at all, he once again lifted her and laid her down on the bed he'd made for the two of them.

Softness below, hardness above, heat from one side and a chill from the other. Sensations overwhelmed her, each seeming to join and augment the hunger he had awakened in her. "Gus…" she whispered, at once feeling weak and yet so strong. Her hands found his powerful shoulders, clinging. Her legs parted, inviting his possession.

Nobody in her life had ever made her feel this hot so swiftly. No one. It was as if he possessed a magic connection to all the nerve endings in her body, so that his least touch made every single one of them tingle with awareness and need.

He kissed her mouth again, deeply but more gently. His hands wandered her shoulders, her neck, and then her breasts. After a few minutes of driving her nearly crazy with longing, his mouth latched onto her nipple, sucking strongly until she arched with each pull of his mouth, feeling devoured but hungrier still. Her hips bucked in response, finding her rhythm, and then, depriving her of breath, he entered her.

Filled, stretched and finding the answer she had so

needed, she stilled for just a moment, needing to savor him, needing the moment to last forever.

He must have felt nearly the same, because he, too, stilled, then caught her face between his hands. Her eyelids fluttered and she looked into his eyes, feeling as if she could see all the way to his soul.

Never had any moment felt so exquisite.

Hunger washed through Gus in powerful waves. He'd had good sex before, but this was beyond any previous experience. Something about Blaire had lit rockets in him, driving him in ways that stole his self-control.

Part of his mind wanted to make this flawless, to give her every possible sensation he could before completion. Most of him refused to listen. There'd be another time for slow exploration, gentle touches and caresses. Time to learn all that delighted her.

Right now he could not ignore the one goal his body drove toward. After those moments of stillness that had seemed to come from somewhere out among the stars, his body took over again, leaving his brain far behind.

A rocket to the moon. A journey beyond the solar system. A careening sense of falling into the center of the universe.

Everything that mattered was here and now. All of it. Blaire and he became the sole occupants in a special world beyond which nothing else existed.

He pumped into her, hearing her gasps, moans and cries, goaded by them and by the way her hips rose to meet his. Her nails dug into his shoulders, the pain so much a part of the pleasure that they were indistinguishable.

He felt culmination overtake her, felt it in the stiffening of her body and the keening cry that escaped her. He held on to the last shred of his self-control until he heard her reach the peak once more.

Then he jetted into her, into the cosmos. Into a place out of time and mind, feeling as if his entire soul spilled into her.

Eventually he came back to their place in time, aware that he had collapsed on her, that his weight might be uncomfortable. But she was still clinging to his shoulders, and when he tried to roll off she made a small sound of protest, trying to hang on, then let him go.

"My God," he whispered.

"Yeah," she murmured in reply.

Perspiration dried quickly in the heat from the fire. He rolled over and draped an arm around her waist. "You okay?"

"Okay? I don't think I've ever been better."

He saw her smile dawn on her puffy lips. He'd kissed her too hard, but at least she wasn't wincing. That kiss had come from deep within him, expressing a desire he'd been trying to bury since he'd first met her.

But since she wasn't complaining, he wasn't going to apologize. She wiggled around a bit until she faced him and placed her hand on his chest. "We can do this again, right?"

If he hadn't spent every ounce of energy he had on her, he'd have laughed and proved it. Instead he returned her smile and said, "Believe it."

She closed her eyes, still smiling, and ran her palm over his smooth skin. "All this time and I never dreamed how perfect you are without clothing."

"Perfect? You're missing the scars."

"Battle scars," she retorted. "I have a few, too. You didn't point them out and I'm blind to yours. Just take the heartfelt compliment. I knew you were in great shape, I just never imagined such a striking package."

"I can say the same. I've been pining for you since day one."

A quiet little laugh escaped her. "We were behaving."

"We wanted to take care of our friendship."

Her eyes opened wider. "I know. Have we blown it?"

He shook his head slowly. "I don't think so."

"Me, either. This feels incredibly right."

He thought so, too. Holding her close was no longer ruled by the passion between them. He felt a different kind of warmth growing in him, the sense that an emptiness had been filled, that places perennially cold in his heart were thawing. He gave himself up to the gift that felt perilously close to a peace he had forgotten existed.

He was not the kind of man who wished for the impossible, but at that moment he wished he could stay in this place forever, with Blaire in his arms, with the warmth in his heart and soul. To cling to feelings he'd lost so long ago, that had become the detritus of war.

He spent a lot of time *not* thinking about the war. Sometimes it was like trying to avoid the elephant in the room, but he tried to focus on the present day and the needs of the forest he protected and the people he served. Just taking care of Mother Nature and offering a bandage to a kid who'd cut his finger on a sharp piece of wood, those things made him feel good about himself.

So he tried not to remember. Still, the demons roared up out of the depths from time to time. They did for Blaire, too, and when it happened they got together whether in town for a trip to the diner or at one of their headquarters. Sometimes they hardly had to speak at all. A simple word or two would convey everything that was necessary.

They'd been balm for each other for a long time. He actually depended on her and she seemed to depend on him. But this was so very different. This wasn't dependence of any kind. This was a meeting of two souls with a hunger for something greater.

She ran her hand over his back, not paying any special attention to the burn scar that wrinkled his back on one side. "Your skin feels so good," she murmured.

He stroked her side in return. "So does yours. Plus your curves. Enough to drive a guy crazy. Did that give you any trouble on duty?" He'd seen more than enough men crossing the line with women in their units.

"Some. Funny thing, though. After infantry training I wasn't an easy target anymore. Most of them wisely didn't press the issue."

He liked the thought of her scaring the bejesus out of some young fool who thought he was entitled to take what he wanted, to expect some woman to be grateful for his attentions.

"I was also luckier than some because my superiors weren't into sexual harassment at all."

"Fortunate. I saw some of that stuff. I'm glad it overlooked you."

And there they were, returning to the safe—safe?—ground of their military experience. He could have sighed, and it was all his fault.

Then he found the escape hatch before he totally destroyed the mood. His stomach growled. A giggle escaped Blaire.

"Yeah," he said. "I guess the soup didn't stick. Want me to wander into the kitchen and find something for both of us?"

In the end, they slipped into jeans and shirts and went barefoot into the kitchen together. She did have a few things handy, things she didn't usually buy in any kind of quantity because they were too tempting. But tucked into her freezer, lying flat beneath a load of other food, was a frozen pizza.

"I can doctor it with canned mushrooms and some fresh bell peppers," she offered. She'd splurged on a couple of peppers at the store. In fact, as she looked inside her fridge, she saw a whole bunch of splurges she'd hardly been aware of making. Her mood? Or because she had hoped that Gus would stay the night again? The latter, she suspected. Regardless, her usually bare refrigerator was stuffed to the gills tonight.

"Mind if I look around?"

She waved him toward the fridge. "Help yourself. And if you like to cook, so much the better."

But cooking never became involved. He found her brick of white Vermont cheddar cheese, an unopened package of pepperoni slices that she'd almost forgotten she had and a box of wheat crackers in the cupboard. He wielded her chef's knife like a pro and soon had a large plate full of sliced, crumbly cheese with crackers and pepperoni. It looked like a professional job.

"I suppose I should have saved the pepperoni for the pizza," he said as he carried the plate into the living room and pulled the end table around to hold it. She followed with two cans of cola.

"That pizza is a desperation measure," she answered. "I can always get more pepperoni."

They curled up on the couch together. She tucked her legs beneath herself.

These moments were heavenly, she thought as she nibbled on crackers and cheese. Everything felt so right. She only wished it could last. And it might, for the rest of the night.

But her PTSD was still gnawing at the edges of her mind, trying to warn her of the threat outside, a threat held at bay only by the violent storm.

Except she couldn't be certain there was any threat at all. Just leftover tatters of her mind from some seriously bad experience.

She tried to shake it off and let her head lean against Gus's shoulder. He didn't seem to mind at all. Every so often he passed her a cracker holding a bit of cheese or pepperoni. Taking care of her.

A sudden loud crack of thunder, sounding as if it were right in the room, caused her to start. The bolt of lightning flashed even through the curtains that were closed against the night.

"Wow," she murmured. It awoke memories she didn't want, causing her to leave the comfort of being close to Gus. She rose and began to pace rapidly, wishing the room were a lot bigger.

"Blaire?"

She glanced at him, taking in his frown, but she suspected he knew exactly what was going on. That crack of thunder had sounded like weapons fire. Too loud, too close. Her hands suddenly itched to be holding her rifle, her body to be ducking down behind something until she could locate the threat.

At least she didn't try to hide. She hadn't lost her sense of where she *really* was, but the sound had awakened deeply ingrained impulses. At least there'd been only one crack of thunder. The grumbling continued, but that's all it was, grumbling.

"It was just thunder," Gus said.

But she could tell he was reminding himself as much as her. Some things, she thought, would never be normal again. She hated the fireworks displays the town put on, so she stayed out here rather than joining the celebration. At least fireworks were forbidden in the state park and in the national forest.

Which, of course, didn't mean she never had to put a stop to them and threaten people with arrest if they didn't listen. But walking up to a campsite where people were setting off bottle rockets, reminiscent of the sound of mortars, and firecrackers that sounded like gunshots... That was an effort of will on her part.

"Yeah," she answered Gus.

"I'd pace along with you but I think we'd collide."

"I'm sorry."

"Don't be. It jolted me, too. I'd been out about six months when a kid lit a string of fireworks right behind me. Firecrackers, probably. I swung around instantly into a crouch and I really didn't see him. Didn't see the fireworks. I hate to think what might have happened if my buddy hadn't been there to call me back."

She nodded, understanding completely. Gradually the tension the bolt had set off in her was easing, and after a couple of more minutes she was able to return to the couch. She sat near him, but not right beside him. She didn't think she was ready to be touched yet.

He still held the plate of crackers and cheese that

they'd made only a moderate dent on. "Have some more," he said, holding it toward her. "Eating something usually brings me back to the present. Especially something I never had overseas."

The fire had begun to burn down and she considered whether to put another log on it. Mundane thoughts. Safe thoughts. Her taste buds were indeed bringing her back from the cliff edge. Tart cheese, crunchy, slightly bitter wheat crackers. An anchor to the present moment.

At last she was able to look at Gus and smile. The magic of the evening was beginning to return.

Jeff gave up. He didn't care if someone spotted him. He popped open a can of paraffin used to heat foods on the trail and lit the flame with his lighter. Then he set it in front of him, holding his freezing hands over it. Within minutes the survival blanket caught some of the flame's heat and began to reflect it back toward his face.

Thank God. He'd begun to think his nose would fall off from frostbite, although he was sure it wasn't *that* cold. Having to sit out here like this was pure misery, and he wondered that he hadn't started shivering. Although his insulated rain jacket was probably capturing his body heat as effectively as it kept the rain out.

As soon as his fingers felt a little better, he reached inside his jacket and pulled out a pack of cigarettes from his breast pocket. They were a little crushed, but still smokable, and damn he needed a smoke.

The misery of the night was beginning to drive him past moral considerations. He hated his friends even more now, but step by step he made up his mind to get Blaire Afton out of the way so he never needed to do this again.

One shot. He was pretty good at several hundred yards. Maybe more. That other ranger wouldn't be able to find him fast enough if he picked his spot and knew all the places for concealment or quick escape. First thing in the morning, he promised himself. Then he was going to shoot Blaire in the same way he would shoot a game animal.

After that, having bought a few days, he was going to move to Timbuktu or some other faraway place so that Will and Karl would leave him alone. Forever. He just wanted to be left alone forever. Dinah and his baby would be better off without him. Yeah, he could run as far as he wanted.

And he didn't care if it was called running because, damn it, he needed to run for his life. He no longer trusted those guys not to kill him anyway. They weren't going to let him go simply because he'd done what he'd been told to do.

Then another thought crept into his brain. Why shoot Blaire if it wasn't going to save his own life?

Double damn, he thought. Why had he needed to think of that? Because, he reminded himself, killing her would give him time to make plans and extricate himself. He couldn't just march out of here tomorrow and be on a plane by midnight. Nothing was that easy, even without thinking of his family.

He started making a mental list as he continued to warm his hands. Passport. Cash. Arranging for his bank and credit cards to accept charges from overseas. Clothes. He needed to take at least some clothing with him. He wasn't rich like the other two and couldn't be needlessly wasteful.

But he *did* have enough to get away to some cheaper

place, and enough to sustain him until he could find some kind of work. He didn't mind getting his hands dirty, he was strong and healthy, and educated. He ought to be able to find something somewhere.

Regardless, he figured if he left the country, Will and Karl would lose all interest in him. He wouldn't be around to make them nervous, or to annoy them. Out of sight, out of mind would most likely apply because he didn't think either one of them would want to waste time tracking him down in some other country.

Yeah. Kill the woman and hightail it. The plan would work. He just needed to take care the other ranger couldn't find him first. Hell, he ought to shoot the man, as well. Will had suggested it. It would certainly buy him time to leave this park behind, to get out of the mountains.

Another thing to hash over in his mind as he sat there in misery. He hardly even noticed that the storm rolled out after midnight. All *that* did was make the night colder.

Damn, his life sucked.

Chapter 11

Blaire and Gus made their way up to her loft bedroom instead of feeding the fire on the stone hearth. Heat rose and it had filled the loft, which captured it. Blaire's predecessor had used the room farthest back in this cabin for a bedroom, but it hadn't taken long for Blaire to figure out the loft stayed warmer on frigid winter nights. She burned less fuel and didn't need to use space heaters. She now used the back room for storage.

Her successor would probably change everything around, a thought that occasionally amused her. As it was, she had a tidy space, big enough for a queen bed, a small chest of drawers, a night table, a chair and a lamp. Inconvenient as far as needing a bathroom, but it was a small price to pay.

She had to warn Gus to watch out for his head, though. The loft ceiling nearly scraped her head.

"This is cozy," he remarked. The light had several settings and she had turned it on low so he was cast in a golden glow.

"*Cozy* is a pleasant word for *tiny*," she answered. "But I like it."

"I can see why. Nice and warm, too."

Three or four minutes later they were both tucked under her comforter, naked and locked in tight embrace.

This time Gus used his mouth and tongue to explore her, at one point disappearing beneath the covers to kiss and lick her sweet center until she thought she was going to lose her mind. When she was sure she couldn't stand it anymore, she turned the tables, rising over him to discover his defined muscles, the hollows between them and finally the silky skin of his erection. It jumped at her first touch, and she felt an incredible sense of power and pleasure, unlike anything she'd ever felt.

But he was doing a lot of that to her, giving her new sensations and a new appreciation of sex. This was in no way the mundane experience she'd had in the past. This was waking her to an entirely new view of being a woman.

She enjoyed his every moan and shudder as her tongue tried to give him the same pleasures he had shared with her earlier. Finally his hands caught her shoulders and pulled her up. Straddling his hips, she took him inside her, then rested on him, feeling as if they truly became one.

Their hips, welded together, moved together, and the rising tide of passion swept her up until it carried her away almost violently. They reached the peak together, both of them crying out simultaneously.

Then, feeling as if she floated on the softest cloud, Blaire closed her eyes and drifted away.

Lying like spoons beneath the covers, Gus cradled her from behind, holding her intimately. She felt his warm breath against the back of her ear, and even as sleep tried to tug at her, she spoke.

"That was heaven."

"If that was heaven, sign me up." Then he gave a whispery laugh. "I'm sure it was better."

She smiled into the dark in response. "I don't think I've ever felt this good."

"Me, either." He pressed a kiss to her cheek, then settled back again. Their heads shared the same pillow and she could feel his every move. "I hate to be the practical one, but the storm has passed and if you want to ride out in the morning…"

She sighed. "We need to sleep. I know. I've been fighting it off because I don't want to miss a minute of this."

"This won't be the last minute," he answered. "Unless you tell me to take a hike, I plan on being right here with you tomorrow night."

She hesitated. "What about Holly?"

"She always wanted to replace me."

Blaire gasped. "Seriously?"

He chuckled. "Not really. But she enjoys ruling the roost sometimes. Which is the only reason I can ever take a vacation or get to town. Holly is the best, but she's told me more than once that she likes being able to point at me when someone's unhappy."

"Ooh, not so nice." She was teasing and she could tell he knew it when he laughed.

"She has her moments, all right." She felt him pull her a little closer. "Sleep," he said. "It's going to be a long day in the saddle."

In the early morning, before the sun had risen when the light was still gray, Gus went to the corral out back to check on the horses. They regarded him almost sleepily and stood close together because the chill had deepened overnight. Remembering summers elsewhere, he sometimes wondered how folks could ever really think of this climate as having a summer. A few hot days, but up here in the forest on the mountain little of that heat reached them. Eighty degrees was a heat wave.

The lean-to over one part of the corral, against the cabin, seemed to have done its job. The wind must have been blowing from a different direction because the feed was dry and if the horses had gotten wet at all, he couldn't tell. Even their blankets seemed mostly dry.

They nickered at him, apparently glad to see a human face. He could well imagine. The night's rain had left a lot of mud behind, and that wasn't good for them to stand in. He needed to move them out of here soon.

He loved the morning scents of the woods after a storm, though. The loamy scent of the forest floor, the pines seeming to exhale their aroma with delight…all of it. Fresh, clean and unsullied by anything else.

Well, except horse poop, he corrected himself with amusement. Grabbing a shovel that leaned against the cabin wall, he scooped up as much as he could find and dumped it into the compost pile on the other side of the fence. He wondered if the compost ever got put to use. He knew some folks came up to grab a load or two of his in the spring for their backyard gardens. Maybe they came here, too. He turned some of it and felt the heat rise. Good. It was aging.

Smelly, though, he thought with amusement. So much for that fresh morning aroma.

The sky had lightened a little more as he returned inside, wondering if he should start breakfast or let Blaire sleep. He was used to running on only a couple of hours of sleep in the field. Today wouldn't be a problem for him. He didn't know about her.

As he stepped inside, he smelled bacon. Well, that answered the question. He passed the kitchen area to the bathroom, where he washed his hands, then returned to Blaire.

"Morning," he said. "I hope I didn't wake you when I got up."

"Not really. I was starting to stir. How are the horses?"

"Champs. They're fine, but they really need a ride today. At the moment they're standing in mud."

She turned from the stove to look at him and he thought he saw a slight pinkening of her cheeks. "Bad for them?"

"Bad for their hooves if they stand too long. A few hours won't cause a problem, I'm sure, but I know they'd feel better if they could dry off their feet."

"Who wouldn't?" She turned back to the stove and flipped some strips of bacon.

"Can I help?"

"Make some toast if you want it. We've got power this morning, amazingly enough. I was sure that storm would have left us blacked out. Anyway, the toaster's over there. We don't have to use the flame on the stove."

He found a loaf of wheat bread next to the toaster and a butter dish with a full stick. He dug out a knife and began by popping two slices of bread into the toaster. "Did you ever see those four-sided metal tents you could use to make toast over a gas flame?"

She thought a moment. "Those things with the little wooden handles so you could pull down the piece that held the bread in place against the grill? My great-grandmother had one, but I never saw her use it."

"I've sometimes thought I'd like to find one somewhere. Power goes out over at my place, too, and I like my toast."

"Then we ought to look for one. Now that you mention it, that would probably help me out a lot in the winter."

He watched her fork bacon onto a plate with a paper towel on it. She immediately placed more strips in the pan. "I stuck my nose outside," she said. "It's cold, isn't it?"

"Relatively. We'll need jackets and gloves for certain."

"Then we should eat hearty. Stoke the internal heater."

He absolutely didn't have any problem with that.

They rode out after the sun crested the mountains far to the east. It hung red and hazy for a while, then brightened to orange. Soon it became too brilliant to look at.

The cold clung beneath the trees, however. At Gus's suggestion they started circling the murder scene about two hundred yards out.

"He had to watch for a while before moving in," Gus said needlessly as they had already discussed this. "So he'd have some kind of hide. Maybe use one left by another hunter."

She was riding beside him as their path through the trees allowed it. A slight shudder escaped her. "I don't like the way you phrased that. *Another* hunter. Like this guy was after deer or elk."

She had a point. "I hope you know I didn't mean it that way."

"I do," she acknowledged.

"You okay?"

"Hell, no," she answered frankly. "Ants of bad memories are crawling up and down my spine, and occasionally all over me. If you mowed this forest to the ground, maybe then I'd be able to believe there isn't an ambush out here waiting for us."

"I read you." Yeah, he did. It might all be PTSD from their time in war, but whether it was didn't matter. They couldn't afford to ignore it until they were *sure* the shooter wasn't out here.

A little farther along, she spoke again. "We started this whole idea to find evidence."

"True."

"How much could be left after that storm last night? Seriously."

He shook his head but refused to give in to the despair that sometimes accompanied the memories. His brain had a kink in it since Afghanistan and all he could do was make the best use of it he might. Ignoring it never won the day.

They used both GPS and a regular compass to navigate their way around a wide arc. The GPS didn't always catch a weak satellite signal through the trees, but as soon as another satellite was in place it would strengthen. In the interim, when the signal failed, they used the old-fashioned method.

About an hour later, Blaire made a sound of disgust. "I haven't yet been able to see the Jasper tent through the trees. If someone was going to observe, he'd need the sight line or he'd have to be a lot closer. What's the smart money?"

Gus reined in Scrappy and waited until Blaire came fully beside him, their legs almost touching.

"Here." He reached into his saddlebag and pulled out a huge pair of binoculars that would have served a sniper's crew well. "Look upslope and see what catches your attention."

"Why up?"

"Because if there's a high spot up there, or even along this arc, those trees aren't necessarily going to matter. We don't have to see *through* them."

She gave him a crooked smile. "Which is why you were special ops and I wasn't." She looked upslope again. "You're right, I'm probably looking in the wrong direction."

"We should look both ways. In case he might have found an open sight line here, too."

"I hope we're not on a fool's errand," she remarked as they moved forward.

"We've got to look. Neither of us is the type to sit on our hands." Nor did he want to tell her that he could swear he felt eyes boring into the back of his neck. Those sensations had never let him down in the 'Stan, but they hadn't always been right, either.

Even so… "You know, Blaire, we're both concerned he's still hanging around, but I can't understand why he would."

"I can't understand why he killed that poor man in the first place. Besides, I've heard criminals like to come back to the scene. To relive their big moment. To see what the cops are doing. We're looking. Maybe he's interested in that. Maybe it makes him feel important."

"Possibly." He tilted his head a little, looking at his display and seeing the GPS was down again. He pulled the compass out of his breast pocket to make sure they were still following their planned route. So far so good. He looked downslope again but saw only trees. A lot of trees. He could have sighed. "That was good reasoning, you know."

She had been looking upslope with the binoculars. "What was?"

He smiled. "Your rationale for why he still might be here. Maybe our senses are completely off-kilter."

She lowered her head for a moment, then said something that made his heart hurt. "I hope not. I'm still learning to trust my perceptions again."

They were getting too close, Jeff thought. He'd made his way back to the hide atop a big boulder from which he'd watched the campground. It would give some hunter a panorama for tracking game. For him it gave a view of the killing field.

He caught himself. That was too dramatic. That called to mind the most god-awful massacre, and he didn't want to associate with that, even in a private moment of thought.

But putting his binoculars to his eyes, he watched the two of them. If he took Blaire out now, the guy might dismount to take care of her. Would he have time to get away before the man came looking for him?

He looked up the slope and recalled the night of the shooting. He'd had to go into the campground that night, right to the tent. This time he could keep a much safer distance and just hightail it. It wasn't as far, and he knew the way. He ought to since he'd covered the path so many times.

Shooting Blaire might spook the horses, too. The guy—Gus, he thought—might get thrown. That would be helpful. Of course, a man could probably run faster over this terrain than a horse could. But would he leave Blaire if she was bleeding?

Yeah, if she was already dead.

Crap.

He rolled over again and watched the two of them. If they came up any higher, he was going to have to retreat from this spot. He had little doubt they'd find it. It worked as a deer blind, not a human blind. The guy who'd built this nest hadn't wanted it to be impossible to find in subsequent years. Too much work had gone into it, such as moving heavy rocks for a base.

Damn, he wanted a cigarette. The thought made him look down and he realized he'd left a heap of butts already. Damn! He scooped them up and began to stuff them into a pocket. Not enough to leave a shell casing behind. No, now he'd leave DNA for sure. Maybe Will was right to scorn him.

No, Will wasn't right. Will wasn't right about a damn thing except he needed to make sure Blaire didn't have a sudden memory of him and make a connection.

Then Jeff was going to clear his butt out of this country.

His thoughts stuttered a bit and he wondered if his thinking was getting screwed up. Energy bars barely staved off the cold and he was almost out of them. Maybe his brain was skipping important things.

But he knew one thing for sure. If he went back without killing that woman, Will and Karl were going to kill *him*. So he had to do it. Just to buy time.

He needed those two to split up a little more. More space between them, more distance. He didn't want to add *two* people to a body count that shouldn't even exist.

He closed his eyes briefly, wishing himself on another planet. Or even dead and buried. Anything but lying here watching a woman he had nothing against, waiting for an opportunity to shoot her as if she were a game animal.

It was self-defense, he told himself. Indirectly, perhaps, but he needed to defend himself and this was the only way. Self-defense. He kept repeating it like a mantra.

Gus drew rein and Scrappy slowed, then stopped. Realizing it, Blaire slowed Lita down and looked over at him. "Something wrong?"

"Scrappy just started to limp. Maybe he's got a loose shoe or something. I need to check. Give me a minute?"

"Of course." She watched him dismount, then turned her attention to the woods around them. She just didn't see any place yet that would have given the shooter a clear view of the campground. They needed to get higher, unless Scrappy was truly lame, in which case they'd have to head back.

Because she was busy telling herself this was a fool's errand, they'd never find anything useful and it was simply born of their military training that required them to act against a threat... Well, she wouldn't necessarily mind if they had to call this off. She loved being out here on horseback, and Lita was a great mount, but the sense of danger lurking around every tree was ruining it and probably ridiculous besides.

Since she'd left the combat zone for the last time, she'd been forced to realize how powerful post-traumatic stress could be. She hadn't been inflicted with it as badly as some of her former comrades, but she had it. Enough to make her uneasy for no damn good reason, like the last few days.

A random murder had occurred. It might not even be random at all. They wouldn't know that until the police collected more evidence. But right now, riding through the woods, hoping to find the place from which the shooter could have observed the campground, had its footing more in her memories than in the present.

Yeah, it was creepy, but *this* creepy? She needed to talk herself down. Needed to accept that the killer was long gone and every bit of the uneasiness she couldn't shake was being internally generated by a heap of bad memories that couldn't quite be buried.

Then maybe she could get back to doing her job, and Gus could get back to doing his. Holly and Dave might not mind standing in for them for a while, but it wasn't fair. They both had jobs to do and they were letting them slide because neither of them could quite believe in the safety of the woods.

That thought caused her to sit back in the saddle. Couldn't believe in the safety of the woods? Seriously? This retreat she had come to in order to escape the bustle of the busy, populated world because it somehow grated on her and kept her on alert too much? It no longer felt safe?

God, this was bad. Maybe she needed to get some counseling. Never had the detritus of her military experience gotten this far out of hand. Nightmares, yeah. Disliking crowds, yeah. But the woods? The safe haven she'd found here?

"It seems he got a stone in his hoof," Gus said, dropping Scrappy's right foreleg to the ground.

"Do we need to go back?"

"Nah. I've got a tool in my saddlebag. I'll get it out in a minute and then we can move on."

She watched him come around Scrappy's left side and unbuckle the saddlebag. "Is he bruised?"

"I don't know yet. He didn't limp for long, so I hope not."

"Well...if he needs a rest..." She trailed off as it hit her how far away they were now from everything. Miles from her cabin. Probably miles from the dirt road. Could they shortcut it through the woods? Maybe. It all depended on how many ravines were lurking between here and there. So far they'd been lucky. At any moment the mountain could throw up a huge stop sign.

"It'll be fine," Gus said as he pulled out the tool. "We can always walk them, but I don't think it'll be necessary."

Blaire felt the punch before she heard the report. She started to fall sideways and grabbed the saddle horn only to feel it slip from her fingers. She felt another blow, this one to her head as she wondered with confusion why she was on the ground. Then everything went black.

Jeff had a clear escape route. He could run up to the cave like a mountain goat, nothing in his way from here. When the guy dismounted his horse and started to check its hoof, it seemed like a fateful opportunity.

He had a clear shot at Blaire, and from over two hundred yards he had no doubt he could make it.

If he was one thing, he was a superb marksman with this rifle. One shot was all he'd need.

He looked downslope and liked what he saw. Damn fool ranger wouldn't be able to reach this spot fast. Too many rocks, a ravine that looked deep enough to swallow him and his horse. It made great protection for Jeff.

Okay, then.

Lifting his rifle to his shoulder, he pulled the bolt to put a shell in the chamber. Then, with his elbows resting on a rock, he looked through the scope. Suddenly Blaire was big, a huge target.

Holding his breath, steadying his hands until the view from the scope grew perfectly still, he fired. He waited just long enough to see Blaire fall from her horse.

Then he grabbed his pack and gun and started to run uphill. He didn't wait to see the result. He didn't need to. He was a damn fine shot.

What he hadn't seen was that the man was looking right in his direction when he fired.

Gus removed the stone from Scrappy's foot and tossed it away. Bending, he looked closely and saw nothing worrisome. He straightened and looked up at Blaire, who was still straddling Lita. "He might be a bit tender later, but he's fine to continue."

"Good," she said.

Then the entire world shifted to slow motion. He saw a flash from up in the woods some distance away. His mind registered it as a muzzle flash. Only then did he hear the familiar *crack*.

Before he could act, he saw red spread across Blaire's

sleeve and begin to drip on her hand. He had to get her down. *Now.*

She reached for the saddle horn, but before he could get there, she tipped sideways and fell off Lita. He heard the thud as her head hit the ground.

Everything inside him froze. The clearheaded state of battle washed over him, curling its ice around everything within him, focusing him as nothing else could.

He left Scrappy standing and dealt with Lita, who was disturbed enough by the sound and Blaire's tumble to be dancing nervously. He feared she might inadvertently trample Blaire as she lay on the ground, so he grabbed her by the bridle, then grabbed Scrappy with his other hand.

He knew horses well enough to know that Scrappy might react to Lita's nervousness and begin to behave the same way. While it wasn't usually necessary, he used the reins to tie Scrappy to a tree trunk along with Lita.

They nickered and huffed, an equine announcement of *let's get out of here*, but he was sure they weren't going anywhere.

Only then, what seemed like years later but couldn't have been more than a half minute, he knelt next to Blaire. She had the rag doll limpness he recognized as unconsciousness, and he feared how badly she might have hit her head.

But there was a sequence, and the first thing he needed to do was stanch the blood from her wound. Time slowed down until it dragged its heels. Only experience had taught him that was adrenaline speeding up his mind, that time still moved at its regular pace.

With adrenaline-powered strength, he ripped the

sleeve of her jacket open and kept tearing until he could see where the blood was heaviest. Then he tore her shirt and revealed her shoulder, turning her partly over to see her back as well as her front.

A through-and-through wound, bleeding from both sides, but not through the artery, thank God. Bad enough, but no spurts. Grabbing the sleeve he had just torn, he ripped it in half and pushed it against the two holes, front and back, as hard as he could.

He could use her jacket sleeve for a tourniquet, he thought, but his mind was only partly on first aid. "Blaire. Blaire?"

Her unconsciousness worried him as much as anything. How hard had she hit her head? Head wounds could be the absolute worst, even though he was sure he could stop the bleeding from her shoulder.

He kept calling her name as he wound the jacket sleeve around her shoulder, making it tight. Stop the bleeding. Find a way to wake her up.

Only then could he search out the shooter, and he damn well knew where he was going to start.

Blaire came to with a throbbing head and a shoulder that was throbbing even harder. She cussed and suddenly saw Gus's face above hers.

"Thank God," he said. "You hit your head."

"How long was I out and who shot me?"

"You were out for about two minutes and I don't know yet who shot you. But I saw the muzzle flash."

"Then go get him, Gus."

"No. I really want to but I'm worried about you. I need to get you help."

She tried to sit up, wincing a bit, so he helped her, propping her against a tree.

"I don't think you lost a lot of blood," he said, "but if you start to get light-headed, you know what to do."

"Not my first rodeo," she said between her teeth. "The blow to my head wasn't that bad. I'm not seeing double or anything. The headache is already lessening. The shoulder... Well, it hurts like hell but I can't feel any serious damage." She moved her arm.

"The shooter messed up," she said after a few moments. "Just a flesh wound. He must have used a full metal jacket." Meaning that the bullet hadn't entered her shattering and spinning, causing a lot of internal damage.

"Blaire..."

She managed a faint smile. "I always wanted to say that."

He flashed a grin in response. "Your head is okay."

"My shoulder's not too bad, either."

He rested his hand on her uninjured shoulder, aware that time was ticking, both for her and for the escaping shooter. "I'm going to radio for help for you. Then, if you think you're okay by yourself for a bit, I'm going after that bastard."

With her good arm, she pushed herself up. "I'm coming with you."

"Stop. Don't be difficult, Blaire. You've been shot."

She caught his gaze with hers. "I've also been in combat. So have you. Trust me, I can judge my own fitness. There's a ravine up there and I know the way around it. What's more, he obviously has a long-range weapon. Do you? Do you really want to go after him alone? He could be perched anywhere."

He frowned at her, a frown that seemed to sink all the way to his soul. "You might start bleeding again."

"If I do, I'll tell you. This feels like you've got me bandaged pretty well. Quit frowning at me. I won't be stupid."

"Riding up there is stupid," he said flatly. But looking at her, he realized he was fighting a losing battle. If she could find a way to get herself back on Lita, she'd follow him. Never had he seen such a stubborn set to a woman's jaw. He wanted to throw up his hands in frustration. "I'm trained for this," he reminded her. "Solo missions."

"I'm trained, too," she retorted. With a shove, she reached her feet and remained steady. "See, I'm not even weak from blood loss. I'm *fine*."

Well, there were different definitions of that word, but he gave up arguing even though he had an urge to tie her to that tree. But, he understood, if that shooter realized she was still alive, he might be circling around right now. He could get in another shot without being seen.

"Hell and damnation," he growled. But he gave in. Better to keep her close.

He had to help her mount Lita since she had only one workable arm, but once she was astride the horse, feet in the stirrups, she looked fine. No paleness to her face, no sagging. Maybe the wound wasn't that awful.

It was her left shoulder that was injured and she was right-handed. Like many of the rangers out here who needed to go into the woods, she carried a shotgun as well as a pistol. The shotgun was settled into a holster in front of her right thigh, and before he would allow her to move, he asked her to prove she could pull it out and use it with one arm. She obliged while giving him an annoyed look.

"It's a shotgun," she said. "I hardly have to be accurate."

If he weren't getting hopping mad, he might have smiled. "I just need to be sure you can use it. And I'm radioing this in, like it or not. We aren't going to play solitary superheroes out here."

Damn! He'd gone from violent fear that she was dead into relief that she was reasonably okay and now he was so mad he was ready to kill.

Someone had shot her. Why? Hell, he didn't care why. Whoever it was, needed to be grabbed by the short and curlies, tied up in handcuffs and marched to jail.

As they moved farther upslope, his radio found an area with clear satellite transmission, and he gave the sheriff's office a rundown as they rode, including that Blaire had been wounded but was riding at his side. He asked they be tracked, and dispatch promised they would.

Insofar as possible, he thought as he hooked the radio onto his belt again. He kept glancing at Blaire to be sure she was still all right and wondered if she had any idea how distracting she was. This wasn't helping the search much. His concern for her wasn't making him a better hunter.

He would have liked to be able to shield her with his body, but since there was no way to know if the guy might circle around and take another shot, there was no safe place for her to ride. He suggested she lead the way because she knew how to get around the ravine, and all he had to do was point out where he had seen the muzzle flash. Plus, he could see if she started to weaken.

She was a born navigator with a lot of experience. She guided with surety, part of the trip taking them away from the area from which he'd seen the flash, much more of it angling toward it and up as they left the ravine behind.

He glanced down into that ravine as they crossed a narrow ledge of rock and realized there'd have been no way to cross it directly. None. The shooter was probably counting on it to slow them down.

But their horses moved swiftly when the terrain allowed. Soon they found a trampled muddy place that he'd probably been using. From there his trail was clear for about twenty feet or so, giving them direction, then it disappeared in the sopping duff and loam beneath the trees.

She drew rein and waited for him to catch up to her. "He probably followed as straight a path uphill as he could. For speed?"

He nodded. "I agree."

"And there's a road on the other side of that ridge," she said, pointing. "Not much of one, little more than a cart track used by hunters, but he could have left a vehicle there."

"I bet." He paused. "Let's speed up. This is a rough climb. He had to get winded. To slow down."

But the horses wouldn't, he thought. They'd just keep climbing steadily and as quickly as they could, as if they sensed the urgency. They probably did. Horses were sensitive animals.

He kept one eye on Blaire while he scanned the area around them. The guy might have angled away from a straight path. It all depended on how scared he was and how much time he thought he'd have. If the shooter thought Blaire was down, he might think he had a lot of time.

He hoped so. The fury in him had grown cold, a feeling he remembered from other conflicts. He was riding its wave, heedless of danger to himself, focused on the mission, focused on Blaire's safety. Nothing else mattered.

She, too, was scanning around them, but he had little hope they'd see much. The shooter probably had the sense to wear woodland camouflage, although the higher they climbed the thinner the trees grew. They were nowhere near the tree line, but for some reason the growth here was thinner. He tried to remember if there'd been a fire here at some point. The ground was plenty brushy, but the trees didn't seem as big or as stout as they had farther below.

Then he saw it. A flash of movement above them.

"Blaire."

She halted and looked back at him.

"I think I saw him. We're sitting ducks right now. We'd better split up." He hated to suggest it, given that she was wounded, probably suffering a great deal of pain and maybe even weakening. But together they made a great target.

"Where?" she asked quietly.

"Eleven o'clock. About three hundred yards upslope."

"Got it."

Then with a brief nod she turned Lita a bit, angling away from where he'd seen the movement. Misleading as if she were going to look elsewhere.

He did the same heading the other direction, but not too much, teeth clenched until his jaw screamed, hoping that their split wouldn't tell the guy they'd seen him.

Then Blaire called, "I think I saw something over here."

Did she want him to come her way? Or was she sending their intended misdirection up to the shooter?

"I'll be there in a minute," he called back. "Need room to turn around."

"Yo," she answered, her voice sounding a little fainter.

The brief conversation gave him the chance to look up again to the spot where he'd seen movement. There was more movement now. Rapid. Then something happened and he heard rocks falling. A man's shape, suddenly visible, lost its upward momentum and instead he seemed to be scrambling frantically.

Gotcha, he thought with burning satisfaction. "Now, Scrappy." He touched the horse with his heels, speeding him up. If ever he had needed this horse to be surefooted, he needed it now. Scrappy didn't disappoint.

With amazing speed, the horse covered the ground toward the man, who was still struggling as more rocks tumbled on him from above. The guy had evidently made a serious misstep and gotten into a patch of very loose scree.

Taking it as a warning, Gus halted Scrappy about two hundred feet back, then dismounted, carrying his shotgun with him. He approached cautiously, aware that the guy was armed and desperate.

Then he swore as he saw Blaire emerge from the trees on the other side. He was hoping to have dealt with this before she entered the danger zone. He was, however, glad to see she'd unholstered her shotgun and angled Lita so she could use it.

"Keep a bead on him," Gus called to her as he hurried carefully toward the man.

The guy turned over, his rifle in his hands, looking as if he were ready to shoot. Gus instantly squatted and prepared to take aim, but the man evidently realized he was outnumbered. If he shot in any direction, one of two shotguns would fire at him.

"Put the rifle away," Gus demanded, rising and making it clear that he was ready to shoot. "Now."

He could see the guy's face clearly, reflecting panic. He looked around wildly, his feet pushing at the scree beneath him but gaining no purchase.

"Give up," Blaire called. "You wouldn't be the first man I've shot."

Well, that was blunt, Gus thought, easing closer to their quarry. Vets didn't like to say things like that. He hoped to hell that wasn't the blow to her head talking.

"I've got him," Gus called when he was ten feet away. Resignation had replaced panic on the guy's face. He took one hand from his rifle, and with the other tossed the weapon to the side.

Then he said the strangest thing: "I'm so glad I didn't kill her."

Chapter 12

A half hour later, with Jeff Walston securely bound in zip ties, Gus heard the sound of helicopter rotors from overhead. Medevac was on the way, and as he'd been told over the radio, a couple of cops were riding along.

Good. He needed to be away from the source of his anger. He had enough experience to know he wouldn't take it out on his prisoner, but he had never liked the uncomfortable, conflicting emotions the situation brought out in him. The guy could have killed Blaire. Maybe had wanted to. It would have been easy for Gus to treat him like a soccer ball.

But he didn't. Instead he sat beside Blaire, whom he'd helped to dismount and sit against a tree. For all she had claimed it was just a flesh wound, it was taking a toll on her. He was amazed at the strength and determination that had brought her this far.

"I wouldn't have minded having you on my team over there," he told her.

"That's quite a compliment," she murmured. "Thanks, Gus."

"You're remarkable."

"I'm a soldier." That seemed to be all she needed to say. From his perspective, it was quite enough.

Because of the chaotic winds aloft so near the peak of the mountain, the helicopter couldn't come very close or low. Through the trees he caught glimpses of three people sliding down ropes to the ground, and after them came a Stokes basket.

Then another wait.

"I wish I could go to the hospital with you," Gus said. "But the horses…"

"I know. Take care of the horses. They were good comrades today, weren't they?" She smiled wanly. "Gus?"

"Yeah?"

"I think I was running on adrenaline."

That didn't surprise him at all, but before he could respond, three men burst out of the trees in tan overalls. He instantly recognized Seth Hardin, a retired Navy SEAL who'd helped build the local rescue operations into a finely honed operation.

They shook hands briefly as the other two put Blaire on the basket and strapped her in. Gus repeated her injuries to the two EMTs, then watched them race back through the woods to get Blaire onto the helicopter.

Seth remained with him. "I'll keep watch over the prisoner if you want to head back."

Gus nodded. "I need to take care of two horses. But

FYI, I didn't touch the guy's weapon or much of anything except to put the zip ties on him."

Seth arched a brow. "That must have required some restraint."

"Exactly." They shared a look of understanding, then Gus rose. "You armed?"

Seth patted his side, pointing out the rather obvious pistol attached to his belt. "Of course."

"You want one of our shotguns? He said he's alone but…"

"Hey, you know what we're capable of. I'll be fine. I'm just going to make sure this creep can't move an inch, then I'll stand back and pay attention. It won't be for long. The second chopper is supposed to be following with some more cops. You just get out of here. You don't need to wear a neon sign to tell me how worried you are about Blaire."

Jeff Walston wanted to spill his guts. He started talking in the helicopter and by the time Gus was able to reach town, they had a pretty clear picture of the so-called Hunt Club.

It was an ugly one. Micah Parish filled him in as Gus drove to the hospital. Gus listened with only one ear. He could get the nitty-gritty later, but right now he was badly worried about Blaire. Blood on the outside of the body didn't necessarily mean there wasn't internal bleeding. She'd held on, probably longer than she would have without a flood of adrenaline coursing through her, but now the question was how much damage had she worsened with her stubbornness.

At the hospital they wouldn't tell him much except

that she was now in recovery. He could see her when she woke up.

The wait was endless. His pacing could have worn a path in the waiting room floor. Still, pieces began to fall together in his mind. He began to see exactly where he wanted to go.

It kind of shocked him, but as it settled in, he knew it was right.

Before Blaire even opened her eyes she knew where she was. She'd been in the hospital before, and the odors plus the steady beeping of equipment placed her firmly in her present location.

As she surfaced slowly from the drugs, memory returned. Being shot, the insane ride through the woods that she would have been smarter not to do, helping Gus capture the bad guy. The ride in the Stokes basket up to the helicopter. Then nothing.

She moved a little and felt that her wound had changed. Probably surgery, she thought groggily. Yeah, her throat felt raw, so there'd been a breathing tube.

It was over. She'd be fine. She didn't need a doctor to tell her that. She'd been in worse condition once before from a roadside incendiary device. That time she'd been saved by luck as much as anything, being on the far side of the vehicle.

"Blaire."

A quiet voice. Gus. He was here. Warmth suffused her, and a contradictory sense of happiness. Lying post-op in a hospital bed seemed like an odd place to feel that warmth.

At last the anesthesia wore off enough that she could

open her eyes. They lighted instantly on Gus, who was sitting beside her bed.

"Blaire," he said again, and smiled. A wide, genuine smile that communicated more than words. She was okay and he was happy and relieved about it. Then she sensed him gently taking her hand.

"Welcome back," he said. "You're fine."

"What was that all about?" she asked, her voice thick. "The guy. What was he doing?"

He told her about The Hunt Club, about how the man they had captured had been forced into committing two murders by threats against his life.

"Sport?" That almost made her mind whirl. "They were doing this for sport?"

"Two of them, evidently. They've been rounded up. The full truth will come out with time, but right now the man we caught seems eager to talk."

"Good." Then she slipped away again, still under the influence of surgical medications.

She had no sense of how much time had passed, but when she came to again, her shoulder throbbed like mad. "Damn," she said.

"Blaire?" Gus's voice again. "What's wrong?"

"My shoulder hurts worse than when I was shot."

"I'm not surprised. No adrenaline now, plus I guess they had to do some work inside you. One of the docs said you were lucky your lung didn't collapse."

Those words woke her up completely. "What?"

"You were bleeding internally. Next time you want to ride a horse when you've been shot, please reconsider." Then he pressed a tube into her hand. "Top button. Call the nurse for some painkiller."

She certainly needed some. She pressed the button and a voice came over the speaker over her head. "Nurse's station."

"Something for pain, please."

"Be there shortly."

Then she dropped the tube and her fingers reached for Gus. He replied by clasping her hand.

"Listen," he said. "You were tough. You *are* tough, as tough as anyone I've known."

Something important was coming. She could sense it. All of a sudden she didn't want that nurse to hurry. She wanted to listen to him.

"I know we've avoided this," Gus continued. "But I refuse to avoid it any longer. Nearly losing you... Well, it kind of yanked me out of stasis."

"You, too?"

He nodded. "We don't have long. I'm sure you're about to get knocked out again. But tuck this away for when you're feeling better because I don't want to take advantage of you."

"How could you?" She thought she heard the nurse's rubbery steps in the hall. Her heart began to accelerate. "Gus?"

"I love you," he said simply. "And if you don't mind, I'd like to marry you. But don't answer now. Just put it away until you're back on your feet. I promise not to pressure you. I just needed you to know."

Just as the nurse wearing blue scrubs appeared in the doorway, she felt her heart take flight. "Pressure away," she said. Then the needle went into the IV port. "I love you, too," she said before she vanished into the haze again.

A month later, they stood before Judge Wyatt Carter

and took their vows. They'd agreed to keep their jobs, to feel out their path into the future.

And they'd promised each other they were going to attend the trials of The Hunt Club. A game? Just a game had cost five lives? It was an appalling idea. It appalled Blaire even more to recognize Jeff Walston and remember they'd served briefly together. A man known to her!

But that faded as they stepped out of the courthouse into a sunny August morning. The bride wore a street-length white dress and the groom wore his best Forest Service uniform.

A surprising number of people awaited them outside and began to clap. Turning to each other, they kissed, drawing more applause.

They had friends and had found love and a new way of life.

"Upward," he murmured. "Always. I love you."

* * * * *

Jenna Kernan has penned over two dozen novels and received two RITA® Award nominations. Jenna is every bit as adventurous as her heroines. Her hobbies include recreational gold prospecting, scuba diving and gem hunting. Jenna grew up in the Catskills and currently lives in the Hudson Valley in New York State with her husband. Follow Jenna on Twitter, @jennakernan, on Facebook or at jennakernan.com.

Books by Jenna Kernan

Harlequin Intrigue

Protectors at Heart

Defensive Action
Adirondack Attack
Warning Shot
Dangerous Conditions

Apache Protectors

Shadow Wolf
Hunter Moon
Tribal Law
Native Born

Harlequin Historical

Gold Rush Groom
The Texas Ranger's Daughter
Wild West Christmas
A Family for the Rancher
Running Wolf

Visit the Author Profile page
at Harlequin.com for more titles.

WARNING SHOT

Jenna Kernan

For Jim, always.

Chapter 1

Homeland Security Agent Rylee Hockings paused on the way into the sheriff's office at the foul language booming from the side of the building. The deep baritone voice continued in a colorful string of obscenities that made her think the speaker had been in some branch of the armed services.

A military brat herself, she had heard her fair share of cussing during her formative years while being dragged from one base to another, Kyoto to Hawaii to Germany and back to Hawaii. The youngest of six, she had the distinction of being the only one of her family not to join the US Marines. Some of the military upbringing had worn off on her because she still believed that one was judged on performance. It was one of many reasons she planned to kill this assignment and show her supervisor she had what it took to be a field operative.

It was just past noon on Labor Day. Because of the federal holiday, she had not expected to find the sheriff in his office, but stopped as a courtesy. The second day of September and sunny, but the sunshine did not warm this frozen block of a county in upstate New York. Here it already felt like November. The leaves were pretty. Already at peak leaf-peeping season.

She rounded the building and found a tall man with strands of honey-blond hair falling over his flushed face as he jammed a coat hanger in the slot between the weather stripping and the driver's side window of the vehicle before him.

The vehicle was a white SUV and on the side panel in gold paint was the county seal and the word *Sheriff.*

The man had his back to her and he had not heard her approach due to the swearing and stomping of his feet on the frozen ground. His breath showed in the blast of cold air. The collar of his jacket was turned up against the chill. His distraction gave her a moment to admire an unobstructed view of one of the nicest looking butts she had seen in some time. His uniform slacks were just tight enough and his posterior just muscular enough to keep her interest for a little too long. He wore a brown nylon jacket, heavily padded and flapping at his sides as he threw the coat hanger to the ground.

"Unsat," she said, using the US Marine jargon for unsatisfactory.

He whirled and met her gaze by pinning her with eyes so blue they should have belonged to a husky. Her smile dropped with her stomach. Straight nose, square chin and a sensual mouth, the guy was the complete package, and then he opened his mouth.

"Sneaking up on a sheriff is a bad idea."

"As bad as locking your keys inside?" She squinted her eyes and dragged her sunglasses down her nose. "I could have had an entire unit with me, and you wouldn't have heard."

He stooped to retrieve his twisted coat hanger, snatching it from the ground with long elegant fingers.

"FUBAR," she said.

"You in the Corps?" he asked, referring to the US Marine Corps.

"My father, two brothers and a sister." She motioned to the sheriff's vehicle. "No spare?"

"Lost them," he admitted.

"Why not use a Slim Jim?"

He scowled and thumbed over his shoulder. "It's in the back."

She wished she'd checked into the background of the sheriff of Onutake County before this meeting, but time had been limited. Knowing what he looked like would have been helpful right about now. For all she knew, this guy was a car thief.

She made a note to do some background checking as soon as she found a moment.

"You Sheriff Trace?"

"Who's asking?"

"Rylee Hockings, Department of Homeland Security." She retrieved her business card case from her blazer and offered him a card, leaning forward instead of stepping closer. There was something other than his vocabulary that urged her to keep her distance. She listened to that voice instead of the one that wondered if he were single. But her traitorous eyes dropped to his bare hands and the left one, which held no wedding band.

He nodded, not looking at her card.

"Didn't expect to find you on the job today, Sheriff."

"More calls on weekends and holidays. Just the way of the world."

He'd have trouble responding without his car, she thought.

"What can I do you for?"

"Just an introduction. Courtesy visit."

"Uh-huh," he said, his expression turning skeptical. "So, you plan on treating me like I'm still a marine?"

"Excuse me?"

"Muscles are required, intelligence not essential," he said, choosing one of the tired jokes members of the army often leveled at the marines.

"So you were army, then." She knew that much from the jibe toward her family's branch of the military.

"Once." He smiled and her heart jumped as if hit with a jolt of electricity. The smile and those eyes and jaw and, holy smokes, she was in trouble. She forced a scowl.

"You know, you should always run a check of your equipment before you lock up."

"You a newbie, reading manuals, going by the book?"

She was and the assumption was insulting.

"Why do you ask?"

"You still have that new car smell."

Her scowl was no longer forced. What did that even mean? "I'm not the one locked out of my unit."

"It isn't even locked. The alarm is just on and I didn't want to set it off again."

Again. How often did he do this? she wondered. "I'll be doing some investigating in your county."

"What kind of investigating?"

She smiled. "Nice to meet you, Sheriff."

"You want an escort?"

"From a sheriff careless enough to leave his keys and—" she glanced through the windshield to verify her suspicion "—his phone in his unit? Thank you but I'll manage."

She turned to go. *New car smell.* She growled and marched away.

"You got a Slim Jim in your vehicle, Hockings?" he called after her.

"I do, but I wouldn't want to chance damaging yours. Maybe try Triple A."

"Where you headed?"

"Kowa Nation," she said and then wished she hadn't.

"Hey!"

Rylee turned back. Throwing her arms out in exasperation. "What?"

"They know you're coming?"

"Where's the fun in that?"

"Agent Hockings, I advise you to call the tribal leadership and make a formal request to visit."

She cast him the kind of wave that she knew was dismissive. Those damn blue eyes narrowed. They were still enthralling. As blue as the waters of the Caribbean.

Rylee straightened her shoulders and kept going. When she reached the front of the building, she heard the sheriff's car alarm blare and then cut short.

From her official vehicle, Rylee logged in to the laptop affixed to the dash and checked out the sheriff's official records. Sheriff Axel Trace had been taken into state custody at thirteen and listed as orphaned. She gazed at the entry. There was a hole there big enough to drive a truck through. No birth record or school records. His paper trail, as they used to call it, began with the entry by the sheriff of this very county when he took custody of the lad. Axel's parents were listed as deceased, but no names for her to search. No cause of their deaths or circumstances, no guardians noted, no relatives. Just record of Axel's temporary placement with Kurt Rogers, the county sheriff at the time. The placement lasted five years until Axel enlisted out of high school. Rylee scanned and clicked and scanned some more. Impressed didn't quite cover it. There were plenty of records now, and all exemplary. She'd read them more carefully later. But on a fast pass, the man had distinguished himself in the US Army as an MP and reaching the rank of captain in Iraq. She scanned his records and noted his transfer to Hanau, Germany.

"Oh, no," she said.

Captain Axel Trace had broken up a brawl in a bar that had resulted in the death of two servicemen. She would read all the details later. For now, she skimmed and noted that Trace had been attacked and engaged with appropriate use of force.

"And two months later, you chose discharge rather than reenlistment." She wondered if the incident had been the cause of his decision to leave the service and his prospects behind.

He seemed to have had a great opportunity for advancement and she wondered why he had instead elected discharge and returned to his home county to run for sheriff, replacing the man who had held the position until retirement six years ago. It seemed an odd choice.

Perhaps it was just her ambition talking, but the sheriff could have done a lot better than this frozen Klon-

dike Bar of a county. The entire northern border was
Canada and, other than the St. Lawrence River, she saw
nothing but trees and more trees. She didn't understand
why anyone with his training would allow himself to get
stuck in a crappy, freezing county where you reached
the highest possible position at thirty. Sheriff Trace had
no family up here, none anywhere according to his records. And now he had nowhere to go but sideways
and no increase in salary unless the good people of the
county wanted their taxes raised.

Meanwhile, Rylee had nothing but advancement in
her sights. Her plans included filling in that blank spot
in her résumé under field experience. Eliminating the
possible terrorist threats up here was a good start. She
wasn't fooled that this was a great opportunity. This
county had been tagged by the DHS analysts as the
least likely spot for the crossing. But that didn't make
it impossible. This morning she had gotten her break.
Her initial assignment was to speak to four groups who
might be connected with the terrorist organization calling itself Siming's Army. Just initial interviews, but it
was a start. But en route, Border Patrol called her to
report an illegal crossing: a single male who was carrying a canvas duffel bag. The contents of that bag were
her objective. Until she knew otherwise, she'd act as
if the contents of the bag was the object for which her
entire department hunted. They had abandoned pursuit
when the target entered onto Mohawk land. She had a
chance now, a possible break in the search for the entry
point of this threat.

Her attempt to reach her boss, Catherine Ohr, ended
in a voice mail message, and she had yet to hear back.
She had lost the GPS signal with her directions to the

Kowa Mohawk Nation just outside of town. Not that it mattered. One of the things her father had taught her was how to read a map.

Federal officers investigating leads did not need appointments to visit federal land. Sheriff Axel Trace should have known that, but it wasn't her job to tell him what he should know.

Newbie. New car smell. First field assignment.

Rylee lowered her chin and stepped on the gas.

Chapter 2

Sheriff Trace responded to the call from the Kowa Nation one hour later, passing the border patrol checkpoint just off their rez and knowing that would only further ruffle feathers. Likely, this was also the work of Rylee Hockings.

Homeland Security Agent Hockings didn't look like trouble, as she sat small and sullen in the seat beside the desk of the Kowa Mohawk Reservation's acting chief of police. But having already met her, he could not help but take in the moment. Having ignored his advice and dismissed him like the help, there was a certain satisfaction in seeing her in wrist restraints.

He didn't know the exact point when his moment to gloat changed into a completely different kind of study, but he now noticed that Rylee Hockings had a heart-shaped face, lips the color of the flesh of a ripe watermelon and large, expressive brown eyes with elegant arching brows that were the brown of dry pine needles. Her straight, fine blond hair fell forward, making her flushed cheeks seem even pinker. Their eyes met, and her brow descended. Her lids cinched as she squinted at him with open hostility.

Axel could not resist smiling. "The next time I ask you if you'd like an escort, maybe don't flip me the bird."

"I didn't flip you off." Her reply was a bark, like a dog that might be either frightened or angry but either way sent clear signs for him to back off.

"No, I believe you said that when you wanted the help of a sheriff who was dumb enough to lock his keys in his cruiser, you'd ask for it."

He glanced at her wrists, secured with a wide plastic zip tie and hammering up and down on the knees of her navy slacks as if sending him a message in Morse code. He wondered why federal agents always advertised their profession with the same outfits. A blazer, dress shirt and slacks with a practical heel was just not what folks wore up here.

"I didn't say dumb enough. I said *careless enough*."

He glanced to the acting chief of police, Sorrel Vasta, who said, "Potato, Pa-tot-o."

"I also mentioned that the Kowa tribe does not do drop-in visits," said Axel.

"Especially from feds," added Vasta. He folded his arms across his chest, which just showed off how very thin and young he really was.

"This," said Agent Hockings, "is federal land. As a federal officer, I do not need permission—"

"You are a trespasser on the Mohawk Nation. We are within our rights to—"

Whatever rights Vasta might have been about to delineate were cut short by the blast of a shotgun.

Hockings threw herself from the chair to the floor as Vasta ducked behind the metal desk. Axel dropped, landing beside Hockings, pressed shoulder to shoulder.

"Shots fired," she called, reaching for her empty holster with her joined hands and then swearing under her breath.

"Who are you yelling to exactly?" Axel asked. "We all heard it."

She pressed those pink lips together and scowled, then she scrambled along the floor, undulating in a way that made his hairs stand up and electricity shiver over his skin. He hadn't felt that drumbeat of sexual awareness since that day in high school when Tonya Sawyer wore a turquoise lace bra under a T-shirt that was as transparent as a bridal veil. She'd been sent home, of course, to change, but it hadn't mattered. Images like that stuck in the memory like a bug on a fly strip. He had a feeling that the sight of Hockings's rippling across the floor like a wave was going to stick just like that turquoise bra.

"Out of the way," Hockings said, her thigh brushing his shoulder.

The electricity now scrambled his brain as the current shot up and then down to finally settle, like a buzzing transformer, in his groin. High school all over again.

Vasta squatted at the window and peeked out. The only thing he held was the venetian blinds. His gun remained on his hip. He glanced back at Axel and cocked his head.

Axel realized his own mouth was hanging open as if Agent Hockings had slapped him, which she would have, if she knew what he had been thinking.

"They shot her car. Peppered the side," said Vasta.

Her head popped up like a carnival target from behind the desk.

"Who did?" Her perfect blond hair was now mussed. Axel resisted the urge to lay the strands back in order. Was her hair silky or soft like angora?

"I dunno, but they are long gone," said Vasta. "Even took the shell."

"How do you know that?" She reached his side.

"Shells are green and red, mostly. Easy to spot on the snow."

Agent Hockings moved to the opposite side of the window. "There is a whole group of people out there. Witnesses."

Axel's laugh gleaned another scowl from Hockings. Vasta's mouth quirked but then fell back to reveal no hint of humor when Hockings turned from Axel to him.

Now Axel was scowling. Vasta was making him look bad, or perhaps he was doing that all on his own.

Axel reached the pair who now stood flanking the window like bookends. He pressed his arm to hers, muscling her out of the way in order to get a glimpse outside. Her athletic frame brought her head to his shoulder, and he was only five foot ten. She was what Mrs. Shubert, the librarian of the Kinsley Public Library, would have called petite. Mrs. Shubert had also been petite and was as mighty as a superhero in Axel's mind. He knew not to judge ferocity in inches.

"Or," said Hockings, "you could see if any of the

spectators have a shotgun in their hand or shell casing in their pocket."

"Illegal search," said Vasta. "And none of them have a shotgun any longer. So, here's what's going to happen. Sheriff Trace is going to escort you out in restraints and put you in the back of his unit. Then he's going to drive you outta here. If you are smart, you will keep your head down and look ashamed, because you should be."

"I will not."

"Then they will likely break every window in Axel's cruiser and possibly turn it over with you both inside."

Hockings stiffened as her eyes went wide with shock. The brown of her irises, he now saw, were flecked with copper. She looked to him, as if asking if Vasta were pulling her leg.

He hoped his expression said that the acting chief of police was not.

She turned back to Vasta. "You'd have to stop them."

"Listen, Agent Hockings, it's just me here. Last week, I was an officer, and now this." He motioned to his chief's badge. "Besides, I'm tempted to help them."

Hockings looked from Vasta to Trace and then back to Vasta.

"Are you pressing charges against Hockings?" Axel asked Vasta.

"Are you serious?" she asked the sheriff.

He gave her a look he hoped said that he was very serious. "They have tribal courts and you do *not* want to go there."

"They can't prosecute a federal agent."

"But can hold you until your people find out."

Her fingers went straight, flexing and then lacing

together to create a weapon that he believed she was wise enough not to use.

"Fine. So contrite. That will get us out of here?"

The acting chief of police nodded.

"What about my vehicle?"

"I'll drive it to the border and leave it for you."

"The border?" To Rylee, the border was Canada. Vasta enlightened her.

"The border of our reservation."

Her gaze flicked between them and her full mouth went thin and miserly. But she thought about it. Axel just loved the way the tips of her nose and ears went pink as a rabbit's in her silent fury.

"Fine. Let's get going, if you have your keys," she said, pushing past him.

The acting chief of police was faster, beating them to the door to the main squad room. There, two officers sat on a desk and table respectively, both kicking their legs from their perches where they had been watching the drama playing out through the glass door of the chief's office.

"Josh and Noah, you two have point," said Vasta, instructing the men to lead the escort.

Both men rose, grinning. Each wore tight-fitting uniforms. Josh's hair was black and bristly short. Noah wore his brown hair in a knot at his neck.

They headed out behind the officers, with Axel holding Hockings's taut arm as if she were his prisoner. Behind them came the acting chief of police. Trace tried and failed not to notice that he could nearly encircle Rylee's bicep with his thumb and index finger and that included her wool coat. She glared up at him and her muscle bunched beneath his grip. Hockings clearly did not like role-play.

The crowd that Hockings had insisted Vasta question were now calling rude suggestions and booing. Vasta waved and spoke to them in Kowa, a form of the Iroquoian language. The officers before them peeled away, giving Axel a view of his cruiser and the rear door. For reasons he did not completely understand, his squad car was untouched. Axel hit the fob, unlocking his unit. Noah swept the rear door open.

Axel made a show of putting his hand on Hockings's head to see that she was safely ensconced in the rear of his unit. The effect brought a cheer from the peanut gallery and allowed him to get the answer to one of his many questions about Hockings.

Her hair was soft as the ear of an Irish setter and blond right to the roots. Hockings fell to her side across the rear seat and remained on her side. *Wise beyond her years*, he thought.

The booing resumed as he climbed behind the wheel. It pleased him that Josh and Noah now stood between his unit and the gathering of pissed-off Mohawks.

And off they went. They were outside of Salmon River, the tribe's main settlement, but still on rez land before Rylee sat up and laced her fingers through the mesh guard that separated his front from the back seat. Her fingernails were shiny with clearish pink polish and neatly filed into appealing ovals. Her wrists were no longer secured.

"How did you get out of that?" he asked.

"My father says you can measure a person's IQ by whether or not they carry a pocketknife."

"With the exception being at airports?" he asked.

"You going to keep me back here the entire way?"

"Not if you want to sit beside me."

She didn't answer that, just threw herself back into the upholstery and growled. Then she looked out the side window.

"They better not damage my car," she muttered.

"More," he said.

"What?"

She wasn't looking at him. He knew because he was staring at her in the rearview until the grooves in the shoulder's pavement vibrated his attention back to the road.

"Damage your car more," he clarified. "They already shot at it. So, you find who you were looking for?"

She folded her arms over her chest. Just below her lovely small breasts, angry fists balled. She was throwing so much shade the cab went dark.

"How do you know I was looking for someone?"

"What Home Security does, isn't it, here on the border?"

"In this case, yes. We have an illegal crossing and the suspect fled onto Kowa lands."

"They have your suspect?"

"Denied any knowledge."

Homeland Security Agent Rylee Hockings was about as welcome in Salmon River as a spring snowstorm.

"Maybe Border Patrol has your guy."

"No. They lost 'em. That's why they called me. They abandoned pursuit when our suspect crossed onto Mohawk land. Both the suspect and the cargo have vanished." She glanced back the way they had come. "I need my car."

What she needed were social skills. She didn't want

his help, but she might need it. And he needed to get her out of his county before she got into something way more dangerous than ruffled Mohawk regalia. Up here on the border, waving a badge at the wrong people could get you killed.

The woman might have federal authority and a mission, but she didn't know his county or the people here. Folks who lived on the border did it for one of three reasons. Either it was as far away from whatever trouble they had left as they could get, or they had business on the other side. He'd survived up here by knowing the difference, doing his job and not poking his nose into the issues that were not under his purview.

There was one other reason to be up here. If you had no other choice. Rylee had a choice. So she needed to go. Sooner was better.

He considered himself to be both brave and smart, but that would be little to no protection from Rylee's alluring brown eyes and watermelon-pink mouth. Best way he knew to keep clear of her was to get her south as soon as possible.

"The Mohawk are required to report illegal entry onto US soil," she said. "And detain if possible. They did neither."

"Maybe they aren't interested in our business or our borders."

"America's business? Is that what you mean?"

He scratched the side of his head and realized he needed a haircut. "It's just my experience that the Mohawk people consider themselves separate from the United States and Canada." He half turned to look back at her. "You know they have territory in both countries."

"Yes, I was briefed. And smuggling, human trafficking and dope running happen in your county."

She'd left out moonshining. But border security was thankfully not his job. Neither were the vices that were handled by ATF—the federal agency responsible for alcohol, tobacco, firearms and recently explosives. He was glad because enforcement was a dangerous, impossible and thankless assignment. His responsibilities, answering calls from citizens via EMS, traffic stops and accidents made up the bulk of his duties. He was occasionally involved with federal authorities, collaborating only when asked, and Agent Hockings seemed thrilled to do everything herself. He should leave it at that.

"Borders bring their own unique troubles."

"Yet, you have made limited arrests related to these activities. Mostly minor ones, at that, despite the uptick in illegal activities, especially in winter when the river freezes."

He ignored the jibe. He did his duty and that was enough to let him sleep most nights.

"It doesn't always freeze," he said.

"Hmm? What doesn't?"

"The river. Some years it doesn't freeze."

She cocked her head and gave him a look as if he puzzled her. "How long have you been sheriff?"

If she were any kind of an agent, she knew that already, but he answered anyway.

"Going on six years this January."

"You seem young."

"Old enough to know better and halfway to collecting social security."

"You grew up here, didn't you?"

"I've never lived anywhere else."

"You have family up here?"

His smile faltered, and he swerved to the shoulder. He gripped the wheel with more force than necessary and glanced back at her, his teeth snapping together with a click.

One thing he was not doing was speaking about his past. Not his time in the military, not the men he'd killed or the ones he couldn't save. And he wasn't ever speaking of the time before the sheriff got him clear of the compound. He needed to get this question machine out of his county, so he could go back to being the well-respected public servant again.

As far as he knew, only two men knew where he came from—his father and the former sheriff. And he looked nothing like that scrawny kid Sheriff Rogers had saved. So changed, in fact, he believed his own father would not know him. At least that was what he prayed for, every damn day. All he wanted in this world was to live in a place where the rules made sense, where he had some control. And where, maybe someday, he and a nice, normal woman could create a family that didn't make his stomach knot. But for now, he needed to be here, watching his father. Here to stop him if he switched from preaching his unhinged religious vision to creating it.

She opened her copper-flecked brown eyes even wider, feigning a look of innocence.

"What?" she asked.

He unlocked his teeth, grinding them, and then pivoted in his seat to stare back at her.

"Two hours ago, you showed up in the city of Kinsley at city hall, making it very clear that you did not want the assistance of the county sheriff. Now you want my résumé."

"Local law enforcement is obliged to assist in federal investigations."

"Which I will do. But you asked about my family. Like to fill in some blanks, that right? Something before I turned thirteen?" She was digging for the details that were not in public records or, perhaps, just filling time. Either way, he was not acting as the ant under her magnifying glass.

She met his stare and did not flinch or look away from the venom that must have been clear in his expression. Instead, she shrugged. "What I want is out of this back seat."

He threw open his door and then yanked open hers. She stared up at him with a contrite expression that did not match the gleam of victory shimmering in the dark waters of her eyes. *Dangerous waters*, he thought. Even through his annoyance, he could not completely squelch the visceral ache caused by her proximity.

"You prefer to drive?" he said.

She slipped out of his vehicle to stand on the road before him. "Not this time. When do I get my vehicle back?"

He drew out his phone and sent a text. By the time she had settled into the passenger side, adjusted both the seat and safety belt, he received a reply.

"It's there now," he said. The photo appeared a moment later and he plastered his hand across his mouth to keep her from seeing his grin. Axel slipped behind the wheel and performed an illegal turn on a double solid, a privilege of his position, and took them back the way they had come.

"Why are you whistling?" she asked.

Was he? Perhaps. It was just that such moments of glee were hard to contain. By the time they reached the sign indicating the border of the Mohawk rez, she caught sight of her vehicle.

Someone had poured red paint over the roof and it was dripping down over both the windows and doors on one side. There were handprints all over the front side panel.

"My car!" she cried, leaning forward for a good look. Then she pointed. "That's damaging federal property."

"Looks like a war horse," he said, admiring the paint job. It was so rare that people got exactly what they deserved.

Chapter 3

Rylee Hockings stood beside the surly sheriff with hands on hips as she regarded the gooey paint oozing from the metallic door panel of her official vehicle and onto the road. She struggled to keep her chin up. Her first field assignment had headed south the minute she headed north. When her boss, Lieutenant Catherine Ohr, saw this car, she would be livid.

Her vehicle had been towed and left just outside the reservation land and abandoned beneath the sign welcoming visitors to the Kowa Nation.

"Maybe the paint will fill in the bullet holes," offered Sheriff Trace.

His chuckle vibrated through her like a call issued into an empty cave. Something about the tenor and pitch made her stomach do a funny little tremble. She rested a hand flat against her abdomen to discourage her body from getting ideas.

"I could use those prints as evidence," she said to Sheriff Trace.

"Or you could accept the life lesson that you might be the big cheese where you come from but to the Kowa, you are an outsider. Up here, your position will get you more trouble than respect. Which is why I offered you an escort."

And she had turned him down flat. Despite his mirthful blue eyes, extremely handsome face, brown hair bleached blond from what she presumed was the summer sun, and a body that was in exceptionally good shape, something about this man rubbed her the wrong way. The sheriff seemed to think the entire county belonged to him personally.

"I need to call Border Patrol." She left him to gloat and made her call. Border Patrol had lost their suspects after they entered Mohawk territory yesterday, Sunday, at three in the afternoon and had had no further sightings. Now she understood why they ceased pursuit at their border of the reservation and called her field office. They had set up a perimeter, so the suspect was either still on Mohawk land or had slipped off and into the general population. The chances that this man was *her* man were slim, but until she had word that the package and courier had been apprehended elsewhere, she would treat each illegal border crossing as if the carrier came from Siming's Army.

Her conversation and update yielded nothing further. The perimeter remained in place. All vehicles entering or leaving the American side of the Kowa lands were being checked. They had not found their man.

She stowed her phone and returned the few steps to

find her escort watching the clouds as if he had not a thing to do.

"They tell you they wouldn't go on Mohawk land?" he asked.

She didn't answer his question, for he seemed to already know their reply. "So, anyone who wants to avoid apprehension from federal authorities just has to make it onto Mohawk land as if they had reached some home-free base, like in tag."

"No, they have to reach Mohawk's sovereign land and the Mohawk have to be willing to allow them to stay. The Kowa people have rights granted to them under treaties signed by our government."

They had reached another impasse. Silence stretched, and she noticed that his eyes were really a stunning blue-gray.

"You want me to hang around?" he asked, his body language signaling his wish to leave.

"Escort me to a place that can get this paint off," she said.

He touched the paint and then rubbed it between thumb and forefinger. He wiped his finger and thumb on the hood, then tapped his finger up and down to add his fingerprints to the others.

"Stop that!"

He did, holding up his paint-stained hand in surrender. "Oil based. Can't use the car wash. Body shop, I suppose."

"You have one?"

"Not personally, but there is one in town."

"I'll follow." She used her fob to open the door and nothing happened.

He lowered his chin and lifted his brows. The corners of his mouth lifted before he twisted his lips in a poorly veiled attempt to hide his smile.

Had the vandals disconnected her battery or helped themselves to the entire thing?

"Tow truck," he said.

She faced the reservation sign, lifted a stone from the road and threw it. The rock made a satisfying *thwack* against the metal surface.

He placed the call and she checked in with her office. No messages.

"Tow truck will be here in twenty minutes. Want to wait or grab a ride with me?"

"What do I do with the keys?"

"Tow truck doesn't need those," he said.

She nodded. "I knew that."

Did she sound as green as she felt? How much more experience in the field did Trace have? He'd been an army MP and now was a sheriff.

"How did you decide to run for sheriff?" she asked.

His mouth tipped downward. He didn't seem fond of speaking about his past. She decided to find out why that was. She'd missed something in her hasty check.

"My friend and mentor, Kurt Rogers, was retiring. He held on until I got out of the service and threw his support behind me. Been reelected once since then."

Rylee managed to retrieve her briefcase and suitcase from the trunk, half surprised to see them there and not covered with paint. They walked back to his sheriff's unit side by side.

"Must be hard to be popular in this sort of work."

He cocked his head. "I don't find it so."

He helped her place her luggage in the rear seat and

then held the passenger door for her. She had her belt clipped as they pulled back on the highway.

They did not speak on the ride into town. The air in the cruiser seemed to hold an invisible charge. She shifted uncomfortably in her seat and he rubbed his neck.

"Motel or the body shop?" he asked as they hit the limits of the town of Kinsley, which was the county seat.

"Motel."

It bothered her that, of the three possible choices, he took her directly to the place where she was staying. She didn't ask how he knew.

The sheriff pulled to a stop and she retrieved her bags.

He stood on his side of the vehicle, staring across the roof at her. "You feel like telling me where you'll be next, or should I just follow the sound of gunfire?"

She refused to take the bait and only thanked him for the lift.

"Don't mention it," he said and then added, as he slipped back into his unit, "I surely wouldn't."

She stooped to glare at him through the open passenger door. "Why not?"

"You won't need to. Soon everyone in the county will know you are here and what happened on Mohawk land, because a good story spreads faster than wildfire and because you used exactly the sort of strong-arm tactics I'd expect from a rookie agent. What I can't figure is why your supervisor sent you up here without a baby-sitter. You that unpopular he couldn't even find you a partner? Or is he just that stupid?"

"*She* is not stupid and it's an honor to be given a solo

assignment," she said, feeling her face heat. "A show of respect."

"Is that what she told you?"

She slammed the door and he laughed. Rylee stood, fuming, as he cruised out of the lot.

What did she care what he thought? She had work to do. Important work. And she didn't need the approval of the sheriff of one of the most sparsely populated counties in the state.

Kowa Mohawk people were on her watch list along with a motorcycle gang calling themselves the North Country Riders. This gang was known to smuggle marijuana across the Canadian border. Additionally, she needed to investigate a family of moonshiners. The Mondellos had for years avoided federal tax on their product by making and distributing liquor. Finally, and most troubling of all, was a survivalist compound headed by Stanley Coopersmith. Their doomsday predictions and arsenal of unknown weapons made them dangerous.

This was Rylee's first real field assignment and they had sent her solo, which was an honor, no matter what the sheriff said. She was unhappy to be given such an out-of-the-way placement because all the analysis indicated this as the least likely spot for Siming's Army to use for smuggling. Most of department had moved to the Buffalo and Niagara Falls regions where the analysis believed Siming's Army would attempt infiltration.

She let herself into her room and went to work on her laptop. She took a break at midafternoon to head out to the mini-mart across the street to buy some drinks and snacks.

Her car arrived from the body shop just after six

o'clock, the telltale outline of the red paint still visible along with the outline of three handprints.

"Couldn't get those out without buffing. Best we could do," said the gaunt tow truck driver in navy blue coveralls. "Also replaced the battery."

"Dead?" she asked.

"Gone," he said.

He clutched a smoldering half-finished cigarette at his side and her invoice in the other. The edges of the brown clipboard upon which her paperwork sat were worn, rounded with age.

She offered her credit card. He copied the numbers and she signed the slip.

The tow truck operator cocked his head to study the vehicle's new look with watery eyes gone yellow with jaundice. "Almost looks intentional. Like those cave paintings in France. You know?"

Rylee flicked her gaze to the handprints and then back to the driver.

"Like a warrior car. I might try something like it with an airbrush."

Rylee her held out her hand for the receipt.

"If I were you, I'd stay off Mohawk land. Maybe stick to the casino from now on."

She accepted the paperwork without comment. The driver folded the pages and handed them to her. Rylee returned to her room and her laptop. It was too late to head out to the next group on her watch list. That would have to wait until tomorrow.

Her phone chimed, alerting her to an incoming call. The screen display read *Catherine Ohr*, and she groaned. She couldn't know about the car already.

"Did you not understand the Mohawk are a sovereign nation?" said her boss.

"On federal land."

"On Kowa Mohawk Nation land. When I asked you to speak to them, I meant you should make an appointment."

"At eight a.m., Border Patrol notified me of a runner. A single male who crossed the border on foot carrying a large navy blue duffel bag. He was believed to have been dropped off by his courier on the Canadian side. That same courier then picked him up on the US side. They were sighted on River Road. Border Patrol detained the pickup driver thirty minutes later just outside Mohawk lands. The passenger fled on foot onto the reservation, carrying the large duffel on his back."

"They questioned the driver?"

"Yes. He denies picking anyone up."

"Name?"

"Quinton Mondello. Oldest son of Hal Mondello."

"How many sons does he have?"

"Four. Quinton runs things with his father. He's the heir apparent, in my opinion."

"So, the moonshiners were carrying moonshine. Made a drop in Canada and were heading home with an empty truck."

"Then why run?"

"You believe the passenger was an illegal immigrant?"

"At the very least," said Rylee.

"You believe the Mondello family is engaged in human trafficking?"

"Or they are assisting the Siming terrorist."

"That's a stretch. Border Patrol saw the passenger flee?"

Rylee's stomach knotted. "No. They were acting on an anonymous tip who reported seeing the passenger flee prior to Border Patrol's arrival. Border Patrol stopped a truck of similar description just outside Mohawk lands."

"Could have been a Mohawk carrying cigarettes from Canada. Could have been a moonshiner. Pot grower. Poacher. And their tip could have been a rival poacher, moonshiner or pot grower. Any of those individuals would have reason to flee. Hell, they have ginseng hunters up here trespassing all the time."

"Not in the fall."

Ohr made a sound like a growl that did not bode well for Rylee's career advancement plans.

"It could also be a suspect," added Rylee, pushing her luck.

"Therefore, we don't really know if there even was a passenger."

"Quinton Mondello denies carrying a passenger."

"Of course, he does. And he may be telling the truth."

Rylee didn't believe that for a minute.

"So, you decided to follow, alone, without backup and without notifying the tribal police," said Ohr.

Rylee dropped her gaze to the neatly made bed and swallowed, knowing that speaking now would reveal an unwanted tremor in her voice.

"Hockings?"

"Border Patrol didn't pursue." There was that darn tremor.

"Because they understand the law. That is also why

they had to release Quinton Mondello. No evidence of wrongdoing."

Silence stretched.

"Do I need to pull you?"

"No, ma'am."

"I do not have time to clean up your messes, Hockings."

Rylee thought of the handprints on her federal vehicle and her head hung in shame.

"Do not go on Mohawk land again for any reason."

"Yes, ma'am."

Ohr hung up on her.

Rylee needed some air. She gathered her personal weapon, wallet, shield and keys before heading out. The September night had turned cooler than she realized, and she ducked inside to grab a lined jacket. She stepped outside again and glanced about. The night had fallen like a curtain, so much blacker than her suburban neighborhood with the streetlights lining every road. Here, only the parking lot and the mini-mart across the road glowed against the consuming dark. She'd seen an ice-cream place, the kind that had a grill, on their arrival. A burger and fries with a shake would hit the spot. It wasn't until she was driving toward her destination that she realized she had snatched the blue windbreaker that had bold white letters across the back, announcing that she was Homeland Security.

The dash clock told her it was nearly 8:00 p.m. and she wondered how long the ice-cream joint might stay open. The answer turned out to be eight o'clock. She arrived to see the lot empty except for one familiar sheriff's vehicle and a clear view of the solitary worker inside, cleaning the grill. Out front, sitting on the picnic table surface with his feet on the bench, was Sheriff Trace and a very young man.

She ignored them, which wasn't easy, as she had to walk from her vehicle to the order window.

"Ms. Hockings," said the sheriff.

She nodded and glanced at the pair.

"Who's that?" asked the young man. The sheriff's companion had peach fuzz on his jaw and hair shaved so short that it was impossible to know if his hair was blond or light brown and a stunned expression. There was an old crescent scar on his scalp where the hair did not grow.

The sheriff mumbled something as she reached the order window and was greeted by a red-faced woman who said, "Just cleaned the grill. You want something to eat, have to be the fryer."

"All right. So…what are my choices?"

"Fried shrimp, mozzarella sticks or French fries."

"Ice cream?"

"Yup." She motioned a damp rag at the menu board behind her. "Ain't cleaned that yet."

Rylee ordered the shrimp and fries with a vanilla shake. The woman had the order up in less than four minutes and the counter light flicked off as Rylee retreated with her dinner in a box lined with a red-and-white-checked paper already turning transparent in the grease.

The sheriff called to her before she could reach her car.

"Agent Hockings. Join us?" he asked.

She let her shoulders deflate. Rylee wanted only to eat and have a shower. But she forced a smile. Establishing working relationships with local law enforcement was part of the job. Unfortunately, this local made her skin tingle when she got too close. She hated knowing from the heat of her face that she was blushing. He returned her smile and her mind wandered to questions that were none of her business, like what Axel Trace's chest looked like beneath that uniform.

Two months ago, Rylee had had a steady boyfriend but that ended when she got promoted and he didn't. The help she'd given him on course work might have worked against him in the written testing when he didn't know the information required. In any case, he blamed her, and she'd broken things off. Showing his true colors made getting over him easy. Except at night. She missed the feel of him in her bed; that had been the only place they had gotten along just fine. Now she knew that attraction was not enough of a foundation for a relationship. So why was she staring at the sheriff's jawline and admiring the gap between his throat and the white undershirt that edged his uniform?

Because, Rylee, you haven't been with a man in a long time. She swept him with a gaze and dismissed this attraction as the second worst idea of the day. The first being pursuit onto Mohawk land.

Rylee sat across from the pair, who slipped from the surface of the picnic table and onto the opposite bench, staring at her in silence as she ate the curling brown breading that must have had a shrimp in there somewhere. The second bite told her the shellfish was still frozen in the center. She pushed it aside.

"Want my second burger?" asked Axel.

"You have a spare?"

"Bought it for Morris, here. But two ought to do him."

Morris gave the burger in the sheriff's hands a look

of regret before dipping the last of his fries into his ice-cream sundae.

"This is Morris Coopersmith," said Trace. "Morris, this is Rylee Hockings. She's with Homeland Security."

Stanley Coopersmith was one of the persons of interest.

Morris's brows lifted, and his hand stilled. When he spoke, his voice broke. "Nice to meet you."

"Likewise." Rylee accepted the wrapped burger Sheriff Trace extended. "Any relationship to Stanley Coopersmith?"

Morris grinned and nodded. "That's my dad." Then the smile waned. "He doesn't like comics."

Morris's dad was on her watch list. He led a colony of like-minded doomsday survivalists, who had their camp right on the New York side of the border. It would be simple for such a group to transport anything or anyone they liked through the woods and over the border in either direction.

"Want some pickles?" asked Morris, offering the ones he had plucked from his burgers.

"No, thank you," she said to Morris. Her phone chimed and she checked to see the incoming text was unimportant.

Morris pointed. "Do you have a camera on that?"

Rylee nodded.

"Take our picture," he insisted and moved closer to the sheriff.

Rylee gave the sheriff a questioning look and received a shrug in response, so she opened the camera app and took a photo.

Morris reached for her phone and she allowed him

to take it and watched closely as he admired the shot. At last, he handed her back her phone.

She asked the sheriff, "Are you two related?"

It was a blind guess. Morris was pink and lanky; his body type more like a basketball player. Axel's blond hair, sun-kissed skin and muscular physique seemed nearly opposite to the boy's.

She wasn't sure why she didn't delete the photo, but she left it and tucked her phone away. Then she turned her attention to her meal. She had a mouthful of burger when the sheriff dispelled her first guess.

"I'm transporting Morris from his home to the jail in Kinsley due to failure to report to his last hearing. He's got to be in court in the morning."

"Oh," she said, forcing the word past the mouthful of food. She knew the shock was clear on her face. Did he usually stop to buy suspects dinner? She had so many questions but turned to Morris. "I'm sorry for your trouble. I hope the hearing goes well."

"Doubtful. Not the first time I got picked up."

"Oh, I see." The investigator portion of her was dying to ask what exactly he had repeatedly been picked up for.

"I steal things," said Morris and grinned.

"Morris," said the sheriff, his tone an admonition. "What did I say?"

"Let my lawyer do the talking?" said the boy.

"And?"

"Don't discuss the case."

Axel Trace nodded solemnly.

Morris turned to Rylee. "But I wasn't stealing for me this time. So that will be all right." He glanced to the sheriff for reassurance and received none.

Axel Trace looked as if he were taking his dog to the vet to be put down. His mouth tugged tight and his eyes... Were they glistening? His repeat blinking and the large swallow of soda he took seemed answer enough. Sheriff Trace cared for this boy.

Rylee choked down the rest of the burger in haste. Morris finished his sundae and grinned, smacking his lips in satisfaction. On closer inspection, he did not seem quite a boy but a man acting like a boy. He certainly didn't have a grip on the seriousness of his position. Why hadn't the information on Stanley Coopersmith included that he had a boy with special needs?

"How old are you, Morris?" she asked.

"Twenty." He showed a gap-toothed smile.

That was bad news. "I see."

She glanced to Trace, whose mouth went tight. Then she looked back to Morris. Her gaze slid to the sheriff.

He motioned to Morris with two fingers. "Come on, sport. Time to go."

Morris stood, towering over the sheriff by six inches. He was painfully thin. He wore neither handcuffs nor zip ties on his wrists. Trace pointed at his unit. Morris wadded up his paper wrappers and shot them basketball-style, as if hitting a foul shot. Then he cheered for his success and finally slipped into the passenger side of the sheriff's car.

"Is that wise? Having him up front with you?" she asked.

"Morris and I have an agreement."

Morris called from inside the cruiser. "Coke and comic for good behavior."

She stared at the young man and staunched the urge to open the door and release him.

"You have a good evening, Rylee."

"Thank you for the burger, Axel." The intentional use of his first name seemed all right. He'd used her given name first. But he just stood there, staring at her. And her breath was coming in short staccato bursts; she regretted dropping the distance of formality.

He gave her the kind of smile that twisted her heart and then returned to his duty, delivering a boy who should be entering a group home to the court systems.

Rylee headed back to her motel but then veered instead into the Walmart parking lot. It wasn't until she found herself in the books section that she realized she was looking at comics. The boy was spending the night in jail; he could at least have another superhero to keep him company.

Rylee made her purchase and used the GPS to find the jail in Kinsley. There, she was buzzed in and escorted back by a patrolman who allowed her to give Morris the graphic novel.

"You are a nice lady." Morris beamed. Then his voice held a note of chastisement. "Did you pay for this?"

She would have laughed if not faced with a boy who should not have been there in the first place.

Chapter 4

Observe and report. Rylee took her chief's directive to heart as she set off the next morning, the first Tuesday of September, to observe the next group on the watch list. The survivalists headed by Stanley Coopersmith. The group's rhetoric centered around surviving the apocalypse triggered by foreign terrorists. Ironic, as that scenario might turn out much more plausible than anyone in federal law enforcement had thought until a few months ago and the very reason she was here today.

It was hard to believe that such a group might aid foreign terrorists until you recalled your history and cult leader Charles Manson's attempts to begin a race war by murdering innocent affluent white victims, including Sharon Tate. It was terrifying, the lengths individuals might go to bring about their worldview.

At 7:00 a.m., Rylee left her car on the shoulder and

hiked through the woods to a place where she could observe the central compound. Even though she was dressed all in earth colors for camouflage and was wearing a forest green wool sweater and a brown leather jacket atop her gray jeans and brown work boots with thick socks, she had underestimated the chill in the morning air. She had plenty of time to think about her inadequate wardrobe, among other things, as she lay on her belly in the pale green ferns. A cool September breeze shook the leaves overhead, sending down a cascade of yellow leaves through the fog.

"Should have worn a wool cap," she muttered to herself.

Maple leaves fluttered through the shafts of sunlight, giving hope that the fog would lift, as she watched the compound through binoculars. From this position, she had a clear line of sight to a large crumbling former dairy barn that might have once been yellow, two new prefab outbuildings with metal exteriors and roofs and a weathered farmhouse, looking patchy with the graying wood peeking out beneath flaking white paint.

One of the newer structures was a dock with a covered large boathouse on the St. Regis River that flowed into the St. Lawrence. That structure meant that it was reasonable to assume that the survivalists did leave their land. Did they use their boats to traffic in illegal drugs or human beings? Operations needed funding and she had yet to discover theirs. They were no longer farmers. That much was certain.

Had Stanley Coopersmith headed to court to defend his son?

Her reports on this group said that their leader never left the facility and his younger brothers, Joseph and Daniel, both married with children, rarely left their land. Stanley, who was married to Judy Cooper-smith, had two grown boys—Edward, who they called "Eddie," and Morris, whom she had met on the night of her arrival.

She shivered with the cold as she counted occupants, noted physical descriptions into a digital recorder and snapped shots through her telephoto lens. As the morning stretched on and the sunlight finally reached her, she daydreamed about making a major arrest. Was it possible her runner had left Mohawk land? The Mohawk reservation land ended at the St. Regis River, just a short distance from Coopersmith's property. Had this been the runner's destination? The journey along would have been easy overland, or on the St. Lawrence River, with an escort of survivalists.

If she intercepted the shipment from Siming's Army, her boss would have to promote her. Then Rylee might ask for an assignment in New York City. What would her father think of that?

She sighed. Would he be proud?

The sound of a trigger's click dropped her from her daydreams like an acorn from an oak and made her stiffen. Her skin flushed hot and her fingers tingled. She held the binoculars; making a grab for her weapon seemed like suicide. Why hadn't she placed her weapon nearer to hand?

"Lace your fingers behind your head," came the order from a male voice behind her. The smell of the earth beneath her now turned her stomach and the ground seemed to churn as if heaved by an earthquake.

"Roll over," ordered her captor.

"I'm a federal agent. Homeland Security." For once, her voice did not shake.

There was a pause and then the command to roll over again.

She pushed off and rolled, coming to her seat. The man holding a rifle was the brother of the family's leader—Daniel Coopersmith. She recognized him by his ginger beard and the scar across the bridge of his nose. He held the rifle stock pressed to his cheek and the barrel aimed at her chest.

"Stand up."

She released her laced fingers as she did so. The blood pounding through her veins made her skin itch. This might be her only chance to reach her weapon. Her only chance to avoid capture.

"Don't," he advised.

The roar in her ears nearly deafened her.

He wasn't taking her. That much she knew, because she was not creating a hostage situation on her first assignment. As she came upright, she swept her leg behind his and knocked him from his feet. As his arms jerked outward in reflex, she seized the barrel of the rifle and yanked. By the time Daniel recovered enough to scramble backward, she had his rifle pointed at him.

"It ain't loaded," he said.

She felt the weight of the firearm and gave him a look of disappointment.

"Daniel, have you had any visitors, other than me, recently?"

"What kind of visitors?"

"Smugglers."

"Anyone crosses our land we know it. Got cameras everywhere. How we spotted you."

"Your family likes their privacy?"

"We don't assist illegals if that's what you mean."

"Why is that?"

"They're carriers. Part of the scourge to come."

She knew the dogma.

"You know your nephew is in court this morning?" she asked.

Daniel curled his fingers around his beard and tugged.

"I knew he run off again. He get arrested?"

"Shoplifting."

"Comics again?"

She shrugged.

"Stan is gonna tan his hide."

"Not if he's in prison. Second offense."

Daniel seemed to forget she was pointing his rifle at him as he turned to go.

"I gotta go tell Judy." He glanced at her over his shoulder. "You best git. Leave my rifle on the road by your vehicle. That is if Stan don't already got your car."

"Stop." She had her weapon out and it *was* loaded.

He stopped and glanced back at her.

"You threatened a federal agent," she said to her retreating would-be opponent.

"I threatened a trespasser who's also an agent. We got constitutional rights. Illegal search. Illegal surveillance. Just cause. Illegal seizure." He continued speaking about rights and threats as he wound through the trees and out of sight.

She watched him go.

As it happened, when she reached her vehicle, she found Stanley Coopersmith waiting with his wife, Judy. Coopersmith was a man in his sixties, silver-haired, slim and muscular with a mustache that would have made any rodeo cowboy proud. His wife's hair was short and streaked with silver. She had the body of a woman accustomed to physical work and the lined face of a smoker.

Coopersmith did not move the rifle he held resting over his shoulder at her approach. She kept her personal weapon drawn but lowered.

"You holding my boy?"

"Sir, I'm Homeland Security—"

"We know who you are," said Judy Coopersmith, her chin now aimed at Rylee like a knife. "You holding my boy?"

"No, ma'am. Morris was arrested for shoplifting by local law enforcement. He has a hearing scheduled for this morning."

"You come here to tell us this?" said Coopersmith.

"No. I'm here investigating a case."

"You here to shut us down?"

Visions of Waco, Texas, flared like a dumpster fire in her mind.

"I am not. My job is to secure our borders."

"Well, we can assure you that this border is secure. Nobody sneaks through this patch of ground without us knowing. Yourself included."

"That's reassuring," said Rylee. "Has anyone tried recently?"

The two exchanged a look but did not reply. *No answer is still an answer*, she thought.

She took a leap of faith that their mutual threat made her, if not an ally, at least not an enemy. "We have intelligence that indicates something dangerous might be coming over from Canada. I'd ask you to be extra vigi-

lant and hope that you will alert me if there is anything
that threatens our national security."

Another long look blazed between the two.

"Why do you think we're up here?" asked Coopersmith. "Just a bunch of crazies playing war games in
the woods? We know what's coming."

"And you do not think the federal government is capable of stopping threats from foreigners."

"If I did, why would I build a bunker?"

Rylee glanced toward her vehicle. "I'd best get back."

It was a long, long walk…to her vehicle. She did not
draw an easy breath until she was safely behind the
wheel. However, when she pressed the starter, her vehicle gave only an impotent click. The engine did not
turn over on any of her next three attempts. There was
no motor sound. In fact, the only sound was the thumping drumbeat of her heart.

The fog had settled into a steady drizzle by midday.
Axel reached the stretch of old timber bordering Coopersmith land. He'd received a tip from Hal Mondello,
who knew how to spot a fed's car if anyone alive did,
that Rylee had headed past his place. Beyond Mondello
land was the cult that called itself the Congregation of
Eternal Wisdom. Beyond that was Hal Coopersmith's
spread and his survivalist family. He didn't know which
was a worse place for Rylee. For personal reasons, he
decided to try Coopersmith's first and backtrack if necessary.

Hal Mondello was not a friend, but he protected his
self-interest. Having the sheriff rein in a fed nosing
around would be to his benefit. Hence, the call.

Mondello called himself a farmer, but everything he

raised went into his cash crop, moonshine. Hal supplied most of the entire region with hard liquor. His brew was popular for its potency and the fact that it was cheap, due to Hal's complete avoidance of paying any federal tax. That made his moonshine a working man's favorite. Thankfully, that sort of violation fell under the auspices of the ATF, who had found his operation too small to be bothered with.

Axel raced out to the Coopersmiths' main gate, running silent, but exceeding the speed limit the entire way. He understood the Coopersmiths' desire to live off the grid, be largely self-sufficient, but he didn't understand living in a constant state of fear of some upcoming disaster from which only you and yours would survive. What kind of a world would that be, anyway? The thought of only Axel and his family surviving such a calamity gave him a shudder.

On the other hand, he did admire the Coopersmith family. Before they'd taken to their compound and ceased interacting with the outside world, Axel had been to their farm and respected the close-knit group. Anything could be taken too far. Religion came to his mind and he shuddered again.

He'd just be happy to have a family that didn't scare him so much that he didn't dare leave them out of his sight. And he owed Stanley Coopersmith for getting him out of his abysmal situation and helping him take his GED. Without him and Kurt Rogers, Axel didn't know where he might be now.

Axel was pleased to find Stanley's oldest son, Edward Coopersmith, minding the gate when he roared up. He and Eddie had enlisted in the army together and the two had been friends up until a year ago when his father had shut the family up on their land.

By the time Axel had left his sheriff's unit, the dust he'd raised was falling about them in a fine mist, settling on his hat and the hood of his car. Here, beneath the cover of trees, the drizzle had not succeeded in reaching.

He and his former comrade stood on opposite sides of a closed metal gate.

"Where is she, Eddie?"

"Who?"

"The homeland security agent your family is detaining."

Eddie could not meet his gaze.

"No concern of yours, I reckon."

"Eddie!"

His friend gripped the shoulder strap of the rifle slung over his shoulder so tightly his knuckles went bloodless.

"She's up at the farm," Eddie admitted.

"Under duress?"

"Not that I could see. But they was armed. So was she, come to that."

"Trespassing?"

"Well, she was."

"Eddie, she's a federal agent. You do not want her harmed."

His friend offered no reassurance.

"Bring me up."

"No outsiders."

"I'm not an outsider. I've eaten at your table. Your ma taught me algebra."

"Still…she ain't your concern."

Axel imagined the news crews and federal helicopters circling the compound. He had to stop this right now. Looking back, he didn't know why he did it. Perhaps because it was the only idea that popped into his head.

"She's my girl," said Axel.

"She's what now?" Eddie cocked his head.

Axel doubled down. "That's why she's up here, berry picking."

"With binoculars?"

"She's my fiancée and I won't have her touched."

"If she's your girl, why she up here alone?"

"Rylee is deciding if she wants to live up this way. I imagine she got…confused. Turned around."

"She was armed."

"Everyone up here is armed. We got bear and moose and elk." *And survivalists with semi-automatic assault rifles*, he finished silently.

Eddie released his grip on the rifle strap to scratch under his jaw at the coarse black beard. He looked so much different than from just a few years back when he was muscular and fit. Now his body looked undernourished and his face gaunt.

Axel watched Eddie as the man considered his options in silence.

After a long silent stretch, Axel had had about enough. "Open the gate or I'm ramming it."

"You can't do that." Their eyes met.

"I'm getting my girl so open up or stand aside."

Chapter 5

"Your girl, huh?" His old friend did little to hide his disappointment and Axel wondered if perhaps Eddie was attracted to Rylee. His answer came a moment later.

"She's very pretty. Kind of prickly, though."

"True on both accounts."

He realized that here on the compound, Eddie had little opportunity to meet eligible women. Rylee was a beauty and smart and he was certain she would have zero interest in locking herself up on nine hundred acres to wait for disaster.

Rylee was here to stop that impending doom from arriving. He admired her for that.

"Eddie, I'm getting in my vehicle. That gate best be open before I get there."

It wasn't a bluff. He knew that his modest yearly budget did not include major damage to his vehicle, but he was getting up to the farm. By the time he had his unit in drive, Eddie was swinging back the gate.

Axel paused just inside to speak to Eddie. "Why don't you come to my place for dinner one day?"

"Can't." Eddie made a face.

"Open invitation," he said and headed off. Axel bounced along the twin groves that served as the access road to the compound, his windshield wipers screeching over the glass as he tried to clear the mist and mud.

Rylee had been stripped of her weapons and now accepted escort to one of the outbuildings. Judy Coopersmith had left her to see to her youngest son, Morris, who was heading to court today. Before leaving, she warned her husband, Stanley, that *this little gal is a guest and is to be treated like one.*

Stanley Coopersmith had his brother Joseph working on her car that had either a bad starter or a bad battery. Stanley thought Rylee should see something in his garage before leaving. She had time on her hands and so if Mr. Coopersmith wanted to give her a tour, she was happy to take it.

The garage turned out to be a huge prefab carport of aluminum, with a vertical roof that looked wide enough to park two tractor trailers in.

"We use it to repair our vehicles and construction. It's right in here."

The odor of motor oil, mildew and rust assaulted her before they'd cleared the single door that stood beside the huge twin garage doors. Inside, two pickup trucks stood end to end, one on blocks and the other with the hood open and a greasy tarp draped over one side.

Beside these casualties sat a backhoe with the bucket

removed and showing one broken tooth. Along the back was a long tool bench. She picked her way past various replacement parts that littered the grease-stained concrete. On the cluttered surface of the tool bench sat one pristine device. It was a drone—white, approximately thirty-four inches with eight rotors, one of which had been damaged. She glanced at Coopersmith, who motioned her forward.

"Go on," he said.

"Where did this come from?"

"Darned if I know, but I took that shot. It was carrying something, like a duffel bag. It dropped it across the river before I made that shot. Crashed out back and we scooped it up."

"What's across the river?" she asked.

He looked startled. "That's the Mohawk Nation."

"Do you believe that it is theirs?"

"No saying. I didn't shoot it until it was over my place."

"And its cargo?"

"Dropped on the Kowa side of the river."

"Did they retrieve what the drone was carrying?"

"Can't say. But I know someone has been trying to activate that drone remotely."

"How do you know that?"

"Because the damn thing keeps moving around the garage. It's why I chained her down."

Rylee used a cloth to lift the drone. "Heavy."

"Thirty pounds and no serial number. No markings at all that I can see."

"When did you find it?"

"Yesterday."

Monday, she realized, and the same day that Border

Patrol followed a small man dropped off on the Canadian side, who crossed the border through a wooded area and then fled onto Mohawk land carrying a duffel bag. Had their suspect had the drone to carry out the cargo or did he have outside help?

"Were you planning to report it?"

"No. I was planning to take it apart and keep it. But if you want it, I'll accept offers."

"Offers?" She did a poor job holding back her surprise. "How much?"

"Take five hundred for it."

"Done."

She reached for her wallet, zipped in her blazer.

"You carry that much?"

She nodded, opening the billfold.

"Should have asked for six," he said.

"I'll give you seven." And she did.

Stanley accepted the cash.

"Has this happened before?"

"Trespassers? Sure. Just today, for instance." He gave her a pointed look and she flushed as he continued on. "But drones. That's a new one for me."

A voice came from behind the pickup.

"Pop?"

"Back here."

Edward Coopersmith appeared, red-faced and unable to make eye contact with her. Behind him came Sheriff Trace. He had no trouble making eye contact and the result was an instant acceleration of her heartbeat. The physical reaction to this man was getting bothersome. She scowled at the pair as they continued toward them.

"Axel, what a surprise." Stanley offered his hand to Trace and cast a scowl at his son.

"I wouldn't have brung him, but this here is his gal and he's worried."

Stanley looked from Axel, whose jaw was locked tight, to Rylee, whose mouth swung open.

"Interesting news, seeing she's only been here a day and a half."

Edward glared at Axel, who shrugged.

Stanley Coopersmith spoke again. "We aren't detaining her, Axel. Fact, she's leaving anytime. You want to give her a lift?"

"I'll need my weapons," said Rylee.

"'Fraid our policy is to confiscate the firearms of trespassers."

"And my vehicle?"

"Also confiscated."

"It was on a county road."

"The road belongs to the county. The land is ours. You left the government land when you left the road."

"Taking a federal vehicle might be a problem for you," said Rylee.

Coopersmith did not blink. She looked to the damaged drone, itching to get it to her people. A glance at Trace told her he was worried. He motioned with his head toward the exit.

Rylee looked to Coopersmith. "What do you want for them?"

"Money is good."

"What about shotgun shells? I have ten boxes in my trunk."

"You don't anymore."

Here, Axel stepped in, looping an arm around her waist and cinching her tight. Her side pressed against his and even though their skin never touched, her body tingled with awareness and she temporarily lost the ability to speak. His scent enveloped her. He smelled of pine soap and leather.

"I appreciate you looking out for my girl, Mr. Coopersmith. And for all you did for me when I was a boy. I'd appreciate you allowing us safe passage through your land."

"Very fact she's up here shows I'm right. It's coming. I feel it in my bones."

Rylee glanced to Trace to see what *it* might be. His hand rested familiarly on her hip and she found it harder to think as her body pressed to his.

"What about two cases of MREs for your trouble?" he offered, referring to the military Meals Ready to Eat. The food staple stored for years and he thought might just appeal to a man ready to hide in a bunker.

"I'll take six for the drone and safe passage off our lands."

"And her vehicle, weapons and anything else you took from her car."

"Done."

Axel released her to shake on the deal. Rylee stepped away from both men and headed toward the door.

She resented being bargained for like a milk cow. But she said nothing. Safely clear of Axel's embrace, her mind began functioning again. She retrieved the drone and carried it with her as they left the garage.

Edward hovered by her opposite side. "If things don't work out for you two, you could give me a call."

She blinked at the strange offer. "You have phones out here?"

"No, but Axel can get a message to me."

Axel chose this moment to press a hand to her lower

back. The gesture was intimate. "We best be on our way, sweetheart."

The endearment sounded forced but made Edward flinch. Inexplicably, she felt a tightening in her throat and her breath came in tiny gasps. She forced her mouth closed and breathed through her nose all the way to her vehicle, parked before the main house.

There, she watched her weapons loaded back in her trunk. Everything went back in place except the shotgun shells. She placed the drone on top and accepted the keys from Stanley.

"You understand this is a one-time deal on account of my wife saying you was to be treated as a guest."

"Do you always ransom your guest's belongings?"

Stanley Coopersmith's smile was wily. "Generally, I just keep them."

"You will have to notify me if you apprehend or spot any more trespassers or see any unusual activity."

"Actually, I don't have to." Stanley accepted her card.

Axel held open her door and cast her an impatient look. Those gray-blue eyes relayed messages that she could not decipher other than his impatience and a possible brewing storm.

Rylee allowed Axel to walk her alongside of the sedan and tuck her into her seat as if she were a child unable to successfully open or close a car door. Then she followed his vehicle off the property and out of a gate that was the only gap in a perimeter fence that stretched into the woods in either direction.

A chill now lifted the hairs on her arms and neck. Had Stanley actually been considering ransoming her? She was a federal agent and taking her hostage would have brought the FBI straight to his property line. There, federal authorities would have waited during negotiations that she realized might have stretched on and on. For the first time, her annoyance with Axel turned to the realization that she might just owe him her thanks. If that situation had escalated, the ramifications could have been disastrous for all parties.

Axel had gotten her out of a survivalist camp without bloodshed, quickly and with only the merest gesture of a bargain. Just the dashboard computer was worth far more than a few cases of prepackaged food and shotgun shells.

That was twice now he'd pulled her fanny from the fire. Rylee gripped the wheel as she followed Axel onto the highway and back toward Kinsley. Perhaps a collaboration with the locals was not just some empty gesture and words from her department. She might get farther with his help if she included him in her investigation and, perhaps, keep custody of her car.

Trouble was she didn't trust him. All she really knew was that he was a local guy, generally liked, with an impressive military career that he had left to come here. His background information was general at best. But where had he been before he was fostered to Kurt Rogers at age thirteen? And what had happened to make him leave the army shortly after his fatal shooting of fellow servicemen?

As an army brat, she didn't approve of his taking the early discharge option. Her father, sister and brothers were all career Marine Corp so she shared her father's aversion for the army.

"One way to get to know someone is to speak to them," she said to the car's interior.

Rylee was not a joiner. An introvert by nature, she

was comfortable only with her siblings, and some more than others. They were nearly back to Kinsley before her phone picked up cellular service. She used the vehicle's communication system to call her boss.

Someone from the Glens Falls office would pick up the drone. Hopefully, they could glean some information from the navigation system. She'd seen her share of drones during professional training and recognized this one was not the garden-variety hobbyist craft. Too sophisticated and too expensive for the average operator.

By the time she reached her motel, she realized she had missed lunch and was starving. In the motel lot, the sheriff peeled off to park in the guest area. She checked the drone in the trunk. It was not in the spot she had placed it and there were scrape marks on the inner surface of the trunk. The blades began to whir, and she slammed the trunk closed.

This was a safer spot to hold the device than the motel room and she wasn't sure she could get it in there without it getting away. She glanced around. You usually had to be within sight of a drone to effectively operate it. This sort might have a longer range and all sorts of navigational upgrades.

Axel was beside her car as she locked the vehicle.

"You know, I do have other things to do besides collect you from private property."

She turned and met him with a bright smile. "And I appreciate your efforts and I'd like to take you out to lunch as a thank-you."

It was as if she'd frozen him in some tractor beam. He stood with his mouth half open, a finger raised to continue his lecture, and now seemed unsure how to proceed.

She closed her hand around his extended index finger and lowered his hand to his waist. He frowned before drawing his hand back. She doubted he intended the action of gliding his digit from her closed palm to be sexual, but from the startled gaze and the drop of her stomach, the friction had done just that.

He stood speechless, and she was finding a lack of oxygen in this corner of the parking lot. *Oh, no,* she thought. Not this one. He's overbearing and judgmental. He's in a dead-end career at the top of the world. She had the impression he played fast and loose with the law and enforced only the regulations that fell under his auspices. But those blue-gray eyes. They reminded her of a winter sky. Axel lifted his hands and for a moment she thought he would hold her again. The little show for Coopersmith replayed in her mind with the firm feel of his fit body.

She stepped closer. He grasped her shoulders and for just a second he seemed unsure if he should push or pull. Rylee leaned toward him and he extended his arms, sending her back a step.

"Separate cars. You follow me," he said and whirled away. His retreat came as close to a jog as a man could manage and still be walking. She'd never seen someone in such a hurry to be rid of her.

It only then occurred to her that the sheriff might be as hesitant of her as she was of him.

Her hands went to her hips. "We'll see about that."

Chapter 6

Axel checked the rearview every ten seconds to be sure that Rylee was following him. His heart was thumping as if he had run all the way to Bear Creek Café. He tried and failed to convince himself he was just anxious that she not veer off to find herself in another jam that required an extraction.

But it was a lie. He wanted her in his arms again. That little stunt for the benefit of the Coopersmiths had been a mistake. He'd been close enough to smell the light floral scent of her hair and feel the fit of her body against his. Both made him hungry for far more than lunch.

He realized, with a sinking feeling, that he was spending so much time minding her business because she was so appealing. Even her false bravado came across as charming. He groaned aloud as he set his blinker tapping and made a slow turn into the lot. Rylee was parked and out of her car before he even had his turned off.

"Fast woman," he muttered.

He tried to hold the door for her, but she made it inside unassisted and told Bonnie they'd prefer a booth. Then she took the one farthest from the counter.

"Waitresses have ears like elephants," she told him as she slid into her side and used a napkin from the metal dispenser to send the crumbs from the last patron's meal onto the floor.

She sat to give herself a clear view of her vehicle out the window.

Smart, he thought. *Keep an eye on that drone.*

Bonnie followed them back with menus and a wet cloth to finish the job Rylee had started.

"Drinks?" Bonnie said, grinning broadly at Axel as she wiggled her eyebrows at him.

His scowl only made her smile broaden. Bonnie was short and round and the pink apples of her cheeks seemed more responsible than her nose for keeping her owlish glasses in place. Her hair was blond, short and starched straight as the rails on a fence. She stood on tiny feet, balancing her girth with the skill of an acrobat.

"Iced tea," said Rylee, flipping the laminated menu over and over as if something new might appear.

Bonnie didn't ask Axel what he wanted but did pause to give him a "what's her deal?" look before departing. She returned a moment later with black coffee and Rylee's iced tea.

Axel removed his jacket and set it beside him in the booth. They ordered—a burger with fries for her, an egg salad sandwich with fresh fruit for him. She lifted her brow at his choice but said nothing.

"Any news from your home office?" he asked.

"None that I can discuss."

"They coming for the drone?"

"Of course."

She glanced out the window as a line of bikers roared past, rattling the window.

"They part of the North Country Riders group?" she asked, making the question seem casual.

The fact that she knew not only that they had a motorcycle gang—or "club," as they self-identified—up here but also their name did not bode well.

"How you know of them?"

"Briefings. They bring weed over the border. How is up for debate. You made any arrests in that department?" She sounded as if she already knew the answer and did not approve. He switched from wanting to kiss her to wanting to ditch her.

"Smuggling is your department. Best leave the borders to BP boys and ICE, right?" he said, referring to Border Patrol and Immigration and Customs Enforcement, the two branches of Homeland Security working on drug enforcement up here.

"Not if they sell it in your county," she countered.

"They don't."

"So it just passes through here like the water through the aquifer?"

"More like the St. Lawrence. What travels past us and down state isn't my concern."

"Maybe it should be."

"You have no idea what I do up here all day. Do you?"

"Eat barbecue and gamble at the casino?" she guessed.

"I cover up to thirty calls a day. Mostly folks who smeared themselves and their vehicles all over our roads. Drunk drivers, texting drivers, sleepy and distracted drivers and then we have the domestic violence calls, drunk and disorderly, and you might not be surprised to hear that most of those last ones are guests on vacay. But the winters up here are hard, lonely, and we have suicides. I also accompany Child Protective Services and they are way too busy here." He took a sip of coffee, burned his tongue and quickly chased the brew with ice water.

"You okay?"

"I will be when you head back down to Glens Falls."

"You got a particular reason you want me gone?" That one sounded like an accusation.

"You insinuating I'm dirty?"

"Just that you work up here without much supervision."

"I'm supervised by the town council and elected by the citizens I serve."

"Eloquent." She pursed her lips and his blood surged in all the wrong places.

Truth was, just sitting this close made his nerves jangle like a jar full of quarters rolling along the floor.

"Anything else?" she asked.

"I don't like your brand of cooperation."

"How's that?"

"The kind where you expect me to assist in an investigation of which I have no information."

She sat back and folded her arms. Her posture said that she wasn't interested in any sort of cooperation. Then, unexpectedly, her arms dropped to her sides and she leaned in until her torso pressed to the edge of the table. He leaned in as well, close enough to smell her skin and the spicy, earthy scent of something that seemed wildly erotic. His fingers, resting on his knees, curled, wadding the fabric of his trousers in his fists, and he told himself to sit back. But he didn't.

"All you need to know is that I am searching for illegal border crossings."

"You looking for a person or what they carry?"

"Both."

The lines on her face told him the rest.

"It's soon?"

"Any time."

"So why you?"

"Why not me?"

"You clearly don't have experience in the field. Either that or your method of investigation is to piss everyone off. Are you trying to rattle them into doing something stupid?"

Her chin lifted and she said nothing. But her cheeks blazed, indicating to him that her technique was no ploy. The high color bloomed on her throat and the vee of skin visible above her buttoned-up blouse. His blood sizzled and turned to ash.

"I volunteered." She clasped her drink between both hands, lacing her fingers around the glass. "Most of my department is assigned elsewhere."

He pictured the briefing and this county being mentioned and her hand shooting in the air. She wasn't up to it. Now he felt irritated at her supervisors for sending her and annoyed that he'd have to babysit her during her little field trip.

"Were you that kid with her hand in the air, asking if there was homework?"

The flush bloomed brighter. "Homework is important." She cleared her throat. "This assignment is important."

"If that's true, why send you up here all alone?"

"Who said I'm alone?"

Did she have contacts, informants or undercover agents up here? He tried to think of any new arrivals. But the fall season brought many visitors to watch the leaves turn and boat on the St. Lawrence.

"Still, if this were a likely place for your illegal border jumpers, I'd expect a higher presence."

She conceded the point with a slight incline of her head. "Intel indicates that this crossing will be at the other end of the state."

"Buffalo?"

"Most likely. But this area is still a possibility."

"How possible?"

"Least likely, according to the analysts' report."

"So they sent you in the opposite direction of trouble. That about it?" In other words, her department was trying to get rid of her. He had a few thoughts of his own on why. Where he came from they called that a snipe hunt.

He waited for an answer.

She glanced away.

"I see." He hadn't meant that to sound so insulting. But it had.

Rylee sat back as if she'd slapped him. The arms came up and around her chest again. Her face hardened, and her eyes went cold as frozen ground.

"I know it can be difficult, having federal involvement in your county."

No use holding back. He laid it out there. "You're what's difficult. And I'm guessing that is exactly why they sent you up here. Not the most popular agent down there in Glens Falls. Am I right?"

"From my perspective, I'm thorough."

He continued to stare, and she glanced away.

"You can rub folks wrong."

She nodded, forcing a smile that struck him as sad. She was the know-it-all in the office. Least popular because she was often right. And she had the social skills of a bull shark.

So why did he feel the need to help her?

"You could get better cooperation if you turned down the aggression a notch."

The arms slid back to her sides and she clasped her hands before her on the table. Her perfectly shaped pink nails with the white French tips tapped restlessly. She eased back into the vinyl seat. Their eyes met and a chill danced over his skin.

"I wanted a field assignment and I got one. I'll admit that I don't play well with others. Abrasive and dictatorial were the words my supervisor used just before shipping me up here."

"I can see that. I might have said headstrong." He sipped his coffee, now just the right temperature to scald his throat without leaving any permanent damage. "Thank you for telling me all that."

"I'm sure you are even more anxious to see my back than she was."

He lowered his chin. "No, I think your analysis might be wrong."

Her eyes lit up and looked at him as if for the first time.

"Were you sent here, or did you choose to come here?" he asked.

"I chose because I think the analysis is wrong. This border is a strong possibility."

"But the boss went with the numbers and was happy to let you take a field trip."

She puffed out her cheeks and blew away a breath. He waited and at last she said, "Yes."

"How big a load?"

Her brows rose and studied him. Judged him, he thought. Then she shook her head.

No details for the sheriff, he realized.

"I'd like to ask you about some of the organizations in your county."

The path between them was back to a one-way road, he realized. She didn't trust him, and he wasn't sure if that was standard or if she had something on him. The obvious reared up inside him like a jab to his belly. How thorough had her research been before her arrival?

He studied her and decided she likely knew it all. He sank down in the booth seat, bracing his hands on either side of him so they acted like flying buttresses to the cathedral.

She continued, all business again, "The Kowa Mohawks are on my watch list because of their known smuggling activities."

"Cigarettes."

"What?"

"They buy in Canada and sell on their reservation and skip the federal tobacco tax."

"They transport merchandise through New York State without declaring them. It's trafficking."

"I guess they figure that since they are a sovereign nation, they don't pay income tax."

"Sovereign nations don't import goods over federal and state highways."

"They have land on both sides of the St. Lawrence and all this land was theirs once."

"Agree to disagree," she said.

"Okay."

She made a face. "I don't want to win the argument. I want you to understand that some of their members are radical in ideology and could, conceivably, be convinced to assist in a domestic attack."

"Not buying it. I've never seen them bringing in more than smokes. Next?"

"The North Country Riders?"

He nodded. The motorcycle gang did a lot worse than smuggling tobacco. They carried weed from Canada into New York. They also carried illegal pharmaceuticals.

"Possibly. For the right price, I believe they'd carry anything or anyone."

"The Mondellos?"

"Moonshiners? They are all about avoiding taxation and the feds. That family has been in business since prohibition."

"They have property directly on the river, facilitating their illegal distribution. They have the means and the opportunity."

"Motive?"

"Same as for the booze. Money."

He shrugged. "I can't rule them out. Who else?"

"The Coopersmith family. Survivalists are one thing, but what if they feel it is necessary to give the coming Armageddon a little shove?"

"I've known them since I was a boy. They are all

about protecting their own, protecting this country. I can't see them doing anything to jeopardize either. Who else?"

"That's it." Her eyes still twinkled, and he felt for all the world like he was in an interrogation room. Sitting here, under the guise of helping her out when actually he was on her little list. She knew. He was convinced. But some tiny part of him did not want to say it aloud.

He shook his head. "You left out the congregation."

"A religious order?" she said, but her eyes narrowed as if just considering them.

He shifted in his seat, realized he was relaying his discomfort and forced himself to sit still.

"You know about them?"

"Some." She gave nothing away.

"They are also on the St. Regis River, between the Mondellos and the Coopersmiths, just a stone's throw from the St. Lawrence."

"That's true."

"Father Wayne heads the outfit. Call themselves the Congregation of Eternal Wisdom." He waited for her eyes to light up with recognition or her brows to lower in disapproval. But instead, her expression remained open.

"Go on," she said.

He didn't want to. The coffee now sloshed in his stomach like waves tossed by an angry sea. This storm's origin came from deep within himself, out of the sight of his DHS observer. Funny how something that had been his entire world for so many years, to her, meant nothing at all.

"It's a cult. They call themselves a congregation but it's a cult. They also live in a fenced compound. You might see some of the men outside the complex. They wear simple clothing. The top is a brown tunic. Bottom is baggy pants. No pockets, just a satchel, if they need to carry anything. Their heads are shaved and most wear beards."

"I haven't seen anyone like that. Is it an all-male order?"

He dropped his gaze to his half-finished coffee. "No. But you won't see the women. They stay put."

"Are they a radical group?"

"No. But their ideas are untraditional. Their leader says he is preparing them for ascension. They consider themselves the chosen and they consider children communal property."

"Many cultures share in raising children."

The small hairs on his neck lifted. "These kids don't know which of the women is their birth mother."

Now she was frowning but her notebook was out.

"They practice polygamy and some of the males undergo voluntary castration."

She stiffened. "What? Why?"

"Preparation for the afterlife. No sex there, according to Father Wayne. You'll know which ones have done this because they shave all their hair away." Axel lifted his mug and swallowed, tasting the remains of the coffee mingled with bitter memories. He should tell her the reverend's last name, but he just couldn't summon the courage.

"They sound like the Branch Davidians," she said.

"Except for the UFOs."

She sat back, leaving the pad open on the table. "Are you pulling my leg?"

He wished that were so. Axel pressed the flat of his palm to his middle, trying to settle his stomach.

"No joke. They live, farm, sing and dance out there on the river. And their leader has twisted theories of UFO visitations with God and scripture. The jumble is confusing but the gist is that reported alien visitations are actual angels sent by God in preparation for the end of the world. Only they call it the Rising."

"How many?"

"Hard to get an exact count. Thirty adults, maybe."

"How many children?"

"Social services go out there to check on them. The cult won't let kids be inoculated or register their births. They're homeschooled, or they tell us they are." He knew that schooling included creationism, their version of scripture and little else. "They collect the necessary textbooks and fill in all the correct paperwork." He locked his jaw so tight there was a distortion in his hearing, so he eased up.

"How do they fund their order?"

"Selling books and junk online. Taking donations and offering religious retreats. They recruit from the guests and once you are in, everything you own becomes theirs. Communal property."

"How do you know so much about them?"

Because I was born there.

"It's my business to know who lives in my county."

She lifted her pen and began writing. "I'll check them out."

And then she'd discover exactly where he came from.

"If you are going out there, you need me along."

"I don't."

"Rylee, trust me. You won't get past the gate without me. Let me help you."

She held his gaze and he held his breath.

"All right. I won't go out there without you."

Chapter 7

On the third night in Onutake County, Rylee roared into the lot of the roadhouse favored by the North Country Riders on a red Harley Low Rider. The neon advertising for various beers sent colorful light gleaming across the chrome on the line of Harleys parked in a neat row along the front of the establishment, including the handicapped spots.

She parked her motorcycle at the end of the line of bikes and walked it back in preparation for a quick getaway that she hoped would not be necessary. Once the sled was leaning on its stand, Rylee tugged off the helmet and braced it under one arm, keeping her gun hand free.

She had prepared for her meet with the undercover agent from DHS stationed up here, dressing in clothing appropriate for a roadhouse in the territory of the

North Country Riders. The tan slacks were tapered so
she wore her calf-hugging suede boots over them. Her
suede-fringed top covered all her assets and her brown
leather jacket covered her service weapon. Under her
bike helmet, she wore a black woolen cap.

She paused to take in her surroundings. Or was she
just stalling?

That thought sent her forward, as she wondered again
if she should have called the sheriff to request backup.

"It's just a meet. Make contact and get out." She
tugged the wool cap lower over her ears, hoping to hide
the most obvious of attributes, her blond hair.

No disguising she was female, because of her height.
The longer she stood, the faster her heart beat.

"Did you ask for this field assignment or not?" she
scolded. Despite the lecture, she suddenly missed her
desk and her data with the kind of wistful longing usually reserved for departed friends.

Squaring her shoulders, she marched to the door,
paused and then reached for the handle. The interior
stank of stale beer and the thumping beat of music assaulted her eardrums. She swept the groups of occupants, seeing that the motorcycle gang occupied most
of the tables and the area of the bar closest to that seating. There was a stage at the opposite side with a band
playing '80s metal. No one seemed to be paying any
attention to them as they shouted in each other's ears
and tipped long-necked bottles back.

She made for the area of the bar closest to the band,
farthest from the bikers and closest to the spot the serv-
ers picked up their orders for the tables.

The sticky floor made it seem she was walking
across a surface slathered with glue. She set her hel-

met on the scarred surface of the bar, beside the heart someone had scratched into it.

As she waited to order, she busied herself looking for her contact. She did not know her, but Rylee's image had been sent to the agent. She still had five minutes to go before the meet.

Reaching into her coat pocket for her mace, she made sure it was close at hand. Then she retrieved her mobile phone and glanced at it because the screen showed she had made a call, connected and had been connected for three minutes. Had her helmet made the call?

She glanced at the caller information and groaned. Sheriff Axel Trace. Rylee lifted the phone to her ear but could hear nothing.

"Trace?" she asked.

"Rylee? Where are you? I was just having your phone geolocated."

"I'm fine. Sorry. Must have pocket dialed you."

"Fine? What's that music?"

"'Bye, Trace. I have to go."

"Rylee, where—" She disconnected and shoved the phone back in her pocket.

"What'll ya have?" The bartender was young with a bushy beard that did not disguise how painfully thin he was, or cover the tattoos on one side of his throat. It seemed to be a wing and the word *blessed.* The tips of the wing flew up behind his ear, which sported a plug the size of a nickel. Above his eyebrow was a musical note.

She ordered what most of the patrons were drinking.

"Glass or bottle?"

"Bottle."

The beer arrived and her server made a nice show

of flipping the opener before uncapping the bottle and sliding it across the marred surface.

"What you riding?" he asked.

"Harley. 2016 Low Rider."

"Sweet."

A woman across the bar at the table extracted herself from the lap of a big man with a stomach that left her little room. She knew him. He was Lloyd Fudderman, head of the North Country Riders. But Rylee did not know that woman. The brunette wore a black T-shirt modified with a slice down the center to expose the tops of her breasts and so short her stomach and navel hardware were in full view. She strode away, swinging her hips to the delight of Fudderman, whose full salt-and-pepper mustache lifted on both sides of his mouth. His beard was stained yellow from tobacco, Rylee assumed, and his black leather vest showed various patches.

His woman wore unlaced biker boots and jeans that had been artfully torn and frayed across the knees and thighs. Her long wavy hair bounced with the rest of her as she passed behind Rylee to the bathrooms.

The lightbulb went off in her head at last and she slapped her money on the table, retrieved her helmet and beer and headed to the toilet. That must be her contact.

Rylee passed through the swinging door and into the brightly lit bathroom. At the row of sinks, a heavyset bottle blonde uncapping a lipstick. The T-shirt she wore indicated that she was one of the staff. The young woman had a florid face that clashed with the lipstick she reapplied. The color of the cosmetic reminded Rylee of a dog's tongue. Rylee's contact was nowhere in sight. Rylee dipped to see under one of the two stalls and spotted the brunette's unlaced boots. She glanced to the employee, who eyed her in the mirror and then broke contact to check her phone.

Rylee's contact emerged, checked her hair and ignored the soap, sink and bottle blonde as she refastened her belt, which unfortunately sported a Rebel flag. Then she glanced at Rylee, scowled and headed out.

Rylee blinked after her in surprise.

"Agent Hockings?" asked the blonde.

Rylee opened her mouth and just managed to keep it from swinging open as she nodded.

"I'm Agent Beverly Diel."

"Yes," she managed, cocking her head as her entire system misfired. "Hello."

"That was Queeny. She's Fudderman's woman, though she's half his age. Seems to be a lot of that going around up here."

"In the gang?"

"And at the cult. Fudderman has been in contact with the head of the Congregation of Eternal Wisdom. You know them?"

"No."

"I haven't been able to contact any of the women out there and the men don't come in here or speak to secular women. I suggest you find out what you can about them. But do not go out to their assembly alone."

"Why not?"

"Because it's a cult. The headman has them all twisted up into believing they're the chosen people and the judgment is coming. They live separately, and they might be armed against what they see as a coming apocalypse. If you go, go with backup."

"I'll do that." She didn't have backup and wouldn't

get any without first showing something to prove she was on the right track.

Beverly gave her a hard look.

"I won't."

"All right, then." She washed her hands and yanked down a paper towel from the dispenser with both hands.

"Did you get my report?"

She rolled her eyes. "Thin in evidence, heavy on speculation."

"I'm an analyst."

"I get that." The woman scanned Rylee's outfit, making her words seem like insults. "What I don't get is why you are up here instead of at your computer terminal."

"It was in my report."

"Rylee—" Her tone was one you used to explain to someone dim-witted. "You're fishing, am I right? Trying to get the attention of the supervisors who are ignoring you?"

"My report—"

"I read your personal file. You don't belong here. You don't have the training or the experience. Go home."

Rylee felt like a swimmer preparing to let go and sink into the deep.

"What do you think will happen if I call your supervisor?"

Rylee felt her skin grow cold and a shiver of fear inched up her spine. It wasn't the prospect of losing her job that frightened. It was the prospect of telling her father that she had lost her job that really made her gut twist.

But what if she were right? There was no turning back. She went home and admitted that she went rogue or she finished this and stopped this threat. Rylee narrowed her eyes, preparing to fight.

Beverly's brows lifted and she looked interested for the first time.

"The man who evaded Border Patrol…"

"The man you followed onto Kowa land?"

Her head dropped.

"Yeah. That's something."

Rylee lifted her gaze to meet Beverly's. The woman no longer seemed harmless. There was something of the hunter flashing in her dark eyes.

"He got away clean because someone from Fudderman's group picked him up. Took him back over the border, what I heard."

"What about his cargo?"

"Missing. The Kowa took it and that's all Fudderman's guys know."

"Did you report this?"

Her mouth went tight, and she gave Rylee a "what do you think?" look.

"So, they *do* carry illegals," Rylee said.

"First I've heard. It's been all weed and Oxy, so far as I can tell. I'm a regular buyer."

"I thought they didn't sell up here."

"Ha," she laughed.

Clearly, the sheriff did not know this. Or did he? It wouldn't be the first time a law enforcement officer had been paid to look the other way.

"What if I can get the cargo from the Kowa?"

Agent Diel cast a look that told Rylee she had no confidence that would happen, but then she gave her a patronizing smile and nodded.

"Sure, hon. You do that. But don't come back here dressed like that."

"Like what?"

"Like a magazine version of how tough girls dress." She shook her head as she scanned her from head to toe. "You see anyone in her wearing suede boots?"

"I came on a motorcycle."

"Every last one of them already knows you are here and who you are and what you are investigating. You'll get no help from that crew," said Diel.

"They running their own organization?"

"I don't know yet. Might find out in time. Now ride it out of here and don't come back. I'll contact you if I have anything."

"My number?"

Her face twisted and she lifted her phone. "I have it."

"So you could have called," asked Rylee.

"Wanted to get a look at you. Worse than I thought," she said. Then she capped her lipstick and shoved it in her front pocket before pausing at the door. "You should keep that outfit for Halloween. Maybe add a temporary tattoo."

Beverly left and the door banged shut.

Rylee braced herself on the counter, allowing her head to drop. When she opened her eyes, it was to see the tile comet—a streamer of toilet paper—fixed to the heel of one suede boot.

The commotion outside brought her up and to full alert.

The music had stopped and there was shouting coming from beyond the door. She recognized one voice. Axel Trace was bellowing her name.

Chapter 8

Dressed in plain clothing tonight, Axel appreciated how quickly his presence inside the roadhouse had been noticed. The jeans, boots and flannel shirt beneath the open canvas jacket did nothing to keep him from being as recognizable as a roast pig at a vegan picnic. *Probably just as welcome, too*, he thought.

The patrons gradually came to rest, pivoting in their seats to face him as all conversation came to a halt. The band caught on last. First, the drummer lost the beat and then the bass player missed the bridge. The singer and lead guitarist opened his eyes, straightened and stepped back from the microphone. Feet shifted uneasily as the gathering cast glances from Fudderman and then back to him.

Fudderman lifted his half-finished longneck to his lips and tipped the bottle, draining the rest. Then he set the bottle down with a heavy crack that made the woman on his lap startle.

He pushed her off and to her feet, eyes never leaving Axel's. A smile came slowly to his lips as he sat back, relaxed, with one hand on his knee and the other on the bottle.

"Evening, Sheriff." He had the courtesy to not ask if the sheriff was lost or crazy, which Axel appreciated. "The fed is in the bathroom."

Axel glanced toward the dark alcove past the bar. Then he headed that way. A big man with a shaved head stepped before him, bringing Axel up short.

"Get out," he said, leaning in so Axel could smell his breath, stale with beer and raw onions.

"That your sled parked in the handicapped spot, Hooter?"

"You and I going to have a problem?"

"I won't. But you have a hundred-and-fifty-dollar fine for parking there."

"The hell you say." He began a string of obscenities that involved at least three suggestions that Axel perform physical impossibilities on himself. Then Hooter reached back for a bottle and began an arching swing toward Axel's head.

Axel kicked out Hooter's feet from beneath him. Top-heavy and drunk was a bad combination in a bar fight. Hooter went down hard. The smaller man who Axel didn't know jumped in, swinging a bottle. It was like being back on base in Germany on any Saturday night. Axel grabbed his attacker's wrist and drew back one finger, causing his opponent to scream as the finger dislocated. Unfortunately, he also dropped the bottle, which bounced off Axel's forehead before shattering on the ground.

"Rylee! Time to go! Rylee!" Axel shouted toward the women's bathroom as Hooter scrambled to his feet. He didn't get all the way up before Axel brought his knee to the man's gut, sending him to his hands and knees on the beer-soaked floor.

The men at the bar closed in, forming an ever-decreasing circle.

"Rylee! Get out here." Still time if she made a quick appearance.

She did, only she had her gun drawn. This brought the other occupants of the bar to their feet. Weapons of all sizes and types were drawn in response.

"You," said Rylee, pointing her weapon at the smaller man with the dislocated thumb. "Back up, now."

Her voice was cold and her demeanor terrifying. She seemed born for this, with a steady hand, calm control and chilling expression of anticipation.

The man backed up, cradling his finger. Hooter reached his feet with the help of a bar stool that he scaled like a child on a jungle gym.

The circle widened as Rylee stepped beside him.

"Which one hit you?" she asked.

Ah, she was going to defend him. He was touched. But he also wasn't crazy.

"Let's go," he said, heading toward the door.

Rylee backed along beside him, her pistol deterring any from closing in.

Outside, she lowered her weapon and faced him. "Where's your personal weapon?"

"I'm off duty."

They kept moving, her keeping an eye on the closed

door to the bar and coming up short as he reached his vehicle. His sheriff's department SUV lay just beyond where he had parked it, only now it sat on its side, driver's door up.

"What the..." His words trailed off. He rounded on Rylee. "I'm done babysitting you."

"Who asked you?"

"You called me from this...this gang hangout and tell me you're fine."

"I was fine until you started screaming."

"I wasn't screaming."

The door behind them banged open and members of the North Country Riders spilled out like floodwater.

"Come on," she said tugging him toward the back side of the bar. He followed, keeping pace as she jogged along.

Behind them, shouts and the sound of beer bottles smashing on the pavement urged them to greater speeds.

"I'm on the other side," she said, leading the way to a Harley Low Rider.

He paused, agog, forgetting everything as he admired the bike, which was all black right down to the fork and tailpipes.

"Wow."

She straddled the seat, righted the bike and rolled it forward off the kickstand. She'd parked the Harley for a quick escape. He eyed the rear seat that was higher and smaller than the saddle she occupied. He'd look like a gorilla riding behind a jaguar, he decided, but when the next bottle landed beside his boot, he made the move.

"I forgot my helmet," she said. Then turned the key. The engine grumbled. "Hold on."

He did, wrapping his arms around her waist and flattening himself over her back like a large bulky coat. She revved the engine and set them in motion, leaving a cloud of smoke and considerable rubber on the pavement.

He finally found the tiny footrests and decided this bike was designed for one person. A glance behind them showed an angry mob in the street.

He felt a pang of separation over leaving his sheriff's vehicle and worry over his SUV's welfare.

"Where are we going?"

"Kowa Nation," she called.

"Bad idea," he said. "They'll take your bike."

"I have to speak to their leadership."

He had to shout to be heard over the wind.

"Then let me call them. Pull over."

"Anyone following?" she asked, glancing in a side mirror.

"No. Pull in up there."

She did as directed, turning into the empty lot of the ice-cream stand now shut up tight for the evening. Drawing up beside one of the picnic tables, she rolled to a stop and braced her feet on either side, steadying the bike as he dismounted.

"That gang of thugs is selling weed in your county," she said.

"How do you know?"

She shook her head. "Can't say."

"Great. Thanks for the useless intel."

"You could use it and shut them down."

"I'm working on that and thanks again for telling me my job. But you see, I must catch them at it and have real evidence. That's how we do it up here."

She made a face and knocked down the kickstand, easing the sled to rest.

"Why didn't you draw your service weapon?" she asked.

He didn't answer but pressed gingerly at the lump emerging on his forehead with two fingers.

"The guy threw a punch. He didn't draw a weapon."

"He attacked a law enforcement officer."

"Just a way of reestablishing his personal space."

"You do know how to use a handgun?"

He blew away a breath through his nose and his teeth stayed firmly locked. His chin inclined just enough to give an affirmative answer.

"Guns, drawing them, shooting them, killing things. It doesn't solve problems. It only makes different ones."

She wondered about that answer. It seemed to come from some personal experience, and she thought of his army service record. Two confirmed kills, she recalled, the line of his personnel records coming back to her in a flash of perfect clarity.

"When was the last time you fired your pistol?"

"Hanau, Germany, 2008."

"You haven't drawn your sidearm in a decade?"

"Not a requirement of my position."

"Was this after you killed two servicemen in Germany?" she said, quoting from his records.

His eyes narrowed, glittering dangerously. "Yes."

"Will you tell me about that?"

"No. But you can read all about it on Google. May 1, 2008, one month before discharge, Hanau, Germany."

"But you would draw your weapon if circumstances demanded it."

"What circumstances?"

"To defend the citizens under your protection?"

"Yes."

"To protect yourself?"

"I don't think so."

She watched him swallow down something that seemed bitter, judging from his expression.

"Was it so terrible?"

"Taking another man's life? It's a scar on your soul."

"Then why pursue law enforcement?"

"More like it pursued me. Sheriff Rogers, the man I replaced at his retirement and for whom I have great respect, asked me to run for sheriff. He said I needed to get back in the saddle and that the county needed me."

"Seems you aren't really back."

"Most lawmen never have to draw their weapon."

That was true. And she really could not judge, because she had never been placed in the kind of situation he had faced.

"But you're not most people."

Axel gave her a long look and she felt, somehow, that he was taking her measure. He used the palms of his hands to scrub his cheeks as if trying to remove some invisible film. When he lifted his gaze to meet hers, he nodded, as if to himself.

"The report said two servicemen were involved in a drunken brawl. That the first serviceman drew his weapon on military police and that I ordered him to put down his weapon. He didn't. Instead, he drew on me and I shot him. Two shots and down he went. His partner charged me and I shot him, as well."

That was exactly what she had read.

Rylee pictured the bar in Germany, the drunken servicemen. The MPs called to restore order. She covered her hand with her mouth and then forced it down. She had asked and the least she could do was listen to him without sending judgment.

"But then there's the part that they don't put in the reports. There is the part that you see at night when you close your eyes. That first serviceman? He was drunk. Really, really drunk, according to his blood alcohol. When I shot him, he fell backward against the bar. He looked at me, and it was as if he suddenly realized what was happening. He seemed to me like a man who had just woken from some kind of a nightmare and into another one, where he had attacked an MP and now he was going to die. He knew it. He started to cry. His partner didn't have the opportunity…" His words trailed off. "He just…" Axel swallowed hard.

Rylee placed her hand on his. He turned his hand palm up and wove their fingers together, squeezing hard. Then he tried again.

"He just died instantly. I found out later, he was a newlywed expecting his first child. He was a boy. They named him after his father." Axel lifted his gaze and held hers. "That's the part they don't put in reports."

Rylee found her voice trembling when she spoke. "But you know that wasn't your fault. You were doing a job, responding to drunk and disorderly. That serviceman raised his weapon. Drew his weapon on you."

"His partner did what any good wingman would do, backed up his friend and it cost him his life."

"He attacked you."

"The price was too high."

"You had a right to defend yourself."

"There are other ways, Rylee. I could have thrown

an empty bottle at him. Especially the second guy. He was drunk and he didn't have a weapon."

"He *was* a weapon, trained by the US Army."

"I think, believe, that a gun isn't the only option."

"It's the safest one."

"Safest?" He gave a mirthless laugh. "Not for the person on the wrong end."

He stared at her with eyes that beseeched her to understand. But she couldn't. Not really. Because she'd never faced such a situation. All she knew was that she was in no position to judge his feelings and that killing those two men had taken a toll on him. The urge to comfort overwhelmed. She stared up into those blue eyes and lost her way. Like a pilot flying in the infinite sky, there was nothing to help her recover her bearings.

She stepped forward, taking their clasped hands and bringing them behind her as she used the other to stroke the back of his neck, threading her fingers into his short thick hair. Rylee stepped closer, pressing her body to his.

He lowered his chin as his arms came around her. Rylee pressed her lips to his. Her urge to comfort dropped with her stomach as her body's reaction to his overwhelmed her. She reveled in the pleasure of his hungry kisses, as his strong hands stroked in a steady rhythm up and down her back. His mouth was velvet. She pressed herself to the solid wall of muscle as his arms enfolded her, taking her mouth with greater urgency.

Looking back on that first kiss, she would have liked to take credit for drawing back first. As an analyst, she should have done some figuring and recognized that kissing the sheriff was a bad idea. But it was Trace that eased her away. He groaned as he broke the kiss, as if it cost him something to do so.

The next thing she knew, she was blinking up at him, missing the comforting heat of his body and the new buzz of desire that made her inch closer. He allowed it but simply knotted his hands behind her back and leaned away.

"What are you doing to me, Rylee?" he whispered. His voice was a soft rumble that seemed to vibrate low and deep inside her.

"Making a mistake." She followed that with a half smile.

"No doubt. And it's the sort of mistake that I might just approve of, but you said something about wanting to go to Kowa land?"

Her brain snapped back into action. How could she have forgotten the information she had been given by Agent Diel?

"They have something. That duffel. I need to get it back."

Chapter 9

"What's so important about that bag?"

Axel waited, marking her indecision by the furrows now appearing on her brow. Apparently, he was good enough to kiss but still not good enough to collaborate with.

She pressed her lips together, giving him a fierce look, and then she dropped her chin and studied the ground. When their eyes met again, he could tell she'd reached a decision.

"That illegal I was after? He was picked up by Fudderman's group after leaving the Kowa Reservation."

"You know this how?"

"I have a contact who also told me that Fudderman's people took him."

"Took him where?"

"My contact believes he was transported back over the border."

"Why bring him over only to take him back?" asked Axel.

"Because he wasn't important. His cargo was."

Axel felt that tingle at the base of his spine. The one that told him things were about to go south. He locked his jaw, not wanting to ask the next question. Turned out he didn't need to.

"Whatever he carried was left behind at the Kowa Nation. They have it. The question is, are they complicit in this carrier's plans or did they intercept him and his goods by accident because of my pursuit?"

"All right, you convinced me." Axel stood before her. The concern that had vibrated along his spine now moved to his stomach, twisting it in a way that told him they needed to move. "I have a friend on the Kowa Nation. We'll give her a call."

Rylee's brow descended on the word *her*. He failed in keeping his smile a secret. Was she concerned with the fact that he had female friends? All sorts of possibilities danced through his mind, distracting him from the task at hand. Primarily, he wanted to kiss her again.

"Her name is Kate Vasta. She's the younger sister of the acting chief of police." He drew out his cell phone and scrolled through his contacts. She answered on the third ring. Her voice was full of light animation and what sounded like delight to hear from him. Kate had been more than a good friend. But that was in the past, at least for him.

"Axel Trace. What can I do for the sheriff of the county?"

"Hi, Kate. I need a favor." Axel went on to explain

what he wanted, and Kate promised to allow them in the rez as her guest. She also offered to meet them at the border and escort them directly to her brother.

Axel ended the call and grinned back at Rylee. "We're in."

"Thank you," said Rylee.

Her words showed gratitude. But her voice carried a very different message. He'd known kissing her had been a mistake, but he just couldn't resist. Now all the complications of a relationship, newly forming, were bubbling between them as they faced this new threat. It was baggage they did not need. In his line of work, distractions were dangerous.

Rylee donned her helmet, straddled the bike and kicked back the stand. She turned over the motor and looked back at him, waiting.

Axel climbed on behind her and tried to ignore the feel of her warm body pressed close to his. He failed. There had been several times in his life when he knew he was in big trouble. This was now one of them.

True to her word, Kate Vasta was waiting for them in a battered green pickup truck at the border of the Kowa Nation. Kate drove Axel, with Rylee following on her bike, taking them directly to her brother's home. Apparently, they were expected because both her brother and one of the executive board members were waiting outside for them. Rylee was off her bike and at his side with cat-like speed.

Kate stepped out of her truck and addressed her brother. "Brother, I brought a guest. You remember Axel Trace, and this is his friend Rylee Hockings."

Her brother looked none too happy as he nodded. "We met."

Kate turned to Axel. "Do you need me?"

Axel spoke to her with his eyes fixed on her older brother. "I don't know. Do we?"

Vasta shook his head and Axel flicked his gaze to Kate. "Thank you for helping us out."

"Anything for a friend. You give me a call sometime. You hear?"

Axel felt a pang of guilt. It was wrong to call a friend only when you needed a favor. He made a mental note to call Kate soon. Then he glanced at Rylee and saw her glaring daggers at Kate as the woman climbed back into her truck and reversed course.

"Would you two like to come inside?" Vasta asked.

Axel motioned Rylee forward and followed her into the Vastas' ranch-style home. They were directed to the living room, where Vasta had to ask his children to leave the room.

Rylee did a good job of briefly explaining that the duffel bag that was, perhaps, in their custody contained something of national interest and possibly posed a significant hazard to his people.

Vasta and Executive Council Member Jeffries exchanged a long, silent look. Then Jeffries rose and asked them to follow him. They returned to Rylee's bike and waited for Jeffries to climb into a new matte black dually pickup. Then they left Vasta behind and followed Jeffries's vehicle out of the drive and past the city center, the casino and through one of the communities where the Kowa people resided. Beyond that, they headed to the St. Lawrence River and several storage facilities, stopping at a nondescript prefab garage.

"It's in here," said Jeffries. He paused only long enough to release the lock on the container door and click on the lights. Inside were storage containers filled with boxes of tobacco and a small desk supporting a computer from the last decade and a phone. Beyond squatted a gray metal filing cabinet that looked to have been kicked down a set of stairs, as the second drawer was too badly bent to close. Jeffries unlocked the filing cabinet with a small key and removed the duffel bag from the bottom drawer. Rylee's entire posture changed. She was on full alert with one hand on her weapon. Axel gave her a nudge and shake of his head. Her hand dropped back to her side.

Executive Council Member Jeffries set the duffel on the desk.

"We confiscated this from the person you pursued here," he said to Rylee. "We let them go. It seems to us that the carrier was Japanese. But I really don't know."

"Could he have been Chinese?" asked Rylee.

"I don't know." Jeffries rubbed the back of his neck. "It's possible."

"Has anyone looked inside this bag?"

Jeffries nodded. "Yes. Executive council and the acting chief of police have all seen the contents of this bag. We are in agreement that we do not want it on our lands but were not in agreement as to what to do with it."

Axel thought of the possibilities. What were the choices?

"Half the council was in favor of destroying it. The other half wanted to deliver it to state officials."

"Has anything been removed from this bag?" she asked.

"No."

She motioned to the bag. "May I?"

Jeffries nodded, extending a hand as he moved away.

"Why now?" asked Axel. "You could have given it to her when she first arrived."

"She didn't arrive. She entered our land without invitation. This negated any option to deal with her. Now she comes with a friend and with the escort of the sister of the chief of police."

Rylee flushed. "I am sorry for my bad manners. If I could, I would have done things differently."

Jeffries nodded. "Do them differently in the future. This is our home. How would you have reacted, if situations were reversed?"

"I would have deemed you a threat. I might not have been as forgiving as you have been."

Rylee turned her attention to the duffel. The way she unzipped the canvas bag gave Axel the chills. She moved as if the entire thing might explode.

"Is it volatile?" he asked.

"No. But if it is what I think it is, the contents are very dangerous."

"In what way?"

"I can't say," she said through clenched teeth, gingerly drawing back the sides of the bag.

Axel glanced in to see a second container of vinyl, rolled with a Velcro fastener. It reminded him of the sort of thing he used to carry lures for fly-fishing, only his version was canvas. Rylee lifted the orange-and-black bag to the desk and released the fastenings. Then she unrolled the container until it lay flat on the desk. The rectangular vinyl was divided into dozens of slots, each containing a glass vial.

"Ampoule transport roll," she said. Her voice had an airy quality and her breathing now came in short, rapid blasts from her nose.

"Get it out of here," said Jefferies.

"The foreign national carried this onto your land?" asked Rylee.

"No. This little guy crossed onto our land and we were in pursuit when we saw the drone with the duffel. Both in the same area, near the river. One of our people shot at the drone and it dropped the duffel, but we lost the thing in the trees near the river. Runner also got away. Recovered the package, though."

"A miracle it didn't break on impact," said Axel."

"Fell through the pine trees. My son caught it. And the guy who was there to retrieve it took off." Jeffries looked grim. "That spy came onto our land to retrieve this," Jeffries motioned at the bag, but now stood well back from the desk.

"Your son is very lucky. It was a good catch," said Axel.

"I was thinking the same thing."

Rylee rolled up the transport container holding the vials and then pointed at the duffel. "Burn that."

The rolled container went inside her leather jacket. She extended her hand to Jeffries and thanked him again. Then she turned and headed out of the storage building like a woman on a mission.

She had been correct, he realized. She had gone against the odds and gotten it right. But her people were all in the wrong place.

Axel thanked Jeffries and then jogged after Rylee.

Chapter 10

The ride to Kinsley was a blur.

They stopped at her motel to switch from the motorcycle to her vehicle and collect the drone given to her by Stanley Coopersmith. Then they headed to his office in Kinsley.

As Rylee pulled to a stop at the curb, he saw his battered SUV parked before the station. Pete, of Pete's Garage, had beaten them here, managing to tow his sheriff's vehicle back. Axel paused on the sidewalk to take in the damage. One side looked as if it had slid a hundred yards on gravel. The sheriff's insignia had all but disappeared, along with most of the paint on the passenger side.

Rylee was like a schoolgirl, nearly skipping the distance between her car and his office. He unlocked the door and held it for her, then flicked on the lights.

Her expression was animated; she seemed to have an external glow, like a halo or aura surrounding her. In his office, she paced as she spoke with an excited ring to her voice. She kept the phone pressed to one ear and her finger in the other.

Rylee seemed to have completely forgotten he was even there, as he took his seat and scrolled through his emails. Why did he care if she knew he was there or not? But he kept glancing her way, hoping to catch her eye. He didn't.

She described the cargo they had recovered. Arrangements were made for a pickup. After the call, she came to rest, collapsing into the big chair beside his battered wooden desk. The chair had been in the former sheriff's home, but when the stuffing began to show in one worn armrest, Rogers's wife had insisted it be banished from the house and it ended up here.

"Can you believe it?" She pressed one palm to her forehead and stared at the tiles of the drop ceiling above his desk. "I wish I could call my dad."

"It's not that late."

"He's in Guam again, I think. But, boy, I'd love to call him. I can't, of course. This isn't public info, but…" She smiled and sighed, happy in the prospect of telling her family of her coup.

"You were right." He moved to sit on the edge of his desk, keeping one foot planted on the floor. It didn't help. Rylee at close range still made him feel slightly motion sick. Did she know how pretty she was? "You gotta be pleased."

"More than pleased. Did I tell you that I'm one of seven? Seven!"

"No, you didn't tell me that."

"Oh, yeah. And as the youngest, I have never successfully commandeered my dad's attention for more than a minute at a time."

"Well, this ought to do it." He had lost his need to gain his father's respect the day he had asked his father which of the women in the compound his mother was and been told that it didn't matter.

Not to his father, maybe, but it sure did matter to Axel.

"What's he do, your dad?" *Besides ignore his daughter,* he wondered. Had he ever been that in need of his father's approval? He hoped not, but he admitted to himself that he had been back before he started sneaking off the compound. Only then did he begin to realize how twisted and aberrant his childhood really was. Early on he began to suspect that the warnings about the outsiders being damned had been a lie. A way to keep them all apart from anything that might undermine his father's control over them all. At first, he had sneaked off for attention. But no one had seemed to notice or care. If he hadn't left, would he right now be dressed in brown robes with his head shaved?

"My dad is a colonel in the US Marines, Indo-Pacific Command. All my brothers and my only sister are marines, too. I'm the black sheep, did not follow my marching orders."

"He wanted you to enlist?"

"Of course. He wanted me to attend officer training school and be a marine. He expected all of his children to serve their country."

"You are serving your country, Rylee. Working with Homeland Security would certainly fit that bill. He must know that," said Axel.

"Not according to my dad. You're either in the US Marines or you are not. There is no other option."

"So, your career choice caused some tension?" asked Axel.

"Oh, yeah," said Rylee. "I just didn't want to live my whole life out of the gunnysack. I wanted…wanted to find a place, one place to call home. Mom said home isn't a place. But you know, it could be."

"Except for my time in the service, I've lived my entire life in this county."

"Meanwhile, I didn't even know that there were families who did that. I saw from your records that you were emancipated. Is your family still here?" asked Rylee.

Why had he mentioned his past? Of course, she would have questions, but that did not mean he was ready or able to answer them. How did you even begin to explain the complicated mess that was his family? Let's just start with his mother. No, that was a terrible place to start. His father? Even worse.

"Just my dad. He's still around. I don't see him often."

Rylee's eager expression fell. She glanced away. "Oh, I see."

She didn't, though. How could she?

Axel forced a tight smile and she glanced away.

"I'm sorry about your mother."

He realized then that his words had led her to believe wrongly that his mom was dead.

Of course, Rylee was sorry for what she saw as a loss but she might be sorrier if she knew that his mother lived not ten miles from him and was not permitted to speak to her son or acknowledge him in any way as she prepared to enter Heaven's Door, as they called it. She had chosen his father's religious dogma over a relationship with him. That kind of rejection caused a sorrow that just never went away.

This would be the time to correct her and explain the situation. Axel groaned inwardly. His stomach knotted, and he knew he would not be doing that. Not today, not ever. Many of the good citizens of the county had forgotten that he was the skinny boy brought out of the Congregation of Eternal Wisdom by social services. They had forgotten that Sheriff Kurt Rogers had removed him from the influence of his father and fostered him for five years before Axel had joined the army.

His father had told Axel to his face that if he did not want to follow the true path to Heaven's Door, he could suffer the Desolation with the rest of the unbelievers. Axel's ears still burned at the memory of his father's scalding condemnation.

"Any brothers or sisters?" asked Rylee.

That was another complicated subject. One that he didn't even know how to begin to answer. Surely, he had brothers and sisters. But which ones were his by blood, who could say? The only way to sort that would be DNA testing and that would never happen.

Axel opted to keep his answer vague and truthful and then change the subject. "Yes. But you… Seven, right?"

"Exactly. I have five older brothers and an older sister, all in the marines."

Uh-oh, he thought. Each one would be glad to knock him in the teeth for what he wanted to do with their baby sister.

Rylee continued, "Oliver, the oldest, is a master sergeant in the Marine Air-Ground Force. Paul is a sergeant major in personnel. It burns Oliver up that Paul has a higher rank. Paul is stationed stateside in California. I have two twin brothers, Joshua and Grant. They're both second lieutenants and both intelligence warrant officers in Hawaii. That's a great posting. Those two have done everything together since as far back as I can remember. Marcus is only two years older than me and an assault vehicles commander. Can you believe my only sister, Stephanie, is a gunnery sergeant in communications? She's working as a cyber-network operator in Germany."

"Your mom?"

"Mom worked in the military schools. She taught music. And I play guitar and strings because of her. But she passed five years ago of a lung infection."

"I'm sorry."

"Yeah." She took Axel's hand. "We have that in common—losing our mothers. Don't we?"

They didn't. He frowned.

"I know. It's hard, right? I think Josh and Grant were glad to reenlist, with her gone. Home isn't a home without a mom. Or at least that's how it was for us. We lived all over. Oceanside, Honolulu, Okinawa and then back to Hawaii, but Kāneʻohe Bay this time. We were in Jacksonville, which I liked, and then Beaufort, South Carolina, which I hated. But I was thirteen. Thirteen-year-olds hate most new things, I think, and moving. I detested moving. Maybe I just hate South Carolina because that's where she died. So, Dad got transferred from Guam to Germany. That way me and Stephanie and Marcus could be with him. My older brothers were all up and out, enlisted by then." She straightened as if someone had put an ice cube down her back. "Sorry, I didn't mean to unload all that baggage."

"It's all right. You know, families can be complicated." He set his teeth and looked at her open expression. Maybe Rylee could understand. She knew grief
and separation and a dad who was emotionally unreach-
able. Only difference was she was still trying to reach
hers. "Listen, about my father—"

Her phone chimed, and she darted to her feet, removing the mobile and staring at the screen.

"My boss," she said and took the call.

Thirteen minutes later there was a helicopter parked
on centerfield of the community baseball field. Rylee
jogged out, keeping low. He didn't know what he had
expected but it was not to see Rylee, carrying both
drone and samples, climb aboard and disappear behind
the door. Before he could take a step in her direction,
the chopper lifted off, sending the dirt on the infield
swirling behind them.

"Didn't even say goodbye," he said, as he covered
his face from the assault of rock and sand.

What was he thinking? That she was staying? This
was a good reminder that she was on to bigger and better things. He told himself it was for the best. Best that
she left before she discovered just where he had come
from. Because if she stayed, sooner or later, she'd learn
the truth and that was something that he just could not
bear.

It was Thursday afternoon. After a long night and
a few hours of sleep, Rylee was back in her office in
Glens Falls. Somehow, everything seemed different, as
if she didn't belong here.

Rylee held her cell phone in her palm, staring down
at the contacts list. She had scored major points, located

the vanguard of the attack and was just aching to crow about her accomplishment.

Her brow wrinkled as she realized that it was Axel she wanted to call. Not her father, who would likely be unavailable. He'd been unavailable emotionally to her for most of her life. Expecting him to suddenly see her as a competent protector of their country was just irrational. So why had she done all this?

If not for praise and advancement and accolades, why? Confusion rattled inside her like a bag of bolts in a barrel.

She hardly knew Axel. So why was she missing him and wanting to tell him everything that had happened since leaving him last night?

He was a bad choice for many reasons, not the least of which was the way he played fast and loose when deciding which laws to enforce.

For just a moment, she allowed herself to imagine an alternate reality. One where she came home to Axel every night. One where she stayed in one place and made a home for them. A garden with tomatoes and a bird feeder. Neighbors whose names you bothered to learn.

Rylee had spent her life moving and, while she'd believed she wanted something different, every decision she'd made climbing up the ranks had involved a move, and there was no end in sight. A promotion, the one she wanted so badly to earn, would require packing again and a new office, new city, new coworkers. Why had she never realized that in choosing to do the opposite, and not joining the US military, she had nevertheless adopted a transient lifestyle?

She sat hard as the realization hit her. She wasn't ever

going to stop moving. She wasn't going to be a team player. Or be a welcome part of a group task force on anything. She was going to live a rootless existence, moving from one apartment to another with whatever she could carry in three suitcases. Just like her father.

She was never going to have that dog or those kids or that husband that she had believed she wanted. Was she?

Rylee scrolled through the contacts, past her family's names and her friends and her professional contacts, stopping on Axel Trace. Was she really going to pick him?

Suddenly, Rylee's accomplishment frightened her. It was what she wanted. To make a splash. To gain attention. To use her analysis skills and new field experience to move onward and upward.

So why was she thinking of a cool autumn night and a picnic table outside an ice-cream stand in the far reaches of New York State and the man who waited there?

Chapter 11

The knock upon Axel's door brought him grudgingly to his feet. Friday nights were busy, and he'd just made it home before eleven o'clock. The hour meant this was not a visitor. Most bad news came lately by phone or text, but some folks, the older ones mostly, stopped by to drop trouble on his door. Usually not after nine in the evening.

He had discovered that the later the hour, the larger the problem. Domestic, he decided as he left the kitchen in the back of the house, thinking the visitor would be a woman carrying her children in her arms, seeking protection. He'd stopped counting the number of such visits he'd taken since being elected as county sheriff.

Axel hiked up his well-worn sweatpants and grabbed a white T-shirt from the peg behind the door on his way past. He had changed for bed after his supper, but he'd cover up before he greeted his visitor. He had the shirt overhead when the knock came again.

He glanced through the window set high on the door and his breath caught. Rylee Hockings stood on his step dressed in a gray woolen jacket, thigh-hugging jeans and scuffed hiking boots. She was looking down at the yellow mums on his steps that had already been nipped by frost. The blossoms drooped and wilted. The angle of her jaw and the overhead light made her skin glow pink. The black knit cap on her head trapped her blond hair beside the slim column of her throat.

His breath caught, and his blood coursed, heated by her nearness. When was the last time a woman took his breath away?

Never was the answer. He'd steered clear of most women, recognizing the trouble they inherently caused and not wanting the complication of explaining the soul-scarring mess that was his family. Why would any woman, especially one as dedicated, smart and pretty as this one, want a man who most resembled the tangled wreckage of a submerged log in the river. He was good for tearing the bottom out of boats and causing other people trouble. So far, his personal life had been nothing but bad.

She lifted her fist, knuckles up, to knock again and glanced up to see him peering down at her.

"Hey! You gonna let me in?" she said, her voice raised to carry through the locked door that separated them.

He shouldn't. Because if he did, he had a fair idea where the evening might lead. She was smiling like a woman satisfied with the world, but he had the feeling he could change that smile, brighten it, perhaps remove the lines of tension bracketing those pink lips.

Axel turned the dead bolt, pulled open the door and stepped back.

"What a nice surprise."

She'd left Wednesday night and there had been no calls, no texts and no emails from her or from Homeland Security. He'd decided that she'd dumped him like an empty beer bottle, and now he didn't know what to think.

"We've assembled a team. They'll be here tomorrow morning. I just wanted to brief you before their arrival on all that's happened."

"Sure." He thought the surprise must have shown on his face. Thus far, she had briefed him on very little.

She breezed inside with the cool air, and he closed the door behind her. She stepped into the neat entry and sank to the bench with his shoes lined up beneath and the variety of coats hanging above on pegs. Above that, the cubbies held his hats, gloves and a softball mitt.

"Boots off?" she asked.

He was happy to have her remove any item of clothing she wanted.

"Sure. And let me take your coat."

He waited as she worked loose the laces while also glancing into the living room. She slipped out of her boots, revealing new woolen gray socks. She was getting the hang of dressing for the weather up here, he thought. But Rylee was quick and used to adjusting to her environment. She must be, after so many moves.

She stood and he took her coat, using the opportunity to lean in to smell the fresh citrus scent at her neck before stepping back. Rylee headed to the living room. He had left it earlier, as he always did, pillows in line on the couch he used only for napping and his book waiting on the table beside his comfortable chair beside the remote.

"You're neat," she said, coming to a stop.

Having things, personal things, was something he never took for granted. Personal property was forbidden at the congregation. He could never have imagined owning a home of his own. Filling it with the overstuffed comforts that were lacking in the austere landscape where he had been raised.

Wooden chairs placed on pegs each night. Floors swept and then mopped. Children assigned tasks on a weekly basis that grew increasingly difficult as they aged.

He'd been approaching that age where he would have been expected to choose the most holy position for males at the compound or the lesser status of men who did not accept the full preparation to be received in Heaven.

"Axel?"

He snapped his attention to her and realized he was clenching her coat in his fist.

"I asked if that was coffee that I smelled?"

The smile was forced but she didn't seem to notice. "Yes. Have you had supper yet?"

"Oh, hours ago, but I'd love a cup of coffee."

He debated where to bring her—the living room with that big couch or the dining room with the large wooden table for a professional conversation?

He motioned to the living room. "Make yourself comfortable. I'll bring you a cup. How do you take it?"

"Black."

He nodded and waited as she slipped into his world in her stocking feet. He was quick in the kitchen, returning with two cups. He tried not to place too much meaning on the fact that she sat on the sofa.

"Do you use the fireplace often?" she asked, gazing at the wood fireplace, screened and flanked with fire tools and a metal crate of kindling. The logs fit in an opening built in the river stone masonry for that purpose. The stone swept up to the twelve-foot ceilings of the old farmhouse and was broken only by the wide mantel crafted with chisels by hands long gone from the living, out of American chestnut back in a time when the tree was a plentiful hardwood.

"Yes, and I keep it set. Would you like a fire?"

"Oh, that's not necessary. It's just I always wanted a house with a fireplace. They don't usually have them in California or Hawaii—or Japan, for that matter."

"Or in South Carolina?"

She laughed, but her eyes were now sad. "That's right. How long have you been here?"

"Let's see, I found this place after I left the service. I bought the home after I finished my probation period with the City of Kinsley."

"Police Department," she said, quoting the part of his history that she obviously knew, the part that was in the records. But Sheriff Rogers had held back enough. Keeping the circumstances of his claim for emancipation listed as abandonment. The truth was worse and more complicated.

"That's right. So that was, wow, six years ago. And I still haven't replaced that back deck."

He set down her coffee and took a seat beside her. She gathered up the mug and took a sip.

"Strong," she said and set the ceramic back on the slate-topped coffee table.

He left her to set the fire. The entire process involved striking a match and lighting the wadded newspaper beneath the tepee of kindling.

He slipped two logs from the collection and waited for the flames to lick along the kindling, catching the splinters in bright bursts of light.

"That's a pretty sight. Warms me up inside and out," said Rylee, gazing first at the fire and then to him.

An internal spark flared inside him and his heart rate thudded heavy and strong.

He knelt beside the fire and glanced back at her, taking in the relaxed smile and the warm glow of the firelight reflected from her cheeks and forehead. The entire world seemed to have taken on a rosy glow and he wasn't at all certain it was the fire's doing.

"Is it too late for a conversation?" she asked.

Did she mean too late in the evening or too late in their relationship? He'd spent the first few days resenting her intrusion, followed by a pervasive annoyance at the extra work she caused him. But just before she left, when they took that wild ride on the motorcycle, and even before that kiss, he knew there was something different about this woman. Perhaps the threat she posed was not professional but strictly personal.

Was that better or worse?

"No, it's not too late."

"Trace, I think I made a mistake with you. I want to apologize for trying to run you. You don't work for me and it was wrong for me to treat you as if you did. To come in here and tell you what to do in your own county. That's not collaboration. It's my first field assignment and I really want to do well. It's important for my career for me to get this experience. But even more important was finding the package. Finding that case will save a lot of lives."

He came to sit beside her on the sofa. "That's a good thing. But you're back, so I have to assume your work isn't finished." He didn't let himself latch on to the possibility that she'd come back to finish their business. "Do you want to tell me what this is all about?"

He waited in the silence that followed as she laced her fingers together and leaned forward until her forearms rested on her knees. Then she stared at the fire as it caught. He had time to add both logs to the blaze and return to his seat before she spoke.

"Yes, I think you deserve that. There was some trouble this summer—July—in the Adirondacks just south of here and in the city of Saratoga Springs." Her brows went up and she looked to him.

He nodded. "I know the area." He'd even gambled at the thoroughbred track a time or two in August.

"There was a CIA operative there. Apparently, he was collecting intel from a foreign agent on US soil, which breaks about fifty rules that I can think of. Regardless, the meet was made at Fort Ticonderoga and he retrieved a thumb drive full of intelligence. However, they were followed and our man had a difficult time getting the information into the hands of federal operatives. There was a civilian involved. A completely untrained, inexperienced woman, and how she survived I do not know. In any case, the intel leads them to believe there was a small sample of a biohazard, which they recovered. That told us what we were looking for. Unfortunately, the actual sample and the helicopter carrying it were shot down. This material went missing for part of August. Apparently, it was discovered in a downed helicopter by an adventure specialist and a New York City homicide detective, who somehow managed to evade pursuit by foreign agents and successfully brought the intelligence to a state police office outside of Saratoga Springs, New York. The sample went to the CDC in Virginia."

The Centers for Disease Control, he knew, took care of all sorts of things, but as the name implied, they all had to do with diseases.

"Is it a pandemic?"

Chapter 12

Rylee's head dropped, and she gave a tired nod. "Yes, a pandemic."

Axel suddenly found it hard to breathe as visions of men and women in yellow hazmat suits cropped up in his mind like goldenrod.

"It's really bad," said Rylee. "What we collected were the samples to be used as prototypes for mass production."

His throat went tight and his breath caught as he remembered the yellow taped vials and the ones capped with red. "We also recovered an active vaccine."

"Vaccine?" asked Axel. That didn't sound too bad.

"The sample is a chemical weapon we have been tracking for months. It's a deadly strain of the flu."

"If it is a weapon," asked Axel, "why bring a vaccine?"

"They would want their people vaccinated before releasing the virus," said Rylee.

"How will it be released?" asked Axel, bracing his hands on his knees as he awaited the answer.

"We don't know," said Rylee. "A subway at rush hour. An outdoor concert. A Renaissance festival. The beach. Anywhere, really, where there is a crowd. It's airborne and does not die on surfaces. Technically, they could dust it on anything—the railing of a cruise ship, the escalator at a mall, a single suitcase on a baggage carousel at Dulles Airport."

A chill went up his back as tiny needles of dread seemed to pierce his skin.

"This is not the average seasonal flu," said Rylee. "It's a whole different animal. A pandemic. Virulent. They compared a possible outbreak to something like the influenza epidemic of 1918, which killed more people than World War I. And it attacked people ages twenty to forty. Not the old or the very young, but healthy adults. It killed fifty million people with a mortality rate of 2.5 percent. The CDC estimates that this strain has a mortality rate of 12.4 percent in unvaccinated populations."

Axel felt sick to his stomach. Why hadn't he helped her from the start?

"My office has been running different scenarios and possible targets. The intelligence that we received indicates that this virus will be used in a biological attack. Prior to the attack, the intelligence collected indicates that the active virus strains would be delivered across the border. We have been on high alert, trying to discover where the crossing would be made."

"And you thought the crossing would be here on my border. And your supervisors thought Buffalo."

"Yes, that's right. We weren't sure if the biological

agent would be coming across in a large container or if the terrorists were planning to incubate the virus here within our borders. We now have our answer. They're going to manufacture here."

Axel placed a hand on her knee. "But you found it. You got the virus before they could turn it over to the manufacturing plant."

"Well, that's partly true. We did get it. But we can say, with fair confidence, that they will try again. This size of a load makes it easy to carry and hard to find. The load will likely not be carried in a tractor trailer, train car or ocean liner, as we theorized. That's why we're deploying here. We think they'll use similar tactics. If they get through, if they put this virus into production, lives will be lost. It would be bad, Axel. Really, really bad."

He sat back in the couch, drew his hands together and wrapped them around his body. His quiet little county had become ground zero.

He thought that he knew this place so well. Now he wondered if he ever knew it at all. His home had become the front line in a war on terror. The truth horrified him. He thought of that virus coming again into his country and getting loose and the lives that would be lost if they did not stop it.

"Who is behind this?" he asked.

"The CIA operative who had secured the intel called the group Siming's Army. Simings are creatures or deities, perhaps, from Chinese mythology. They are referred to as Masters of Fate, and Judges of Life, and as worms—The Three Worms, I believe. These deities are said to enter the body at birth. They are supposed to mark an individual's good and bad actions on earth and use that information to calculate a person's life span. Each worm rules a different body system—mind, body, heart. When your time is up, one of the worms attacks."

"Well, that's terrifying."

"So is this group. Because we had never heard of them before, their motives are murky."

"What do they want?"

"We believe that they think that the US has committed evil on the earth and Siming's Army will exact revenge. Judge us for our actions. We hypothesize that they will attack our heart, mind and body, metaphorically."

"What's the heart?"

"We don't know. Our children. Our citizens. New York City. Congress. The Mall of America. We just don't know."

"The mind?"

"Electrical grid. Internet. The federal government. Again, open to debate."

"This pandemic is the attack of only one of the Masters of Fate. The one on our body?"

"That's right. We believe the virus is the attack meant for that system."

Meaning there were two others, heart and mind, still out there.

"What do we do now?" he asked.

"Go through our suspects again. Find who is helping the motorcycle gang with this cargo."

"You can cross off the Kowa," he said. "At least that's my belief based on their willingness to turn this over to us."

He glanced to her and she nodded. "I agree."

"So, who's on your short list?"

"We are fairly certain that the North Country Riders are involved with the transporting of either foreign nationals, the virus or possibly both. We don't think they're working alone because they don't have the compound or any sort of home base to secure the virus. Also, they have no banking system. Our people can't follow their money because they don't seem to handle any."

"They transport weed. I know they get paid," said Axel.

"Cash, it seems. So who are their bankers?" Rylee blew out a breath in a long audible sigh. "It's my supervisor's opinion that they would be working with someone like the Mondellos."

"The moonshiners?"

"Well, they have a home base and they're well protected. They are an established farm with trusts and way more money than they should have, though we have yet to track it all down. Their money operation was described to me as complicated and sophisticated."

"And they have border perimeter security and boats to cross the St. Lawrence into Canada," said Axel. "But to attack their own country?"

"They're high on our list."

"What about the survival group? Coopersmith has a compound, as well. And he's not only fortified but heavily armed. And they believe that the end of the world is coming. They'd survive a pandemic. I'm certain."

"Yes, they are also contenders. They might have given us the drone as a way of removing suspicion."

"So you are surveilling both groups?"

"Yes."

And he had been annoyed that he had had to pull

her butt out of trouble both times. He should have been helping her. Should have known that there was a credible threat. She wouldn't be here, otherwise.

"I'm sorry, Rylee. I should've been more help. I should have trusted that you had good instincts and good information."

She twisted in her seat so that she was facing him. Her smile was sad and her eyes luminous. He thought of their kiss and wished he could kiss her again.

"Is this a fresh start?" she asked.

"I think so. I'd like it to be."

She reached out and took his hand. He stroked the back of hers with his thumb.

"And you're willing to work with me?" she asked.

"I'll do everything I can to help you."

"Wonderful. One of the groups we are now targeting is the Congregation of Eternal Wisdom. You're familiar?"

Despite the warmth of the room, a chill rolled up Axel's spine and into his chest until his heart iced over. He drew back, leaning against the armrest.

Was he familiar? He was. But he did not want to be the one to bring Rylee to them.

She went on. "They have nonprofit status and are not required to do an annual report. Every nonprofit exempt from income taxes, must file an annual return, except churches."

"What?"

"It's true. Fraud within churches is a major problem, as is mismanagement and money laundering. Very tough to prosecute with the separation of church and state. Most goes unreported. We believe that little of the money collected by this organization from members' estates, donations, retreats and sale of religious products is being used for the congregation's preservation. Numbers don't add up. That means they have established a banking system. They could be the bankers for whatever group is assisting Siming's Army."

"They could launder money collected by the ones paid to carry the load?"

"That's correct."

"That outfit is dangerous. They're especially dangerous to women. You should not be the one to go there. Send some of your men."

She cocked her head as if something now interested her. "You are the second one who's told me that this outfit is dangerous for women. The first was my colleague with DHS. What exactly is going on out there?"

Axel sat back and rested his head on the sofa. He stared up at the ceiling. He didn't remember when he started talking, but he did. He told her what he knew of the cult. He went on and on, but he left out one important detail. One piece of information that he knew would send her out of his house and break their new collaboration. He just did not have the courage to tell her that he'd been born and raised inside the order of the Congregation of Eternal Wisdom.

Chapter 13

Rylee waited as Trace contemplated her question. She knew about the cult. She had even been out there to speak to their leader, Reverend Wayne. From what she could see, the residents there were of an extreme belief but did seem to be content and grounded. They lived communally and from a quick overview, she believed they had adopted some of the tenets from Buddhism, Taoism, and perhaps the old Shaker communities that use to thrive in upstate New York at the turn of the last century, until their tenet toward celibacy brought the group to the obvious end. In this community, both men and women were covered up. All seemed happy. And committed to preparing themselves for what they saw as the upcoming end of humanity's time on earth.

The reverend had left her to speak to the two social strata of men distinguishable by whether they grew facial hair. And to the women, who did not seem subjugated or threatened. She could see the children but had not spoken to them. Her observation was that they were on the thin side but there were no visible indications that they were not well cared for and developing normally.

"Is there something going on out there, Axel, that you want me to be aware of?" asked Rylee.

Trace scrubbed his hand over his mouth and then turned to face her. The fire had taken the chill from the air, leaving her with a pleasant lethargy brought on by a sudden pause in the frantic preparations and debriefing that had been the last two days.

"People up here give them a wide berth," he said. "We know that the folks who come from all over to join them are very committed to their beliefs that the end of the world is near. The reverend, however, seems more committed to being certain that the newest members of his flock are stripped of all personal possessions and assets upon joining. The reverend seizes these for the betterment of his congregation. I have been in contact with the IRS about this but, as he is a nonprofit and a church, investigating him is tricky. A cursory look came back with nothing suspicious."

"I can ask some friends at the Treasury to have another look," said Rylee. "But if they already came back with nothing… Why are you so certain something illicit is happening out there?"

"A feeling that I have. A bad feeling."

The silence settled over them like a warm blanket. She was growing comfortable with him. There was no pressure to fill the warm dry air with useless prattle. She watched a log roll in the flame, sending a shower of sparks below the grate. The embers glowed orange and

gradually faded to gray. She loved the smell of wood
smoke. Somehow, in her traveling from place to place, it
had always been a comfort. Their home in Germany had
had a fireplace and she used to beg her parents to light
the fire. They did very occasionally, as her mother did
not trust that the chimney had been correctly cleaned.

She caught him staring at her, seeing a different kind
of fire in his eyes. The need he stirred in her had gained
in strength. What at first had been an annoyance and
a distraction, had gathered into an internal storm that
was getting out of her control.

She glanced back to the flames. She had told him
everything and that felt good. Instead of making her
anxious, the information felt like what she should have
offered at the start—a collaboration with local law enforcement. If she weren't so suspicious of everyone, she
would have done this earlier.

He was a decorated officer with an exemplary military record. True, he had been in the US Army, but she
wasn't going to hold that against him. She wasn't like
her dad, seeing one branch of the military as superior
to the rest. And he had come home and gotten his edu-
cation, without the help of family to do that, applying
for aid and to colleges. Getting that first job right here
in Kinsley's police force and then being elected by the
county at such a young age. Clearly, his community had
faith in him. Unless those same citizens on his watch
list had made sure that he was elected.

Her smile waned but she pushed back the doubts.

No, there was no evidence or even speculation to that
effect. It was only her problems with trust that made
her so reluctant to believe in him.

Trust. And that was the trouble. Or at least what

the counselor at school had suggested to her. The free mental health service offered through the health and wellness center at her college. The mental health professional who had advised she come weekly and proposed to her that her tendency to avoid relationships might be due to her experience of losing any friends due to the frequent moves. And that her difficulty forming an attachment with a partner might be due to her father's emotional distance and physical absence.

You don't trust men to stick around, she had said.

Yet, this man had stuck around in his county despite having no family here. Parents listed as unknown on official records. Sheriff Rogers's report listed him as abandoned. Yet Axel said his dad was still around. Had his father abandoned him or was he unable to care for his child? It was also possible that his father had been deemed unfit as a parent, but then there would be a record. The entire thing was mysterious. In any case, how complicated must his feelings for his father be?

That blank spot in his past troubled her. Where had he been before his appearance in official reports? The records yielded nothing. Where had he been for thirteen years?

"Would you like something other than coffee? I have beer and white wine."

"You don't seem like a wine guy."

"Former girlfriend," he admitted.

Red flags popped up before her like traffic cones in a construction area.

"Should have improved with age, because she left it over two years ago."

"Anyone since?"

"No one serious. I'm not in a relationship, Rylee, if that's what you're asking."

"I'm not." But of course, she was, and the reason she cared if he were available made her ears buzz and her stomach ache with dread because it meant that she was considering one—a relationship—with Sheriff Axel Trace. *Not him*, she told herself.

"So, wine?"

"No, not her wine. I'll have a beer."

He chuckled and stood, removing the barely touched coffee and heading out. With both hands full, he could do nothing about the low-slung sweatpants and Rylee nearly fell off the couch staring at the dimples at his lower back and the tempting curve of his butt.

"You should get out of here right now," she muttered to herself. She folded her arms over her chest and sat back in the chair. Her gaze fixed on the fire, burning low and giving a soft crackle as the logs surrendered to the flames.

He returned with two beers in glasses. That earned points. He set hers beside her on the table and returned to his seat with his; only this time, he took the center cushion, closer to her. The proximity brought his scent to her.

Wood smoke, something stronger and new. Had he put on cologne while he was gone? Whatever it was, it was sexy as hell. She leaned to retrieve her new drink and took a long swallow. The bubbly brew cooled her throat. They sat quietly, with the outward semblance of calm. Only her heart was thumping like a rabbit caught in a snare, and his jaw clenched as he held a smile that seemed forced.

"This is such a nice room," she said. That brought a

beautiful smile to his face, transforming his usual serious, dour demeanor into something breathtaking. A trickle of excitement moved inside her.

"I picked out everything." The pride was clear in his voice and with good reason. He had an eye for masculine homey touches.

Were they going to do this?

He caught her gaze and held it. He set aside her drink and then his own. Then he extended his hand, palm up, offering himself to her.

"I want to kiss you again," he said.

"Is that right?" she asked.

He nodded, his gaze never wavering from hers. A luscious tingle danced over her skin and her cheeks felt hot.

"It's a bad idea. Long-term, I mean," he said. "I'm staying. You're going. That doesn't give us a lot of time."

"Time is overrated," she said.

His smile broadened. And he gave a dry chuckle that warmed her inside and out.

"Is that a yes on the kissing?" he asked.

She grinned. "That's a yes."

She took his offered hand and he dragged her into his arms. She settled beside him, feet on the sofa and arms hooked around his neck.

"What if we do more than kissing?" he asked.

"I'm open to more."

She waited for him to kiss her, but instead he let his gaze roam over her face, down her neck and then return, retracing his course until his gaze fixed on her mouth. She drew her lips between her teeth and dragged her bottom lip free. She watched him swallow, his Adam's apple bobbing. The room no longer felt warm but hot.

The tension between them coiled like a spring. Still, she waited. She hoped he'd make the first move. Instead, he let his head drop back to the sofa and closed his eyes. Squeezed them tight as if the only way to resist her was to remove her from his sight. She took the opportunity to study his features. The thickness of his dark brow. The length of his feathery lashes. The slight flush that covered his cheeks and neck. The strong muscles that flanked the column of his throat. And the interesting wisp of dark hair that emerged from the top of the shirt. She had caught him dressed in little. She suspected he wore only a T-shirt and not a thing beneath the thin sweatpants. When she'd knocked, had he already been ready for bed? Would he consider taking her along?

Waiting was overrated, too, she thought. If he knew that she was not staying and that she knew he was not going, she did not see any reason why they should not spend the evening together. It was not a conflict of interest. They were no longer on opposite sides. He had agreed to help her with her investigation, and she had shared what information she had. They were both consenting adults.

The more she rationalized her decision, the more she had to push down the demons of doubt. Why was she trying so hard to convince herself that sleeping with Axel Trace would not be a mistake?

Somewhere in her heart, she recognized that starting something she could not finish with this man was dangerous. She should crawl off his sofa, find her boots and march herself out of his house. She should go back to the motel and continue reading through the mountain of paperwork associated with this investigation.

But she couldn't. Some unnamable part of her could do nothing else.

She ignored reason and her better judgment. She ignored caution and fear. She ignored doubt, as she pressed herself against him and lowered her mouth to his.

Chapter 14

Axel's grip about Rylee tightened as she deepened the kiss. Her insides began a persistent aching to touch his skin. The impulse to drag away every barrier that separated them built to a roar, drowning out the receding whisper of doubt.

This was right. This was perfect, and she wanted all of him. Rylee broke the kiss and felt his resistance in the tightening of his grip before he allowed her to lean back. His confused expression made her smile. She could see the rising beat of need tighten his jaw and burn in his hungry gaze.

She wasn't teasing him and it took only an instant to drag the long-sleeved shirt over her head, leaving her in nothing from the waist up except her white lace bra.

His mouth hung open for a moment and he made a sound in his throat, like a sigh, then he reached for her.

Warm hands splayed across her bare back. The contact thrilled, and they shared a smile.

"You really want to do this, Rylee?" he asked.

"Seems so."

"I'm going to need you to give me a definitive answer here."

"Yes, Sheriff Trace, I want to make love to you, right here and now, in front of this lovely fire on this soft leather couch." She ran a finger down his forehead and nose, pausing on his lower lip. "Definitive enough?"

In answer, he took her index finger in his mouth and sucked. The smile fell from her lips as his tongue swirled about the sensitive pad of her finger. Her mind did the rest, anticipating the pleasure he had in store for her. Rylee's eyes fluttered closed and her head fell back. He released her finger as his hands moved to her torso and he leaned her forward, kissing the center of her chest, just below the collarbone. Then his tongue painted tiny swirls on her flesh.

Axel stroked her back as his mouth moved from the top of one breast to the next. She felt the clasp at the back of her bra release. Free from the constraints, she shrugged out of the lace and tossed it aside.

His hands reversed course, coming between them as she straddled his lap. He lifted her. The calloused, rough feel of his palms on her sensitive skin gave her an erotic thrill matched only by the look of longing on his face. His focus dropped from her face to her breasts. She leaned in and he licked one nipple to a hard, aching bud.

This time she groaned. The need that had burned her up now turned liquid and she gave in to the urge to move on top of him, rocking back and forth. Axel sucked one nipple and then the next, taking his time and making her crazy.

She tugged at his shirt, dragging it up to his shoulders and then raking her nails over the exposed skin of his back.

He released her with surprising strength, lifting her effortlessly off his lap and onto the seat beside him. Then he stood and stripped out of his shirt before stooping to strip off her socks. She stood then, and he unfastened her jeans, sliding them down her legs. Dressed in only a tiny scrap of white lace, Rylee waited.

"You're so beautiful," he said, his voice low as if they were in church.

"Back at you," she said and offered her hand. "Rug or couch?"

"Ladies' choice."

Rylee pointed to the sofa. Then stretched out on her back and beckoned to him. He came to her, offering her a small open packet, protecting her again. She rolled the condom over him. He squeezed his eyes shut as he sucked in a breath at her touch. She lay back and he came to her, barrier between them. His body burned. His hot, firm flesh pressed tight to her damp skin. She opened her legs and he glided into her. She savored the steady rhythm and the delicious friction. His spicy scent mingled with the smell of leather and wood smoke.

She wouldn't think about why this was the wrong man at the wrong time. Rylee arched back, closing off all doubts and warnings and, oh, yes… This was what she wanted. Him making love to her here, safely hidden away from the rest of the world and their judgments and rules.

She closed her eyes to savor the perfection of his loving.

And as she moved with him, the rest of her thoughts receded until all she could do was catch the rising wave of pleasure that shattered her to pieces before dropping her safely back between the soft folds of the sofa and the warmth of Axel's embrace.

She dozed. Rousing when his fingers danced up her shoulder as he kissed her neck, humming his pleasure.

They snuggled together on the wide leather sofa, the fire heating the room. Something about the feel of him, his scent and the strength of his big solid body made her feel grounded and at home. She stroked the warm velvet of his back, savoring the feel of his skin when his voice rumbled through his chest.

"Do you like it up here on the river?" he asked.

"It's got a rugged beauty," she said, hearing the languor in the slowness of her voice.

"Would you ever think of staying?"

The languor dissolved, and she stiffened. What was he asking?

"I've got plans, career plans to earn an assignment in New York City."

He made a disapproving sound. "You ever been there? It's noisy and dirty and crowded."

"And a major assignment."

"I thought you said you wanted to stop moving from place to place."

"Well, yes. But after I get promoted."

The rumble in his chest was back, sounding like a growl.

"No end to that. Just like your childhood being dragged from one posting to another. Only this time you are doing it to yourself. Don't you want a home, Rylee?"

She scowled. Her career advancement involved a

willingness to travel. Getting to New York would put her in a place to make a real difference. She looked forward to telling her family, imagined the conversation with her father. It was important to do well, more important since she was not in the military.

She lifted to an elbow to look down at his handsome face, marred only by the frown tugging at his mouth.

"Would you ever consider leaving this county?"

His answer was immediate. "I can't."

"Because of your job. Elected official?"

"I know this place. Everything I am is because I was born in Onutake County. There are real good people here and then there's the ones that bear watching. I'm here for them, to be here when things go bad."

"You sound like it's a foregone conclusion."

"It is."

"Anyone specific?"

"The Congregation of Eternal Wisdom."

"Ah," she said. "We talked about them. They're on my watch list."

"They definitely should be."

"You have information on any illegal activities?"

"Just bilking vulnerable people out of their life's savings and twisting their beliefs to Reverend Wayne's version of faith."

"Not illegal, as I've said."

"Immoral, then."

"That's why you stay? Because of that religious order?"

"It's a cult."

She swallowed back her disappointment. Was that a lump in her throat? What was happening to her?

She had enjoyed sleeping with him, but she wasn't looking for a relationship. Who was she kidding? Sleeping with Axel had been mind-blowing and now that she could think again, she realized she was in real trouble.

"So, you're needed here." Why did she even want to know and why was she holding her breath?

"I am. Maybe someday I'll be free of this place."

Axel woke in the gray predawn light, lying on his back with Rylee beside him. She slept on her side, pressed between the leather back of the couch and his body. One arm lay on his chest, with her palm pressed flat over his heart. Her cheek rested on his shoulder and her mouth was open as she gave a soft snore with each intake of breath. Her top leg was coiled about one of his, so that her foot and ankle threaded beneath his opposite calf.

She'd asked him if he'd ever leave the county. Nothing had tempted him so much as her question. The tug to be with her was new, like some invisible cord drawing him to her.

Then there was his father and his promise to see Axel suffer for daring to leave the fold. He knew exactly how his father might do that; he could call his followers together and, at his word, they would all return to their rooms and take their lives. That included the children, his siblings, who had stayed and the mother he could not even name. She was there among the other women, one of them. He'd tried shutting them down and failed. He didn't have the authority. His father knew that and seemed to bask in Axel's powerlessness.

Rylee's skin was covered in gooseflesh. The fire had burned out and the air in the room held the chill that told him the forecasted cold front had arrived. His arm was under her and his fingers splayed over one perfect orb of her ass. He resisted the urge to squeeze. Instead, he

lifted his opposite hand and dragged the fleece blanket
from the back of the chair, covering their naked bodies.
Rylee hummed her satisfaction and then nestled closer.

One eye opened and she peered up at him.

"Hello, gorgeous," he whispered and brushed a
strand of blond hair from her cheek, tucking it behind
the shell of her ear.

"I've got to pee." She pushed up and groaned. "Freezing in here."

"Take the blanket," he said.

In a moment, he had the fleece around her shoulders.

"What about you?" she asked.

"Heading to my bed. Care to join me?"

"Sounds reasonable." She grinned and then went
down the hall toward the guest bathroom as he headed
to the master.

They reconvened in his king-size bed, where she
dropped the fleece in favor of the down comforter and
flannel sheets and him.

"Oh, the sheets are cold," she said, shivering.

"Not for long," he promised.

When they finally stopped warming the sheets and
each other, the bedding was tangled about his waist, two
of the pillows were somewhere on the floor and they
were both panting. He gathered her in, their moist skin
sticking them together like Post-its. He smiled, tucking
her head under his chin as he embraced her.

He had known they'd be good together, but Rylee in
the flesh was so much better than anything he could
ever have imagined. She was bold and more uninhibited
than he would have guessed. In her professional life,
Rylee was exacting, demanding and a pain in his butt.

In his bed, she was generous, thrilling and the best

thing to happen to him in forever. He wondered if she had an early start and if she didn't, if he could manage to keep up with her.

He grinned like a fool at the ceiling of the quiet room as Rylee's breathing changed. His entire body felt sated and relaxed, and he had the suspicion that it was not just having sex with an amazing woman that he had to thank. It was sleeping with Rylee. He really wanted to please her and to give her a piece of himself that he had kept from all the others. He wanted her to know him as no one else had. The smile began to fade.

Why was that?

He wasn't stupid enough to think that if he were good enough in bed, she might not want to leave him. Was he?

He pressed his free hand to his forehead and groaned. That was exactly what he thought. If they were perfect together, she might just change her mind about this case and her promotion and quit everything to live forever in his arms.

He was, in layman's terms, an idiot.

As if to prove his point, Rylee's phone alarm sounded from the living room and she was up and retrieving the device before he could even drag the pillow from his face. He opened his eyes to see the golden light of morning made richer from the reflection off the yellow leaves of the sugar maple that occupied much of the backyard. The next thing he saw was Rylee dressed in her wrinkled jeans and rumpled shirt, still barefoot as she crossed before the bed, staring at her phone. She disappeared into the bathroom without even glancing at him in the bed.

That was bad, he knew. Really bad. He'd made more

than a few hasty exits after spending the night somewhere that, in the morning, seemed like a mistake.

He dropped back into the pillows. Morning had come,
and he needed to play it cool as if this were just one of
those things, except it wasn't. Maybe he should tell her that.

Or never tell her that. The sound of the water running
brought him to his feet. Images of Rylee, soapy with suds
rolling down her body, sent him to the bathroom door.
His hand on the knob, he paused. Then he realized it was
the water running into the sink and that a closed door
was a clear indicator that she did not want his company.

His hand fell to his side.

"Breakfast?" he called.

"Sorry. I've got to run."

And what had he really thought she would do? Call
her boss and resign?

Axel dragged himself back to bed and realized that
his hamstrings were sore and that he was still naked.
He needed to start running again.

"Run away from Rylee, maybe," he muttered. The
chill in the air made him choose jeans and a flannel
shirt, which he dragged on over a clean white T-shirt.

He headed to the kitchen, hoping that some fresh
brewed coffee would wake him up to the fact that what
had rocked his world had clearly not been an earth-
moving experience to Rylee.

He didn't like being a workout dummy. Question
was, should he tell her so or cross his fingers and hope
she needed him again?

Chapter 15

Rylee blinked at herself in the medicine cabinet mirror. Her hands were on the edge of his sink, only inches from his shaving cream, razor, toothpaste and toothbrush that lined the back of the countertop.

Had she lost her mind?

Obviously, she had lost her mind because the sex with the sheriff had been mind-blowing. Hard as it was to admit she had never experienced that sort of a connection with anyone in her past. Note that her past wasn't littered with hundreds of lovers, but she had had enough of them to know that what she and Axel had shared was unique, and that made her realize it was dangerous.

She wanted to get out of there as quickly as possible and find somewhere she could think. Somewhere where her view did not include the wide, tempting expanse of Axel's bare chest. She needed her brain and not her instincts to guide her.

Certainly, she knew better than to sleep with a co-worker. Axel was not actually a coworker or a subordinate, but he was a local associate and that made this a bad idea. The sort of idea that could end a career. And here she was so close with a real breakthrough and solid evidence that this place had been used by the terrorists to smuggle some of the biohazard.

The troops were on their way. Her boss was on her way. She'd already received a text with Lieutenant Catherine Ohr's ETA. And she'd received them while naked in Axel's bed.

She wanted very much to be dressed in a clean, ironed suit when she met her superior, rather than the rumpled mess of clothing that had clearly been scooped up off the floor and hastily donned on her way out.

Coffee. She needed coffee, but she also needed to get out of here first. She did not want to have a conversation with Axel. She did not want to explain her reluctance to continue with something that was so devastatingly wonderful that she could not wait to see him again and wanted very much to crawl back under that giant fluffy coverlet and explore every inch of that amazing body. It was one thing to have a body that was as perfectly formed as Axel's and was quite another to know how to use it to the best effect. And he ticked every box. She was still ticking as a result. Her leg muscles ached with fatigue and yet, here she was trying to think of a way that she could see him without having any of her colleagues find out. No.

"Bad idea," Rylee said to her reflection, wagging a finger at herself for emphasis.

Rylee found his spray deodorant, pressed the button, sniffed and decided against it. What she needed was a shower. She didn't need to add more of Axel's scent to her skin. She glanced toward the shower and then shook her head. She paused only long enough to draw a long breath and close her eyes before emerging into his bedroom. He was, thankfully, fully dressed in his casual clothes and sitting on his unmade bed. White T-shirt, open blue flannel shirt and faded blue jeans. His feet were bare, and she found the sight of his long toes dusted with hair instantly arousing.

She groaned.

"You okay?" he asked.

"I'm not sure." She forced herself to stop fidgeting and stood still before him. "Axel, did we just make a mistake?"

His mouth went tight, and his brow descended. He glanced away from her and then back. Then he rose to stand before her, close enough to touch, but he did not reach out.

"I don't know, Rylee. Only time will answer that. I do know that I don't regret what happened between us. I'm sorry if you do."

Her hands were clasped, and she spun the titanium ring she had commandeered from her brother Paul that encircled her thumb as if it were a spinner. What to say?

"I'm not sure we have very much in common," she said, feeling it a bad start. Her belief was confirmed by the narrowing of his eyes.

"We have this in common," he said, motioning to his bed. The covers looked as if they had been twisted and tossed by the ocean and then cast ashore to dry. "And we have the fact that you cared enough about me last night to share my bed."

"My timing is bad. My supervisor is en route, and

I only have an hour before she'll expect a briefing. It's not that I don't want to see you again. It just can't interfere with my work."

He quirked a brow and his mouth twisted as if he were reluctant to admit she'd scored a point.

"Honestly, Axel, I knew she was coming today. I just didn't know she was flying and would be here so soon."

She came to sit beside him. "You must think… Well, I don't know what you think."

He turned toward her and stroked her hair, which was still tangled and as wild as he knew she could be. Then he drew her in and she let him. He dropped a kiss on her forehead before stepping away. He took the opportunity to stroke her cheek with his thumb. His touch sent an electric tingle over her skin.

"Let me know if you need anything from Onutake County."

She held her smile. "I'll be in touch."

Then she headed for the door, one hand shoved in her jeans pocket, clutching the key to her motorcycle. In her back pocket, she'd shoved her nearly dead phone. She needed to get to the motel to recharge its battery and her own.

Something popped into her mind and she paused at the door to his bedroom. He watched her, his dark brows lifted.

"Um, I think I'll be going out to the Eternal Wisdom commune today. Maybe I can find some reason to shut them down."

His expression grew stormy and the blood vessel at his neck pulsed dangerously. "Not alone. We discussed this."

"They might be involved in smuggling."

He snorted. "If they are, you'll never catch them."

"And why is that?"

"Too smart."

She picked up the gauntlet he'd tossed. "We'll see about that, won't we?"

"You aren't going alone."

"I'll have my team with me."

"They don't know these people like I do."

"You can ride along, if you like."

The acid in his empty stomach burned at just the thought of going out there with her because he knew that Father Wayne would instantly pick up the vibe between them. Then he would delight in revealing to Rylee that he was Axel's father.

The only thing worse than having that happen was letting her go out to that place without him. She didn't know or understand how very dangerous Father Wayne could be.

His breathing changed, coming in short angry puffs, and his teeth were locked so tight he'd need the Jaws of Life to get them open.

Axel considered and decided that his shame was small compared to Rylee's safety.

"Axel? You all right?"

He unlocked his jaw. "I'm going with you. End of story."

"Okay, let me clear it with my supervisor. I'll get back to you." She glanced at the screen of her phone. "Jeepers. I have to go."

He walked her out and watched as she drove off, knowing he would have to tell her. Father Wayne was more than a cult leader and con man. Rylee had the right to know. His father was why he stayed and, more specifically, because of what he feared his father might do. Axel was imprisoned here as surely as when he had been trapped behind the congregation's walls. He had to stay, to be here to stop his father from ever carrying out his deadly version of the Rapture, which he called the Rising.

Lieutenant Catherine Ohr waited for Rylee in her rented sedan outside a craftsman-style home painted gray. Rylee checked the address again and pulled behind her boss. The two women exited their vehicles simultaneously.

Lieutenant Ohr swung the leather briefcase over one shoulder as she cleared the distance toward Rylee with her long stride. She extended her hand and the two women shook.

"Right on time," said Ohr. "We are gleaning some interesting data from the drone. Good work on its recovery."

"Thanks," said Rylee. "I had some help with that. Wouldn't have gained access to the survivalist camp without the assistance of the sheriff."

Her supervisor's mouth turned down. Ohr was a tall woman, nearly six feet in height, and she was skeletally thin. Rylee had observed her at lunch; generally, Ohr ate a cup of yogurt at her desk and seemed to leave her computer only to smoke cigarettes. As a result, her complexion was sallow and her brown hair thinning and brittle. The lines around her mouth, always prominent, seemed to harden at the mention of the sheriff.

"Yes. Sheriff Trace. I read that in your report. It's generally a good idea to cooperate with local law enforcement. However, in this case, I think you might have done better to speak to the former sheriff, Kurt Rogers. Better information and less entanglements."

Rylee's brow wrinkled and confusion settled over her, along with a twinge of anxiety. Why would she have spoken to the former sheriff? And what entanglements did she mean? Was she talking about her personal relationship with Axel? But how would she know?

Lieutenant Ohr paused on the sidewalk to face Rylee.

"This is where Kurt Rogers lives," said Ohr. "He has some information on Sheriff Trace that I think you need to hear. Shall we?" Ohr motioned toward the house and did not wait for Rylee before extending her long legs and striding up the walkway to the front door. She ignored the bell and knocked briskly. As they waited, her supervisor tightened the sash on her leather jacket. A deep bark told Rylee a large canine had come to the door. Then there was a voice of someone telling the dog to be quiet and a moment later the door swung open.

The man had a full white mustache, rosy cheeks and hair that made Rylee think for a moment that he perhaps belonged at the North Pole. He was slim, however. But the choice of suspenders to hold up his jeans did reconfirm her initial impression. The man looked from one to the other, swept them each with a glance and said, "I see the dress code hasn't changed. But the last time I spoke to the feds, they were both males, so perhaps we are making some forward progress. Come on in, ladies."

He stooped to grab hold of the collar of his black Lab, whose thick tail thumped against his master's leg. Rogers told his dog to sit and she did, her tail now thumping on the carpet runner as the two women stepped inside. Catherine ignored the canine, but Rylee extended the back of her hand to the dog, allowing the animal to take in her scent.

"This is Ruby," said Rogers. The dog's ears perked up at the mention of her name. Rogers released her and she stayed where she was until he guided them from the entry to the living room, at which time she took the opportunity to sniff the legs of both new arrivals before settling in a dog bed beside the recliner.

After the initial chitchat, they were motioned to a sofa. Rogers chose the well-worn and stained brown leather recliner.

"I understand you want some background information on the current sheriff. That right?"

Her supervisor not so much sat as perched on the edge of the sofa, ankles together and hands clasped on her knees.

"I wondered if you could fill in my subordinate on what you told me on the phone and include any additional details you might have recalled." Catherine tapped her clasped hands together as she spoke.

Rogers drew a long breath and then turned to Rylee. The pit of her stomach dropped, and she felt the tightening of the muscles between her shoulders. Whatever he was about to say, she knew it was not good. What would these two think if they knew she had come directly from Sheriff Axel Trace's king-size bed to this meeting? Rylee repressed a shudder.

"Well," said Rogers. "I told Ms. Ohr here that Axel used to walk to Kinsley whenever he could slip away. He didn't talk much but the librarian sort of took him under her wing." He turned to Catherine at this and continued with, "She's retired now, as well. But I can put you in touch, if you'd like. I'm sure she may have some additional information on Axel."

"Not necessary for now."

Rogers turned his attention back to Rylee. "He didn't really fit in with the people. I could see he was unhappy and it bothered me that no one came looking for him. No matter how long he was gone. That got me to call social services. We all went out and had a look at the compound."

Rylee sat forward as if stabbed in the back. Had he said compound?

"Other than their unconventional living situation, we did not find the children in poor health or malnourished. All of them seemed relatively happy and…" Rogers rubbed his neck. "You know, they just have different ideas. Ideas that I'd call dangerous. And not everyone out there toes the line. One of Reverend Wayne's followers was arrested by Border Patrol for transporting an Eastern European into the US."

"A Croatian," said Ohr.

"Leadership denied knowledge and I found nothing to prove otherwise."

"Do you feel they are engaged in human trafficking?"

"Maybe. Might have been an outlier. I couldn't catch them, but for that one time. If folks at the compound are smuggling or trafficking, I never found any evidence."

Rylee interjected here. "You say *the compound*. What exactly are you referring to?" But she knew. She was certain that she already knew.

Rogers brows lifted. "Oh, I thought you knew. Axel was born on the lands belonging to the Congregation of Eternal Wisdom. His dad is the leader of that group. Man named Wayne Trace. Goes by Reverend Wayne."

"His name isn't Trace. It's Faith."

"Changed it."

Ohr gave Rylee a long, critical look. "Thorough background check would have revealed the name change."

Rylee dropped back into the thick padding of the seat cushions. Wayne Faith was Wayne Trace. Cult leader and Axel's father. If she was such a crack investigator, how was it possible that she had missed this?

The knot in her stomach turned into a whirling sea, pitching so hard that she needed to grip the armrest to steady herself.

One of the men on her watch list was the father of the sheriff. How much worse could it be? She knew the answer to that. She could have slept with the son of a man who was about to go on her list of suspects. That would make it worse.

Rylee's supervisor lifted a brow, regarding her. "Is something wrong?"

Rylee forced herself to release the armrest and managed to give her head a shake. She turned her gaze to the former sheriff. She put aside her emotions, pressing them down deep where they threatened to explode like compressed gas. "Mr. Rogers, the sheriff gave me some information on this group, but I would appreciate it if you could you tell me exactly what you mean when you say they have dangerous ideas."

Rogers thought for a minute. His index finger setting the whisker straight in his mustache.

"Yes, I could do that."

Chapter 16

Axel waited for Rylee on the shore of St. Regis River in a park that was a popular launch for small crafts. He suspected that she'd set the location because she did not want to be seen with him. He didn't blame her. He should have told her the truth, even knowing that this was exactly what would happen.

Most women did not like being lied to, but this omission interfered with her case. Could she forgive him?

Maybe she doesn't know. Which meant that she would find out eventually or that he had to tell her.

He liked neither option. They'd already gone too far. His night with Rylee had made him wonder about things that he had no right thinking about. Like what it would be like to wake up to see her in his bed every morning.

I'll bet she'd be a great mom.

Axel wiped the sweat from his upper lip. That was

the kind of thinking that was going to get his heart broken.

What was he doing? He would be a terrible father. The only examples he had of parenting were twisted. All he really knew was what not to do. Could that be enough?

He was out of his unit now without remembering leaving his SUV. He paused in his pacing to look back at his vehicle, the door open and the alarm chiming. He strode back to slam the door. Then he faced the water. The fog was thicker there, rolling toward him like some special effect in a stage production.

This park was too close to the compound of the Congregation of Eternal Wisdom for his liking. The compound was situated on the St. Regis River. Mid-river lay an island belonging to the Kowa tribe, and the shore beyond was also Mohawk land. Beyond that, across a narrower stretch of the St. Lawrence, lay Canada.

Axel shifted, rocking from side to side as he stood between his vehicle and the river. If not for the fog, he could have seen the fence just south of this spot. One had to have lived there to know it wasn't to keep intruders out so much as it was to keep insiders in. He hadn't been back to this spot since the day he'd jumped that fence and walked out that last time.

The cold of the air and the warmth of the water had created a real London-style fog, but the chill he felt had nothing to do with the damp or the fact that he could not see more than fifty feet. He didn't need to see, it was all there in his mind—the layout, the women and children in one building, single men in another and the others, the ones they called most blessed, ensconced in their own house. These were the ones who had made, what his father called the greatest sacrifice, and what Axel called self-mutilation.

The engine sound brought him around. Headlights glowed eerily in the mist. Tires crunched on gravel and he recognized her sedan, the red handprints nearly unnoticeable in the mist. She parked her car at an angle, so her departure would not require her to reverse direction. Her cab light flashed on as she exited her car, shutting her door with more force than necessary.

She paused to lock her car, unnecessarily, he knew. Then she cinched the belt to her coat before marching toward him. One of the large boulders, placed to keep folks from accidentally driving into the river, gave him support as he sagged.

Her expression told him all he needed to know. She knew everything. He could see it in the upward tilt of her chin and the downward tug at the corners of her mouth.

She stopped and glared. Her face flushed. He forced himself not to shift as he held her cold stare.

"I don't even know where to begin," she said.

"I'm sorry, Rylee. I should have told you."

"Yeah! My first field assignment and your father is on my watch list."

"He wasn't. You never mentioned him."

"But you knew that he should be. You knew that one of his followers was arrested by Border Patrol for transporting an Eastern European into the US."

"A Croatian. My father denied knowledge."

"Do you believe him?"

"It doesn't matter what I believe. Only what I can prove."

"It matters to me."

"Part of the indoctrination is to believe that he is one of God's chosen. I believe that none of his followers would take such action without his specifically ordering them to do so. I told ICE exactly that when they questioned me."

Immigration and Customs Enforcement had charged one of Reverend Wayne's followers, William Evers, with human trafficking. The illegal immigrant was deported and, as far as Axel knew, Evers was still in federal prison.

"You lied to me," she said.

"I omitted."

"You were born there, in that compound. I'm looking for a foreign agent on US soil and now I learn that one of your father's followers was engaged in human trafficking. That kind of activity points to the possibility of ongoing human trafficking. The sort of trafficking that might bring my suspect to your county."

"Do you have evidence to that effect?"

"We know a foreign agent carried a deadly virus strain onto US soil. We know that person is missing. Additionally, we know that one of Wayne Faith's followers once transported an Eastern European illegally into this county. And we know that you are the son of Wayne Trace, whose surname was changed to Faith. Do you have any idea what my affiliation with you will do to my career?"

"Who you sleep with is your business, Rylee."

"The trouble is I don't really know who I slept with. Do I?"

He glanced away.

"It's not just that you lied, Axel. It's that I can't trust anything you say, or don't say, again."

He looked back at her. "You ever been ashamed, Rylee? During your years traveling with your family or in college or maybe in your stellar career? You have someone in your past that you'd do anything to distance yourself from?"

"If you wanted distance, why did you move back here after your discharge?"

It was a question he didn't think on because the answers hurt too much.

"Maybe I wanted to be near my mother."

"Who is?"

He looked away again. "I don't know. But if she ever wanted to leave, I wanted her to know I was close. That I could help her if she'd let me."

"Is that all?"

He looked up and then to the river and then to the ground. Everywhere and anywhere but at Rylee.

"Why else, Axel?"

"To stop him. I wanted to be here in case he set a date. I have siblings there. I have childhood friends who never left. If Father Wayne decides that the Rising is coming, I wanted to be here to stop him."

"Stop him from what, Axel?"

"They rehearse their departure to Heaven's Door. That's what he calls mass suicide. Not death, just a door. They have costumes and rituals. He holds their lives in his hand. On his word, they'll all kill themselves."

He hazarded a quick glance to see Rylee's mouth had dropped open.

"Can't you close them down?"

"I told you, I've tried. It's not illegal to believe what they believe. I've had Child Protective Services out there dozens of times. The children show no signs of abuse. And their upbringing is no harder than Fundamentalists or any number of religious subgroups."

"His religious beliefs are crazy."

"But not illegal."

She closed her mouth and gave him a troubled stare. She seemed to be deciding something. Axel held his breath. When she didn't speak, he broke the silence.

"If you have something on him, some law that he's broken, I can help you."

Rylee shook her head. "Perhaps you do really want to stop him. I don't know. But you can't be involved in this investigation any longer and I cannot have anything more to do with you."

"Rylee, please."

"Goodbye, Axel." She started to turn away.

He felt the panic squeezing his heart. He couldn't breathe. Axel's hand shot out and he stopped her, drawing her back.

"You can't tell me you don't have feelings. That what we shared meant nothing to you."

"I can't say that. But I can say it is the reason why this hurts so much. You made a mistake. I can forgive you. But it's over between us. I can't take the chance that you are holding back other secrets or that my association with you won't jeopardize this case. It's too important. Far more important than either of us."

"Then let me help you," he begged.

"Too late for that, Axel. You know it. Now let me go."

He didn't want to. But he did, releasing her and with her, the best chance he'd ever had at a normal life with a woman who made his body quake and his heart sing. Now, both seemed to be burning to ash. What right did he have to a woman like her, anyway?

Axel watched her go back to her sedan. The engine purred to life and she rolled away, looking straight ahead, as if he didn't even exist. In a moment, the fog made her, and her vehicle, disappear.

Axel stood at his office window in the building that held all city offices, including his. Right on time, the charcoal gray sedan arrived driven by an unknown female agent with Lieutenant Catherine Ohr in the passenger seat. Behind them, a second car pulled in, this one announcing Border Patrol. Two officers exited, one male and one female, in uniform. He knew them both. Captain Sarah LeMaitre and Officer Greg Perhay. They'd worked the Ogdensburg Bridge and the forty-eight miles of US coastline along this posting for as long as he'd been sheriff, and today their expressions were all business.

Ohr exited the vehicle and headed across the parking area with the second agent in tow. He lost sight of them as they rounded the building. It gave him time to return to his desk and the computer and the mobile phone that still had no texts or messages from Rylee, despite his making three unanswered calls to her.

The two women appeared in the hallway, visible from his office through the glass panel, and entered, coming to a stop before him in the small seating area beyond his desk. In the hallway, LeMaitre and Perhay flanked the entrance. Axel's unease grew as he turned to his visitors.

Ohr wore a business suit and black leather trench coat with the collar upturned, bright red lipstick and a low-heeled shoe. She was gaunt, even with the coat adding much-needed bulk. Her cheekbones stood out and the makeup she used did not hide the unhealthy color of her complexion.

The second agent, by contrast, was tall and fit with brown skin and dark curling hair clipped close to her head. She wore a thigh-length blue woolen coat with an upturned collar, gloves and a cashmere scarf the color of oatmeal.

Ohr shook his hand. Her long bony fingers clasping his for the briefest time possible. Then she introduced the second agent, Lucille Jackson.

"What can I do for Homeland Security?" he asked, wondering why Rylee was not here with them but unwilling to ask.

"I understand from Kurt Rogers that you were born on the compound of the Congregation of Eternal Wisdom," said Ohr. She might as well have slapped him across the face.

His cordial smile slipped and he straightened, feeling the need to sit down.

"Yes. That's correct." He motioned to the chairs before his desk. "Would you care to sit down?"

Ohr gave a shake of her head but not a hair moved. She stepped in, crowding his personal space.

It was a technique of which he was familiar, and so he forced himself not to step back. She smelled of ash and tobacco. He glanced to Jackson, who had a pad of paper out and was jotting down notes.

"Are you still a member?" asked Ohr.

"No. There are no members outside of the compound. You are either in or out."

"Emancipated at thirteen?" asked Jackson.

"Yes." Axel did not like being on this side of the questioning.

Ohr leveled him with a steady stare. "We have reason to believe that the individual who escaped capture on Monday, September 4, may be here on Congregation's property."

He straightened. "Your source?"

"I'm not able to share that. The message was received by a Border Patrol agent." She lifted a hand and motioned to the agents behind her without turning her head.

Captain LeMaitre stepped forward and handed over the letter, which Ohr passed to Axel. The page was torn from a lined composition book. He recognized the type of paper from his early schooling on a twisted version of the world beyond the compound walls.

He read the note.

The Rising is near. We are prepared and joyful to reach Heaven's Door. Please tell our son, Axel, we will miss him and have missed him greatly. Ask him to come home to us.

"Where did you get this?" he asked.

"One of the brothers from the congregation delivered it to a border agent. Do you want to tell me what this means?" asked Ohr.

"This congregation believes that they are the chosen people and that a great disaster is imminent."

"And they'll be spared?" asked Jackson, her eyes rolling toward the ceiling as if having heard this on too many occasions.

"The opposite. They believe they will be called to the Lord before the Desolation. They prepare by readying themselves to meet God by living according to their leader's mutation of religious scripture."

"Mutation is an interesting choice of word," said Ohr.

Axel absorbed this gut punch with only a twitch of his brow. She knew about the rituals of castration, then?

Ohr smiled and extended her hand for the note. He returned the page, folded as it had been.

"There's something else," said Axel. "Part of their ceremonies are preparations for the Rising. If Father Wayne tells them the Desolation is near, it is possible they might all take their lives."

"You are talking about mass suicide?"

"I am."

"I'm aware of their beliefs. Unfortunately, shutting down this organization is not our objective. We are not interested in another Waco. My objective is recovery of the foreign agent who slipped through Agent Hockings's fingers." She tilted her head in a way that was birdlike. "Are you certain Wayne Trace is your father? I understand that he gives all children born on the compound his name. Isn't that correct?"

"That is because all the children born in the compound are his. He is the chosen one. The only man allowed to touch the women. That means any and all women of age."

Ohr folded her arms as if finding this unsettling. Her expression showed her disapproval. "Your mother is there?"

"As far as I know."

"What is her name?"

It was such an obvious question. But the answer made him sick to his stomach. He wrinkled his nose and swallowed. Trying not to look at Ohr, he spoke.

"I don't know her name. The women who elect to join the cult, they are not allowed to claim their children. All those born there are separated from their birth mother and raised communally by women who have not yet born children or are past the age to bear children."

Ohr's brows rose high on her forehead. She and Jackson exchanged a look. He recognized the silent exchange, having witnessed it before—pity mixed with disgust.

"Why is that?" asked Ohr.

"Part of Reverend Wayne's dictates. Children belong to everyone."

"During your time there, did you ever see any illegal activities?"

"No."

"Funding?"

"Donations to his cause and the assumption of all assets from those who decide to throw in with him."

"You know what Agent Hockings recovered here. You know that we are still in pursuit of the person who transported this package. Our investigation leads us to the conclusion that this individual is still in your county. In your opinion, would your father have any reason to shelter such an individual?"

"Don't call him that."

"But Reverend Wayne Trace *is* your father."

Axel lowered his head. The truth was impossible to bury. He knew because he had tried. He took a moment to breathe, the air heavy with the stink of stale cigarette smoke, and then he answered her question.

"He's been preaching the coming apocalypse, the end of the days, for nearly twenty years now. That's a lot of days gone and his followers all willing and wanting to meet their maker. Eager, even. The outbreak of a plague would give his prophecies more credence. Earn points with his followers. Maybe bring in a pile of more followers. So, yes. I believe it is possible that he would assist and shelter such an individual."

"Our findings exactly. We have the layout and all the information on known members within. What I need from you are details on the life inside and the interior layout of buildings to which we might need access. Drone surveillance shows us that one individual never leaves the women's compound. Is that normal?"

"No. Every one of the members have work assignments. The only exception is illness."

"Thank you."

Axel wondered who was ill or injured. Then another thought struck him.

"Do you think this person, in the women's compound, is the one who transported your package?"

"Not at liberty to say," said Ohr. "Now, your congregation hosts retreats for outsiders."

"It is not *my* congregation."

"Yes. In any case, they allow outsiders in for up to three weeks."

"But they are housed in a separate area."

"For the most part. But not during meals."

"If they wish to join the congregation for prayer or meditation or meals, they are welcome," said Axel. "The congregation makes their way of life look ideal. Pastoral, simple. Wayne is a very charismatic guy and he knows how to sell the soap."

"Soap?"

"His lifestyle. The congregation. Most of the converts are unhappy people who have been on more than one retreat. Folks who don't fit in anywhere else, I guess. He makes the unhappiest among them feel a part of things until they just let go of their old life and join him."

The possibility hit him like a fillet knife to his stomach. He braced as he looked from one woman to the other.

"Which brings me to our next concern. We need to identify the residents there. Do you have a list of some sort?"

"I'm sorry, I don't."

"Then we need agents inside. Drones can only do so much. The members never look up, so there is no way to identify any of the residents. Damn bonnets, hats and veils. And if they are hiding someone, our suspect, we need access to find him."

"You think they'll walk your agents to the very spot where they might be hiding someone?"

"That's the mission. We don't require their cooperation."

"I could assist."

"Your connection with this group makes that impossible. But we will inform you when operations are complete." With that announcement, the lieutenant turned and left his office. Jackson fell in beside and slightly behind her.

"How much personnel do you have up here?" he asked the retreating figures.

"I'm not at liberty to say."

"Because he's got fifty or more. And he's got contacts."

"Who do you mean?"

"The North Country Riders. That adds another thirty. You are badly outnumbered. I'd advise against charging into the lion's den."

"You are being dramatic. They're federal officers. They can handle themselves."

Axel knew his sire was fully committed to his little empire. What he didn't know was what he was capable of, when his kingdom was threatened.

Would he follow through and call for the deaths of all his followers? Would they do as he commanded, go to their bunks and take the cocktail of drugs inducing a sleep from which none would ever awaken?

Axel found himself on the move without even recalling leaving his office. He had to speak to Rylee.

Chapter 17

Rylee looked from one woman to the next. Each wore a brown head covering that allowed her to see no part of her hair color. Their complexions ran the gamut from a deep walnut to a freckled pink. But they all shared the same cautious eyes and rigid posture.

The meeting with Reverend Wayne Faith had not gone well. The man talked in circles, repeating himself and the same quotable truisms.

God's hand will bring justice.

We are the chosen.

This life is the true path to Heaven's Door.

We pray for the souls of the lost.

By the lost, he included Rylee and all who lived outside the walls of his compound.

It was just past 5:00 p.m. on Saturday night and she and Agent Lucille Jackson stood before his stylish desk surrounded by murals depicting people dressed

in shapeless brown garments being lifted into the sky.
The Rising, he had explained in detail. The mechanics
of which seemed to involve the trigger of a great human
disaster followed by God welcoming home only these
few men and women. She'd have laughed if they were
not all so serious and deadly sure. What she didn't know
was if the good reverend would be willing to give his
predicted apocalypse a little shove forward by helping
to smuggle into their country a population-decimating
virus.

"We will need to see the living quarters," said Agent
Jackson, keeping her voice calm while revealing a bit of
the southern accent. She had not removed her mirrored
glasses and so the stare down was one-sided.

Rylee's fellow agent stood five inches taller and had
clear brown skin with russet undertones. She wore her
black hair close-cropped and an impenetrable expression.

The standoff stretched, tight as a stretched rope.

Finally, Wayne spoke. "It would be out of the question to allow two women into the men's quarters."

Rylee had elected to wear a DHS ball cap, in def-
erence and as a reminder of who and what she was.
No need to announce or explain to his followers. They
likely already knew she was a federal agent. Whether
that would attract or repel was an open question.

"We will start with the women's quarters, then,"
Rylee said and turned to go.

Wayne hurried around his desk. The man was thin
with a fleshy face and neck that would make a tom
turkey proud. His hair was sparse, but he had grown
the back out and wore it braided in some aberration of
the elves of Middle-earth. Unlike his followers' drab

attire, Wayne's robes were white. The rest of his congregation wore the more practical brown, which was perfect for the thaw that turned the icy roads here into a muddy quagmire.

He managed to get ahead of them as they reached the lobby beside his office and before his church of death.

"You can't go alone."

"Federal officers," drawled Agent Jackson. She waited as Wayne scowled and stared at his reflection in her glasses. Now his gray complexion had a healthy flush. The man was not used to being challenged. That much was clear.

"An escort, then."

"If they can keep up," said Jackson and headed outside.

Rylee was glad for the hiking boots that remained on despite the sucking mud.

Jackson swore as she lifted her pant leg to reveal a shoe and sock smeared with what Rylee hoped was only mud. There were farm animals wandering about.

Before they had reached the women's quarters, a young female dashed up before them, arms raised to stop them.

Jackson had her hand on her sidearm. "You do not want to do that," she warned.

"Sister Della is coming. She's right there." The woman's wave had changed to a frantic combination of pointing and motioning.

Jackson kept her attention on the young woman and her hand on her weapon while Rylee glanced back the way they had come.

Striding toward them from the stables was a tiny stick of a woman who held her skirts high to avoid the mud. The result was a troubling view of her striped socks and rubber clogs below cadaverous knees. She moved quickly for one so small. Rylee judged her to be in her fifties from the heavily etched lines around her mouth and the fainter ones around her eyes. Unlike her pale legs, her face was ruddy and tanned as if she spent every minute of the day out of doors.

"That's her. Sister Della is an elder," said their obstructer. "She'll take you in."

The woman lifted a hand. "Sister Nicole, I am here. What is the trouble?"

"These two demand access to the women's quarters," said Sister Nicole.

"Demand? Not a pretty start. Ask, children. Just ask." She reached beneath her robes.

"Stop," said Jackson.

Della did and cast her a curious expression. Rylee cocked her head as she stared at familiar blue eyes and that nose... She recognized this woman but was certain they had never met. Had they?

"What are you doing?"

"Getting my keys, girl."

"But slowly," said Jackson, her weapon now out of the holster.

The woman's face did not register fear so much as fury.

"You bring weapons into this holy sanctuary?" asked Sister Nicole.

"We are federal officers and we carry guns," said Rylee.

Sister Nicole tugged at her brown garments, looking affronted. Sister Della lay a hand on the younger woman's shoulder.

"I'll take them from here," said Sister Della.

Sister Nicole opened her mouth as if to raise an objection and then acquiesced, nodding and lowering her gaze. She lifted that gaze to glare at the intruders before returning the way she had come.

Sister Della watched her, the smile on her face peaceful as a summer sky. Then she slowly withdrew the keys. "I'll take you anywhere you wish."

Jackson pointed at the women's quarters and Sister Della led the way. Over the next hour, they wandered in and out of stables, gardens, residences and any outbuilding large enough to hold a shovel. Sister Della gradually lost the reclusive reserve and asked Rylee a few questions about herself and her beliefs.

"Are you enjoying your time here on the St. Lawrence?"

"Working, mostly."

"Have you met our son, Axel Trace?" asked Sister Della.

"Our?" asked Jackson.

"Children belong to all of us," she explained. "We were grieved when he joined the army and now, a sheriff, still using weapons to solve the world's problems. What he never understood is that there is no saving the world. Only yourself—your soul must be clean, you see."

"I have met him," said Rylee.

"Have you? What does he look like?"

Clearly, Axel did not visit.

"Would you like to see a photo? I have one on my phone."

"On a phone? Really?"

She looked mystified, as if she had never seen a mobile phone.

"How long have you been inside these walls, Sister?" asked Rylee, as she pulled up the photo she had taken of Axel and Morris Coopersmith on the bench outside the ice-cream stand her first night in town. She wasn't sure why she had kept the shot instead of deleting it. Axel looked relaxed and had a gentle, sweet smile on his face as he sat with his head inclined toward Morris. Looking back, she realized that it was the first moment when she began to fall in love with Axel.

Sister Della moved in as Rylee stared at Axel's kind, handsome face.

"Hockings? You all right?" Jackson asked.

Rylee shook her head and turned the phone, so the sister could see. Sister Della opened both hands and placed them on either side of the phone, cradling his image and Rylee's hand.

"Oh, he's so handsome. Looks just like his father," said Sister Della.

Rylee glanced back at the image. She didn't see the resemblance between Axel and Reverend Wayne. And she was certain that Axel would do anything to change his lineage.

Sister Della sighed and released Rylee's phone, pressing both hands over her heart. "He looks well."

"He's a strong, capable man." *Despite your efforts*, she thought.

"We've only had three leave us. All boys and all to the army. Can you comprehend? We are pacifists. Killing is against God's law."

"What about killing yourself?" asked Jackson.

"Do you refer to the Rising? That's not killing, Lamb. That is responding to the call of our Lord."

Della's placid smile was disturbing. Rylee shifted uncomfortably in the austere quarters.

"Has the sheriff been helping you to find what you seek?" asked Della.

Rylee took a chance. "He is. We are looking for a person. Foreign national, likely Chinese."

"Really? Here? I've seen no one like that." Her face was troubled and Rylee sensed she did know something.

"Axel has been searching with us. It's important to him."

"What has he done, this Chinese person?"

"He's a threat to national security," said Jackson.

"National." She laughed. "There are no nations. We are all one." The sister turned to Rylee. "May I see that photo again?"

"I can make a copy for you."

"Really? I'd like that. Though we are not supposed to have photos of—well, yes, but he's not my old family, so perhaps... I'm not certain." After this conversation with herself concluded, she beamed at Rylee. "I'd like that."

Dark clouds continued to build throughout the late afternoon. As the sun dipped, so did the air temperature.

"Are there any other buildings on the compound?" asked Jackson, now shivering from the cold and casting a glance skyward.

"None here." Despite her small stature, Rylee thought she noticed the sister straightening, growing and setting her jaw.

"What is it?" asked Rylee.

"Have you been down to the river?"

"Yes. Do you mean here on your grounds?" Rylee

was not looking to the north toward the St. Lawrence but to the west, where the St. Regis River glinted steel gray through the trees.

"That river is a dangerous waterway. We only use our boats in fair weather."

"Boats?" said Jackson. "Here?"

"Yes, they are outside of the compound but belong to Father Wayne. Some of the male members of our congregation are lobstermen who use the boats daily to check their pots. One of the men at the boathouse could show you."

"What do you use the boats for?" asked Rylee.

"I'm sure I don't know. I'm in charge of the animals. And the women are not allowed near the boats."

A few more questions and they discovered where the boats were located. Sister Della walked them back toward the church and sanctuary, where their car was parked.

"Right through there." She pointed toward the open gate. "If you are quick, you might find your...man."

Rylee didn't like her impish smile, as if she were the only party privy to some joke.

"The road to the boathouse is on the north side of the outer wall, judging from the engine noise I hear."

Sister Della offered a wave before she turned and walked toward the barn and the animals in her care.

"Why did she tell us that, about the boathouse?" asked Jackson.

Rylee shook her head, perplexed. She had been wondering exactly the same thing. But Sister Della had told them something else. She had told them to hurry.

"Boathouse?" asked Rylee.

"Oh, yeah," said Jackson. "Calling in our position

and destination," she said, and with that done, they headed to their car and left the compound grounds, turning north to the dirt road that paralleled the high concrete block walls. The afternoon bled into evening, with the gray clouds making the twilight come early. The lights of some buildings beyond the wall and below their position came into view.

"That's right on the river. How did we not see it?" asked Jackson.

"We saw it, but there is no affiliation between that business and this church. I've checked all their holdings. A marina is not among them."

Jackson gripped the wheel over some kidney-jarring ruts and steered the sedan to the shoulder. "Wonder what else Reverend Wayne left off the list."

"Lots of vehicles for this late in the season," said Rylee.

She took out her binoculars. Below them lay a small inlet, cut from the river, with steep banks. On the concrete pad were several cars and trucks and beyond was a metal commercial garage or small warehouse that was likely the marina. Stacks of blue-and-green plastic crates, used to ship live shellfish, lined the docks before a crane. Below the jetty, bobbing in the water, three brightly colored lobster boats were tied.

"What do you see?"

"Looks like a quay with commercial fishing vessels, wharf, lobster traps and crates to ship seafood." She lowered the binoculars. "We need a drone."

"We need a warrant." Jackson put the vehicle in reverse and glanced in the rearview mirror. The curse slipped past her lips. "We've got company."

Chapter 18

"How many?" asked Rylee as she pivoted in her seat. Behind her, she was blinded by the flashing, bouncing headlights.

"Too many!" said Jackson.

"Can't go back."

"What do you think they want?"

The answer came a moment later, when their rear windshield exploded. Rylee screamed as glass fell all about them, pelting the backs of their seats and flying between them, reaching the cup holders and console.

Jackson did not wait, but stepped on the accelerator, sending them jolting forward down the rough unpaved road to the quay. Their pursuers followed. The distinctive sound of bullets pinging off the rear fender sent Rylee ducking behind her headrest.

"Faster," she yelled. Now more in control of herself, she had drawn her service weapon and removed her safety belt. Pivoting until she faced backward and stared out the shattered rear window at the trucks. The flash of headlights was enough for her to identify four pickups, much newer than the old battered models she had seen within the compound.

These might be from the order or someone else altogether.

A flash of gunfire told her which pickup truck was currently shooting at them. She returned fire and was gratified to see the trucks swerve off the twin ruts of a road and bounce into the wooded area to their right. The crash of metal colliding with the trunk of a tree made her flinch.

The rest came on like wolves pursuing the fleeing deer.

"Both dead ends," said Jackson.

Rylee glanced ahead and saw that Jackson had to either veer to the left toward the concrete pad on which sat a commercial metal storage building or to the right and the opposite side of the canal, where the crane, traps and seafood shipping containers sat on a concrete slab above the three fishing boats moored to the jetty. Between the two and beyond both lay the black water of the channel.

"We can't go back," said Rylee. "We're outnumbered and outgunned."

"Right or left?" asked Jackson.

Both bad choices.

"Left," said Rylee, choosing the metal building and the possibility of better cover.

Jackson turned the wheel, committing them to the side that held the commercial garage. As they approached, Rylee saw that the storage facility backed up to the canal on one side and the channel on the other. The building before them was a two-story structure made of sheet metal. On the front sat two bay doors, each large enough to drive a tractor trailer through, but both bay doors were closed. There were no windows that she could see, except in the side door that flanked the structure. Beside the building sat some sort of scaffolding.

"Aim for a garage door?" asked Jackson.

"Likely locked. Left side?"

"It's too close to the river. We might go off into the water."

"We need cover," said Rylee.

"Going through the garage door?"

There was no way to tell if there's a vehicle parked just beyond that door.

"Side door. Right side."

Jackson's elbows extended as she braced. Rylee could not see why but hugged the back of her seat as the car jolted, scraping the undercarriage. Rylee was thrown against her seat and then into the dashboard behind her. When she regained her position, it was to see the pickup trucks fanning out, surrounding them. The smooth ride marked their arrival on a concrete slab that held parking, the metal building and a scaffolding, she now saw, that held six boats at dry dock, parked one above the other and three across.

"Brace yourself," called Jackson. Rylee had time to pivot in her seat as Jackson swerved, sending them careening in a half circle. Rylee lifted her gun arm, still gripping her pistol as she was tossed against her door. The impact jolted her service weapon from her hand.

They now faced their attackers. Jackson's repositioning would allow their car doors to provide them with some cover as they escaped toward the garage's side door.

Where was her gun?

A glance at Jackson showed blood oozed from her nose, running down her chin and disappearing into the navy blue wool of her coat's lapel.

"We have to get inside."

Jackson and Rylee threw open their doors simultaneously. Bullets ricocheted off the grill as Rylee ducked, her hand going to the floor mat. She flinched as her palm landed on something hard. Shifting, she recovered her pistol. Then Rylee exited through the door toward the back of the vehicle.

Jackson was already at the side door and using the butt of her pistol to smash the window glass. Dangerous, Rylee thought until she saw Jackson slip the safety back off.

Rylee reached her as she stretched her arm through the gap and released the door lock from the inside.

The two women slipped inside. Behind them, machine gun fire erupted, closer now, the bullets shrieking through the metal walls all about them.

"I can't see a thing," said Jackson.

Rylee returned her pistol to her hip holster and retrieved her cell phone, gratified to discover that it worked after the jolting exit.

She swiped on the flashlight app and the beam of light swept their surroundings, disappearing into the cavernous space. The shipping containers beside them were neatly stacked and now she realized they were not shipping containers, but the modern version of the clay pots once used to catch lobsters. The more efficient models were each spray-painted with the owner's number. They rose from the floor to the ceiling.

"They're coming!" Jackson pointed toward the bouncing beam of headlights darting through the open side door.

"We need backup."

"Could we take cover under the dock?" asked Jackson as they backed, shoulder to shoulder, farther into the garage.

"There *is* no dock. It's concrete and the seawall. Only way out of here is across the canal or back the way we came."

"Trapped."

That was it. A succinct one-word summary of their situation.

They were pinned and needed to survive long enough for backup to arrive.

Rylee used her phone to send a text with their situation. Then she hit her contacts list, using the mapping app that would send her location with her message. Finally, she added the names to the group text. First, *Catherine Ohr* and *Sarah LeMaitre* from Border Patrol. She swallowed back her doubt before adding the last name, selecting *County Sheriff Axel Trace*. She held her breath and pressed Send.

"This way," said Rylee.

Jackson hesitated. "If they come through the side door, they'll come through one at a time and we'll have a clear shot."

But their pursuers didn't choose the opening through which they had entered. The sound of their bullet punching through the metal garage door before them and the sound of men shouting confirmed that. Rylee's decision to move became more urgent.

"They're destroying the garage lock," said Jackson.

"That's Wayne Faith," said Rylee. "I'm certain."

Rylee led them with her phone through the cavernous structure, past two boats in dry dock stacked one above the other on metal scaffolding. Beside them sat empty racks and a winch. Construction equipment, including a Bobcat and a backhoe, completed the vehicles. They'd never get out of here in either one, Rylee knew.

At the front corner, beside the door, Rylee noticed a framed office with large glass windows reflecting her light back at them.

"That's just where I'd look for us." Jackson paused, searching their surroundings. "What about those stacked boats?"

"You want to hide in one of those wooden bottomed boats?" asked Rylee. It was the kind of choice that left no option.

"It's cover. Hard to reach. A tower, easier to defend."

"Depends on how much ammo we have. And how much time we have to hold them," said Rylee.

"You walked right by those boats. They might as well. And it would put us behind them. We might be able to slip past them and to their vehicle."

"We can't slip out of those boats," said Rylee. "The bottom one is ten feet off the ground. The scaffold is metal. We won't be quiet on descent and they have semi-automatic weapons."

"Your alternative?" asked Jackson.

She had none, except the mission. "We need to find the suspect. It's the only proof that this congregation is involved."

"Shooting at us should be proof enough," said Jackson.

"Let's go out the back." Before them were two more large garage doors and a small door to the right.

Jackson glanced toward the rear exit. "No cover. Nothing out there but the seawall and water. Plus, any men that may have come around to block that way out."

"It's dark outside. We might get past them or get out before they block us in."

Jackson gave her a dubious look, but nodded.

Behind them, the front garage door inched upward.

At the back door, Rylee flicked her phone to mute as a reply came in from her supervisor. Then she tucked away her mobile. Jackson called to her in a whisper.

"Help coming?" she asked.

Rylee nodded.

"Look." Jackson pointed to the narrow window flanking the back entrance. "At the boats."

Two of the trucks had peeled off and their occupants were now disembarking from their vehicles. They headed under the floodlight and straight for the boat with the red hull.

"They must have seen us come in here," said Jackson.

Rylee nodded. "So what are they after over there?"

She knew the answer before she saw two men haul the small dark-haired figure from the wheelhouse of the boat.

Their suspect was getting away.

Behind them came the sound of their pursuers, now inside the garage.

For the past ninety minutes, Axel had tried and failed to reach Rylee. He had stopped at her motel, called and left messages. With each passing minute, he grew more certain that she was at the compound. He was on his way there when his mobile phone chimed, alerting him to an incoming text message.

He stared at the glowing screen and the message from Rylee. 10-33 Shooting.

He had his SUV turned in the direction of the address listed, an address he did not know. That troubled him. GPS in his sheriff's unit showed a small private quay on the river road near the Congregation of Eternal Wisdom. Axel started to sweat as he depressed the accelerator, exceeding the speed limit on the winding road.

A 10-33 was a call for immediate help.

When he spoke, it was to the empty car's interior. "If anything happens to her, I'll…" *Be lost*, he thought.

Because he loved her.

Why did it take this, gunfire and the possibility of losing her forever, for him to realize that keeping her safe was more important that keeping his secrets?

Axel made one phone call en route. One to his trusted friend Kurt Rogers.

"She called you?" asked Rogers.

"Text. They are pinned down at the wharf."

"What wharf?"

Axel gave him the location.

"Rylee says there are a three lobster boats moored beyond the congregation walls on the river."

"Theirs?"

"She says so."

"What's your plan?"

"I'm going in and getting them out," said Axel.

"Sounds good."

"Call Sorrel Vasta. Ask for boats. I don't want them getting the DHS suspect over to the Canada side of the river."

"I'll ask," said Rogers, his voice relaying his uncertainty.

Axel knew that the cult was unpopular among the Kowa people because of Reverend Wayne's attempts to recruit from among members of their tribe, and the Mohawk people had resources Rogers just did not have. Specifically, they had watercrafts, all sorts, from fishing vessels to tour boats.

"I'm on my way out there now. See you in a few," said Rogers and disconnected.

Axel's car radio crackled to life. Border Patrol was requesting assistance for DHS officer Hockings and Jackson and reporting they were thirty minutes out.

"ETA in five," he replied. He was driving too fast to text Rylee back. He'd just have to tell her when he saw her.

If you see her.

Gunfire. Rylee pinned at a marina he never even knew existed during all that time inside those walls. Why had no one ever mentioned a wharf and lobstering operation?

The answer seemed obvious. No one wanted them to know. He knew from the meals he'd had as a child that shellfish, usually crab, was often on the menu. What he hadn't known was what else his father had carried across the St. Lawrence in their little private fleet.

He turned off his lights before reaching the compound. There was no road between Rylee's location on the GPS and the road where he sat. He crept along the narrow country road, approaching the north-side wall of the compound, scanning the weeds to his right, and then he saw it: the obvious tracks of many vehicles and the crushed and broken grass on either side of a rutted road.

He lifted his radio and reported the location of the road. Then he released his rear door. He took only the time it required to toss out a traffic cone and light a flare. Then he was back in his SUV and rattling along the frozen ruts of the road. Temperatures were forecast to dip to the twenties tonight, frost warning in effect. It was a bad time to be in or near the water.

The glow from below the hill alerted him that he was nearing his destination. His heartbeat pounded with his racing blood and his jaw ached from clenching his teeth. He flicked off his headlights and crested the hill.

The beams from the halogen lights mounted on the roofs of the pickups below illuminated the area, making the wharf resemble a Friday night football field. He saw men on the wharf and jetty, all armed with rifles.

A second truck barreled over the hill behind him and he turned to see the familiar turquoise truck of Kurt Rogers. He stood in the headlight's beam and waved. Rogers was beside him in a moment and out of his vehicle, moving well for a man well past sixty.

"Situation?" asked Rogers, settling beside him with his rifle at the ready.

"Unknown," said Axel. He drew out his field glasses and peered at the wharf.

"Who are they?" asked Rogers.

"Don't you recognize that truck?" asked Axel.

Rogers scanned the wharf using the scope on his rifle.

"Looks like Hal Mondello brought his entire crew. Some on the jetty. Some surrounding that building."

The head of the moonshiners was not visible, but Axel knew his truck on sight.

"All this time I thought it was the North Country Riders," said Axel.

"Makes sense. Fishing vessels would make transport of liquor so much easier. Just meet up with another boat out there and load the crates from one to another," said Rogers, as he continued to scan the area using his scope. "Where's your gal?"

He wished she was his. "Likely inside the garage."

"You best get down there, then," said Rogers, still watching the men through his scope. "You got your gun?"

"Of course."

"You aim to use it?" Rogers gave him a hard look.

"If I have to." But he wondered if it were possible. To again use a gun and kill another man. To save Rylee? He hoped he wouldn't.

"Well, now," said Rogers. "Looks like they are transporting more than booze."

Trace followed the direction of Rogers's attention.

"Look on the jetty beside the yellow boat," said his friend.

On the jetty, two men wrestled a small figure from one of the boats.

"That a woman?" asked Rogers.

The figure was diminutive, dressed in black and fighting for all she was worth against the man holding her.

"The one everyone has been looking for."

"I thought the suspect was a Chinese man," said Rogers.

"Can't be a coincidence."

"They have two choices now. Back the way they came or take the boats." Rogers scanned the scene below.

Mondello's men were all scrambling into one boat.

"Looks like they made their choice," said Axel.

"You gonna let them leave?"

"Absolutely. I'm here for Rylee."

"They're taking that gal," said Rogers, indicating the struggling woman. Two men lifted her between them so that her feet never touched the ground as they hustled her along.

"I'm going down there and finding Rylee."

Axel left the trucks and his old friend, using the darkness to move closer through the underbrush that flanked the road.

Below, the men's captive broke free and ran up the jetty. One man lifted his pistol and shot her in the back. The woman's arms flew up. She staggered, her center of gravity now rolling forward, too far before her legs.

Axel ran through the brush as Rogers swore and started shooting. His friend's aim was good, taking down the man who had shot the woman in the back.

The second man now swept his rifle wildly, moving to find the position of the unknown shooter. He ignored the woman crawling on the jetty, running for cover as Rogers's second shot missed the man who leaped from the quay to the yellow-bottomed boat.

The men on the quay now had Rogers's position and returned fire as Axel moved quickly down the hill. Rylee's text had come from inside the garage, so that was his destination.

Behind him came the wail of sirens. Their approaching cacophony drowned out the shouts of the men below. Border Patrol had made good time.

The men below fired on Rogers, who had moved behind his truck. Their bullets punctured the front grate.

The men by the trucks now moved en masse toward the boats on the opposite side of the canal from the marina. Hal Mondello, past the age of running, paused by the woman, who had made it to her hands and knees. With a mighty shove from his boot, Mondello kicked the woman from the lip of the jetty and into the icy water of the canal.

A door banged open and he saw a familiar flash of blond hair as Rylee ran from the cover of the garage and across the open ground on the opposite side of the jetty. The men, now on the boats, lifted their rifles.

"No, no, no," he chanted as he raced toward the canal. Above, Rogers's shots sent the men ducking for cover.

"What's she doing?" he muttered.

But he knew. Even before she jumped from the jetty, he knew.

Chapter 19

Rylee had left Jackson behind her as she'd dashed out into the cold autumn wind. Jackson could not swim and their suspect, the key to the entire case, had been kicked into the water.

How deep was the water? How cold?

Feet first entry, she'd decided. To be on the safe side. Nothing worse than breaking your neck on a shallow bottom or a piling hidden beneath the inky surface. She saw them, the men scrambling into the boats, as she'd leaped out in one giant stride to nowhere. She'd recognized one of them.

Hal Mondello had stared back at her with a surprised expression as she'd sailed out over the canal. She'd looked from him to the black water before it swallowed her up.

A thousand needles of ice pierced her skin as she

struggled with her sodden clothing and waterlogged boots to reach the surface. River water burned her eyes as she realized that this was not like swimming in a lake in July. This water was deadly.

The steel-toed boots and sodden clothing dragged her straight to the bottom. Panic shuddered over her as she fought the urge to gasp against the cold, knowing that one breath of water would be her last. She tipped her head to look back at the surface and saw only deep threatening darkness. The black of a watery tomb. The razor-sharp terror clawed at her, but she forced herself to crouch on the spongy bottom and release her boots. She could not quite feel the laces, double knotted, because of the numbness of her fingers. But one boot came loose and then the next. But now her lungs burned with the need for air.

Rylee tried to release the zipper of her coat, but failing that, she dragged the entire thing over her head and away. The efforts took her sweater with it. Planting her feet, she prepared to push off the bottom when something brushed her cheek.

The blurry image of a woman's face sank before her, the outstretched, lifeless hand gliding over Rylee's chest. Rylee caught the scream of horror in her throat, keeping the precious, nearly exhausted oxygen in her aching lungs. It was her target, the person of interest. Was she dead?

And would Rylee follow her?

She grasped the woman's collar in one fist, locking her fingers around the fabric like the talons of an eagle. She exploded off the bottom with everything she had, kicking toward the surface she could not see. Now she felt the current, dragging her along and out, she realized, to the river.

Sound returned before the light. Gunfire and shouting. The knocking of the vessels against the floats beside the seawall. She couldn't feel her feet or the woman she thought she held. Had she let go?

No time now. Just air, everything centered around that next breath. Now the blackness was punctuated with sparks of light. The surface approaching or her brain preparing to shut down?

She squeezed her eyes shut and kept kicking, willing herself to break the surface, to live, to see Axel Trace again so she could tell him what she should have said the morning he told her about Reverend Wayne. That Wayne wasn't his father and that she was sorry his childhood was so terrible that he felt he needed to hide where he came from. She should have let him know that she didn't care and that she forgave him for the lie because she loved him.

The water gave way to the night and Rylee gasped, inhaling a full breath of sweet cold air. She forgot to kick and just as quickly sank once more. This time she kept kicking, getting her face above and dragging the body of her target with her, struggling until the woman's face broke the surface. Water streamed from the woman's mouth, and she jerked and spasmed as Rylee continued to kick, just managing to keep them both above the surface in the current's pull.

Greedy. That's what the river was. The water making her choose. Take them both to the bottom or just Rylee's prize. A glance to the quay showed they were sweeping out from the mouth of the canal and into the river.

One of the boats left the channel with her, powered

by diesel and heading right for them. Rylee realized they meant to run her down. She imagined the propellers cutting into her flesh, shredding her muscle to hamburger.

Rylee stopped kicking and let the river take her again.

Axel reached the seawall. The gunfire exchange now slowing as those on the vessel redirected their weapons to the river, searching for the woman who had been kicked into it and the one who had jumped in after her.

How cold was that water?

Deadly cold, he knew.

He could not see Rylee, but it was obvious that they could from the shots they unloaded into the river. Each discharge seemed to tear into him.

Mondello's men were aboard the first vessel, now leaving its moorings, and the men from the congregation now drove back the way they had come, back to the compound, where there would be no escape from federal authorities.

A terrible thought struck him. They had an escape. The Rising. If Father Wayne told his followers that this was the night, how many would end their lives in the way they had so long rehearsed? Go to their bed, take the pills, wait for God to bring them to Heaven.

And remove any and all witnesses.

Terror lifted every hair on his body as he pictured them, and him in the years gone-by, dressing in their white robes, swallowing the placebo and lying on the cots in neat rows, like so much cordwood. The tranquilizers taking them quickly to unconsciousness but this time there would be no waking unless they really did wake at Heaven's Door.

Suicide was against God's will. He had learned this

only after leaving—the murdering of one's self was prohibited in the Bible.

Where was Rylee? The lobster boat moved out to deeper water, the men aboard staring back at him and the vehicles from Border Patrol, no longer seeing any of them as a threat. The distraction was why Axel did not see the fast-moving speedboats approaching behind them.

Axel recognized them instantly. The Kowa tribe used these vessels to give tourists exhilarating high-speed rides on the river and perhaps for the occasional tobacco run to Canada. Before the fishing boat was fully underway, it was surrounded by the Mohawk Nation. Gunfire exploded again, and grappling hooks glinted in the air. Axel turned his attention to the water.

A face broke the surface. Rylee, he realized, holding the other woman by the collar of her shirt. Rylee sputtered and struggled to keep her mouth and nose above the surface as she was swept from the boats and downriver. He ran along the seawall, following her course. In a moment, she'd be right in front of him and then, he feared, gone forever.

Chapter 20

Rylee saw the orange ring buoy sailing through the air, over her head and past her. But the rope fell across her shoulder. She tried to grab at it, but her arms were so heavy with her sodden shirt and the cold. Her fingers would not respond to her command to clasp. So she hooked her elbow over the rope and held on. She felt the friction as the rope pulled through her jointed elbow, the pain a relief from the numbing death that stalked her. Someone was trying to save her.

After what seemed hours, the ring struck her. She fumbled to get her arm around the ring but it only dunked and bobbed away. She tried again and the ring upended and then shot farther away. Fear enlivened her efforts. If she didn't get ahold of the ring, she'd die. But to grasp the ring, she needed to release her captive.

Was the woman already dead? The hungry, desperate

voice in her head told her to let go and that only made her grip the more determinedly against the impulse. She would not let go. Like one of those snakes she had heard of that locked their fangs and would not release even if their head were severed from their body. Rylee held on and watched the ring being tugged away.

She pivoted back toward the receding seawall. Someone was there, gathering the rope, preparing for another throw. But this time, the ring buoy fell short.

On shore, the man tied the rope around his waist. A spotlight illuminated him. It was Axel, stripping out of his jacket and holster. Tearing off his boots and flinging aside his hat. What was he doing?

The answer came a moment later when she saw him back up and then run on bare feet down the concrete pad and dive far out over the water.

Shouting reached her, cutting in and out as she bobbed beneath the surface and then kicked on weary legs back to snatch a shallow breath. The shivering had stopped. Was that good or bad?

A bright light blinded her. A spotlight. If it was the lobster boat, she was dead. Should she let them shoot her or sink once more?

Rylee's kicks grew weaker and she feared that if she sank this time, it would be her last.

Axel swam out to Rylee through the freezing water. He could not see her, but he could see the spotlight from one of the boats from the Kowa Nation. He used it like a homing beam, swimming hard and lifting his head only to mark his progress. Behind him, the ring buoy dragged, made noticeable by the slight tug at his waist as he pulled himself along.

He'd learned to swim in the army. A sinker, his drill sergeant had said—too much muscle and little fat. If he stopped kicking, he sank like a stone. But the only way he'd stop was when he and Rylee were safely back on shore. The light danced just before him, so close he could see the entire circle, but he did not see Rylee.

He grabbed a breath of air and dove. Beneath the surface, the light caught the pale glow of her blond hair and skin, now blue in the artificial light.

Rylee reached out her free hand to him as she sank and he grasped her wrist. Reversing course now, he kicked to the surface, breaking first and gasping in the dazzling white light. He dragged her against him with one hand, pressing his chest to hers, keeping her and the second woman before him as he dragged the rope, hand over hand, behind them. The ring buoy hauled closer and closer until he had it behind Rylee. Beside her, the other woman choked on river water and sputtered. Both women had lips the color of raw liver and the shock of that sight was enough to get him swimming.

Shouts reached him. He turned to see Sorrel Vasta waving and motioning him toward the boat. Axel could not even see the shore past the bright light, but he trusted Sorrel and changed course again.

The motor of the boat engine hummed in his ears and then cut abruptly. A second buoy slapped the water beside him and he looped one elbow through the ring. An instant later, he and his charges were gliding along the choppy water toward the stern.

They reached the ladder. Both women were tugged from his arms by many hands. The light flicked off as Axel tried to climb aboard. His hands were stiff with the cold and gripping was difficult. He crooked his wrists and used them, as he might if wearing mittens, to scale the ladder and reach the stern platform. There he sprawled. Heaving and spent.

Vasta kneeled over him, throwing a blanket across his shivering body.

"Axel? We're heading to Kinsley Marina. Ambulance is waiting to take you all to the ER," said Vasta.

Axel nodded. "R-Rylee?"

"She's breathing. The other stopped. We're working on her. Resuscitation. You sit tight."

The engine roared and the boat tipped, cutting through the water like a blade.

"The other b-bo..." His tongue wasn't working, and the shivering was getting worse. That made no sense. He was out of the water and wrapped up tight.

"We stopped Wayne's men before they got inside the walls of their compound. Father Wayne and eight of his men. Trussed up like grouse. My other boat is taking them in to the Border Patrol guys. Ha! Wait until they see what we brought them. They gonna have to cut us some slack. Maybe have to say thank-you. That might about kill them."

"Rye-lee," he whispered.

"We're taking care of your woman, brother. You just sit tight."

A shout and cheer came from behind him.

Vasta grinned. "We got the other lady breathing again."

Rylee woke up to the sound of a vacuum cleaner and found that she lay between two air mattresses. Beside her, a freckle-faced red-headed woman, dressed in violet scrubs, checked a machine that blipped and pinged beside the hospital bed.

She noticed her patient was conscious and smiled at Rylee. "You waking up? Good deal. I'll tell your people. They've been in and out of here, checking on you."

"Where am I?"

"Kinsley General Hospital. I'm Tami, your nurse. You're in our ICU. You came in here about the temperature of an ice pop, but we warmed you right up."

"The woman…"

"The one who came in with you?" Tami grimaced. "She's here, too. Bullet wound and the cold. She has frostbite on both feet. Friend of yours?"

"Not really."

"Good, because they have state police standing right at her cubicle. Whatever she did must be bad. We only get that handling when we treat prisoners from Franklin or Upstate Correctional. What'd she do?"

"Not at liberty—"

"To say." Tami rolled her eyes. "Already heard that one. You with Border Patrol?" she asked.

Rylee shook her head. "Department of Homeland Security."

"Well, I'm eaten up with curiosity. You had a near miss."

Rylee lifted the clear covering on top of her that was swollen with air.

"That's a warming blanket. Got one below you, too. Still trying to bring your core temperature up to normal." She tapped away at her tablet and then smiled at Rylee. "Nothing to eat or drink for you just yet. But soon. Your family has been notified."

"My family?"

She tapped on her tablet. "Father, Colonel Hockings." She paused there to make a face that showed the title impressed. "In... Guam. Army?" she asked.

Rylee flinched. "Marines."

Tami smiled as if it were all the same to her.

"Where is Axel?"

"The sheriff? Next door." Rylee didn't like the smile on Tami's face as Tami glanced in the direction of the hall. "On my way to check his vitals next, which I would do for free. But when I'm done, who will check mine?" She laughed. Then she pointed at the button clipped to Rylee's bed rails. "Press the button if you need anything."

Rylee waited until the nurse left to pull down the air blanket. Immediately, she began to shake and shiver again. She had so many questions to ask and patience was not her strong suit. But she adjusted the blankets and closed her eyes, hoping the blanket did its work quickly. She had not meant to sleep, but when she next opened her eyes, only the light above her bed was on and the blankets both top and bottom continued to reverberate like a vacuum cleaner.

At six o'clock on Sunday morning, Axel checked on Rylee and then checked himself out of the hospital against the doctor's orders. Damned if he'd miss the biggest case this county had ever seen, lying in a hospital bed under an electric blanket. He wasn't leaving without seeing Rylee, though. He discovered from a familiar nurse in purple scrubs that Rylee had been moved to a private room for security. From Tami, he learned that Rylee had been awake part of last night. All her vitals were good, and she would suffer no ill ef-

fects from her dive into the St. Regis. The woman she
rescued had not fared so well. He was informed that
she would likely loose several fingers and both feet to
frostbite. One lung had collapsed from the bullet wound
and she had suffered dangerous blood loss. Whether
that had caused brain damage was still unknown. She
was currently in a medically induced coma to protect
her brain as she healed.

The trooper stationed at Rylee's door checked him
in. They'd been on many traffic fatalities together, so
the ID was unnecessary.

"Do you have any word on what happened at the
compound last night?" he asked.

"None. Been here most of the night," said the trooper.

Axel nodded and left him, pausing when he reached
Rylee's bed, wondering if he could touch her. All the
wires and tubes made him nervous. Even her finger
had a pulse monitor clipped on. He leaned down and
pressed a kiss to her forehead.

"I'm here, Rylee. I'm going to finish this for you."

Her heart rate accelerated and her eyelids fluttered.
He waited, hoping she would open her eyes. But she
did not, and he let himself out.

He was just passing registration when the circus
came to him. The flashing blue-and-red lights of law
enforcement vehicles bounced off the waiting room
walls from the windows overlooking the parking lot. He
reached the main waiting area when the double doors
whooshed open and in marched the federal and state
authorities, moving in formation.

Catherine Ohr led the pack. She was flanked by two
men in dark suits and black woolen overcoats. All that
was missing were fedoras and they could have been ex-

tras in a Bogart and Cagney movie. Behind them, five state police officers stood with sullen expressions and bristly short haircuts, the purple band around their Stetsons matching the purple leg-stripe on their trousers.

"That was a speedy recovery," said Ohr. "They told me you were spending the day." The woman smelled of cigarette smoke.

"Unfortunately, they didn't clear that with me."

"Just coming to see you," said Ohr, pinning him with watery blue bloodshot eyes. Rylee's supervisor had had a long night.

"What a coincidence," said Axel.

"Where's Agent Hockings?" asked Ohr.

"Still in her room, sleeping."

Rylee's boss lifted her thin eyebrows at him, then flashed her shield and ID at the receptionist.

"You have an empty room?"

They were led to a small exam room. Ohr left the troopers milling in the hall. She and her two agents now stood between him and the exit, and for a moment, he thought they were here to arrest him.

"What happened after I went in the river?"

"Quite a lot. The Kowa Nation captured the Mondellos, who were attempting to flee custody in a lobster boat. The Kowa had several boats. The fastest brought you, Hockings and the suspect to Kinsley for treatment."

He remembered that. Speaking to Vasta and wondering if the suspect had died.

Ohr continued her summary. "Border Patrol got the men fleeing the wharf before they reached their compound. My people raided the compound, but Wayne and his council were not among them."

"They got away?"

"He did not. But he tried. Wayne and his people were in a small motorboat on the river trying to flee the country."

"You caught them."

"The Kowa caught them. Initially with Border Patrol." Her smile was broad. "Wayne is in federal custody along with his council, five men who were with him. Two others suffered gunshot wounds and are here in the hospital. My people are interviewing the men and women from the Kowa tribe. Your retired sheriff is helping with a team at the Mondello property. We have all the Mondellos in custody except the eldest of his sons, Quinton. Still searching for that one. Just about finished up there. We still need a formal interview from Rogers. He seems to know everyone in the county."

"Did you get to the compound? Did you stop them from taking the suicide pills?"

"We did. Thanks to you. You told Acting Chief Vasta before they took you to the hospital. They got the word to us."

He vaguely remembered that.

"Seems your father was going to clean house by ridding himself of anyone in the congregation who might have known what he had been up to."

Axel felt sick to his stomach to be associated in any way with that man. To have him as his father was crushing.

"You saved a lot of lives, Sheriff."

Most important of which was Rylee's. Had he saved his mother? The empty place in his insides ached. Maybe now he'd learn who she was.

"Is there anything else, Sheriff? I need to check on

the condition of the woman Rylee dove in to save from the river," Ohr said.

"I've had an update." Axel relayed what he knew about her condition. "I do have one more question. How did Rylee know about the wharf?"

He'd lived inside that compound and didn't know about it.

"According to Agent Jackson, one of the women in the compound suggested they check there for the suspect."

He frowned. It was unlike any of the members to act in a way that would threaten the group.

"Who?"

Ohr referred to her notes again and read. "Sister Della Hartfield."

Della was an elder. Why would she help DHS agents?

"We'll be taking the suspect into federal custody as soon as the paperwork is signed." She motioned to the two agents beside her, who then swept from the room and vanished from his line of sight.

The troopers trailed after them, presumably toward the ICU and their suspect. Axel suspected the doctors and nurses of Kinsley General would put up a fight, but they'd lose.

"Is she the person who carried the duffel?" he asked.

"Yes. Father Wayne confirmed it. He was hiding her at his compound. Waiting, I assume, for the right time to move her. She's the one we wanted. Good work apprehending her."

"I didn't apprehend her. Rylee did that."

Ohr smiled and inclined her chin. "Group effort, then. Retired Sheriff Rogers says that you called him and he called the leaders of the Kowa people."

"That's correct."

"But not Border Patrol. Why is that?"

Axel thought of Rylee's text and his panic at knowing she was in trouble.

"Rylee's text alerted them and you. I called the men and women who I could trust."

"Which included a tribe of Kowa Mohawk and your retired mentor. Not the state police or federal authorities."

"Both too far away to help."

"I should have you fired."

"I'm an elected official."

"Yes. Inconvenient. Likely your county will throw you a parade."

"Probably a pancake breakfast, but I can hope for a spaghetti dinner."

Ohr made a sound in her throat. Then she cleared it and gave him a hard look. "Wayne Faith is your father?"

"So he tells me."

"He's going to prison. Initial overview shows he has offshore holdings and has been playing fast and loose with the congregation's funds for years. In addition to that, as you feared, he called for the followers who remained behind to take some sort of suicide pill."

"But you saved them?"

"Most."

"How many dead?"

"Four. All children. Given the pills before we could reach them."

Axel felt sick.

He turned his back on her and used a paper cup from the dispenser to get some water. The tap water was warm, but it pushed down the bile.

"Additionally, two of Mondello's men were wounded by Rogers. Two Kowas were shot by Mondello's men. No fatalities from the gun battle."

"Who were the wounded?" he asked.

She read the names from a small notebook. He knew each man.

All this, to protect one woman, keep her hidden with his secrets. His father had gone from being a zealot and flimflam man to a federal criminal.

"What will happen to Father Wayne?"

"Espionage charge. It's a capital crime."

Why did he care what they did to him? Was it because he was blood? Blood that had shamed him all his adult life.

"That's why I'm here. Since your father isn't talking."

"Don't call him that."

"Fine. Since Wayne Trace, AKA Father Wayne Faith, isn't cooperating, I need some insight on the congregation. Help sorting and getting those we detained to speak to us."

"He's not even there and he's still controlling them."

"Yes. It's disturbing. He's waiting for an attorney and hoping for some sort of deal."

"Will he get one?" asked Axel, the sour taste in his mouth and pitching stomach now taking much of his attention. Four dead children. He shook his head.

"Not if I have anything to do with it. You all right? You look pale."

He took a few deep breaths, unsure if his condition was physical or a result of being heartsick.

"I'm not all right, but I am willing to help in any way."

She nodded her approval of this.

"We have several members of Hal Mondello's family in custody and are rounding up more of his people. Seems they had some sort of alliance with Wayne Trace. Mondello distributed what Trace smuggled in from Canada, which we, unfortunately, were unable to recover. It's unclear if they knew what they were transporting."

"The duffel Rylee recovered from the Kowa people?"

"That was the second shipment. The first got through. We thought this was the work of Chinese nationals. But that woman you dragged from the river is North Korean. A chemist. We believe Siming's Army was trying to point blame at China, in hopes of increasing tension between nations. That would serve the North Koreans. North Korea would benefit greatly if we lifted sanctions on them while continuing them on China, and even more so if we challenged Chinese control of that region."

"Did you say a chemist?"

"Yes. Possibly here to culture the virus within our borders."

"Culture it where?"

"That's the top question on our list. Most especially if there is a plant currently in operation of this deadly strain of flu as we speak."

That thought chilled.

"But you've stopped them?"

"I'm afraid they don't need the chemist to reproduce what she carried."

"Biohazard?"

"It's a pathogen, Axel. Called a virus seed stock because they use it to propagate more of the virus. Some of it is here. This disease is a powerful killer, the likes of which we haven't seen since the Middle Ages. If it gets loose, we will suffer the worst pandemic ever faced in America."

"A plague?"

"Of sorts. But much, much faster. My experts liken it to the influenza epidemic of 1918."

"But we have the vaccine?"

"Which takes time to produce. In the meantime, we need to find virus seed stock and kill it before Siming's Army can turn that seed sample into an epidemic."

She reached in her pocket, removed a pack of cigarettes and then dropped it back in place. Axel was certain she longed for a smoke. Who could blame her?

"Now, if you would come with me, you can get me up to speed on this cult on the way."

Chapter 21

Axel had been back within the compound all day speaking to members of the cult individually, with Catherine Ohr there for each interview. The ashtray before her smoldered with the last stubbed-out cigarette.

"Only a few more," she said. "Let's take a break."

They walked out together into the grassy quad. DHS had set up a mobile operations station complete with multiple trailers within the compound's central courtyard. They had even erected a mess hall between the church and living quarters. Generators hummed, powering the mobile light towers that illuminated their way. The entire area now had a distinctly military feel.

Male members of the congregation were being held in the worship hall and the female members were detained in the congregation's dining hall.

As they continued past yet another trailer, Ohr reached for another cigarette and glanced at her phone.

"Seven p.m.," she muttered. "I need coffee." She pointed at him. "Want one?"

"Sure."

"They have pastries and coffee in the mess tent. I'll bring you something."

She strode off toward her people, who moved in and out of the buildings, carrying off computers and other bagged evidence.

Agent Rylee Hockings stepped from the sanctuary beside the main worship hall, where he had just been.

"You're here!" he said, sweeping over her and finding her pale and circles under her eyes.

"For several hours now. I've been interviewing the female members of the cult."

They clasped hands and he smiled at her, his heart dancing a percussive rhythm of joy at the sight of her.

"Rylee, you gave me such a scare." He had so much to tell her, to say. He wanted to rush forward and tell her that he loved her and that he wanted her in his life. Then he saw two of his father's men marched past them in handcuffs. The shame of his association with this congregation broke inside him like a drinking glass dropped on ceramic tile. Millions of shards of doubt splintered out in all directions.

"I need to thank you for coming after me. I was losing to the river," she said and gave his hands a squeeze before letting go. Her smile held. "But we got her. Thanks to you. Who knows what we'll learn."

"Ohr told me she's a North Korean national."

"What? Really?"

"She also told me that Sister Della was the one who directed you to the wharf."

"That's true." Rylee was glancing about as if searching for someone. Her supervisor?

"That surprises me," he said. "It seems hard to believe that a congregation elder would do something that jeopardized the group. Any idea why she would do that?"

"Just a theory. I haven't spoken to her yet."

"What's your theory?" he asked.

"I think she did it to help you."

"Me? Why would she want to help me?"

"Ah... I need to find my supervisor."

And just like that, his opportunity fled. Rylee was back on her mission. It would be easier to stop a runaway toboggan than to prevent her from moving forward with her investigation.

There will be other opportunities, he told himself. Better ones, ones when he rehearsed what to say. No woman wanted to be proposed to in a time and place like this.

He could imagine her telling their kids. *Yes, your mother was just out of the hospital after nearly drowning and on her way to interview human trafficking suspects when I proposed.*

He shook his head, dismayed at the ease with which he produced a mental picture of them together with children. What if he waited and there was no other chance?

"Rylee, I need to tell you something."

She was glancing about them now. No longer looking at him, searching, he thought, for her supervisor among the men and women moving across the yard.

"Take a walk with me?" he asked.

"All right. But I have to get back."

"Just a few minutes."

She fell into step beside him away from the aroma of roasting coffee issued from the mess tent. They walked along the worship hall and sat together on a bench that now faced the back of one of the newly placed mobile operation trailers. At least this spot was not directly under one of the many mobile light towers.

He looked toward the empty women's quarters. Already the conversation had veered off track. Rylee was asking about the living situations for the females in the congregation.

"Yes," he said, in response to her question. "The men lived in one building and the women and young children in another."

"But Wayne kept some women in a private enclosure for himself," she added.

"He insisted on celibacy among the males. As for the females, they were celibate, too, for the most part."

"Unless he deemed otherwise," she said and scowled. "They said it was only so they could bring him children. As if that were some high honor." She shook her head, her expression angry. "A blessing, they called it. For the men, castration was the highest show of devotion. For women to be *most blessed*, they needed to give birth."

"Yes," said Axel. Could he have been thinking of proposing to her during this? He must have lost his mind.

"And the males went along with this," she said.

"*If* they wanted to stay. Father Wayne can be very convincing. Made sure it was a status symbol for the males to lop off their junk and the women to sleep with him. Told his followers that it made them closer to God. Prepared to meet the Lord without lustful, earthly thoughts. But I…"

"Did he tell you that?" she asked.

Axel nodded, head bowed and the palm of his hand pressed to the back of his own neck.

"When I turned thirteen, my own father told me that he wanted me to mutilate myself on my eighteenth birthday. It's why I ran."

"What happened?"

"Sheriff Rogers picked me up. He went out there and my father denied the entire thing. He claimed I made the whole thing up, but I know whom the sheriff believed. He told my dad that Child Protective Services would be out there to check every child and regularly. But despite all that, we haven't gotten more than a few children out of their hands."

"They got you out."

He dropped his hand. "It's why I stay. To watch over the children, help the ones who run and make certain he never called for them to enter Heaven's Door. I come out here and I never say when. They let me in because I was a member, hoping, I think, that I would change my mind and come back. As if…" He blew away a breath and then continued. "I'd file a notice of indication with Child Protective Services at any sign the caregivers weren't meeting basic needs. Then I got out with CPS to check the kids with them, make sure they were safe."

"He knew you were watching him."

"Yes."

"It's why they were never harmed."

"Maybe," said Axel. "But he liked having me come back here. I think he knew how hard it was for me. How much I hated it here. And he enjoyed that my leaving caused me suffering and that he'd managed to trap me in this place despite my desertion. He used me as an example of how you can walk away but you can never leave. He says I'm tied to them despite what I might say or do."

"You know, I always thought I had it hard, trying to

earn my father's approval. And he could be exacting, difficult, but nothing like yours."

"A fanatic. A con man and now a terrorist. I came from him. What does that make me?" It made him unable to propose to her. That much was certain.

"I can answer that. It makes you the complete opposite. He takes advantage and you protect. He exploits and you defend."

"With him gone, I won't be tied here any longer, Rylee. I can go."

She blinked at him and for a heart-stopping moment, he thought he'd misread her. That what he'd seen as love was just sympathy.

"What about your mother?"

He couldn't even lift his head. "I don't know which one of the women is my mother."

"What do you mean?"

"We were separated at birth. She could not claim me and stay with them."

"There is no *them* anymore. We've been explaining that to the members. They're starting to come to grips with what's happening. Most of them, thankfully, are innocent in all of this. Just misguided."

"What will happen to them?"

"Reconnect with families when possible. We'll process them and release them. Where they go will be up to them."

"Will you help them?"

"If we can." She laid a small hand on his shoulder and he lifted his chin until he met her sympathetic gaze. "Axel? I know who she is."

His heart beat so loud that he thought it might bruise his ribs. "How?"

"She looks just like you. I met her on Saturday, here at the compound. I thought at first that I knew her. It didn't take long to recognize why she looked so familiar. I asked her and she confirmed that she gave birth to you. Would you like to speak to her?"

"Yes!" Axel was on his feet. He leaped at the chance and then thought about confronting a woman who had had many opportunities to reveal who she was—and hadn't. "Maybe you should speak to her first and see if she wants to speak to me."

"All right." She stood and faced him, offering her hand.

"Now?"

Her smile was sympathetic. "Yes, now. They won't be here much longer." She was nearly to the sanctuary's dining hall door when he called her back.

"Rylee? Which one?"

"Della Hartfield."

He blinked and nodded. "Della." It seemed right, somehow. "Do I just wait here?"

"Yes. If she's willing, I'll bring her to you."

Axel raked a hand through his hair and tugged at his shirt, momentarily dragging out the wrinkles.

"You look fine, Axel. Just wait. I'll be right back."

He sat on the bench facing the compound's dining hall as his legs bounced up and down with nervous energy. The next eighteen minutes were the longest of his life. Finally, the door opened and out stepped Della, small and pale, her head still draped in the brown covering she had worn for more than thirty years.

Axel stood. The word tore from him like a cry. "Mom?"

She nodded and swept forward, holding out both

hands to him. He took them in something that was not the embrace he had imagined.

He had pictured this meeting so many times, but he was always a boy and she always held him. Instead, this tiny birdlike woman beamed up at him with a smile that seemed to blend contentment with something like madness.

Della had always appeared to have only one foot on the earth and the other somewhere else entirely, as if her spirit was too light to allow her to ever be completely grounded.

She kept him at arm's length as she stared at him. Why had he never seen the similarities until now? Her color matched his, as did her long nose and blue eyes. He pushed back her head covering, expecting to see his blond hair, but her hair was entirely white.

"I'm so sorry that I never defied him. He told me that God would strike you down if I broke my oath and, God forgive me, I believed him." Fat tears coursed down her wind-burned cheeks. Her hands were raw from working outdoors and her spine bent slightly.

"I'm glad my father is under arrest."

Her eyes went wide with shock. "Father Wayne?"

"Yes. I hate him." Hated that he shared the same blood and that his father's deadly legacy would cast a shadow across his heart forever.

Della clasped one of his hands in both of hers and gave a little shake to draw his attention. Then she looked behind her and, seeing only Rylee, she turned back to him. When she spoke, her voice was hushed as if she still feared the retribution of the man who was gone.

"Father Wayne is not your father," she said.

Every nerve in his body fired. Blood surged past his ears and he blinked in stupefaction at her.

"What?" he whispered.

"He's not your father, not really. He claims all the children, but there were a few that were not his by blood. Claiming them was preferable to exposing our failings."

Failings? Did she mean their failing to remain celibate?

"Those of us not chosen to share his bed, well, some of us wanted children. So…"

"Did he know?"

"In some cases, and suspected in others. But he never admitted it."

Rylee spoke now. "Because to do that would be to admit he did not have complete control of his congregation."

Della turned to her and nodded. "I always thought so."

"He's not my father," said Axel, the words spoken aloud as if to convince himself of what he was still afraid to believe.

"Yes, son."

"You are certain?"

"I never slept with the man and I am your mother. So, yes, I'm sure."

Axel released Della and stumbled back, colliding with a wooden bench. He placed a hand on the seat as he fell and thus managed to avoid hitting the ground. The bench shuddered with the force of his landing.

He stared up at his mother as the icy pain in his heart melted away like frost on a spring thaw.

"Who is he, then?"

Her smile faltered. "Do you remember Jack Pritcher?"

Other than Kurt Rogers, Jack Pritcher had been as close to a father as a man could be. In Axel's mind, the big man came back to life. The father figure merging into a father.

"Jack died when I was ten," he said to Rylee.

"He was our carpenter," Della told Rylee and patted the bench as if this were one of Pritcher's creations. "Came from Schenectady. Wife had died, he was older than I was, but he had a kind heart."

A weak heart, Axel remembered, because it was his heart that failed him.

"He came up here after his wife and child died in a terrible car accident. He was a lost soul. I'm sure he never intended to be a father again, but then you came along."

"He never told me," said Axel.

"Not in words. But in other ways. And you have his build. Very trim and muscular. His hair was quite red as a young man, so he told me. And your beard has red highlights."

Axel rubbed the stubble on his cheek.

"Did you two ever think of leaving?"

"Why, no. I loved my work with the animals. I understand them in a way I never understood people. They are more straightforward and no facial expressions to confuse me. Jack seemed content keeping the buildings in good condition. It gave him a purpose. You know what he did back there in Schenectady?"

Axel shook his head.

"He was a fireman. A protector, just like you."

That made his heart ache all over again.

"Della?" asked Rylee. "Why did you tell me where to find the suspect?"

"Suspect?" Her placid expression changed to one of confusion. "I didn't."

"You told us about the wharf," Rylee said, reminding her.

"Yes." Her peaceful smile returned.

"Why?"

Della gave a chuckle as if the question were silly. "Well, because your friend asked me, child. 'Are there any other buildings on the compound?' Those were her exact words. I merely answered her question."

"Because she asked you?" asked Rylee.

Della nodded, seemingly pleased that Rylee now understood.

"What will you do now, Della?" he asked.

"Well, that's a good question. I'm not sure if my older brother is still with us. Perhaps I'll start there. He used to live in Altamont. I remember his address. Also, I've been considering becoming a nun." She swept the veil back up over her hair, wrapping it expertly to cover her head.

Right back into a structured religious community, Axel realized.

"You don't have to, Della. I can take care of you," said Axel.

"Now you sound like my brother. And I don't need taking care of just yet. And though you were always the sweetest boy," she said, "and I'm proud to be your mother, I never really knew how to be one, or a wife. I'm not sure how to explain it, except that I loved Jack, in my way, but I was not in love with him. I don't connect to people in that way. I'm afraid he stayed, hoping I'd change my mind."

Had his father died of a broken heart? Twice broken,

he realized. First, at the loss of his wife and child and then, by Della's rejection.

"And he stayed for you, of course." Della beamed at him, her small hands clasped as if in prayer. "He was proud of you. Do you remember carrying his tools? You were his little helper."

Della patted him on the cheek. "I'll write you when I'm settled, shall I?"

"Della, you don't need to join an order," said Rylee. "Our social workers explained that."

"But I will. Perhaps one with animals. That would be nice. I must be somewhere safe for the Rising. Have to be ready." She was now moving back toward the dining hall. Whatever he had expected, it wasn't this. He followed, trailing her back to the entrance. Della paused at the door handle, only because it was metal and she didn't like metal. He remembered that about her, as well.

Rylee opened the door and the trooper within took charge of Della. She never even said goodbye.

The door clicked shut. "I'm sorry, Axel. She's troubled."

He nodded, his teeth tight together and the muscles at his jaw working hard.

"One of our people told me that she's on the spectrum."

It explained everything and nothing. He looked to the empty place where his mother had been. "Yes. I see."

Chapter 22

Rylee managed to catch a few hours' sleep and was back at work before nine the next day. They finished up at the compound at noon. Ohr had one final interview with Axel in his office in Kinsley. When Rylee arrived, they were already in the conference room. When she tried to join in, Ohr told her to head back to their offices in Glens Falls.

Rylee just blinked at the order. Instead of moving out, she held the doorknob like it was her last friend and stood momentarily petrified. This was not how she had pictured their goodbye.

"I'll finish up here," said Ohr. "See you back at the office."

Rylee stared at Trace, who stared mutely back, his look expectant.

"All right," she said and closed the door.

Trace's head bowed.

She made it outside, but her footsteps slowed. She wasn't going like this. Instead, she waited outside in the cold for Ohr to emerge. Then she planned to see Axel alone. She had to tell him thank-you, at the very least. And tell him that she loved him? Not that it would change anything; he was staying and she was going.

Kurt Rogers emerged from the coffee shop across the street and ambled over to her.

"They still got him in there?" asked Rogers.

"Yes. Thought we might get a late lunch, but heck. It's closer to dinner now."

Rylee could not keep from fidgeting. She tapped her fingers and sighed. The longer Ohr kept him, the less time she'd have to say goodbye.

"My cat paces like that when she's on the wrong side of the door from her kittens," said Rogers.

Rylee stopped pacing.

"It's the cold."

Rogers leaned against the bench on the sidewalk and glanced at the entrance of the administration building in Kinsley. Dressed in a lambskin coat and wearing gloves, he looked broader and younger. She could see for a moment the stature of the sheriff he must have been.

"What are they doing?" asked Rogers.

"Final interview."

Rogers looked back at the agent in the sedan waiting to drive Ohr back to Glens Falls. Rylee's vehicle was parked just behind that one. In a little while, she'd be in that car, driving away. She should be so happy and proud. Instead, she wanted to scream.

The thought made her heart ache. But what was the choice? He was an elected official here and she'd already been told she was being promoted. New York City, if she wanted, or DC.

Soon, she'd have her choice of postings. It was what she wanted. Wasn't it?

Rogers ambled over to the agent in the vehicle, who lowered the window so they could speak.

Ohr finally emerged from the outer doors, followed by Sheriff Trace.

"You still here?" asked Ohr.

She nodded and turned her attention to Trace, painfully aware of their audience. Her driver had left the vehicle and both she and Rogers watched them. Ohr looked from her to Trace, waiting.

"Hello, Sheriff," Rylee said.

His hesitant smile faded. "Agent Hockings," he said, formally. "Thought maybe you left. What can I do for you?"

"I wanted to thank you for rescuing me from the river."

"You already have. And you're welcome."

She couldn't read him. The tension was clear from his expression and the caution in his eyes.

"So, you got what you came here for," he said.

Had she? It seemed something was still missing. Why couldn't she say it to him? She glanced to Rogers and then to Ohr. Finally, she returned her attention to him. Her mouth was so dry.

"Yes, most of it."

"It doesn't all come out like in the movies," he said.

Ohr interjected here. "Our people will be moving to locate and eradicate the manufacturing site. Meanwhile, CDC is creating and stockpiling a vaccine against a possible outbreak. Our diplomatic channels will advocate pursuit of sanctions against North Korea based on evidence that you found."

"You know where they are manufacturing?" asked Axel.

"We have Hal Mondello and Wayne Trace, and both are eager to make a deal. I'm sure our investigation will turn up that information."

She did not mention that they had not succeeded in capturing Hal Mondello's oldest boy, Quinton, thought to have fled to Canada. That bothered Rylee, because he seemed very much in charge of the moonshining operation during her investigation.

Her supervisor turned to Rylee. "Did you tell him you're in line for promotion?"

Rylee's cheeks burned with what felt like shame. It was in part due to Axel's efforts that she'd succeeded. She could not have done any of this without him and the Kowa people. Without them, she'd likely be dead.

Her supervisor continued, "You have done an above-average job here, Agent Hockings. Proved me wrong and far exceeded my expectations. You've more than earned that promotion."

Rylee felt none of the pride she had anticipated. She'd spent enough time imagining this moment to know that the twisting dread that tugged at her stomach was not the jubilation she should have been experiencing.

"Congratulations," said Axel, his voice flat and his expression strained.

The time had come to say goodbye. To get on her horse and ride off into the sunset. Specifically, she needed to slip into the faux leather seat of the sedan still sporting the handprints of the Mohawk tribe and point her vehicle south. Instead, she lingered.

Ohr shook Axel's hand and swept away as if in a race-walking competition and finding herself far behind.

Trace watched her go. "Does she always walk like that?"

"Yes, except on inclines."

"Smoking. Steals the wind," he said.

The odor of burning tobacco clung to her clothing and hair the way the tar likely clung to her skin.

He returned his attention to Rylee, moving closer until she could smell the wood smoke that clung to his flannel and the enticing earthy musk of him.

"Where will you go with your promotion? Do you have an office in mind?"

"I was thinking I'd like a bigger posting. New York, of course, or LA, New Orleans because of the port, or Tampa because of the weather."

None of those included the frozen landscape that now surrounded them. And this was only the preview of what winter held in store, when chunks of ice the size of barges would hamper maritime traffic.

"Tampa seems nice," he said with no enthusiasm.

Snowflakes continued to drift down from the blue sky as if confused as to where they had come from and where they belonged. The grass between the sidewalk and curb had become stiff and crunched with each of her shifting steps. But the snow stuck only to the automobiles and the hard cold blacktop of the road surfaces.

Would he ask her to stay? She tilted her chin to look up into his face, blinking at the snowflakes that landed in her eyes.

"No reason to stay here," he said.

She met his stare. "Would you ever leave?"

Had she really said that aloud? The door of possibilities cracked open a bit.

His brows lifted, disappearing into the wool lip of his ski hat.

"I've never lived anywhere else," he said.

"And I've lived everywhere else." She tried for a laugh, failed and cleared her throat. "Funny that trying to get this promotion, and the last one, kept me on the move. When what I said I've wanted was to settle in one place."

"Your job keeps you mobile."

"I might as well be in the army…moving like a migrating bird."

"Maybe the next posting will be a more permanent one."

Rylee felt the tears misting her eyes and choking her throat. Her nose began to run and she wiped it with her leather glove.

"This is all wrong," she said.

"I know. Crazy, right?"

When she imagined a man making a commitment to her, it wasn't in the form of question. As if he were wondering if she could extend her visit for a day or two.

"You can't stay. Can you?" he asked.

He didn't confess his true feelings or express his devotion. His expression looked pained and she wondered if perhaps he'd be happy to see her go and be done with this… Whatever it was they had shared.

They had known each other only a little over a week. It wasn't long enough to fall in love. Was it? This had to be the stress of the case and the danger. Just an encounter.

She scowled. "I should go."

His nod was exaggerated. "Yes, right."

It was looking more and more as if the emotions that were kicking her like a mule were distinctly one-sided.

"Thank you, Sheriff, for all you've done to help me with this case." She extended her gloved hand.

He stared down at it, frowning like a kid who was expecting something specific on Christmas morning and instead got socks.

"Yeah, you're welcome." The handshake was mechanical.

She smiled. "I hope you'll call us if you see anything of which we should be aware."

He held her hand motionless, as if reluctant to let go. Finally, he dropped his hand to his side and then shoved it into his pocket. She could see the balled fist there.

Rylee walked on brittle legs to the driver's side door, gripping the keys as if they were the neck of a snake. She managed to wait until she left the town of Kinsley before the tears began to roll down her cheeks. The sobs came next.

Kurt Rogers came to stand beside Axel as the caravan of sedans pulled out like a motorcade.

"You should go after her," said Rogers.

"Nothing for her here, Kurt."

"Just you, I guess." He rested a hand on Axel's shoulder and squeezed. "You tell her you love her?"

He shook his head, knowing that words were just impossible.

"Never took you for a fool, son. Until now, that is."

"Maybe I ought to follow her."

"Sure. Plenty of nice places to go. You two could make a home anywhere." His hand slipped away and he faced the river. "Still, this place is awful pretty, with the snow falling like glitter in the sunlight." He studied the fast-flowing, wide river. "Never get tired of that view. All that water rolling toward the sea and here we sit on this shore, letting it pass by. That's the job, I guess, watching over the folks up here on this side of the river. But you can watch over folks anyplace, Axel. Doesn't need to be here. Follow her and you two can decide where to settle later."

"The town needs me," he said.

"Sure. But what I'm wondering is what *you* need. If it's a woman, all well and good. If it's *that* woman, you best go after her."

Chapter 23

Rogers was right again. Axel was letting her get away. He stood in the road, the flurries bringing a dusting of snow. This was his county. He'd been elected to serve as sheriff, and he'd done his job. But he'd stayed to watch over the congregation and stand between the madman at their head and the flock he exploited.

But now they were gone. The women who had raised him had spread out among social services, returning to families or making a lateral move into the arms of another commune. His mother had said her goodbyes and Axel now believed that she had done all she was able to for him. His mother was smart but that part of her that allowed her to connect with people was simply absent. He didn't blame her, but it made him worry. What if he weren't capable of being the kind of parent he had missed? What if he were too damaged by his upbringing?

"What's holding you back, son?" asked Rogers. "Your father is gone. Taken into federal custody, and with all the charges, the only time you'll see him again is on visiting days."

"I won't be visiting. He's not my father."

Rogers lifted his thick white eyebrows. Axel told him the tale.

"You going to change your name? Make it Axel Pritcher?"

"It didn't occur to me."

"Might make a fresh start."

"Maybe. As to Father Wayne, I'll lay odds that he finds his own following in federal prison, but he can't lure vulnerable folks out here. The man was a regular pied piper."

"That's true. But he's gone. That means you can go, too."

Axel turned to look at the old lawman. "You knew that's why I came back?"

"Suspected, is all."

"I still have two years left on my term."

"If you're hanging up your star, I'm not too old to step in until they can do a special election. But try to talk her into coming on back here, if you can."

"Why?"

"Nice place to raise a family. Make me a grandfather, of sorts."

Axel blanched. "I don't even know if she wants a family. And I'm sure I don't know how to be a father."

"The heck you don't. I taught you all you need. Good sense of humor, patience and love. It's not hard, boy. Not as hard as telling the woman you love that you can't live without her. Now that is a job only for the brave at heart."

Axel nodded, glancing back at the empty road.

"Your military record says you are a brave man. Guess we'll find out if that's so. Get going or you won't catch her until she leaves the county."

The flurries had changed to a light snow that required intermittent wiper blade action. Rylee peered out through the windshield at the precipitation that made visibility difficult. Beyond her windshield, the world looked cold and the road lonely. Time to think about the case and not about Axel. She swallowed the lump of regret, but it stayed wedged like a large cough drop accidentally swallowed.

All the way out of Onutake County, she fought the urge to turn her car around and go back to him. Tell him that she wanted… What? To live at the edge of a northern wasteland? She wanted a home and she wanted Axel. She wanted to stop moving all over the world, but she also wanted a career. How did she make this work? What compromises would she need and which of her objectives would be sacrificed to get the other? It was seldom in life that you reached a point where you could so clearly see two paths.

When she decided not to enlist, she had known it was one such juncture. When she had finished college and joined DHS, she had seen her path and taken charge. But how many of those choices were made not to please herself but to make her father proud?

All of them, she realized. Every one. And if he was proud, he had certainly never told her. Not even when she called him to report that her investigation had led to the arrest of the prime suspect. She could share little else, as the investigation and details were both classified, but his reaction had been typically underwhelming.

"Just part of the job, isn't it?" he had asked her during the brief phone conversation.

Risking her life, getting shot at, diving into a frozen river, just part of the job? It was. But even her supervisors recognized she had gone above and beyond, offered congratulations. They were also putting in for a promotion on her behalf, showing with actions how valuable they considered her service.

The conversation with her father had crystalized that searching for praise from him was pointless. He didn't know how, didn't understand her need for it or just refused to offer even the merest encouragement.

So why was she still acting to please him?

She wasn't. Would not. From this moment she would make choices on what was in *her* best interest.

The wiper blades couldn't keep up with the snow, so she adjusted them again to the next higher setting. The other vehicles from her office had left her behind as they sped along, obviously anxious to be home before dark, while she was in no such hurry.

All she knew for certain was that she had made a huge case, her career was on track and she had never been so miserable.

The misery was the clue to the puzzle. Nothing good should make her feel this sad. Why didn't she see before that leaving Axel would not be like leaving one case for another? He was too important to leave behind. And a week was long enough, obviously, because she was certain that she loved him. But uncertain if he loved her.

At the very least, she should have told him that she

had fallen in love with him. The risk of finding out he did not share her feelings now seemed less chilling than not taking the risk and never knowing.

Rylee glanced at the road ahead, the southbound lane of the Northway, searching for an exit or a turnaround that would allow her to change direction. A few miles back, the highway had been a single lane divided only by a yellow line. Now the two directions ran parallel with a median ditch between them.

She considered trying her luck on the snow-covered grass, but the possibility of ending up in the ditch between the divided highway kept her rolling along. Finally, she spotted her chance. The green sign with white letters indicated that the upcoming exit for Exit 26—toward Pottersville and Schroon Lake. Her chance to change direction lay only one mile ahead.

Rylee had been so deep in thought that she had not even noticed that the vehicle behind her was a trooper until the driver hit his lights.

"Really?" she said, glancing from her speedometer to the rearview. "I was only five miles over."

The Northway traffic was light on the two-lane highway, and she easily glided to the shoulder of the exit ramp to Pottersville, followed by the trooper.

It wasn't until the man approached her vehicle that she recognized that he was not in a trooper's uniform and was approaching with his handgun out and raised. She reached for her pistol as she adjusted her view in the side mirror to see the man's face.

Quinton Mondello. Eldest son of Hal Mondello, she realized. The new head of the Mondello family of moonshiners and the one suspected of transporting their North Korean detainee over the US–Canadian border.

With no solid evidence of human trafficking, Quinton had been released. He had not been present on the attack at the wharf and had also evaded federal custody at the raid of his family's compound, slipping through the net when they had come to make arrests after the shooting.

He took aim, plainly deciding to shoot her from the back before ever reaching her window. Headlights flashed as a second vehicle pulled in behind Mondello's. His backup, she assumed.

Mondello's first shot missed its mark. Rylee had left her seat and scrambled to the passenger's side as the bullet punctured the rear window and then cleanly through her headrest before shattering the windshield. The fractured windshield was held in place by the protective film but was now a mosaic of tiny cubes of glass.

Rylee exited her vehicle with her pistol drawn and the safety switched off. She used the open door as a shield. Mondello had reached her rear bumper. He had no cover.

She aimed at center mass, making a guess on his position because the light made it impossible to see him clearly.

Her shot broke the side window, showing her that he'd moved. Where was he?

She listened and heard only a vehicle's chime, indicating a door was open. His backup, she realized.

No time to call it in. She needed to move. Rylee reached the front of her vehicle, the engine block providing cover.

"Drop it, Quinton." She recognized the familiar male voice.

"She ruined my family. My father is in jail because of her," said Mondello.

"Your father is in jail for human trafficking that North Korean across the border, and for manslaughter for kicking her into the canal. Did you know what she carried could have killed your whole family?"

Quinton Mondello's voice rose an octave, making him sound crazed. "You're on my list, too, Axel, and you just jumped to the number one spot."

"Drop it or I will shoot you."

Quinton laughed. "You haven't shot at anything or anybody since coming home from the Sandbox. Everyone knows you are scared to shoot. A regular basket case, I hear."

Rylee moved to look around the fender. The two men faced off like gunfighters at high noon. Only Axel's pistol was aimed at Mondello and Mondello's was still pointed in her direction.

Mondello spotted her now and smiled. Their eyes met. He had her now in his sights, and the fact that Axel would kill him after he made his shot seemed to make no difference. Mondello lifted his pistol and two shots fired.

She registered the surprised expression as she put a bullet in his chest. The second one, the one that removed the smug expression along with part of his face, had come from Axel's weapon.

Mondello dropped, inert and lifeless, to the pavement with a sickening whack. Rylee flinched.

Axel ran forward, gun still aimed at Mondello. He reached the still body and placed his foot over the pistol that lay just beyond his curled hand. He stowed the gun in the pocket of his jacket. He made a quick check of Mondello. The sight of his ruined face told Rylee that no one could have survived such a grievous head injury.

Only then did Axel holster his personal weapon and run toward her. She stood to meet him, with time only to slip her gun back into the nylon case.

Then he had her in a crushing embrace. His kisses, frantic, began at her forehead and moved down to her cheek and then to her neck. There he tucked his face into her nape and muttered disjointed words.

"Almost too late… Could have… Almost… My God, Rylee."

"I'm here." She drew back to look at him.

In all the days and all the times they had been together, she had never seen him so pale. He was trembling.

"My hand was shaking. I didn't know if I could make that shot."

And then she remembered that this peace officer had never drawn his pistol since coming home from serving. He had told her he didn't think he could take another life, not even to save his own. Yet, he had done it, to save hers.

"It was my bullet," she said. Trying to take the blame. But they both knew that the way Quintin had dropped, as if his head were no longer connected to his body, meant that it had been Axel's headshot that had killed him.

Her shot had been deadly but not incapacitating. Mondello would have had time to take that shot at Rylee.

Axel seemed to come back into possession of himself. He still looked pale as moonlight, but his gaze was steady as he cradled her head between his two strong hands.

"No. It was mine."

"You saved my life," she said.

"Thank God." He dragged her in for another hug. "Thank God," he whispered into her hair.

"How did you know?"

She drew back, needing answers and to call this in. Axel blinked at her.

"How did you know Quinton Mondello was following me or that he planned to kill me?"

"I didn't."

She wrinkled her brow, trying to make sense of this.

"Then how did you get here? Why are you here, Axel?"

He let her go and glanced down at the dead body oozing blood onto the road. The thick red fluid oozed along the cracks in the tired pavement.

"Not a good time. Wrong place. Really wrong."

He was muttering again.

"Axel. Look at me."

He did. The trembling had ceased but he looked miserable.

"Why are you here?"

Axel looked at the pavement and the body again. He grasped her hand and pulled her away from the corpse of Quinton Mondello.

"Axel, I have to call this in."

He raked a hand through his hair. "Yes. Call it in. I'll use my radio."

Rylee watched him go. He remained in his vehicle for a long while after lowering the radio. Finally, Rylee headed back to him.

"Climb in," he said. "It's cold outside. Troopers are en route. Be here in ten."

She climbed into the quiet cab and the two waited in silence. Discussing the events would only taint their statements.

"Thank you for coming for me."

Axel nodded but said nothing.

The sound of sirens was almost immediate.

"How is that possible?" she said, spotting the flashing lights of a large vehicle. Her hand went to the handle of her gun.

"There is a voluntary fire company at the southern half of the exit."

And sure enough, the EMS vehicle rolled down the northbound ramp and across a utility road she had not seen beneath the snow cover. Clearly, this was a well-traveled route by the volunteers.

Soon the quiet stretch of road became an active crime scene and Rylee felt grateful that it was not her corpse being tucked in a body bag and rolled into the back of the emergency vehicle.

Axel opted to spend the night in a hotel, rather than drive back home. He didn't sleep well and woke with that dull throbbing headache that came from too much caffeine and too little sleep.

He made it to the troopers' station, reviewed and signed his statement. That left one piece of unfinished business and the reason he'd come in the first place: to speak to Rylee.

A text message, a reply and a location chosen, he headed to the small pub and bistro in Schroon Lake. Inside, he was nestled in the aroma of bacon and frying foods. The interior was all knotty pine bedecked with snowshoes and skis from another century. Hand-hewn beams stretched above him, and a kayak hung from between the ceiling fans. Rustic wooden furniture sat before a blazing fireplace and several customers occupied high stools at the bar, cradling their drinks. The men's attention flicked from their drinks to the television, before returning to watch the busy woman behind the bar.

"Welcome," she called. "Sit wherever you like."

He scanned the room but did not find Rylee, so he took a place at a circular table near the stone fireplace and beneath a chandelier made of antlers. Out of habit, he took a seat facing the door and the wide windows that showed the parking lot and the road beyond. The light flurry was now making progress in coating the windshields of the cars parked before the bistro.

He had a cup of coffee that had been refilled once before he saw her step from a vehicle. It wasn't the one she'd driven last night. That one was now in evidence, part of an active investigation. His first shooting and his first kill, at least since coming home from Iraq, or as he thought of it, the Sandbox.

Axel didn't recall leaving the table or the room or the restaurant. But there he was in the lot with the snow floating down lazily and his breath visible in the cold air.

She was talking to herself. Then she sighted him and hesitated in her purposeful stride. Her steps became awkward, as she slipped on the icy pavement before she recovered and continued her forward momentum at a slower pace. She seemed in no hurry to reach him and glanced back at her vehicle with a look he thought might be longing.

Was this meeting an obligation for her, a duty to be discharged? The thought cooled him more than the wintery air. His coat was in his hand. He must have grabbed it on the way out. Axel slipped into it and waited.

"Hello, there," she said. "I didn't expect an escort in."

They faced each other, him feeling uncomfortable

in his own skin and her waiting. Should he hug her or kiss her cheek?

Instead, he fell in beside her, grasping her elbow and helping her toward the sidewalk. Her boots were gone and instead she wore the sort of shoes that corporate folks wore. She was changing back to the data analyst she had been.

Already leaving him, he realized. He had to stop her. Suddenly, he forgot how to breathe.

"I'm glad you're all right," she said. "I was just rehearsing how to tell you how grateful I am. That's twice in one week you've backed me up."

It was a job he wouldn't mind taking full-time.

"Getting to be a habit."

"Thank you, Axel, for saving my life. Again."

"You're welcome."

They reached the door to the restaurant and he opened it for her. Like many places in the north, this establishment had a double-door system and a small room that was for waiting in the summer and, in the winter, for keeping the warm air from escaping when guests came and went. Here, they paused between the inside and the outside to face each other.

"You all finished here?" she asked.

"For now. Lots of paperwork, you know."

"I imagine so."

"What about you?" he asked.

"I am all packed up."

She glanced past him to the second door, which led inside, catching a glimpse, he knew, of the log and pine interior.

"It looks like a nice place."

It might be the place they would come back to over

the years. That special place where he asked her to be his wife. Or, he thought, it might be that place he avoided forever, never to return.

They moved inside and he led the way back to his table and the cold cup of coffee that waited there.

Rylee took her seat beside him at the pine table. She held her smile as she turned her gaze back on him. Her hand snaked out and clasped one of his, her fingers icy. Their palms slipped over one another and he closed his hand. She gave a little squeeze.

"I know you don't draw your weapon. Haven't, I mean."

"Quinton was right. Not since the Sandbox," he added.

"You fired your weapon. Took the necessary shot. Are you going to be all right with that?" she asked.

"I will be, because I had no other option and my actions kept you here on this earth."

"That just makes me doubly grateful."

Gratitude was not the emotion he wished to engender within her heart.

"I wasn't going to let him hurt you, Rylee. I don't want anything to ever hurt you." And if she'd let him, he'd be there for her, to keep her safe and watch her back. Why couldn't he find the words to tell her so?

Her hand slipped away and the heat of their joined flesh melted from his tingling palm.

"When are you heading back to Kinsley?" she asked.

"That depends."

Outside the windows to their right and left, the snow swirled in the gray afternoon.

"I've been wondering something, Axel." She cocked her head, her eyebrows lifting. Did she know how beautiful she was? Just a look was like a dart piercing his heart.

"You said before that you didn't know about Quinton. That he was coming for me."

The jig was up, he realized. Of course, she'd come back around to that question. "That's true."

"Then why were you there?"

"I love you. I followed you yesterday to tell you that. To get on my knees and ask you to marry me."

"You followed…" Her brow wrinkled, and the corners of her mouth dipped.

Panic seized his heart with sharp incisors.

"Rylee, don't go."

"What?"

"I love you. I don't want you to go."

Now it was her turn to stammer and stare. "Y-you… what? Axel, you've only known me a week."

"Nine days."

"It's not very long."

"Engaged, then. Going steady. Dating. Just not going away."

"My job is in Glens Falls. I'll be transferred soon."

"Yes. I know that. And I don't care. Let me come with you."

Her mouth dropped open and she stared.

"That is a very different offer than asking me to stay."

"It is."

"Axel, are you sure?"

"I'll follow you anywhere, Rylee. If you let me."

She shook her head now, as if not able to understand his words.

"What about your job? You're a county sheriff."

He looked north, perhaps seeing the county and the people there.

"Special election. They'll fill the spot." Now he was looking at her again. "Rylee, I went back there after the military, stayed there because of him."

"Father Wayne?"

"I needed to stop him from killing his followers, my mother, all of them. I knew he'd do it. It was part of his personality. The power of life and death, the ultimate test of his control."

Axel pressed his palms flat to the table.

"I don't need to watch him anymore. End of watch. Mission complete." He stared across the table at her. "Do you understand? I'm free. For the first time in my life I can go anywhere I like, do anything I like and be with whomever I choose." He reached out and she took his hand. "I choose you, Rylee."

"But the county. Your home."

"I hate it there. Hate everything about it, especially the memories. Let someone else take the job. Someone who is there for reasons other than duty."

"Is that really how you feel?"

"Yes."

"What about Kurt Rogers?"

"He'll always be a mentor. I'll visit or he'll visit. But I won't stay in that county. No more."

He'd been through so much. Raised in a cult and then fostered. Held in the county by fear and obligation. She thanked God for Kurt Rogers, who had helped Axel find his way. Then the military, where he'd nearly lost himself again. Back to his county, a self-appointed guardian, giving himself the impossible job of curbing a madman, a man who, until recently, he'd believed to be his father.

"Rylee? Say something."

She leaned forward, reaching for him until her fingers stroked the red stubble on his cheek.

"I love you, too, Axel. I just didn't know how we could make this work between us. But now I see nothing but possibilities."

"Is that a yes?" he asked.

"Yes to the engagement."

He rose from his seat and pulled her into his arms, kissing her with passion before the great stone fireplace in the middle of a restaurant with few customers to witness their union.

When she drew back, her face was flushed and she beamed up at him.

"What should we do now?" he asked.

"I was hoping to buy you lunch." She smiled and offered her hand.

"Yes. Lunch."

She stood beside him, still holding his hand as she spoke. "And after that, a life together."

Together, they would make the permanent home that she had always wanted and raise the family for which he had always longed. They were together at last and forever, just as they were always meant to be.

* * * * *

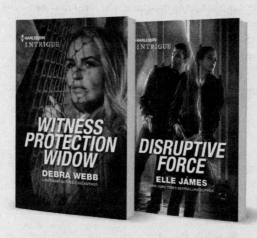

Prologue

The tears leaked out of Kay Duvall's eyes, even as she tried to
focus on what she had to do. *Had* to do to bring Ben home safe.

She fumbled with her ID and punched in the code that
would open the side door, usually only used for a guard taking a
smoke break. It would be easy for the men behind her to escape
from this side of the prison.

It went against everything she was supposed to do.
Everything she considered right and good.

A quiet sob escaped her lips. They had her son. How could
she not help them escape? Nothing mattered beyond her son's
life.

"Would you stop already?" one of the prisoners muttered.
He'd made her give him her gun, which he now jabbed into her
back. "Crying isn't going to change anything. So just shut up."

She didn't care so much about her own life or if she'd be
fired. She didn't care what happened to her as long as they let
her son go. So she swallowed down the sobs and blinked out as
many tears as she could, hoping to stem the tide of them.

HIEXP0121

She got the door open and slid out first—because the man holding the gun pushed it into her back until she moved forward.

They came through the door behind her, dressed in the clothes she'd stolen from the locker room and Lost and Found. Anything warm she could get her hands on to help them escape into the frigid February night.

Help them escape. Help three dangerous men escape prison. When she was supposed to keep them inside.

It didn't matter anymore. She just wanted them gone. If they were gone, they'd let her baby go. They had to let her baby go.

Kay forced her legs to move, one foot in front of the other, toward the gate she could unlock without setting off any alarms. She unlocked it, steadier this time if only because she kept thinking that once they were gone, she could get in contact with Ben.

She flung open the gate and gestured them out into the parking lot. "Stay out of the safety lights and no one should bug you."

"You better hope not," one of the men growled.

"The minute you sound that alarm, your kid is dead. You got it?" This one was the ringleader. The one who'd been in for murder. Who else would he kill out there in the world?

Guilt pooled in Kay's belly, but she had to ignore it. She had to live with it. Whatever guilt she felt would be survivable. Living without her son wouldn't be. Besides, she had to believe they'd be caught. They'd do something else terrible and be caught.

As long as her son was alive, she didn't care.

Don't miss
Hunting a Killer *by Nicole Helm,*
available February 2021 wherever
Harlequin Intrigue books and ebooks are sold.

Harlequin.com

Love Harlequin romance?

DISCOVER.

Be the first to find out about promotions,
news and exclusive content!

f Facebook.com/HarlequinBooks

🐦 Twitter.com/HarlequinBooks

📷 Instagram.com/HarlequinBooks

📌 Pinterest.com/HarlequinBooks

You Tube YouTube.com/HarlequinBooks

ReaderService.com

EXPLORE.

Sign up for the Harlequin e-newsletter and
download a free book from any series at
TryHarlequin.com

CONNECT.

Join our Harlequin community to
share your thoughts and connect
with other romance readers!
Facebook.com/groups/HarlequinConnection